where the north ends

QUERENCIAS SERIES

Miguel A. Gandert and Enrique R. Lamadrid, Series Editors

Querencia is a popular term in the Spanish-speaking world that is used to express a deeply rooted love of place and people. This series promotes a transnational, humanistic, and creative vision of the US-Mexico borderlands based on all aspects of expressive culture, both material and intangible.

Also available in the Querencias Series:

Martíneztown, 1945: Tales of Life and Loss in an Albuquerque Barrio by Nasario García

The Latino Big Bang in California: The Diary of Justo Veytia, a Mexican Forty-Niner edited by David E. Hayes-Bautista, Cynthia L. Chamberlin, and Paul Bryan Gray

Dichos en Nichos by Sage Vogel

New Mexico's Moses: Reies López Tijerina and the Religious Origins of the Mexican American Civil Rights Movement by Ramón A. Gutiérrez

The Poetics of Fire: Metaphors of Chile Eating in the Borderlands by Victor M. Valle

El Camino Real de California: From Ancient Pathways to Modern Byways by Joseph P. Sánchez

Chasing Dichos through Chimayó by Don J. Usner

Nación Genízara: Ethnogenesis, Place, and Identity in New Mexico edited by Moises Gonzales and Enrique R. Lamadrid

Querencia: Reflections on the New Mexico Homeland edited by Vanessa Fonseca-Chávez, Levi Romero, and Spencer R. Herrera

Imagine a City That Remembers: The Albuquerque Rephotography Project by Anthony Anella and Mark C. Childs

For additional titles in the Querencias Series, please visit unmpress.com.

HUGO MORENO

where the north ends

a novel

Foreword by FRANCISCO A. LOMELÍ

UNIVERSITY OF NEW MEXICO PRESS ALBUQUERQUE

© 2025 by Sergio Hugo Moreno
All rights reserved. Published 2025
Printed in the United States of America

ISBN 978-0-8263-6836-2 (paper)
ISBN 978-0-8263-6837-9 (ePub)

Library of Congress Control Number: 2025006820

Founded in 1889, the University of New Mexico sits on the traditional homelands of the Pueblo of Sandia. The original peoples of New Mexico—Pueblo, Navajo, and Apache—since time immemorial have deep connections to the land and have made significant contributions to the broader community statewide. We honor the land itself and those who remain stewards of this land throughout the generations and also acknowledge our committed relationship to Indigenous peoples. We gratefully recognize our history.

Cover image courtesy of the Library of Congress
Designed by Isaac Morris
Composed in Sabon and Vendetta

For Debbie Castillo:

In appreciation and recognition for the positive difference she has made in my life and that of many others as mentor, advisor, professor, scholar, author, editor, humanist, community member, and friend.

Contents

Hugo Moreno's Where the North Ends

A ROSARY OF INTERTEXTUAL DREAMSCAPES

Where the North Ends offers a multifaced narrative difficult to classify. It touches on many realms: from the historical during the 1660s (and leading the stage into 1680 when the Pueblo Revolt that pushed the Spaniards south into the El Paso area occurred) to the surreal (the oneiric qualities that prevail in both the protagonist and the narration), then into magical realism (where María Tzitza ascends into the sky; Lucius the mule speaks much like a centaur; the shaman Refugio turns into a tree; a Blue Lady from the colonial period experiences dislocation between Spain and New Mexico; and a human figure melts like plastic). It works as a psychological novel (where the narrator experiences trances and out-of-body transmigrations as he questions his mental state and sanity); a narrative about myth (without mentioning it, Aztlán, known as the spiritual homeland, is invoked subconsciously); and, finally, a mystery novel (about the self and culture as ruminated via time, history, and space).

As one can see, intertextuality dominates at many levels and planes. The novel is part of Chicano literature in its attempts to return to the far historical past while representing a modern character who finds himself between various timescapes and the liminal spaces between two cultures. It is also a crossover narrative into Native American literature for its many elements and symbols (including numerous examples of Indigenous languages—especially Apache and some Piro) and its many allusions to social practices, beliefs, rituals, and characters. Either way, the work is an exemplary piece that deals with subjectivities thanks to the realms of dreams, metamorphosis, spirituality, and self-knowledge. Here we see traces of Rudolfo Anaya (witchcraft, owls, sorcerers, dreams), Carlos Castaneda (self-exploration into authenticity, alternative realities, the power of nature), and Tony Hillerman (highlighting numerous genuine Native American subjects and the mystery novel). The novel, then, is in part historical, part antihistorical, part surreal, part modern realism, and part mundane coexistence. The leaps into a far past give the impression that New Mexico's historical past still exists as a subjacent cultural matrix that cannot be totally suppressed.

Uriel, the protagonist (sometimes known as Diego), seems to be the key to unlocking this mysterious realm. At one point, the psychotherapist Dr. Hogan tells Uriel about the nature of his dreams of wakefulness, which synthesizes his deep motivations and process for writing his manuscript:

> Existence is an illusion, a dream, Uriel. Human beings are unconscious fabulists, dreamers who don't realize they are only dreaming. You are not crazy, Uriel. You are simply a dreamer who has acquired a degree of lucidity about illusory existence. (251)

This highly experimental work is, indeed, meritorious for its many innovations. Despite the challenging nature of sustaining multiple dreamscapes, the narrative binds together as a continuous but meandering storyline. The plot structure, in spirit, resembles the short story "La noche boca arriba" ("The Night Upside Down") by the Argentine Julio Cortázar, where the protagonist riding a motorcycle has an accident, ending up with a concussion and a broken arm. This leads to a series of dreams at the end of which he finds himself in a brutal scene in which he is about to be sacrificed by a group of Aztec warriors. Likewise, Moreno's protagonist experiences a comparable accident on a bicycle, but the unfolding action takes him into wild swings of (day)dreams, illusions, delusions, hallucinations, imaginings, visions, nightmares, and fantasies through switching spaces and historical times. The fundamental difference between Cortázar's story and Moreno's is that the latter's is substantially more developed and extensive, while leaping through various timespaces that are often parallel but also strikingly different. Ultimately, both the reader and the protagonist can't help asking themselves: Is this real or a mirage?

It would appear that the dreams (et al.) generate their own energy and raison d'être to the point that these illusive notions of reality get confused, tangled, and mixed up into a surreal ultrareality of fogginess, *Twilight Zone* style. There exist hints of allusions to the Spanish baroque dramaturgist Pedro Calderón de la Barca, who wrote in *La vida es sueño* (*Life Is a Dream*, 1651) the following:

> ¿Qué es la vida? Un frenesí. / ¿Qué es la vida? Una ilusión. / Una sombra, una ficción, / y el mayor bien es pequeño. / Que toda la vida es sueño, / y los sueños, sueños son.
>
> [What is a dream? 'Tis but a madness. / What is a dream? A thing that seems, / A mirage that false gleams, / Phantom joy, delusive rest. / Since is life a dream at best, / and even dreams themselves are dreams.][1]

Although the plot initially follows the basic format of Cortázar's story, Moreno's work is more inspired philosophically by Calderón de la Barca's famous play because of the many intertwined subthemes contained within: struggles with predestination, free will, knowledge, superstition, love, justice, and order/disorder. All this is layered by a guiding principle that moves the novel within the context of a metafictional narrative that expresses self-awareness as Uriel tries to get a handle on his own life story, often depending on dreams to create and motivate his writing of a manuscript. The labyrinthine structure of the oneiric reminds us of Octavio Paz's sense of metaphysical solitude, which he tries to resolve. In one instance, Uriel asks: "Is my mind deceived and my soul dreaming?" (149) In other words, he is a character in search of a narrative: partly his own, but mainly the meaning for the distinct threads of his dreams, divagations and digressions that can explain his existence. In the process, he finds himself as a novice monk in a cell in the 1660s in colonial New Mexico, seeking to adhere to the monastic rituals, exigencies, and demands of an orthodox religious order as partly dictated by Fray Antonio. Confusion prevails for the protagonist as he goes in and out of such slices of life from colonial New Mexico to contemporary times, deeply concerned with incarnations and reincarnations. He also gets involved with a shaman of dreams (Refugio) who helps Uriel abandon the mission and escape New Mexico by giving him survival training and performing a ceremony to cure him of "ghost sickness." In addition, he consults Dr. Hogan, a psychotherapist of dreams. The narrative keeps interrupting his flashes of dreams when his wife, Alma, appears and disappears from various scenes, knowing full well that she already committed suicide. All this contributes to a bubbling storyline that defies logic and rationality because he is unable to juggle times as a time traveler with places and people that populate his mind, thus resembling Jorge Luis Borges's concept of Aleph, where all points converge in one place. The mind, then, becomes the epicenter of infinity that can intersect time and history, space and cultures—together becoming the substance of his manuscript in progress for the protagonist wherever his dreams lead him. Even though the novel is titled *Where the North Ends*, that is only the location where an arrow points. In reality, neither limitations nor barriers exist—only amorphous qualities that manifest themselves as ethereal specters through an intertextual lens.

The novel expresses tantalizing thoughts about the nature of dreams and their origins, except, in this case, dreams (along with visions, delusions, confabulations, imaginings, comas, selective memories, etc.) dominate Uriel's existence where he doesn't know when a dream begins or ends. In a sense it is a *Groundhog Day* (1993) of recurrent dreams driven by a Jungian power of the unconscious. Moreno creates a series of rabbit holes with contours of unreality in the form of a dream-within-a-dream scheme. In sum, the work represents a journey into the interior self of Uriel—his last name, Romero, suggesting a roamer—as he navigates his far past into the 1660s and back into the 1980s, though he often also moves within the atemporality of myth, legend, ahistoricity, and his psyche. He is interested in absolute truth but quickly realizes the elusive nature of such a phenomenon. For that reason, he slips back and forth from one dream state to another to the point he recalls experiences he did not live in the 1660s and at the same time intuits what the future will bring. Similar to Jorge Luis Borges's short story "La biblioteca de Babel" ("The Library of Babel"), the protagonist here describes the hexagonal galleries as a universe unto itself that encompasses all reality via dreams. The aimless, and unreliable, narrator makes the reader contemplate the relativity of existence and how the subconscious brings everything together between the physical and the intangible. His greatest ambition, he confesses, is to achieve perfect and complete awakening.

The novel is both provocative and disturbing in that the narrator gets caught between different historical time periods and his difficulties in overcoming such a situation is determined by factors beyond his control. His main anchor to measuring reality is dreams and nightmares, which is in itself perplexing. More than a time traveler, he might be characterized as trapped, even victimized, by being in limbo between different eras and liminal spaces. There emerges a strong sense of cultural atavism where he senses a purpose behind his travels or uninduced trips regarding his ancestors, his New Mexican culture (orthodox religious thought vs. agnosticism), and the different forces that helped shape New Mexico as a unique, multicultural entity. Hugo Moreno unlocks much of this cultural heritage from the past to inject purpose and meaning for Uriel Romero as he tries to unpack the significance of his own life.

Francisco A. Lomelí (July 9, 2024)
University of California, Santa Barbara

Notes

1. See *Dramas of Calderón, Tragic, Comic and Legendary: Translated from the Spanish Principally in the Metre of the Original*, translated by Denis Florence MacCarthy, 2 vols. (London: Charles Dolman, 1853), 67.

where the north ends

1

HOW LONG HAVE I BEEN LIKE THIS? HOURS? DAYS? YEARS? Centuries? Am I dead or asleep? Sometimes I embrace the hope that, one of these days, I'm going to wake up; other times I'm afraid that day will never come.

My body materialized one night in a foggy forest. I was trudging like a sleepwalker, without a sense of direction. It was windy but not cold. I was wearing a black tailcoat and brown moccasins. My body felt heavy, as if it were made of lead. A funeral march marked the rhythm of my steps. I pressed on, stumbling with languor, listening to the solemn music with a cloudy mind.

When dawn began to tear at the veil of night, I reached a crossroads. It was a forest clearing with an old and contorted juniper at the center, firmly entrenched in the bedrock. From one of its branches hung a sign made of wood with an inscription faded by the rain. I approached it to decipher it. It said: "To know the origin is to find the way." I paused to decide which way to go. I looked around and realized that I wasn't alone. The forest glade had been suddenly transformed into the stage of a carnival.

There was a multitude of people from different epochs and cultures dressed in extravagant costumes. An orchestra was playing an enchanting *ländler*. I recognized Alma amid the crowd. She was dressed like an Andalusian *maja*. When she saw me she walked toward me, stood in front of me, and greeted me without saying a word. She simply looked at me, smiled, and asked me to dance by extending her left hand. I accepted with trepidation, remembering that she was dead. But when I held her hand, my sadness disappeared like magic.

"I can't believe you're back. I thought you had gone to a better place. I missed you!" I said, smiling as we waltz-walked toward the stage.

We danced like María and Captain Von Trapp in *The Sound of Music* to both the ländler and an exquisite scherzo that the orchestra played to everyone's delight. We were enjoying each other's company like two young lovers. But, when we were about to kiss, she suddenly stepped back and told me, alarmed, "I don't know who you are. Let go of me!" She then vanished. Everyone else also disappeared and the sylvan glade became desolate again. I stood motionless by the juniper, not knowing what to do or where to go.

"Where are you, Alma?"

A gust of wind answered me with a cold and impersonal silence that chilled me to the marrow. I fell on my knees and started to cry like a little boy. Then a ghost spoke to me and tried to convince me to go back whence I came. I don't know why I replied, "I've reached the point of no return in life."

After a while, when I thought everything was lost, an angelic song burst from the sky and miraculously opened up a clearing in the thicket.

O Röschen roth!
Der Mensch liegt in größter Noth,
Der Mensch liegt in größter Pein,
Ja lieber möcht ich im Himmel rein.
Da kam ich auf einen breiten Weg,
Da kam ein Engellein und wollt mich abweisen;
Ach nein, Ich ließ mich nicht abweisen!
Ich bin von Gott, ich will wieder zu Gott!
Der liebe Gott wird mir ein Lichtchen geben,
Wird mir leuchten bis in das ewige selige Leben.[1]

Believing that I would find salvation, I followed the trail that the music opened. I went through the underbrush until I reached a mighty river and a towering mountain. I climbed up the riverbank, following the sublime symphony that enveloped the sierra like a thick blanket of autumnal fog. Wild beasts, vermin, sylphs, fairies, nymphs, dryads, fauns, and specters galore tried to block and detour me. But the power of music pushed me forward, and its spirit guided me through this ethereal forest.

The closer I got to the foot of the mountain, the whiter the water of the rapids became. When I had almost reached the mountain, I saw from afar a human figure standing by the river. I approached him stealthily. He was an old man of medium height and lean body, with long, sparse, gray hair and a white beard. He was bald with a large forehead and had a protuberance at the top of the skull. His face was long and bony. He had rings under his large, brown, droopy eyes and long eyelashes and thick, arching eyebrows. He was naked and used a Judas tree branch as a walking stick. He contemplated the light of dawn and sang at the top of his voice:

Auferstehn, ja auferstehn wirst du,
Mein Staub, nach kurzer Ruh!
Unsterblich's Leben
Wird, der dich schuf, dir geben![2]

His tenor harmonized with the invisible chorus. He was absorbed in singing and didn't notice my presence. The whole choir was immersed in the climax of the finale of this symphony to eternal life. The blast of the timpani, cymbals, trumpets, horns, and bells crowned the elevated voices of the soprano and the mezzo soprano. When the symphony ended there was a complete silence that lasted only a few moments before a cloud of screechy bats began to obscure the light of dawn. When I turned around to look at this marvel, I made a slight noise that startled the old man or ghostly being. Visibly confused, he turned and stared at me completely still and speechless.

"Have mercy on me, whether you are of bone and flesh or a mere shadow. Help me, please. I don't know where I am."

"What are you doing here? Don't you know it is forbidden to climb the heights of the Zaphon?" he asked me curtly.

"I'm sorry. It wasn't my intention to trespass. I don't know where I am nor where I'm going."

"You are standing on sacred ground. You are at the top of the clouds where the North ends. Why are you looking so wretched, poor souls? Take off your clothes and immerse yourselves in the divine Id."

I wondered why he addressed me as if I were several people, but a more urgent question popped up in my mind.

"But isn't it dangerous?" I was appalled by his request, as it was unsafe to take a plunge in those turbulent waters.

"That is your problem. You must purify yourselves if you want me to help you."

I overcame my fear and shame. When I unbuttoned my shirt, I realized that it was stained with blood. I touched my head and felt that my hair was wet and sticky. What happened to me? I asked myself. But nothing hurt. It was strange. When I unfastened my belt, I noticed a putrid smell. I closed my eyes to avoid seeing my own blood and filth. I threw my clothes behind some bushes and dipped myself in the river, terrified.

I don't know how long I stayed underwater. But when I came out, I felt transformed and full of strength. The man helped me get out with his flowery branch.

"You passed the ordeal. The river did not devour you. You all are innocent," he said. He reached for a towel that was on a rock and handed it to me.

"Why do you address me in the plural?" I ventured to ask him while I was drying myself off.

"You and your shadows are all innocent."

"Me and my shadows? Innocent of what?"

"Do not ask me those questions. Ask Him. I am just doing my duty," he said in a condescending tone, pointing to the sky. Then he gave me a hug. When stepping back, he grabbed me by the arms and, looking me in the eyes, he added:

"Now tell me, who are you?"

"I don't know," I said, surprised, realizing that I didn't remember anything about myself.

"If you do not know anything about yourselves, how do you want me to help you? Your ignorance will prevent you from reaching your destiny," he said and started to walk away.

"Wait! All I know is that I don't belong in this world," I responded without reflecting. And remembering the music that guided me to this place, and trying to get this mysterious man on my side, I pointed to the sun and added:

"My homeland is not here. It is yonder."

"Ah!" he said with a tone of relief and satisfaction and crossed his arms. Holding his chin with his left hand and assuming a solemn attitude, he asked me:

"Did you fulfill the mission with which the Lord entrusted you? Know that you will not be able to take flight toward the light until you fulfill your mission on Earth."

I admitted that I'd never known my mission or purpose on Earth.

"Then it is not yet your destiny to go to the celestial homeland," he affirmed categorically. "You are going to have to return to the world of shadows to discover who you are and where you are from. Only then will you be able to dispel darkness and enjoy the incomparable splendor of the eternal light."

After he said this, he softened his voice and facial expression and asked me:

"Will you allow me a few questions to test the state of your mind so that I may learn how to set about your cure?"

"Sure, ask what you will."

"Do you know the universal end toward which the aim of all nature is directed?"

"No, I don't," I said immediately.

He looked at me with dismay.

"Hmm, let me think about it," I said, worried, and took a lengthy pause to reflect.

He leaned on his walking stick and waited for my answer.

"Other than realizing its infinite potential, I'm not sure if nature has a set goal in its creative acts," I said tentatively.

"Interesting," he said, caressing his beard with his right hand and making an expression of worry.

After a brief pause, he assumed a pensive posture and asked me:

"This world of ours, is it governed fortuitously, or is there any rational guidance in it?"

"I don't know. I've always wondered that. It seems to me that Mother Nature is intelligent and imaginative and that it guides itself as much by reason as by chance."

He made a gesture of disapproval and crossed his arms again.

"Do you know whence all things have proceeded?"

"No, I don't," I answered in all honesty.

"Ah!" he exclaimed, raising his eyebrows and lifting his right arm while pointing at the sky with his index finger. "Then I already know the cause of your sickness. Your vision of truth is hindered by your lack of understanding. Not only do you ignore the origin and the end of all things but you also believe that the demons of chance are the lords of the universe. Come with me. I will give you shelter, clothing, and food, for all strangers and beggars are sent from Him. I will try to disperse these misleading notions by mild and soothing application so that you may come to discern the splendor of the true light."

2

THE MAN TOOK ME BY THE HAND AND LED ME TO A JUDAS TREE that was teeming with purple flowers. Two tunics swayed gently from its branches and two pairs of sandals rested near its trunk. He reached for one of the tunics, wrapped it around his left side so his right shoulder and chest remained uncovered. Then he grabbed a pair of sandals and tied them up. After that, he handed me the other tunic and sandals and asked me to put them on and follow him.

We descended a rugged slope filled with evergreen oaks, firs, junipers, and menacing predators. Their vigilant eyes would light up the dense fog every now and again. I descended with difficulty and was scared for my life. I would have been petrified had it not been for the music of a guitar that accompanied us along the way, playing sad songs like "Estrellita," "Lágrima," "Melancolía," and "Una limosna por el amor de Dios."

"Who's the guitar player?" I asked.

"Do you see how the wild oaks align themselves, the hard rocks soften, and the wild beasts hold back when they see us? It is the guardian angel of all those who believe that the true life is absent," said the man enthusiastically.

We continued our descent in silence. Once we crossed the blanket of fog, a mountain valley unfolded before our eyes. I stared at the landscape in awe, then turned to look at the old man and was stunned by his sudden new appearance. His hair was tonsured, his beard was shaved, and he wore a Franciscan habit. The flowery branch had turned into a large Christian cross. Strangely, we were now standing on a mountain peak.

"Do not be scared, son. Times are hard." He spoke to me as if I were a child, and as though he were attempting to soothe my fear.

"The Indians do not know the Gospel, and they need to be saved from the claw of the Infernal Enemy."

"But where are we? Where are you taking me?" I asked, feeling confused and betrayed.

"We are going home. You need to rest, son."

"And who are you?" I said, trying to hide my anguish.

He stopped and, looking me straight in the eye, replied:

"I am Brother Antonio de San Pablo, professing friar of the Order of Our Seraphic Father Saint Francis of Assisi, provincial of Convento Grande and native of Belvís de Monroy."

"Ah!" I answered, not knowing what to say. Facing east, I looked toward the valley.

There was a chain of mountains that stretched from north to south. Toward the north it was tall and green; toward the south, pale and barren. Behind it, at the end of the horizon, there was another mountain chain, barely visible. Below us there was a canyon with red rock formations and a river that ran in a north-south direction. On the bank of the river, toward the north, there was a wooded strip of land; toward the south, an endless wasteland. The sun was starting to burn its way up the horizon.

"Where are we?" I asked hesitantly.

"We are at the top of the San Mateo Mountains. The tall ones in the northeast are the Magdalena Mountains and behind them are the Manzano Mountains. Over there, on the west side, at the end of the horizon, that is the Sierra Oscura. In the southwest, that is the Fra Cristobal Sierra. Over there, in the south, those are the Caballo Mountains, and the wasteland next to them is the Jornada del Muerto."

That landscape and those names jogged me out of my state of amnesia. They brought up memories of the time when I lived in Albuquerque with Alma. We used to camp and hike in this area. While the man was talking, I recalled the time when she and I had camped on this very mountain. She had been studying for her PhD qualifying exams and was so exhausted and stressed that she was unable to sleep. I suggested that we go to Cíbola National Park. Previously, we had gone camping in the Sandía Mountains. I cherished the idea of hiking in the southern part of the park, particularly in the San Mateo Mountains. I was hoping to see a spotted owl in its natural habitat. I also wanted to hike in the Apache Kid Wilderness, where the riches of the flora, fauna, geology, and history of New Mexico are intimately intertwined. At first, Alma refused to take the weekend off, arguing that she had too much studying to do. However, the thought of being in a remote place that few hikers visited convinced her in the end.

We camped near here, I thought to myself, near the Shipman Trail. The evening we arrived I set out, flashlight in hand, to find a spotted owl. Alma tried to dissuade me, but I reminded her that it was one of the reasons why I had come to this place. I had a map and a detailed guide that included all the trails of the San Mateo Mountains. I was confident I would not get lost. Moreover, I assured her, I would only explore the area around our camp. She said good night and went to sleep.

I was lucky to hear the hooting of an owl almost as soon as I left the tent. I walked cautiously toward the place where I heard it. But I tripped, and the owl flew to another tree. I stopped and waited, hoping to hear it again. Sure enough, it started to hoot from a tree that was taller and deeper in the forest. I decided to follow it, knowing that I had a chance of getting lost, but telling myself that I wouldn't venture too far from the camp.

The owl hooted and hooted, as if aware I was looking for him.

I walked stealthily toward the owl. Fortunately, the ground was relatively flat, and I didn't run the risk of falling off a cliff. I got close to the tree that sounded like the source of the hooting. When I was about to locate the owl with my flashlight, he flew to another tree, where the terrain was more rugged.

I didn't hesitate to follow him. This time the owl was making screeching noises that sounded like a burst of cackles. Guided by my flashlight and the shrieks, I walked deeper into the forest until I reached a rocky point on uneven ground. I proceeded with extreme caution, making sure I didn't get anywhere near a cliff. The sky was clear, there was a full moon, I had plenty of food and water in my backpack, it wasn't cold, and the weather forecast was good. I couldn't miss the rare opportunity to see a spotted owl in its natural habitat with my own eyes.

I kept walking on the rocky point with extreme care, but I stumbled and dropped the flashlight. It fell down the rocks until it disappeared. The owl was still resting on the same tree and kept teasing me with his screeches.

I thought that I was going to find him with the moonlight, but I could not. I had to find solace in the dubious merit of having found an owl, spotted or not, in its native grounds. When he stopped screeching and flew away, I decided to return to the camp.

As one would expect, I found neither the trail back to the camp nor any other. I wandered lost in the mountain for several hours until I found a meadow. I lay down to rest and, without realizing it, I fell asleep and had a dream that I would never forget.

An Apache man was chasing me in the woods. He was riding a horse, and I was running barefoot. At times I seemed to escape, but he always reappeared. After a long chase I fell down, exhausted. The soles of my feet were wounded and covered in mud. Once again, the Apache man appeared on his horse and yelled from afar:

"Do you remember me? I'm Refugio."

An owl that hovered over him flew toward me, landed on a ledge that was behind me, and spoke:

"You fool! Why do you run away? I'll destroy you if I want, or I might let you go. Only an idiot struggles against his superiors!"

Then I awoke. The day was dawning.

"I remember very well that I fell asleep on a mountain peak like this one," I said to myself when I ended my remembrance. "The landscape was identical."

Brother Antonio was still next to me, and he was also contemplating the landscape.

"Are we in New Mexico?"

"Yes, these mountains are located in the province of New Mexico."

"Have you been to Albuquerque?" I asked to show him I knew the area.

"In the province of Extremadura?"

"No, in New Mexico."

"You must be confused, son," he said emphatically. "There is no place with that name around here."

"Albuquerque is located between Socorro and Santa Fe," I said with certainty.

"Santa Fe? Are you talking about the Real Villa de la Santa Fe de San Francisco de Asís?" He spelled out the full name of the capital, as if he wanted me to speak more properly.

"I suppose that's what they used to call it in the olden times."

"In the olden times? The village was founded by Don Pedro de Peralta only fifty-five years ago."

He must have escaped from an asylum, I thought to myself. Or I must be dreaming.

I tried to wake myself up. I was used to doing this whenever I was in the midst of a nightmare or anxiety dream and needed to analyze my situation. The fact of knowing that it was only a dream helped me wake up. What a relief, it was only a dream, I would tell myself. Sometimes I would fall back asleep and the nightmare would continue. But as soon as I realized it was only a dream, I would wake up again, and the nightmare would dissipate. I would return to normality, to my everyday life.

However, this time I couldn't wake myself up. No matter how much I pinched my arm and rubbed my eyes, Brother Antonio remained next to me, looking at me like a psychiatrist trying to help an amnesiac.

It's true that I had forgotten who I was momentarily, I thought. But that could happen to anyone after a whack in the head.

"Are you hungry, Diego?" Brother Antonio asked me, uttering a name that I seemed to recognize as mine.

"Yes, hungry and thirsty. And how did you know my name?"

"Why wouldn't I? I am your father."

"You, my father?" I asked with incredulity. But Brother Antonio pretended not to hear me. He took out a prickly pear from his haversack. He peeled it deftly with a knife and offered it to me. I savored the succulent fruit. It tasted like it had been taken from the Tree of Life itself. Then he gave me water from his gourd. I saw his dusty, calloused feet, his dirty sackcloth, his haversack, his hollow-cheeked, wrinkled face, and the cross.

"Let us go home," he said. "Soon the heat will become unbearable."

I scanned the entire valley and couldn't see a single hamlet.

"All I can see are mountains and wasteland," I said, getting a bit worried.

"Do not fret, son. The Divine Providence has foreseen everything. When I came here for the first time to this province with Brother Isidro Ordóñez and others, I also thought that I would never get out of this place alive. Now I wonder if I'll ever be able to leave this place at all. In this kingdom you have to be very patient. Here time can move as slowly as a snail and as fast as a peregrine falcon."

"And how are we going to get home?"

"On horseback. Refugio is waiting for us."

At that precise moment appeared the Apache man of my nightmare riding a pinto horse and pulling a brown one. He was shirtless and donned a medicine wheel necklace. He was thin and solid like a cedar tree. Although he was probably in his late forties, his face was marked by the cruelty of life and the elements. He had lost his left eye and a scar in his left cheek deformed his face with its angular features and prominent chin.

"You were right!" Brother Antonio said. "I found Diego in trail-with-junipers-that-forks-and-disappears-in-crest!"

"*Goozhoo doleeł*!" he replied.

"Yes," said Brother Antonio, "the Lord's blessings will come to us!"

Brother Antonio took me by the arm so that we could get closer to Refugio.

"He is a witch," I said, trying to lower my voice. "He wants to kill me."

"Do not fear, son. He is your relative. Furthermore, you have done nothing bad. You entered Apache territory by mistake. It was he who let me know you were here."

"And how did he know? He has been chasing me."

"He had a revelation," said Brother Antonio, lowering his voice, as if it were a dangerous secret.

"Revelation, my foot! You must be confused," I replied angrily. "Or I must be dreaming," I said to myself.

"You have had a concussion. Let us go. I will explain everything along the way," he said, pulling me gently by the arm.

"And how do you know he is not deceiving you?" I asked, resisting his pull.

"Refugio is worthy of trust. He prides himself on always uttering the truth. Moreover, I have not told anyone about you," he said, looking me in the eyes. "Let us go. The journey is long."

I assented listlessly. We approached Refugio and the horses. While Brother Antonio checked the tack of the brown horse, Refugio asked me:

"Remember the sign and the code word?"

"Pardon me?" I said, puzzled.

"The sign and the code word. Remember?"

He spoke to me as if we already knew each other, and as if I should know what he was talking about. His voice sounded feminine, ethereal, and strangely familiar. I tried to remember who this person was and what the sign and the code word were, but I couldn't.

Unfrazzled by my lack of response, he made an odd gesture. He placed the medicine wheel pendant on his heart and, pointing at it with his right index finger, he made a harsh, guttural sound: "Aaaaaaaaaaaaaaaaah."

I found his behavior extremely odd and didn't know what to make of it. I smiled out of politeness and moved away.

When Brother Antonio finished checking the tack, he approached me. He handed me the cross, hopped on the horse with ease, and ordered me to sit behind him. I gave the cross back to him and placed my left foot on the stirrup. He took the cross with his right hand and offered me his left one so that I would hold on to him. Making a huge effort, I mounted and sat behind him clumsily, ashamed at my lack of skill.

"It's been a while since I got on a horse," I said, trying to justify myself. But Brother Antonio didn't seem to hear me.

"*Kadi-i!*" yelled Refugio, and we started the journey.

3

WE DESCENDED IN SILENCE THROUGH A ROUGH AND NARROW path that converged with a pebbly rivulet along some stretches. When we arrived at a meadow with a stream, we dismounted to drink water and filled our calabashes. Brother Antonio took out a chunk of beef jerky from his haversack and handed some pieces to Refugio and me.

"*Ahiy'e*," said Refugio.

"*Gracias*," said I.

We both ate our portion. Brother Antonio only drank water and apportioned in equal parts the rest of the beef jerky.

As we were eating, it dawned on me that my psychotherapist wore a medicine wheel necklace like Refugio's. I caught a glimpse of him and noticed their uncanny resemblance. Both made a similar facial expression when pensive, and both had an angular jaw and a cleft chin. I tried to recall her name but couldn't. I remembered that she had been teaching me dream yoga and conjectured that maybe Refugio was her avatar. Realizing that I was having a lucid dream, I made a mental note to write it down in my journal as soon as I woke up and promised myself to recount her my dream the next time we had a session.

It will amuse her, I said to myself, laughing quietly.

Knowing that I was dreaming comforted me and allowed me to feel more at ease near Refugio.

When we finished our snack and the horses grazed sufficiently, we continued our descent down the mountain. After a while, I sank into sleep and dreamed I was walking with Alma along a gorge following the course of the Río Grande. We were holding hands happily and silently enjoying the beautiful view and the cozy warmth of the autumnal afternoon.

Suddenly, some voices and hoorays woke me up. A bunch of people were gathering around and welcoming us to their pueblo. They were clearly waiting for us. Their leader, who seemed more than a hundred years old, approached us. We dismounted, greeted him, and exchanged pleasantries of friendship and good will. They welcomed us and served us watermelon juice in clay mugs. The pueblo was called San Marcial. The blocks of two-story adobe dwellings formed a small, hexagonal fortress. We entered the village through an alley that led us to the central plaza. Some houses had a kiva in front of them, a dome-like structure with an opening and a ladder in the middle to access its interior. Later I found out that the Franciscans called them "stoves" and regarded them as demonic temples. The pueblo leader and his cohort led us to the center of the plaza where there was a row of makeshift ramadas that had tables with clay pots and terracotta ware filled with food.

The cacique invited us to sit down on some palm-leaf mats they had reserved for us. They served us tamales, beans, and roasted squash. Refugio and I started eating eagerly, but Brother Antonio kneeled and prayed.

When Refugio and I emptied our plates, Brother Antonio stopped praying, signaled us that he wasn't going to eat, encouraged us to split his meal, and went back to his praying. We obliged, divided his lunch in equal portions, and continued to eat in silence.

When we finished eating, Refugio moved closer to me and asked me a question that astonished me:

"You had a nightmare with an owl the other night, right?"

"Say what?" I asked in disbelief.

"Remember the dream you had with me and an owl?" he said, pointing at my nose with his index finger.

I couldn't believe that he knew the dream I had when I got lost in the Apache Kid Wilderness. His revelation gave me the chills and left me dumbfounded.

"Holy Wind knows everything," he said, raising his eyebrows and nodding. Then he confessed in a reassuring tone, "Wind's Child told me your nightmare and asked me to help you."

"Why?" I asked incredulously but trying to sound solicitous.

"Because I'm a medicine man and you're sick. Owls give Enemy Ghost sickness," he stated matter-of-factly. "But don't worry, I'm gonna heal you. I'm gonna beat the Enemy Ghost into the ground."

When he said this, Brother Antonio stood up. He requested the attention of our hosts and people started to gather around us. He thanked them for their generous welcome and related the parable of the lost sheep. Thanks to the help of an interpreter, some of the people that surrounded us heeded his message and seemed to receive it enthusiastically. Others, however, observed us with curiosity and puzzlement. It must have seemed odd to them, both our trio and Brother Antonio's story, which he finished by quoting the Gospel: "Rejoice with me, because I have found my sheep that was lost. Luke 15:6."

Then the leader of San Marcial spoke. He thanked us for our visit and invited his people to deem our arrival an honor. When he ended his short speech, everyone applauded and made a racket.

Afterward the pueblo leader and some companions led us toward a small chapel that was embedded on the east wing of one of the main buildings of the pueblo. Brother Antonio asked me to walk beside him. When we entered the chapel, we went straight to the baptismal font. Three neatly dressed young couples, each carrying a baby, approached the font. Brother Antonio requested me to be their godfather and asked me how "the nurslings" should be named. I accepted cheerfully, forgetting that I was no longer Catholic, and uttered the first forenames that came to mind, María Guadalupe, María Lourdes, and José Antonio, which pleased Brother Antonio.

At the end of the ceremony, our hosts invited us to stay and celebrate with them. But they must have understood that we needed to get going, since they didn't insist. As soon as we returned to the plaza, they brought us four horses: Refugio's pinto, the brown one, which was only wearing a rein, an old perlino they assigned to me, and an ash-gray horse that was carrying provisions for the trip.

It must have been about five o'clock when we left. The sun was no longer scorching the llano, but it still burned. Refugio accompanied us only until we reached the bank of the river. There he said good-bye. He was riding his pinto and was pulling the brown horse.

Brother Antonio and I continued our *jornada* along a road that ran parallel to the river. He remarked that we were on the Camino Real and assured me that I had traversed this same road on a mule all the way from Mexico City. At that point, I was already wondering whether what I was experiencing with Brother Antonio was a long dream or whether what I had been remembering from my previous existence were mere fabulations that a playful or malicious spirit had put in my head to deceive me.

"It's a miracle that you survived," he said solemnly. "We owe it all to the most glorious and pious thaumaturge, the apostle San Antonio de Padua, protector of travelers and finder of lost objects."

"Ahem, yes, of course," I answered without conviction.

"I owe San Antonio a great deal: life itself. When I arrived here, gravely ill from Spain, the physicians in Mexico City had given up all hope for me. I owe San Antonio also my entrance into the Franciscan order and my venture in these New World missions. Now I owe him your trip to these provinces as well as rescuing you alive in the San Mateo Mountains. You were lost for seven days! The intendant told me that you got lost when you strayed from the caravan's route after crossing the Jornada del Muerto, about ten leagues from here. What were you thinking? Why did you not follow the Camino Real?"

"I got lost in a strange forest," I answered curtly, remembering my encounter with him.

"Luckily, Refugio knew the exact place where I would find you. An angel must have revealed it to him, the same one that appeared to me a few months ago telling me that you would come to New Mexico. As soon as we arrive in Senecú, I will send a messenger to inform your mother that we have found you. She will be happy to know that you have arrived safely."

"My mother is here?" I was surprised.

"She lives in the Real Villa de la Santa Fe. You will meet her one of these days when she visits Senecú. You will meet your mother and, most likely, your *tía* Juana and other relatives too. The Romeros are prominent people of Río Abajo. Your *bisabuelo* Don Bartolomé Romero, God rest his soul, was a captain in Don Juan de Oñate's army."

"And who is the man that accompanied us?" I asked with trepidation.

"Refugio is an illegitimate son of Don Bartolomé. His Apache name is Iłní'yee. He lives with his people, the Gilas, fourteen leagues away from Senecú Pueblo, on the western slope of the Magdalena Mountains. His maternal grandfather was a Navajo medicine man called Sanaba, whom I converted thirty-five years ago and who lived in Ojo Caliente because he married a Gila woman. Refugio attends Mass in Senecú every now and then. He is facilitating our conversion efforts in his camp. We are trying to catechize the Gila people, but the Apache are very reluctant to convert. They have been the crucible of our work in these provinces."

"And what were you doing on the mountain with him?" I asked, still incredulous of his account.

"When you got lost, everyone believed you were a dead man, except me. That night an angel appeared in one of my dreams. He told me I would receive news of your whereabouts soon. The next morning, I went to Refugio's camp in Ojo Caliente. He told me that, the night before, he had received a revelation after he took peyote. Not only did he know that you were traveling on the caravan from Mexico City and that you had disappeared in the San Mateo Mountains but it was revealed to him the exact location where I would find you. I knew immediately that the Lord had made Refugio an instrument of his infinite greatness and mercy. I asked him to take me to that place. He said he would do it if I gave him El Pardo and the saddle as payment for his services. I accepted, of course. We went up the mountain, and the rest of the story you must know well."

Fortunately, I did and could nod in comprehension this time.

We stopped to rest and refresh ourselves in a wooded area. We let the horses graze in a grassy patch and sat down under a pinyon pine. After having a drink of water, Brother Antonio began to comb the area looking for pinecones with seeds. While doing that he spoke to me about the origins of Native Americans. He claimed that they were the descendants of the ten tribes that Yahweh expelled from Israel during the time of King Hoshea.

"Yahweh sent them off to these overseas lands called Arzareth in the Scriptures. The lost tribes of Israel had been worshipping the Devil until we arrived. They still practice all kinds of idolatrous ceremonies and rites. However, thanks to our evangelizing labor, they are starting to respect the covenant that their ancestors made with Yahweh and, little by little, they are adopting our Christian beliefs and customs. Did you notice how well they received and appreciated the Gospel?" He turned around and looked at me to get my assent.

"Yes, Father," I replied, trying to sound convinced.

"The nation of the Piro is one of the last ones to be converted. They are clothed and civilized, and they till the soil like the Mexicans. They have irrigated and rain-fed lands with good water utilization. Thirty years ago, Brothers Antonio de Arteaga and García de San Francisco began the catechizing labor with the Piro when they founded the Mission of San Antonio de Padua in Senecú Pueblo. As you surely know, Brother García is now building the Mission de Guadalupe at El Paso del Río del Norte to catechize the Manso. Sadly, Brother Antonio de Arteaga passed away last year. Brother Román de la Cruz is now the guardian of the Senecú mission. But he got sick and the custos asked me to be in charge of the mission for a few months."

When he concluded his account, he had finished combing the ground beneath the *piñoneros*. He expressed his disappointment that, although there were many pinecones, none of them had nuts.

"They are all empty. Too bad. It must be due to the drought."

We proceeded on our journey. Along the way he continued his account of the missionary work of the Spaniards in New Mexico. He also spoke to me about his long missionary trajectory in the province. He said he had arrived in 1612 to the Villa Real de la Santa Fe, and that he founded a mission in the Tano pueblo of Galisteo and another in the Tompiro pueblo of San Isidro. He spoke to me about the importance he had always given to music in his instruction.

"It is not true that the Word enters with blood. The Word enters with music."

He praised the intellect of the Pueblo people and the facility with which they learn not just the Christian doctrine but also the mechanical and the liberal arts.

"In the mechanical trades they have learned to forge iron and carve wood. There are carpenters, stonecutters, and sculptors. The children of the caciques, *capitanes*, *fiscales*, and other authority figures have learned to read and write, both in Romance and in Latin. They recite the catechism aloud and in chorus. They know the Pater Noster, the Ave María, the Salve Regina, and pray the entire Creed. Some of them have learned to sing so well that they have become members of the school choir. Antonio Lorenzo, the choir director, composed a complete Mass with concerted flutes. It was a marvel listening to him officiate the Easter Mass."

We continued our journey to Senecú Pueblo. At about midnight we passed by some dry fields. Brother Antonio commented that it had not rained since April, but he assured me that when it rained everything turned green.

Soon after, we finally began to approach the pueblo. We turned right at a fork, ascended a rocky slope, and ran into some famished dogs that barked at us without conviction. Gradually, a row of dwellings with two- and three-story apartments became faintly visible. When we reached the top of the slope, we turned right and entered a narrow street. To the left there was a churchyard and, next to it, on the eastern side, was the mission church, the convent, and, a few meters ahead, the Casa Real. The block of apartments covered the entire right side of the street, forming a fortress wall.

We entered the mission compound through a big wooden gate. Two armed men welcomed us and helped us dismount. The enclosure had a small square with an orchard and a wooden statue of San Antonio de Padua. The church was rustic like the pueblo houses. Despite his old age, Brother Antonio didn't seem tired. As for me, I could hardly move. My legs were asleep and my tailbone and inner thighs were sore. One of the guards had to help me walk. He wore a poncho and a red kerchief. He was stocky, had a patchy moustache and long hair, and was about thirty years old. His name was Pedro Granillo.

We walked toward the convent and crossed a threshold that Pedro called *la portería*. He led me to the ambulatory, which encircled an interior patio covered with flowers and ornamental plants. We turned right and walked through a corridor until we reached the cloister. At the end of the hallway was my cell. Pedro showed it to me briefly and said good night.

The cell had two distinct areas: a small anteroom with a few rustic pieces of wood furniture and a tiny alcove that had a wooden frame covered with a black wool blanket. There I lay down and fell asleep immediately.

4

THAT NIGHT I DREAMED I HAD AN AWFUL CRASH. I WAS AT WORK, at the Cornell Olin Library, and my lunch break was about to start. I needed to send some documents to my mother, and I decided to skip lunch to go to the National Express office downtown. When I went out to get my bike, I noticed two guys staring at me. They were wearing the typical outfit of a border *chero*: a plaid western shirt with pearl snap-on buttons, denim jeans, cowboy boots, a baseball cap, and aviation sunglasses. Their insistent gazes gave me the chills, but I didn't make much of it. I needed to return to work in less than thirty minutes, so I focused on the task at hand. I unlocked my bike and rode toward Day Hall. As soon as I turned right on East Avenue, a black Suburban with dark windows took off, screeching its tires, and started following me. At first I thought I was being paranoid and tried to ignore it. But the Suburban was getting too close to me. I should have slowed down, moved to the side, and let them pass me, but I refused to be intimated and harassed. I pedaled faster and didn't make any stops. When I entered College Town, I thought I had lost them because the campus traffic forced the Suburban to slow down. However, when I reached East Buffalo Street, the Suburban caught up with me. I pedaled as fast as I could, hoping that I would leave it behind. But suddenly, when I was about halfway down the hill, I lost control of my bike and hit a tree, head on.

I woke up horrified but relieved that it had been only a nightmare. Then the tolling of a bell and the beating of some drums reminded me where I was.

"I must still be in Senecú. Damn!" I couldn't believe it. My mind was full of confusing images: the cheros, the Suburban, Ithaca, Alma, Cíbola National Park, Brother Antonio, Refugio, Senecú. The tolling of the bell and the beating of the drums reverberated in my head. The light of dawn was barely beginning to shine.

I had a terrible headache. It felt as if I really had received a whack in the head recently. I remembered that my hair was wet and sticky and that my clothes were stained with blood before I dipped in the river yesterday. Maybe the bicycle accident had been real. After all, it was the last memory I had. I couldn't remember anything after riding down the hill on my bike on Buffalo Street the other day.

I didn't know what to make of this dream. I decided that maybe my headache was due to lack of sleep and caffeine withdrawal.

Brother Antonio entered my room without knocking and stood at the foot of my pallet.

"Good morning, Diego. You must be tired and sore. Are you hungry?"

"Yes, I'm starving. I need a cup of coffee," I said, rubbing my eyes and resigned to play my role in this nightmare, hoping that the coffee would help me wake up to reality.

"Coffee? What is that?"

I got up, sat down at the foot of the pallet, and tried my best to explain what coffee is. "It's a dark brown, aromatic drink, served hot. It helps you wake up."

"That's strange," he said, looking puzzled. "I have never heard of such a drink. It must be a new custom in Mexico City. We do not have it around here. We Franciscans kindle the spirit differently. Each morning, as soon as the bell rings, we get up and, before laziness and the Devil attempt to tempt and control us, we make a punctual discipline of twenty lashes. By the way, because today is a holiday and you just arrived, I have allowed you to get up late. But starting tomorrow you will get up at midnight to pray matins and, afterward, you get up again at five to participate in the Divine Office of Lauds. This afternoon I will give you instructions regarding the Divine Office and about how to conduct yourself during the liturgical hours."

I didn't understand what all of this meant or implied and changed the subject.

"What are you celebrating today?" I asked in a casual tone.

"Are you asking because of the clangor outside?" he said in a sarcastic tone. "Today it is the Día de San Lorenzo. Some Christian Piro are dancing and wearing masks and traditional costumes, like their pagan ancestors did to pay homage to their idols. They are making a *manda* to San Lorenzo so that he intercedes for them before God Our Lord. They are pleading for rain and other boons."

"Of course," I replied, thinking of the Juárez of the youth that I remembered, which did not appear to be the youth that this man seemed to think I had had, where some people celebrated the Day of Saint Lawrence this way.

"Of course?" he said in a tone of stern surprise. "Maybe these *zarambeques* are allowed in Mexico City and other parts of New Spain, but here in New Mexico they are strictly forbidden. These masked dancers are taking advantage of the fact that Brother de la Cruz is in the hospital of San Felipe. They know that they will not be punished so long as I am in charge of the mission."

"These dances don't bother you?"

"I am one of the few Franciscans in this province who thinks it is better to allow the Indians to dance as long as they embrace our religion and pay homage to our saints."

"I believe you are right," I commented with all the naivete of the newcomer.

"That may be, but if you want to avoid having problems with the Inquisition, you better keep your opinions to yourself, especially regarding the topic of Native dances."

"I didn't realize this was a controversial matter. Thanks for the advice, Father."

Taking advantage of the fact that I needed to relieve myself, I changed the topic.

"Can you please tell me where the bathrooms are?"

"Bathrooms? We have no bathrooms here. We are neither in Jemez nor in Algiers."

"I need to do my business."

"Oh, in that case, the latrine is right behind this wall. The door to access it is in the backyard. Put on the tunic and habit of mine that I have left for you on the table by the entrance. Your household goods will arrive later. The mission supply caravan is stuck in San Felipe because Don Juan Manso, the intendent, did not allow us to unload anything in Socorro. The rascal uses the caravan for his personal profit. Hopefully, we will be able to resolve this issue within the next few days. As soon as you get dressed, I will show you the latrine."

"Thank you, Father."

"Please call me Brother. From now on I'm going to be your fellow Franciscan Brother Antonio."

"Alright, Brother," I acquiesced, the same way that I accepted everything else that was happening to me, reluctantly but without protest, as often happens when we are dreaming.

He walked out of the room and closed the door. I got up to grab the garb. It was an aniline-blue habit with a hood made of *sayal* wool, a white cincture with three knots, a wooden Tau cross, and a devotional scapular. The woolen fabric of the habit was as rough as sackcloth.

Partly out of sheer curiosity and partly to avoid conflict, I decided to put on the vestment. I felt uncomfortable and annoyed when I put it on. There was not a Franciscan square inch of my body, I thought, irritated, not even the calluses on my feet. Even though I had been a devout Catholic as a child, I had become an agnostic at the age of twenty-three. Catholicism and other monotheistic religions seemed to me tyrannical and retrograde, an invention of fanatical and intolerant men avid of earthly power.

I exited my cell ill humored. Brother Antonio was waiting in the hallway. First, he showed me the way to the latrine, and then to the refectory. He said he was going to wait for me at the patio and went to the storage room to fetch a watering can.

I walked back to the latrine. It was a small room, wide and narrow. It had a row of four limestone basins without dividers. When I sat down to do my business, I started to hear the voices and laughs of some children. Then the voice of an adult yelling at them. He was demanding them to be quiet and to form two lines. As soon as the children quieted down, he checked the roll.

Upon exiting the latrine, I washed my hands using a bronze bowl and a ceramic pitcher with clean water that were lying on a table outside. I was happy to also find a bar of soap and a clean towel.

I walked toward the patio of the ambulatory and found Brother Antonio watering some flowers in front of the refectory. He invited me to have breakfast. Before crossing the threshold of the refectory, he asked me to bow halfway before the crucifix that was hanging above. Then he led me to the table that was farthest from the entrance.

The refectory was small. It had a series of narrow tables that were aligned parallel to the wall. The seats were attached to it and were made of whitewashed adobe bricks. On two of the walls a fragment of Psalm 21 was inscribed in Latin in large, gothic letters: "The poor shall eat and shall be filled: and they shall praise the Lord that seek him: their hearts shall live for ever and ever." Another wall sported a small window in the center and a corner fireplace in the back. The floor was made of compacted mud, and the ceiling boasted hand-hewn beams.

Breakfast was served. Before having a bite, he asked me to put my hands inside my sleeves and on my chest, to look downward, and, with my heart set on God Our Lord, to entrust to Him those who had produced this food by the sweat of their brow and to those who had given it to us as alms.

Noticing that there were no plates in front of him, after our brief prayer I asked him if he would eat. He replied that he always fasted in the morning. I, on the contrary, couldn't wait any longer. "Pardon me," I said, and took a sip of the frothy hot chocolate, which was getting cold. Brother Antonio scolded me for not waiting for him to bless the meal.

"I see that you didn't learn anything in the convent."

I gave him a blank look that he chose to ignore. He ordered me to get up and kneel down in front of him, bowing my head. He told me not to move until he said so, and to say amen after he finished saying grace.

When I returned to my seat, he let me know that the hot chocolate I was about to drink was a luxury reserved for special occasions.

"What is today's date?" I asked timidly.

He moved away from me and made a mockingly discreet gesture of incredulity mixed with disapproval. He informed me that it was "the Tuesday in which we count ten days of the month of August of the year sixteen sixty-five."

I gave a sip to my hot chocolate. Suddenly, it dawned on me what was happening. All of this must be a dream, I said to myself. Probably the nightmare I had last night was a replay of an actual accident. I must be in a coma or, maybe, I was anesthetized. This was what must be happening. Otherwise, how to explain these hallucinations?

I recalled that my maternal grandfather had published a journal article about the history of the missions of Senecú, Socorro, and Ysleta. I remembered it very well. In a footnote he stated that one of his ancestors had arrived from Socorro to El Paso del Norte in 1680, when the Pueblo Indians revolted and expelled the Spaniards from

New Mexico. Could Brother Antonio be my ancestor? He claimed to be my father. If this was the case, why had he brought me to this mission? Didn't he run the risk of being expelled from the order for having broken his vow of chastity? At his age? I doubted it. This happened many years ago. They must have pardoned him by now.

"What are you thinking, Diego? Have you lost your appetite? You have not tasted the tamales yet."

"Nothing in particular, Brother." I opened the corn leaves and savored the dense texture of the *tamal* mixed with raisins and toasted pine nuts. "Mmm, they're yummy. I've never had them with pine nuts. Who made them?"

"Concha, an Otomí woman from Tlaxcala. Cooooonchaaaaaaaa!" he yelled loudly, asking her to come over.

A mildly wrinkled, round-faced, short, stocky woman with long, salt-and-pepper braids approached us. She was wearing a white cotton blouse that was finely embroidered with red flowers and deer figures. An embroidered white belt with red figures secured her black skirt.

"Concha, Brother Diego likes your tamales."

"Yes, Concha, your tamales are delicious. Thank you very much."

"Thank you, Father," she replied with a discreet smile and, bending her knees slightly, she bowed and left in haste.

Brother Antonio commented that she had arrived from Tlaxcala with Don Pablo Baxcajay, her husband, along with other relatives, about fifty years ago. They had worked at the Senecú mission since Brothers Antonio de Arteaga and García de San Francisco founded it in 1626. Along with other Otomí, they built the Hermita of San Miguel in Analco, a settlement located south of the village of Santa Fe, where many of them lived.

"Don't they live in Senecú?"

"No, Concha and Don Pablo live here in the convent. Neither the Piro nor other Pueblo people allow outsiders to live in their communities. They want to keep their autonomy."

"Why is that?" I asked while unwrapping another tamal.

"They want to preserve their customs and traditions, and surely also to continue practicing their pagan rites and idolatrous superstitions secretly. They are like the sick who refuse to be cured. Despite all they have suffered in exile for worshipping the Devil, famines, pestilences, droughts, storms, hail, wars, and all sorts of hardships and tribulations, they continue to cling to their idols. But, little by little, we are curing their soul with the Gospel and good deeds. Catechizing them with love and benevolence will cure them. Only then will they be able to enjoy the eternal bliss that awaits them. For it is written that God Our Lord has promised us the Kingdom of Jerusalem. I tell them over again: Be ready to receive the gifts of this kingdom. When Christ Our Lord returns, a perpetual light will illuminate us forever. We will no longer have to toil nor worry about anything. The Tree of Life will perfume with its fragrance all the pueblos and the fields. Trees laden with fruits, fields full of grain and vegetables, and rivers brimming with milk and honey will nourish us. All the mountains will be perpetually adorned with lilies and roses."

"And what do they say?"

"Those whose hearts are not hardened are filled with hope and receive the Word of God, like plants drinking water in the drought season. But others have the soul bedeviled and resist conversion. Those who wish to keep practicing their wicked idolatries are ineluctably punished. Fortunately, these are few. Most of them accept our spiritual medicine if we sweeten it with temporal benefits. They allow us to baptize their children and attend Mass so that God brings them good harvests and we protect them from the Apache."

"The Apache?"

"Yes, sometimes they attack and raid us. To avoid this, and to keep peace with them, periodically we give them corn and cotton fabric. We are also teaching them to sow and, of course, to learn and love the Word of God. Now that you have arrived, God bless us, we will be able to intensify our labor, pacifying and evangelizing them."

"What do you mean, Brother?" I asked in disbelief.

"Brother Alonso de Benavides started the pacifying labor of the Gila Apache more than thirty years ago. He converted the leader of a band whose winter encampment is about fourteen leagues from here. Since then, a few Apache have converted. Now that you have arrived, we trust that many more will." He said it in a tone that suggested I was fully aware of why I had come to New Mexico.

"Me? Convert the Apache? Christianize them?"

"Yes, of course. That is why you came. Is it not?" he said, surprised and a bit irritated. "You will have many opportunities to serve God and earn your place in Heaven by taking away from the Devil his dominion over their souls. The Gila Apache are inclined to being converted. Every time I speak to them about God, they listen attentively. While they are bellicose, once you earn their trust, they are peaceful and generous."

This is absurd. Me, a missionary? How ridiculous! I thought to myself.

I got up, walked toward the window, and looked outside. There was a vegetable garden in the patio with planted tomatoes, watermelons, lettuce, squash, and chili peppers.

"What if I am not dreaming?" I said to myself. "What am I going to tell this man? That I don't believe in God? That I don't know what I'm doing here? That I'm from another era?"

But everything seemed real. Nothing seemed ethereal or an illusion. Brother Antonio was sitting on the chair, cross-armed, waiting for me to say something. I remained standing by the window, confused. I fixed my eyes on the vegetable garden and lost myself in thought. It occurred to me that the price for heresy was, in this epoch, death. I started to be afraid.

Brother Antonio got up and approached me. He laid his hand on my shoulder and, looking me straight in the eyes, told me:

"I understand you, Brother. All of us, when we arrive in New Mexico for the first time, want to go back whence we came. There is nothing here but desolation and poverty. There are four hibernal months and eight infernal ones. There is neither gold nor silver nor natural riches here as in other parts of New Spain. We live off the alms that the king and the viceroy give us every three years. But we missionaries are not here to find earthly riches. We are here to save the souls of the Indians. It is a pitiful thing to see these human beings, who were created in the image and likeness of God, living as if they were brutes and, even worse, serving the Devil. We are here to make war on the Infernal Enemy and to take away his dominion over their souls."

"But I don't know what I'm doing here," I confessed candidly.

"All the newly arrived have doubts. When I came for the first time to New Mexico on the Camino Real, riding a mule like you did, I also wanted to desert like my other newly ordained brothers. The journey from Zacatecas seemed endless: a wasteland. We were furious with the *procurador*, Brother Isidro Ordóñez, who had recruited us through lies and deception. Worse still, Ordóñez was a tyrant. On one occasion, a brother and I decided to escape to Mexico City to denounce him, but he set a trap for us and arrested us. He locked us in separate cells and laid upon us a regimen of rigorous bread and water fasting. In the cell, my spirit got so agitated that I started to question the wisdom of God. I asked Him why He had put our mission in the hands of such vile and corrupt men. From the moment I arrived in New Mexico, I had seen nothing but conflict and animosity between the custos and the governor. Both seemed more interested in acquiring greater power, riches, and privileges for themselves than in serving God or the king. I asked God why, everywhere I went, we were governed by corrupt and sinful men who committed with impunity all kinds of abuses and injustices against the weak and against those of us who followed His law. Why did He always seem to punish the innocent and reward the wicked? Why did He let the Devil rule in this territory for so long and so freely without any opposition? Why did he allow the Infernal Enemy to take control over the souls of the people of the ten tribes of Israel? Did He not promise Abraham that He would never abandon his descendants? Had he not given us the power to reason, to question everything, including Him? I spent seven days and seven nights in such a state of mind until an angel, dressed in Franciscan garb, appeared in my cell and told me: 'Your understanding about worldly matters is flawed. Do you really believe you can understand God's conduct? They have sent me to present you three problems. If you solve one of them, I will reveal to you all you wish to know.' I replied, 'As you wish, my Lord.' And the angel said to me: 'How much does fire weigh? What is the length of a gust of wind? How many grains of sand are there at the bottom of the sea?' I replied that nobody in this world could possibly know any of those things. Then he admonished me: 'If you are incapable of knowing such worldly matters, how can you possibly fathom the way of God? How can a mind that has been debased by a corrupt world understand goodness and perfection itself?' After he said this, he disappeared. I immediately understood my grave mistake and impertinence. I asked God to forgive me and promised Him to do His will from then on, even if I did not comprehend the nature of things. That day, I finally understood the meaning of the vow of obedience that we Franciscans make and put myself at the service of Ordóñez, unconditionally."

At that point, I decided that it was time to set the record straight once and for all, and replied:

"Brother, but I have not made any religious vows, and I do not know the will of God."

He reacted with a mixture of appalment and anger, but he quickly softened his facial expression and invited me to sit down again. He asked Concha to serve me another cup of chocolate and, after a few moments of tense silence, he said in a stern voice:

"Do you think that I don't know your story, Diego?"

I thought about telling him that my name wasn't Diego and was about to confess to him who I really was. But my survival instinct kicked in. What if this was not a dream? What if he took my account as an act of defiance, or as a sign that I was crazy, possessed, or who knows what else? So I lowered my head, looked down, and remained silent.

"I am not unaware of the fact that you were almost expelled from the Order. Brother Juan de Paz gave me a full report of your activities and conduct in the convent. I also know that they found in your notebooks several passages of the *Encomion Moriae* and other dangerous ideas. The former custos, Brother Alonso de Posadas, and the conventual prior both intervened and asked the council not to send your dossier to the Holy Office. Thanks to them, the council approved your transfer to New Mexico so that you can complete both the novitiate and apostolate under my tutelage. But be warned: If you abandon or are expelled from your mission, you will be sent back to Mexico City, and the Holy Office will hold you accountable for all your transgressions. Notwithstanding these, I trust that you will atone them with your apostolate and your work in this province. Brother Román de la Cruz and I have been waiting for you with great expectation. You will be able to do great deeds and make numerous sacrifices here. For just as the Lord rejoices in the fruit of the cross, which are the souls of those who shall be saved, so will you, Brother Diego Romero, as a sensible and loyal *Siervo de Dios*, and as my son and heir, rejoice saving the souls of the Gentiles and strengthening the faith of the converts in this province of New Mexico."

After saying these words, he got up and bent over to give me a hug. However, I wasn't able to reciprocate it and remained motionless in my seat. I was at a loss as to the unbelievable and ridiculous situation in which I inexplicably found myself.

"Now, I must retire to do my prayers. In a few minutes they will ring the bell to call us to Mass. You can now go to your cell so that you can pray. As soon as the bell rings, I will come by so that we go to Mass together. Afterward, you will meet me in the office. I will show you the mission and will give you all the details of your tasks and responsibilities in this house. You will start fulfilling them tomorrow. Late this afternoon, you will return to your cell. You will have the rest of the day off so that you can pray, rest, and put your thoughts in order."

Brother Antonio left, and I stayed in the refectory a few more minutes, lost in my thoughts.

5

I WENT BACK TO MY CELL, LAY DOWN ON MY PALLET, AND attempted to calm down. I felt dizzy, nauseous, and hot. The habit was itchy, so I took it off to scratch myself.

I must be in the hospital, I thought. Brother Antonio must be my physician. He is neither a Franciscan friar nor my father. I must have fractured my skull in the accident. Yes, that's it! They operated on me and I'm still under the effect of the anesthesia. Or I'm in a coma, sleeping, connected to a respirator. Or could it be that I'm dead? Is this possible? Am I in Purgatory? In Hell? Is God punishing me? What have I done to deserve this?

Everything was spinning around me. I needed to calm down, relax, sleep, and go back to reality. I attempted to meditate. I closed my eyes. First, I focused on my breathing. I inhaled and exhaled deeply several times. Then I hummed the mantra Om in silence. I tried to visualize and focus my mind on the third eye, drew a mental circle with two lotus petals on each side, and attempted to focus my mind on this image to stop thinking, all in vain. A cacophony of voices and thoughts overpowered my efforts.

"Every stranger and beggar comes from Him . . . Do not be scared, Diego. Such are the times we live in. The Indians are ignorant of the Gospel . . . We must save them from the claws of the Devil . . . The Infernal Enemy . . . The Apache have been the crucible of our efforts in these provinces . . .The crucible of our efforts . . . The crucible . . . What does crucible mean? . . . We must save them . . . They are ready to be converted . . . You must serve God . . . You must earn your place in Heaven by taking away from the Devil his dominion over their souls . . . Numerous sacrifices . . . All the newly arrived have doubts . . . They found dangerous ideas in your notebooks . . . You will atone your sins with your apostolate . . . Or else the Holy Office will hold you accountable . . . I am warning you."

I tried not to feel scared. This was all absurd. These were my own fabulations. Brother Antonio was my physician, or maybe my psychotherapist. Where had I seen that gaunt and emaciated face, those droopy eyes?

I remembered the request that Mom made of me yesterday in an email:

"Protect what is yours. He shouldn't appropriate the inheritance that your grandfather left you. Don't delay signing and mailing us back the documents."

"I don't care if I don't get anything," I remembered saying to myself after I got her email.

I didn't want to sign the lawsuit that my mother and her siblings were going to file against their own brother, accusing him of fraud and dispossession.

"If he wants to keep everything, so be it. I don't want you to get me involved in this legal battle. I don't want anything. I'm living life on my own terms."

"Attempting to sell the family's estate behind our back is unforgivable," my mother said in a previous email. "Even though he is my brother, he should go to jail. Even if I sully the family's good name by filing a lawsuit."

I would have liked to call my mother by phone to tell her that I signed the documents, that I was on my way to National Express when I had the bicycle accident. "I'm sorry, Mom. I had an accident.

I hope that someone recovered the documents and shipped them back to you. There are no phones here, no electricity, no Internet."

Anyhow, this was better. I'd rather stay away from the family drama. They probably already published the letter in the local newspaper. The entire city of Juárez must know our personal business by now.

"Prominent family enmeshed in an inheritance scandal," the headline of *El Diario de la Frontera* must say.

I wondered how *abuelito* would react. If he heard anything, he'd have a heart attack. Or maybe he'd remain blissfully oblivious of this scandal. *Pobre* abuelito. Because of his senile dementia, he hadn't been able to leave the house for the past twenty-five years. He had been disconnected from the world. Like me? No. He didn't remember anything after President López Portillo nationalized commercial banks. I did not lose my memory. On the contrary, the accident made me remember things that I had forgotten. Abuelito forgot that Leonid Brezhnev had already died. In his mind, the Cold War continued. The Berlin Wall hadn't fallen. Mexico was a nonaligned, developing country. Juárez was the best border city of Mexico. The College of Agriculture, his alma mater, was still producing scientists and engineers who would help Mexico reach food self-sufficiency. The Juárez Valley continued to grow and export its fine cotton. His ranches were still productive; his businesses were flourishing; his whole family was united; all of his children lived in harmony and were model citizens. His grandchildren were all great kids. If only he knew. My brother Pepe was a drug dealer. Worse still, evil tongues said that my cousin Miguel was an associate of Luisfer and Damián and that they killed several women, including some little girls. I didn't know if this was true, but one thing was certain: Luisfer and Damián tortured and killed Lupita Gualtoye. Alma told me that Miguel was present when Luisfer tortured and killed Hermes García, her uncle's accountant, for revealing secrets of the Holy Brotherhood to her. It was no news that Miguel was going down the wrong path. But it was hard to believe that he practiced satanic rites and filmed snuff movies with Luisfer and Damián . . . I didn't know. I guess it wasn't entirely impossible. Those friends of Miguel's were capable of anything. I always told him: He who keeps company with wolves will learn to howl. But he never listened. He should have gone with me to Las Cruces. He should have stayed away from his friends, the Narco Richies. He was never interested in studying, or working at the ranch or elsewhere. He only wanted to live the good life, being a social butterfly, hanging out with the children or siblings of drug traffickers, politicians, and millionaires. Sex, drugs, and rock and roll, and some country music and *norteñas*. Black Sabbath, Queen, David Bowie, Willie Nelson, Vicente Fernández, Los Tigres del Norte. Easy money, easy women, living off weed, snow, and black tar. Look where Miguel, Abuelito's favorite, ended up. And my uncle's too. Look where the Romeros ended up.

I was able to forget about Brother Antonio and the mission for a few moments, but the ringing of the bells brought to a standstill my trip down memory lane.

I got up and put on the habit quickly. Fast. Fast. Brother Antonio entered just as I was putting on the sandals.

"You look agitated. Were you not praying? Why did you take off the cincture?"

"I had to lie down. I have a headache. I didn't sleep well last night," I explained as I was trying to tie the cincture.

"I see that you still have not learned how to tie the cincture. Did they not teach you this at the convent?"

"I have no idea," I replied.

"I understand. I almost forgot that you have not taken your temporal vows yet. In other circumstances you would not be wearing a habit but, since you had almost finished the novitiate, the council authorized you to use it here. Let me teach you how to tie it."

Brother Antonio showed me, step by step, how to tie the cincture so that the three knots that symbolize the Franciscan vows of poverty, chastity, and obedience would hang over my right leg without dragging.

"See the ingenious way I tied and adjusted the cincture? You can tighten or loosen it easily. See? It fits you perfectly. And if you want to take it off, you do not need to undo the knot. You simply slide it down your legs. Now, let us go. It is getting late."

We walked toward the church via the ambulatory and entered through a side door. I sat on the front pew and he went to the sacristy to get ready for Mass.

The temple was still empty. The nave was small and austere. The floor was made of compacted mud, and the wood ceiling was supported by square, hand-hewn beams carved with floral and geometric figures.

The altar had a modest but graceful retable. In the central panel was a statue of Saint Anthony of Padua with Baby Jesus in his arms. On the right panel was a painting of Saint Francis of Assisi and, on the left, a canvas of Saint Bonaventure. Corinthian columns with twisted shafts adorned the triptych. The top panel had an oil painting of the Immaculate Conception framed between a pair of columns with twisted shafts and crowned by an open pediment with the seal of the Virgin Mary at the center.

The altarpiece also enclosed a painting of the Final Judgment. At the center, the Archangel Saint Michael weighed souls on a scale. Next to him the Virgin Mary advocated for the salvation of the righteous. The condemned souls walked northward toward Hell, and the saved ones ascended to Heaven. At the top, Christ the King was surrounded by the celestial choruses with Moses and Saint Peter in the front, next to him.

I felt out of place being in a church and, especially, dressed in a Franciscan habit. I had not set foot in a Catholic temple in a long time. Years, maybe decades. I made an effort to remember and realized that the last time was the day I married Alma in the San Antonio de Senecú Mission chapel in Ciudad Juárez. I was twenty-two. It was the year 1988. A 323-year temporal abyss separated me from that period of my life when I was still a Catholic and thought that a life without God had no meaning. I recalled a moment in my wedding when I was kneeling in front of the altar. Our godparents had just placed the wedding lasso over Alma and me, and I was praying with fervor. At the center of the altarpiece was a statue of Saint Anthony of Padua, identical to the one standing in front of me. Was it the same statue? I remembered Abuelito used to say that the only relic that the Franciscans were able to save from the original temple, when the Apache burned it in 1675, was precisely the statue of San Antonio.

6

A GROUP OF CHILDREN GARBED IN WHITE AND ESCORTED BY A sacristan entered through the main door of the church and went up the stairs to the triforium. A little later the worshipers started to arrive, and the boys' choir welcomed them, singing "Juste Judex Jesu Christe." Feeling homesick, I remembered that I was also in the boys' choir of Ciudad Juárez and that we sung in the Mission de Guadalupe of El Paso a couple of times. Both temples looked the same. One time we sang during the Día de San Lorenzo, the year when they demolished the cathedral to reconstruct it. I was ten then. The temple was flooded with people. While we were singing, a stream of worshipers circulated around the building, and Father Payán sprinkled holy water over the river of people from the presbytery. The cacophony of the rolling of drums coming from the street was in disharmony with the song of our timid chorus, just as it was now.

I imagined that outside there was a sea of people gathered in front of the temple and that various groups of dancers were paying tribute to San Lorenzo, as it was customary in Juárez on his day. I heard what seemed like party fireworks, but the bangs silenced the chorus immediately. The worshipers that were inside the temple scrambled to the church entrance, and I did the same. There was chaotic screaming and more bangs. Soon after, the shouting got eerily quenched. A Franciscan friar accompanied by several armed men had arrived to interrupt the ceremony of the Piro dancers in front of the temple.

"Get out of here! This is the house of the Lord! There is no worshipping the Devil here!" the friar yelled and whipped one of the dancers on the back.

"Why do you beat him? We're not worshipping the Devil!" one of the drummers protested.

"Don't talk back at me, you bastard son of a bitch!" replied the friar and gave him a vicious lash in the abdomen that wounded him. The lash ricocheted on the skin of the drum, making it resound. Then he added in a solemn tone: "God says in the Scriptures: 'My house shall be called the house of prayer,' but you are making it a den of demons."

"We are pleading with San Lorenzo to bring us rain," said the wounded drummer. He was trying to stop the bleeding with his left hand without success. "We are losing our crops for lack of rain."

"Ask San Lorenzo as God commands us to do," said the friar. "Those dances and those masks invoke the Devil. It will rain fire if you keep paying homage to the Infernal Enemy. God will punish you. He will attack you with all his might."

"We don't want to offend God. We are here to praise Him and San Lorenzo," said the other drummer.

"Do it with Christian rites. You know these dances and those infernal masks are forbidden."

"God has not listened to our prayers," said one of the dancers. "The fields are dry, and the ground is cracked. It has not rained since April. The river is almost empty. We don't know what to do!"

"You need to pray with greater devotion. Do you really believe that God will be moved by your pagan rites? You are paying tribute to the Devil and his abhorrent coterie with those dances and those masks." Addressing one of the armed men that accompanied him, he added: "Chief constable, take these idolaters to the prison cell and confiscate their masks and instruments."

"Yes, Mr. Secretary," replied the officer.

At that point, the chief constable's men were holding and beating the four dancers and the two drummers. They handcuffed them and forcibly put them in a jail wagon pulled by four mules.

When the young Piro men were being taken away, the friar addressed those who had gathered around him:

"Let us now enter the house of the Lord. We are going to pay tribute to San Lorenzo as God commands. San Lorenzo received the crown of martyrdom thanks to his unwavering loyalty to the Pope and to the true Christian cult. Let us learn from him and follow his example."

Brother Antonio witnessed this abuse like everyone else, without intervening in any way. But he looked dejected, as if he himself had been wronged. He headed back to the sacristy, followed by his acolyte. I returned to my seat and the parishioners slowly began to enter the church.

The friar who had participated in the incident sat next to me and greeted me without warmth. Later I found out that he was Brother Salvador Guerra, the secretary of the Holy Custody of the Conversion of Saint Paul of New Mexico. He was a tall and stout man in his fifties. His bald head shone and the little hair that grew on the sides and back was meticulously shaved. He had murky hazel eyes, a straight nose, and full lips. His large, hairy hands rested on his lap like two tamed tarantulas. When he turned to look at me, he smiled with a peevish expression. His eyes exuded fire.

The organist hit a few notes and started to play a toccata that served as a prelude to the processional hymn. A pubescent boy came out of the sacristy attired as a Sybil. He was wearing a long scarlet robe that dragged on the floor and a pointed hood that covered a midlength, disheveled wig. The boy held a sword with both hands in front of him. Two little boys dressed as angels, each carrying a lit candle holder, strode behind him. Accompanied by the organ music, the three boys walked in procession around the nave. When they reached the presbytery, they genuflected. The one carrying the sword went up the stair and, when he arrived at the pulpit, he intoned the first lines of "The Chant of the Sybil":

Audite quid dixerit Sibilla:
Iudici signum, tellus sudore madescet.

"Listen to what the Sybil said to signal the Judgment," he warned us with his sweet voice. "The earth will soak in sweat."

Then he sang in plainchant the verses of this famous chant that prophesies what will happen on the Day of Judgment.

I was surprised to hear this medieval song in Senecú. I had been fascinated by it ever since I discovered it on the shelves of the University of New Mexico library. It was featured on a disc that contained "A Mass for the End of Time," which I liked to listen to in my apartment when I sat down to write. Once I attended a performance of a Catalan version of this chant in the cathedral of Mallorca when I went to Palma to visit my friend Jaime during the Christmas season. In that beautiful and imposing gothic temple, the "Cant de la Sibil-la" seemed to me solemn and majestic. However, in Senecú and under those odd circumstances, it inspired terror. I started to shake and let out a sob as if those choir boys were dictating my death sentence. Brother Salvador grabbed my arm firmly and scrutinized me with disapproval. But I couldn't control myself. My panic attack lasted almost until the end of the song. When it ended, the Sybil drew in the air a cross with the sword and retired with the angels the same way they entered. When they crossed the threshold of the sacristy, I had recomposed myself almost completely, but I felt deeply ashamed.

Fortunately, the temple isn't full, I thought, trying to console myself.

But Brother Salvador made sure I didn't calm down. He turned to look at me intently with his poisonous viper eyes. I had no idea what to do with myself. I was ignorant of the role I was expected to play in this nightmare. I had an infinite yearning to flee but didn't know where to go. My survival instinct forced me to accept my situation and let myself be taken by the current. Still, I clung to the hope that I would wake up soon.

The acolyte exited the sacristy and rang the bell to alert the congregation that the Mass was about to begin. He processioned to the altar with his hands to his chest. Brother Antonio followed him. He was wearing the traditional Latin Mass vestment, including a biretta. He held the chalice with his left hand and pressed the top of the burse with his right hand. When they passed by the tabernacle, they genuflected and continued the procession to the center of the altar. Brother Antonio took off the biretta and handed it to the acolyte. After placing the chalice on the altar and making some preparations, he descended the steps of the altar, turned around to face the tabernacle, crossed himself, and began to recite a prayer in Latin. The acolyte, who was kneeling on his left side, seconded him. The parishioners also repeated the prayer. I had to mumble it for appearance's sake. Looking at Brother Salvador askance, I aped his movements, which only increased his animosity toward me.

Brother Antonio conducted the Tridentine Mass in the traditional manner, facing the altar and adopting a formulaic and solemn tone. However, when he approached the pulpit to give the homily, he assumed an energetic and somber demeanor.

He brought up the subject of the rumors that circulated in Senecú about the imminent end of the world and the advent of the Antichrist in the year 1666. He also spoke about a prophetic appearance:

"Many of you have heard the rumor that, in recent days, a giant appeared to a Socorro resident who claimed he was a soldier of King Gog of the Land of Magog, the former lord of all the Pueblo people. He announced that King Gog was going to form an alliance with all the pagan nations to attack and destroy the Holy Mother

Church, and that King Gog was going to rule the whole world from then on. He proclaimed that all the Pueblo people needed to unite and fall on the Spaniards, especially on the priests, and that they should not spare our lives. He promised that, with the help of King Gog's army, the Pueblo people would escape their slavish state of subjection and recuperate their old customs and traditions. He declared that everyone needed to be ready because this event was going to take place during next August's full moon."

Each time Brother Antonio made a pause, Santiago Mutanama, the acolyte, translated the sermon in the Piro language. He was a striking man in his fifties with prominent eyes and firm gestures whose deep voice resounded forcefully in the temple.

Rather than denying or refuting the rumor, Brother Antonio claimed that these events had been prophesized in the Letter-Apocalypse of Saint John:

"The Book of Revelation is a prophetic story disguised in figures. Many people say it is unintelligible or that it is only an allegory. But I ask, if it were indecipherable, why did Our Redeemer give it to the Church? Everyone should know that we are living in the end of times. Blessed are those who heed and know the words of this prophecy. Those who have ears and understanding listen to what the Holy Spirit says in the Book of Revelation: Whoever fights against Satan shall eat from the Tree of Life, and whoever fights against the Beast shall not suffer eternal punishment in Hell. For this reason, do not be afraid of the trials and tribulations that we are going to encounter in New Mexico. For it was announced many centuries ago that the Holy Spirit would send us the Antichrist for our own benefit."

The parishioners listened attentively to the sermon and looked distressed, as if Brother Antonio and the acolyte corroborated the fears of the calamities that they already knew they were going to suffer soon. Brother Salvador, on the contrary, seemed furious. Every now and then he would cover his mouth with his fist and clear his throat loudly; other times he would sit at the edge of the pew as if he were about to stand up and leave. But then he would lean against the back of the pew again. At times he seemed to calm down. Nonetheless, his clasped, tense hands betrayed his anger.

Brother Antonio also explained the meaning of the seven cups mentioned in the Book of Revelation. He said they were the seven hardships we would all undergo before the second advent: drought, famine, plagues, pestilence, enemy incursions, fratricidal wars, and persecution of the just. He recalled the "glorious martyrdom" of San Lorenzo and pointed out that the Beast described at the beginning of chapter thirteen of the Book of Revelation was a representation of the Emperor Valerian, who, "in addition to butchering the saints, roared blasphemies against God." He concluded the homily by inviting everyone to await with resignation and hope the second coming of Jesus Christ, then declared:

"Just like San Lorenzo shed his own blood and proclaimed his loyalty to Jesus Christ and the Pope, whose dwelling, the Holy Mother Church, Emperor Valerian damaged and desecrated by forbidding the Christian cult and by persecuting its faithful followers, we need to offer today our loyalty and our life to our Redeemer."

Brother Antonio and the acolyte crossed themselves, went down the pulpit, and walked toward the altar. The chorus accompanied them, singing Victoria's "Domine, ad Adjuvandum Me Festina." Thereafter, the Mass proceeded with the customary prayers and rites.

When we arrived at the communion rite, I decided to kneel and meditate in silence with my eyes closed. This allowed me to avoid Brother Salvador's condemning look, given I couldn't take communion. He left his seat before the farewell rite concluded.

At the end of the Mass, he signaled me to follow him and exited the temple without waiting for me. I trailed him and headed toward the ambulatory. I saw him standing by the door of an office that was located near the refectory. When I approached him, he didn't look at me. He simply ordered me to enter and wait for him there, and then he left.

7

THE OFFICE WAS SMALL AND AUSTERELY FURNISHED WITH A DESK, a bookshelf, and a few chairs. While waiting, I browsed the shelves and leafed through some books.

Brother Salvador returned accompanied by Brother Antonio. The secretary of the Holy Custody had a pair of scissors in his left hand, which he placed on the desk. Both stood in front of me and looked at me with a ceremonious paternalism that made me feel uncomfortable. Brother Salvador asked me to kneel in the middle of the room. As soon as I complied, he asked me why I had come to New Mexico. I didn't know what to reply. After an uncomfortable and, for me, anxiety-ridden moment of silence, Brother Antonio asked me to repeat after him:

"Father, I have wanted to serve our Lord in this Holy Religion for a long time, and so, even though I am not worthy, I humbly ask and beg Your Reverence and all the members of this Holy Custody to admit me to your Holy Company. With the Divine favor, I intend and propose to pursue your holy mission until my death."

After repeating these words, Brother Salvador spoke to me about "the great favor that the Lord was giving me by admitting me to his service and by allowing me to be among such faithful servants." He explained that the Custody would put me to the test for "only a one-year period."

"I exhort and encourage thee to carry on with manly courage the labors of the apostolate, for the Lord's yoke is easy to bear and the burden is light for those who desire to serve him with love and out of their own free will. I warn thee that the Devil, our capital enemy, seeks to harass especially the new servants of the Lord with an array of temptations and thoughts. Thou shalt have to cross this difficult road, just as all of us have done before thee."

When he finished his speech, Brother Salvador gave me his blessing and asked me to rise and give him and Brother Antonio an embrace. Then Brother Salvador grabbed the scissors and said it was now necessary to give me the clerical tonsure as a symbol of my entrance into the religious state.

"From now on, thou shalt devote thyself entirely to God, to the edification of the Church, and to the salvation of the world. Thou shalt observe perfect continence in celibacy and shalt lead a life devoid of riches and subjected to the will of your superiors, who act in the name of God when they command thee to do something according to the rules of our order."

After reciting some prayers he proceeded to clip several tufts of hair off my crown. I accepted the tonsure with the same resignation that I accepted being shorn by my senior schoolmates when I started high school at the Juárez College of Agriculture. As he tonsured me, Brother Salvador reminded me of what Brother Antonio had said in the refectory. He warned me that he would personally be responsible for sending me to the tribunals of the Holy Inquisition in Mexico City if anybody noticed "the smallest hint of Judaizing ideas" my superiors had found in my notebooks at the convent.

"I don't know how you avoided being burned at the stake," Brother Salvador added in a contemptuous tone. "You should feel fortunate that we need more missionaries in this province. If more virtuous devotees were willing to come to New Mexico, you would not be among the living. Here we get all the scum of the viceroyalty. To populate, guard, and govern this territory, the viceroy dispatches to us the thieves and criminals that encumber his duties. And now our superiors have instructed us to receive an *alboraico* in our Holy Custody."

"Please be more generous," Brother Antonio intervened. "Do not forget it was Sister María de Jesús de Ágreda herself who interceded for him before passing away to a better life. The Venerable appeared to the father custodian of the convent. She pleaded for him in the name of the Lord so that his superiors would pardon him and announced that he and Brother Diego are destined to serve God in this province."

"I know perfectly well Brother Diego's dossier, Brother Antonio. I am even aware who his forebearers are," he said, pausing and placing a guilt-ridden tone on the phrase. "I also know who his adoptive parents are, as well as where and how they raised him. The father was a wealthy Portuguese merchant, most probably a Crypto-Jew, and a sodomite to boot. Rumor has it that he was the duck of an influential courtier." Brimming with amour propre, Brother Salvador added, I thought unnecessarily, "I have my informants. Not for nothing am I the secretary of this Holy Custody. As such, I will make sure to file a report of the grievous events that I witnessed today in this mission. Being indulgent with the Indian dances is giving them license to worship the Devil. I will add this incident to your file, Brother Antonio. When the Holy Office finds out that you allowed a group of Christian Piro to practice their diabolical dances in front of the House of the Lord, no doubt they will order your arrest. You know well what happened to the former governor López Mendizábal. As soon as I return to San Diego de Jémez, I will submit my report to the father custodian. This is a notification, by the way."

"You are slandering me," Brother Antonio replied. "'Thou shalt not bear false witness against thy neighbor.' Neither did I give them permission to dance, nor did they request it. They took advantage of the fact that Brother de la Cruz is not in Senecú."

"Are you not in charge?"

"I am neither the guardian of this mission nor the guardian of the law in Senecú. I am only a visiting cleric here."

"This does not free you from the responsibility you have of helping this mission fulfill its task."

"My obligation consists of fulfilling my apostolate by preaching the Gospel to the Gentiles, devoting myself to curing their souls, and administering the Divine Cult and the sacraments. I have consecrated my life to prayer and penance and have always followed the discipline of our order. It is not my duty to enforce the laws of New Mexico."

"Your responsibilities include obeying and making others obey the divine law."

"The divine law, but not the human law. The Sacred Scriptures do not prohibit dancing when paying homage to God."

"You are mistaken. Moses destroyed the Tablets of the Law when he discovered that the Israelites had danced before the golden calf."

"What infuriated Moses was that they were worshiping an idol, not that they were dancing. The Holy Scriptures do not forbid dancing when worshiping God. A passage of Psalm 149 says: 'Let them praise his name in the dance: let them sing praises unto him with the timbrel and harp.'"

"Be that as it may, the pagan dances have been strictly prohibited in New Mexico since four years ago."

"The Kachinas."

"The Kachinas and all the idolatrous dances that the Indians practice in this kingdom."

"The dancers were paying homage to San Lorenzo. They were pleading for rain and other blessings."

"Lies! They were embodying the Kachinas. Why do you think they were wearing those diabolical masks? If they wanted to ask God or San Lorenzo to send us rain, they would have prayed and done penance. And if you wished to help them, you would have given a special Mass. That is what all law-abiding priests do. By the way, your interpretation of the Book of Revelation is another matter you will have to clear before the tribunals of the Holy Office."

"It is not my interpretation. A Siervo de Dios, the venerable Don Gregorio López, championed it. I learned it from Father Don Nicolás Martínez, who is a doctor of theology, a minister of the Cathedral of Mexico City, and the rector of the Hospital of the Holy Faith where my body and soul were cured."

"Do not give me any explanations. Keep them to yourself for when the commissar interrogates you."

"I will. I will also tell him that you want to take revenge because I testified against you ten years ago when you killed Juan Cuna in Orayvi. I will also inform him about the lashes that you gave the dancers today."

"I know that you put on airs as the protector of the Indians, but your threats do not scare me. Nobody has ever called into question the integrity of my Catholic faith. As to yours, there are some doubts."

"Doubts that you have spread. I have spent more than fifty years in this province, and nobody has ever called into question my faith, my devotion, or my beliefs."

"Do not be so sure about that. I know your record from beginning to end."

"And I yours, Brother."

Brother Antonio, to my slow and begrudging admiration, wasn't standing down. For my part I found it interesting that Brother Antonio was getting the same I-know-your-story treatment from Brother Salvador as Brother Antonio had given me.

"It is time to stop arguing," said Brother Salvador. "Both of you must have things to do and I must conduct some inquiries in Senecú before I return to El Paso del Río del Norte. Welcome to our brotherhood, Brother Diego. Have a good afternoon."

Brother Salvador exited the office abruptly. Brother Antonio did not make a single comment. He simply asked me to sit in a chair, took the scissors that Brother Salvador left on the desk, and proceeded to complete the tonsuring of my hair in the monastic crown style. When he finished, he stepped out of the office for a few moments and returned accompanied by two women, each of them carrying a pot of water, one hot and one cold. They left as soon as they put the pots on the desk. Then Brother Antonio opened a chest, took out some razors that were wrapped in a cloth, and started to shave my head and face. When he finished, he dried me with a towel.

I was curious about how I looked and asked him for a mirror. He opened the chest again and handed me one. I looked at my face and was shocked. I could not recognize myself. My face was that of a stranger, a twenty-something male with an oblong face, green eyes, arched eyebrows, straight nose, thick lips, and prominent chin. My teeth were uneven, yellowish, and covered in tartar.

"What is the matter, Brother Diego? You are looking at yourself as if you have never seen your face. Do you dislike my barbering skills so much?" He said it in a joking tone.

"No, it's not that," I said, still baffled. "I just don't recognize myself with this haircut."

"Behold yourself carefully, Brother Diego, for you are, indeed, a new creature. The old life is gone; a new life has begun."

8

IT WAS THE AFTERNOON OF THURSDAY, AUGUST 10 OF 1665, IN Old Senecú Pueblo. After rearranging the shape and look of all the hair on my skull, Brother Antonio led me to my cell. There he went over my chores and responsibilities at the convent. He also cleared up some of the most pressing doubts I had about the person who I was mysteriously incarnating. He told me who he was by recounting a strange parable:

"Once there was a green caterpillar that was looking for a safe and auspicious place to realize its dream of becoming a white butterfly. It found a branch at the top of a tree that seemed perfect. There it stayed still and waited patiently and expectantly for its chrysalis to emerge. But it did not notice that a parasitic wasp was prowling the tree in search of tender flesh to deposit its eggs. When it saw the caterpillar lying still, the wasp waited for the opportune moment. It waited and waited and, as soon as the chrysalis started to emerge from its cocoon, the wasp mounted it and injected its eggs in its body. The eggs incubated and hatched, and the wasp larvae slowly devoured the chrysalis. At the end of the cycle, instead of a radiant butterfly, a multitude of young wasps came out and dispersed themselves in the field, searching for nectar and chrysalises to continue propagating their parasitic species."

I did not understand the meaning of the parable and asked him to explain it to me. He invited me to sit down so I could listen more attentively and said:

"The chrysalis is the pure soul that searches for God. The wasp is the appetite of the flesh. The young wasps are the temptations of the soul invaded by the spirit of the Wicked One. Just as the young wasps devour and kill the chrysalis and survive at its expense when they develop inside its body, so the appetites of the flesh consumed my soul and almost condemned it forever. When you were born, I was practically dead inside, because I allowed myself to be carried away by my carnal desires on multiple occasions. One of my victims was your mother, who was an innocent maiden thirsty for knowledge. My soul fell many times to the snares of the Infernal Enemy. But, thanks to my faith in God Almighty, our merciful Lord manifested his infinite love and rescued me from the hell of sin. The grace of God saved me and welcomed me again in his abode. The same happened to you, my son," he added.

"I don't understand," I said, both displeased by and uncertain about the implication of what he was saying.

"With their daughter's honor stained, and to avoid being themselves dishonored, Don Gaspar Bandama and Doña María Romero forced your mother to give you up for adoption. I was an accomplice in this plot. It was the summer of 1642. A merchant of Portuguese origin by the name of Don Valerio Rosales had arrived on the triennial wagon train. He was married to one of the daughters of Don Tomás de Mendoza and Doña Elena Ramírez. Her name was Margarita. Don Valerio was a Portuguese merchant who had come to New Mexico to consolidate some dealings he had made with the governor. Because Don Valerio was unable to fill his wife with happiness, for, apparently, he was incapable of physical love, he accepted my proposal to adopt you in exchange for an indulgence that would grant full remission of the punishment of certain sins he had committed, which included trafficking slaves. Don Valerio promised that he would make you a good Siervo de Dios and an honest man. Thus, we snatched you away from your mother's arms when you were three months old and sent you to Parral with Don Valerio. He bought a Genízara wet nurse named Flora so that she could feed you and assist your adoptive mother. Unfortunately, when you turned nine, your adoptive mother contracted a mortal illness. Given that your itinerant father spoiled you with luxuries and raised you unchecked by the power of reason, you entered adolescence pinched by the joys of the flesh. When you were fifteen, Don Valerio took you to the grand and opulent City of Mexico, where he amassed a fortune thanks to both his industry and his relations with a court member of Viceroy Juan Francisco de Leyva. At the age of eighteen you befriended a son of the viceroy and, following his example, you gave yourself over to gambling and sinning. Within a couple of years, you squandered what took Don Valerio a lifetime to earn. This sent him to his grave and forced you to enter the Convent of San Diego, where Don Valerio had previously deposited some jewels. There, a pious brother, Father Melchor Rondero, agreed to take you under his wing. With him you learned to love the rational life and, little by little, your soul acquired the true riches: virtue and knowledge. You also learned to relinquish your own volition and to subject yourself to the will of your superiors, which is a more heroic act than vanquishing and taking by force Jerusalem itself. Just as you had lived before in the state of error, wearing the vestments of the Prince of Darkness, the garments of arrogance, conceit, pride, greed, lust, and all the other ornaments of the habit of Evil, so now, in your new state, you have left behind the sinful man and have promised to follow the example of the Heavenly Man, Jesus Christ. That is why you are now wearing the habit of faith, hope, love, joy, peace, goodness, and all the other adornments of the divine vestments. And while it is true that you drank from forbidden sources of knowledge at the convent of the Dieguinos, this water only increased your thirst for prayer, contemplation, and the sacred Franciscan mission."

I listened to Brother Antonio quietly and attentively. When he finished his account, he stared at me and waited for my reaction. I did not know what to say or how to react. I could not stop thinking about my first encounter with him at the foot of that mysterious mountain and how he suddenly transformed himself into a Franciscan monk. He seemed to have forgotten this encounter. I wanted to ask him what had happened to him and why he was making up this story. But I remained quiet and still. He continued to stare at me with his inquisitive eyes, as if he were trying to decipher a veiled message in my eyes. I wanted to get up from my chair to distract myself and reflect, but Brother Antonio kept me glued to my seat with his inquiring look.

"Are you sure you do not remember anything of what I have told you?" he asked me with an expression of incredulity and skepticism.

"Yes, Brother, I do not remember anything," I answered firmly, making an enormous effort to not display the slightest doubt through my eyes or my gestures.

Then he asked me if I recalled the instruction and the doctrine I had learned in the convent. I answered negatively.

"How about the prayers?"

"I don't remember them either."

"The noble arts?"

"I don't either."

"The sublime sciences?"

"I don't."

"Moral philosophy?"

"I don't remember anything."

"Logic? Rhetoric? Physics?"

"Absolutely nothing."

"Arithmetic? Geometry? History? Music?"

Given his insistence, I wondered if I should admit that I knew something about these subjects. However, I replied negatively again to avoid arousing any suspicions.

Perplexed by my amnesia and my absolute lack of knowledge and self-knowledge, Brother Antonio opened a book he was holding and asked me if I still knew how to read. I said I was not sure. He opened it, put his index finger on a passage, and asked me to read it. I realized it would be advantageous to admit that I had not lost this skill. I read slowly:

"How the novice shall prepare for the Divine Office."

A smile spread on his face and he urged me to continue reading.

"There if no picture on Earth that difplays in a livelier manner . . ."

He interrupted my reading to correct me:

"It does not say 'difplays' but 'displays.' You are confusing the letter 's' with the letter 'f.'" He asked me to begin the passage again.

"There is no picture on Earth that displays in a livelier manner what happens in Heaven before the divine assembly than in the choir. For just as all the angels and celestial dwellers continually praise, worship, and glorify our Lord Almighty God in Heaven, so we do in the choir, day and night. Notwithstanding our weak possibility, we make our utmost effort to imitate the angelic spirits. For this reason, Brother, you need to prepare with due diligence and humility so that with holy fear and reverence, inside and outside the choir, at all times and in all places, day and night, you worship and bless . . ."

He interrupted me and said cheerfully:

"Well done, well done, Diego. Now, let us test your memory."

He took the book away from my sight and asked me to repeat what I had just read.

Without any hesitation, I repeated the passage exactly, word for word.

"Bless the Lord! Your house is empty, but the roof remains intact!" he exclaimed, surprised. Then he pronounced a passage of Psalm 31 and asked me to repeat it.

Esto mihi in Deum protectorem,
et in locum refugii, ut salvum me facias:
quoniam firmamentum meum, et refugium meum es tu:
et propter nomen tuum dux mihi eris, enutries me.
In te, Domine, speravi, non confundar in aeternum:
in justitia tua libera me, et eripeme.

Even though I did not know their meaning, I was able to repeat these lines accurately. Brother Antonio expressed relief when he verified that I had not lost the prodigious memory that his superiors had mentioned in their reports. This not only surprised me but made me feel immense joy because I had always suffered from poor memory. Inhabiting Diego's body, by contrast, I only had to listen, see, or practice something once or twice and was able to repeat or do it in a competent manner, particularly those things that I had supposedly learned at the convent. I finally understood what Plato said, that learning was nothing but remembering what we already knew in a previous life.

When he expressed his relief that I had not lost my faculties, he told me something that I did not understand at first but that alluded to our first encounter. He said:

"You expressed anguish that morning, your eyes languished out of sadness, your strength diminished due to so much pain. They forgot about you as a dead person. They left you behind as one leaves a useless object. They plotted to take away your life."

"Who did, Brother?" I asked, confused.

"Your enemies, Diego."

"My enemies?"

"The subjects of the Accuser. They abandoned you."

"They abandoned me? I thought it had been an accident."

"It was not an accident. The Accuser asked Him to subject you to the implacable river ordeal. The subjects of the Accuser led you to the bank of the sacred river. It was me who executed the order to dip you in the waters of the Id. Do you not remember?"

"Of course I remember," I said, relieved.

"Everybody knows that the guilty ones are swallowed by the Water Beast and that the innocent ones are saved."

"I did not know it."

"As a reward for surviving the river ordeal, the one who is falsely accused takes possession of the house of the Accuser. The Almighty, who is just, protected you. He saved you from the trap that your enemies set for you."

"Who are my enemies?"

"Very powerful people. They are the Accuser's servants. They are the custodians of the assets of the City of Man and the Carnal Church. But God is your protector and we, the custodians of the City of God and of the Spiritual Church, are your allies. Even though you still are the king's and the pope's subject, the Celestial Lord is your cornerstone, your shelter, and your way. You have entrusted your spirit to him. Your destiny is in his hands. He has given you one last opportunity."

"One last opportunity? I don't understand."

"To fulfill your mission in this world. You will not be able to reach your final destiny until you fulfill it."

"What mission?" I asked with both naivete and frankness.

"The worst kind of blind man is the one that does not want to see, Diego. God traced the path that each one of us needs to follow. He imprinted in our hearts the map of this itinerary. You need to learn to decipher this message. Learn to listen to the wise silence of your heart. There, you will find the signals that will guide you to your destiny."

At that moment, I decided to open my heart to him. I thought he would understand and that he would help me get out of this mysterious situation. I was not sure I could trust him, but I decided to take the risk. I summoned the courage and told him:

"Brother, I do not want to be a monk. I just want to awaken from this dream."

"Awakening is the reward of the wise, Diego," he replied. "I am also devoted to attaining awakening. I aspire to achieve perfect awakening and to assist others like you who are in search of the path of salvation. Are you familiar with the Parable of the Two Sons?"

"No, Brother, I am not," I replied, exasperated.

"A man who had two sons asked them to go to work in his vineyard. One said no, but he repented later and went. The other said he would go but never went. You are like the former, Diego. Just now, when the day of the world is waning at the eleventh hour, you have come to help your father to work in the vineyard of the Lord. My son, you and I have not come to this land in search of our own things but those that belong to the Lord Our God. We are Saint Paul's disciples. We are here to announce to the pagans the inestimable wealth of Christ's reign so that the Gospel reaches the corners of the earth. We have been entrusted to bring the Good News to New Mexico. Let your mind become more spiritual so that you enjoy a new life. Says Saint Paul: 'Rise thou that sleepest, and arise from the dead: and Christ shall enlighten thee.'"

"I did not come here on my own volition. You brought me here, Brother," I insisted. "You promised you would help me find my way home, but now you want to give me a mission that does not belong to me."

"Diego, you must leave behind the old man. Those deceiving desires will lead you to your own destruction. This is your home. Here you will find the way to true liberation. To attain it you will have to fight against and defeat your greatest enemy: yourself and your own volition. You must subject yourself to the will of your superiors who act in the name and with the authority of God. Behold us with the same respect as God, for we occupy his place.

You will do yourself great harm if you do not conduct yourself with obedience in everything you do. For God wants more obedience than sacrifice, and the actions of the religious man are those of obedience."

I realized that I was not going to get anywhere if I insisted.

"Alright, Brother."

9

DURING THOSE MONTHS, ALMOST EVERY NIGHT, I SEEMED TO return to my previous life. In one recurrent dream, I was still living in Albuquerque. I had been evicted from my apartment; my bank account and credit cards had been closed. I had lost everything. I didn't even have a few coins to make a phone call to my parents. I asked my friends, my coworkers, and the government for help. All in vain. Nobody noticed my presence. I had no choice but to beg for alms at the central plaza. At first I was very polite and wished passersby a good day and heavenly blessings. But everyone ignored me, and I started to insult and curse the whole world. I yelled obscenities, sang rancheras, relieved myself wherever I pleased. Still nobody heeded my presence nor cared what I did or suffered.

In another dream I had returned to Juárez, the city where I grew up. I wanted to start a new life, claim the inheritance my grandfather left me, buy a little house on the outskirts of El Paso. I dreamed of devoting myself to writing, learning to play the guitar again in my free time, and finding a partner with whom to share the rest of my days. But everyone behaved as if I were made of thin air. I lodged in my parents' house. However, neither my mom nor my dad talked to me. They seemed to be upset with me or something. I would have left home if I had another place to go, but none of my siblings, relatives, and friends talked to me. On top of it all, my uncle had claimed the inheritance that my grandfather left me, and I was stone broke.

When I woke up from those nightmares and realized that I was still in Senecú, I felt a mixture of relief and despair. Ironically, what seemed to be a nightmare was becoming a refuge in my dreamworld, and the life to which I yearned to return was turning into a series of anxiety dreams from which I was happy to wake up. I started to understand that what I was going through was more than just a simple dream.

The days and nights went by, and I remained in Senecú in the seventeenth century, living the life of a stranger, clinging to the hope that I would wake up from this nightmare.

I resolved to take refuge in my cell to study and memorize the manual for novices that Brother Antonio lent me. This book contained all the necessary norms I needed to learn to survive in the convent, particularly during the first few months.

My daily routine seemed unendurable in the beginning, but I got used to it as time went by. In addition to attending Mass and the Divine Office, my main responsibilities were praying, meditating, doing penance, and studying the Bible. As a result, I spent most of the day alone in my cell. I had to pray at least three hours a day: one hour after matins, at about one o'clock in the morning; another during nones, between two o'clock and three o'clock in the afternoon; and another one after compline, at about seven o'clock in the evening. In addition, every day I had to do an hour and a half of chores. Sometimes I assisted in the preparation and the administration of the religious services; other times I swept the floors, washed the dishes, helped in the orchard, the vineyard, the pen, or cleaned the latrine.

All my movements were meticulously regulated, not only in public places but also in my own cell. For instance, I had to sleep on my right side with the hood on and the habit tidied and arranged. The cincture had to be extended between my legs and I needed to form a cross with my arms. Lying in bed face up or face down was deemed indecent because it stimulated erotic thoughts and dreams. Walking down the corridors of the convent, I always had to stay close to the wall, looking down, with the hood on and the arms crossed against the chest. If I ran into Brother Antonio, or any other superior, I had to step aside, take off my hood, bow respectfully, and let them pass. Likewise, if any of my superiors happened to ask or say anything to me, I was only allowed to reply yes or no. If they asked me to elaborate, I had to keep my head down and use discreet gestures and speak concisely. If they scolded me, I had to kneel and stay down until they ordered me to stand up. I was not allowed to defend or justify myself, even if they reprimanded me for no reason.

Despite everything, I got used to life in the convent with relative ease. In Ithaca I had lost my attachment to luxuries and most unnecessary things. The studio apartment I had rented in the attic of an old house was small, austere, and sparsely furnished. I slept on a futon that lay on the floor close to my desk. I stored my folded clothes on a shelf with sisal baskets. My parka, my raincoat, a couple of light jackets, and other garments were hung in a canvas-covered rack that closed with a zipper. My dinette was a coffee table with cushions. The kitchenette had an electric stove with four burners, a small refrigerator, a sink, and cupboards made of pressed wood where I kept four dishes, a dozen glasses, cups, mugs, two pans, and a few basic utensils. The rare guests that visited me had to sit on cushions because I did not have any chairs.

My diet was not that different either. Apart from coffee and some processed foods that were an integral part of my diet in Ithaca, in New Mexico I ate similar things, but less frequently and in smaller quantities. In Ithaca I rarely ate meat or fish and occasionally drank hot chocolate and atole. Most of the time I drank water, coffee, and tea of various kinds. In addition to a variety of grain products, I ate beans, lentils, nuts, eggs, cheese, fresh or frozen fruits and vegetables, dried fruits and cookies for dessert or snack, and fine chocolates every now and then.

Even though in Senecú there were none of the luxuries that I had always considered indispensable—especially electricity, sewage, and potable running water in abundance—almost everything I consumed in Senecú was freshly made and grown at the convent or in the vicinity. I ate plenty of beans and, every now and then, fresh trout or catfish, or dried shrimp or oysters, as well as bacon. Meat was always available, except on Fridays and during Lent and other holidays when fasting was compulsory.

In El Porvenir, my grandfather's ranch—which was located in the Juárez Valley, near the village of San Agustín—I had learned to appreciate the simple life in the countryside since I was little. I learned to live without the amenities and complications of urban life. When I graduated from NMSU at the age of twenty-one, my first and last job in agriculture was as the manager of my grandfather's ranch. Although my failure was resounding, for the ranch eventually went bankrupt under my unskilled direction, the experience came in handy at the convent.

In Senecú different stages and facets of my life converged in a strange way, as if I had arrived there to rediscover or know myself by reliving the life of a distant ancestor. The greatest challenge I had was following the regimen of silence that, according to the manual, all novices had to keep for a whole year. Given the circumstances and the fact that the mission needed my services, Brother Antonio said that I only had to keep it for six months. Even though it was difficult to follow it, this regimen helped me adapt to the monastic life. Above all, it protected me against the religious zeal of the epoch and the people with whom I lived. If I had been able to talk to someone other than Brother Antonio, probably I would have said something scandalous or heretical that would have cost me my freedom, if not my life. The most difficult part was not being able to share with others my suffering, my doubts, my memories, and my beliefs. It helped that I knew that if I did, they would regard me as a heretic, a possessed, a demon, or even the Antichrist himself. I was no longer sure who I was or why I was there.

Fortunately, my previous experience with meditation helped me maintain calm in the most critical and challenging moments of my stay at the convent. Moreover, I was amply familiar with Catholic prayers and doctrine. So long as I did not lose my calm or my concentration, I was able to empty my mind and immerse myself in purifying emptiness both when I prayed aloud and when I meditated in silence. Other than in my own conscience and in my dreams, the confessional and my diary were the other two spaces where I was able to air my complaints and my censored thoughts, if only in a cryptic and figurative manner.

Brother Antonio was strict, but he was not a tyrant, and he did not compel me to follow each rule to the letter. For a priest he was open-minded. He listened attentively and did not condemn or become scandalized by my criticisms of Church dogmas and practices, no matter how unorthodox or radical these were. He was never harsh or haughty with his subordinates, as was the norm among those who occupied a position of authority in this place; on the contrary, he was almost always courteous, patient, and understanding. Nor was he violent nor physically or verbally abusive. He forbade the aide and the taskmaster from lashing anyone and the teachers from using corporal punishment with their pupils, as was standard practice in other missions. Although he did practice self-flagellation, he told me that I was not obligated to punish the flesh this way if I did not want to do so. Likewise, unless I committed a reprehensible blunder, he rarely scolded or disciplined me.

One of these instances was the day when he assigned me bell-ringer duty and I overslept. Although Bernardo, the staff bell ringer, woke up and rang the matins bell on time, Brother Antonio considered it necessary to discipline me. In addition to only allowing me to eat bread and drink water that day, I had to kneel by the table before he blessed the meal. I also had to eat my slice of bread "happily" while squatting with a napkin on my lap. After each course was served to everyone but me, I had to take off my hood and clink my bowl with a spoon. When the refectory keeper asked me what I wanted, I had to reply: "I beg forgiveness for not having rung the matins bell." Then I had to put my hood back on and wait in a squatting position until everybody finished their course. I was not allowed to stand up until everybody finished their last bite and Brother Antonio gave me permission.

Under his benevolent but firm command and faultless example, the mission operated with punctual efficiency. At midnight the bell ringer called us to pray the matins. All the residents of the convent who performed religious tasks had to attend, excepting the choir boys. At one o'clock in the morning we returned to our sleeping quarters to pray and sleep a little more. At four forty-five we got up to pray the lauds. Then, after having breakfast, each of us proceeded to carry out his or her duties. By five o'clock the gatekeeper, the baker, the cook, the refectory keeper, the nurse, and their respective assistants, as well as the washerwomen, the cleaners, the taskmaster, the stockmen, the tillers, and all other farm laborers were already at work. At seven the choir boys rose and got ready to participate in the liturgical prayer of the hours at seven thirty. At eight o'clock everyone had to stop working and attend Mass. The aide took attendance and marked those who were absent. Those who missed Mass more than once were reprimanded or punished.

Like any missionary in these lands, Brother Antonio had to be a jack-of-all-trades. First and foremost, he was an evangelist, a church minister, and, much to his regret, an agent of the Spanish Crown. But to fulfill his duties, he had to be many more things. In the midthirties, when he founded the Humanas Pueblo mission, he had to be the designer, the architect, the construction supervisor, and the decorator of the church compound. Much to his displeasure, he also had to be a callous administrator and an abusive boss, for he had to manage a sizable agricultural enterprise with scant resources and his superiors ordered him to pay the mission laborers below the one real per day that, according to law, they were entitled to earn for working from dawn to dusk under harsh, if not deplorable, conditions. At various stages of his missionary service, he had been an instructor of Spanish language, culture, cooking, and customs, as well as an instructor of sacred music, wool spinning, fabric, and garment manufacture. He also had to know carpentry, blacksmithing, animal husbandry, irrigation management, viniculture, as well as Western techniques for cultivating nonnative grains, fruits, and vegetables. He had been both physician and apothecary, albeit, in this case, his knowledge and skills were inadequate, useless, and sometimes hazardous, such as when he treated a wide range of conditions and ailments with bloodletting. As a healer of bodies, Brother Antonio, like most medical practitioners of his time, did more harm than good. For this reason, often he wisely delegated this task to the Native medicine men and women whose curative arts and techniques were frequently, though not always, more efficacious than his. The efficacy of the missionaries as healers of the soul was perhaps even worse than their efficacy as healers of the body. However, in this domain the typical missionary not only forbade any assistance from the Native healers but annihilated it by asking the Holy Office to execute them, accusing them of being sorcerers. In this regard, Brother Antonio also deviated from the norm, for he defended and practiced the peaceful apostolate championed by Motolinía and other Franciscan leaders in the New World. He said that the Indigenous people needed to be converted with good deeds and wise teachings rather than by means of intimidation, force, or violence.

Like all missionaries, Brother Antonio was only a spoke of the wheel of the imperial carriage that brought him to these remote lands to indoctrinate the Indigenous inhabitants and to make them submissive and exploitable subjects. Nevertheless, within this oppressive and repressive system, he embodied some of the most admirable virtues of the Franciscan missionary. Although he was not a saint, for he had broken his chastity and obedience vows on numerous occasions, he was pious, selfless, and hard working. Above all, he practiced the vow of poverty and love for the neighbor that Franciscans professed. Day after day he renounced anything that could sidetrack him from his mission. At the convent he was the first one to get up and the last one to go to bed. He ate once a day and only what was necessary to allow him to bear the heavy burden of his daily chores. He neither socialized nor fraternized with anyone. He assisted social events with the purpose of administering sacraments and preaching the Gospel. He met with his fellow Franciscan brothers only if it was compulsory to do so, and he avoided any responsibility and conversation that was not related to his religious duties. His passion was preaching, and his obsession was the imminent coming of the end of the world. He wanted to save the souls of those good or innocent pagans who, according to him, because they did not know the Gospel and were not baptized, were going to perish in Hell.

Brother Antonio had served in the Franciscan Custody of the Conversion of Saint Paul of New Mexico for forty-seven years, since 1619. From the beginning he displayed a resolute determination to lead a life that was in keeping with his beliefs and his Franciscan vows. He had come to sow the vineyard of the Lord in New Mexico with the intention of following the lifestyle of prayer, poverty, and charity prescribed by the Gospel. However, he soon realized that he would not be able to live according to this ideal. The Franciscan missionary was forced to serve two masters. In addition to serving God, he had to serve the people. On the pretext of helping the poor and acquiring economic self-sufficiency, the missions were becoming a source of material wealth and political power that competed with the interests of the local political leaders and the owners of the haciendas and encomiendas. This had provoked a long series of conflicts and had endangered on various occasions the colonizing and missionary enterprise of the Spaniards in New Mexico.

The guardian of the Senecú mission, Brother Román de la Cruz, whom Brother Antonio was substituting temporarily, had been accused by the former governor of exploiting the Indigenous population and of using the mission's resources for his personal benefit and profit. Such conflicts between missionaries and governors were causing a severe political crisis in the region to the point that many Franciscans and Hispanic colonists were threatening to leave this remote and neglected province. For this reason, Brother Antonio had requested the head of New Mexico's Franciscan Custody to allow him to spend the rest of his days pacifying and evangelizing the Gila Apache. In his view, this endeavor was key to the survival of the missionary project in these territories. However, since Brother Román de la Cruz had contracted whooping cough and had been hospitalized in the San Felipe mission since March, Brother Antonio was asked to be in charge of the Senecú mission.

Brother Antonio maintained that the various Indigenous communities should support and govern themselves without the intervention and the subjugation of the Spaniards. He believed that the missionaries should devote themselves to praising God, praying, meditating, and edifying their souls and those of others, and that the Indigenous communities should provide for themselves and give alms to the missionaries. He was against the policy that entitled encomienda owners to extract tribute from the Indigenous pueblos. He also believed that all the work that Indigenous laborers did for the mission should be paid adequately, without exceptions. His Franciscan brothers and superiors viewed with condescension, and sometimes outrage, his impractical ideas. What many of them viewed as intolerable was his insistence that the missionaries should follow a strict and scrupulous ascetic regimen of absolute poverty, focused exclusively on spiritual concerns. They regarded it as being not just impractical but potentially heretical and subversive.

While Brother Antonio carried out his duties conscientiously, he disliked being mission guardian because he was burdened with responsibilities and did not have much time left to preach the Gospel. He would occasionally remark that God had entrusted him to save souls and not to administer material goods. He criticized his fellow missionaries who, he said, with the pretext of assisting the poor, devoted most of their efforts to addressing earthly affairs and, as a result, neglected heavenly concerns and forgot what Jesus said to the apostles: that they should be like the birds who neither sow nor reap nor gather into barns. At the end of the day, he commented, whatever the missions accumulated would be destroyed and looted by the throng of the Enemy.

Brother Antonio wished with all his heart to build a City of God. He was one of the last few Joachimites still lingering in the order who believed that New Mexico was the last hope to found a true Christian utopia where the doctrine of the Gospel would be put into rigorous practice. According to him, the fact that the Ten Lost Tribes of Israel had been found in New Mexico meant that the end of the world and the Last Judgment were near. The throng of the Beast was going to attack in our time, and we needed to be prepared. They were going to plunder and burn the churches, the haciendas, the houses of Christians, and torture and kill all those who loved and feared God. At that moment, however, he claimed, the jaws of the earth were going to open and devour all the impious ones and confine their souls in Hell. Only the true believers would be saved and led by the angels and the archangels to the Promised Land, where they would recover their angelic nature and live in a state of perfect harmony with God and nature, as Adam and Eve did before the Fall. For this reason, we needed to be prepared and ready for the hecatomb like the chrysalises awaited the glorious day of their transformation and elevation. We had to fast, pray, meditate, and do penance. The pious ones who loved God and obeyed his commandments and the precepts of the Church had nothing to fear. But those who were burdened by their sins and iniquities needed to mend their ways or else condemn themselves forevermore.

Given his old age and the shortage of missionaries in New Mexico, the custodio and other members of the Definitorio tolerated him so long as he obeyed them and did not try to put his ideas into practice. Nonetheless, as a preventive measure, over the past couple of decades they had opted to give him posts as visiting missionary in remote places where he would be most beneficial and least dangerous to the Custody's mission and the viceroyalty's colonizing efforts. However, now that circumstances had forced them to transfer him to Senecú, they were worried, particularly the vice custodio, Brother García de San Francisco, who was one of the founders of this mission, and who had devoted many years of his life to expanding and maintaining it. The recent events during the Day of San Lorenzo and other decisions he had made worried Brother García. According to Brother Salvador Guerra, Brother Antonio was inciting the Piro to rebel against the authorities. These Pueblo people had been, thus far, not only the most faithful Christian converts in all of New Mexico but also the most loyal supporters of the Franciscans' missions. For instance, over the past five years several Piro families had migrated to El Paso de Río del Norte to help him found the Mission de Guadalupe of the Manso. For this reason, Brother García had requested the custodio to remove Brother Antonio from this post and send him to Apache country as soon as possible. However, given that nobody else was available to replace him, they were going to have to wait until Brother Román de la Cruz's health improved. This would require at least another three months.

10

DURING MY NIGHTS OF INSOMNIA, I WOULD READ ST. JOHN OF the Cross's *The Dark Night of the Soul*. Brother Antonio had lent me this book of poems for my edification. In addition to the "Songs of the Soul," it contained an appendix in which the author commented on his poems and explained diverse aspects of the path to God using the *via negativa* in which the soul negates everything to be at one with God. Although sometimes I entertained myself reading the glosses, one night I decided to whisper the poem as if it were a mantra with the idea of falling asleep. When I reached the line "on the secret stairway, in disguise," someone knocked on the door gently. I thought it was Brother Antonio. I was a bit surprised because it was past eleven and he was usually asleep by then. When I opened the door, I was stunned.

"Oh, joyous feat!" I couldn't believe my eyes. It was Alma. She was wearing a wedding gown. Not knowing what to do, I stood motionless. I did not want to fall into the trap of this seductive vision, even though it seemed to me the most real and wonderful thing I had seen in a long time. I must be dreaming, I thought to myself. It must be a wish fulfillment, a trick of my stubborn unconscious that never accepted Alma's death as a final and irrevocable fact.

Alma was holding with both hands a bouquet of white poppies. She waited for me to invite her in, but she lost patience quickly.

"Are you going to let me in or stand me up?"

"No, Alma, I'm sorry! Please, come in." I felt ashamed of my rudeness and incredulity.

She came in and offered me the bouquet as a gift. I closed the door gently and put the bouquet on a nightstand that was by the door. She lifted her veil and we looked at each other silently for a moment. She dazzled me with her beauty. She was wearing a floral, laced headdress embedded with pearls and porcelain lilies, a juniper-green bodice that enfolded a white blouse with a square neckline and virago sleeves, and a long, bell-shaped, forest-green skirt that matched the bodice's intricate embroidery composed of bright-red poppies and dark-green foliage.

"I can't believe you're here, Alma. I know I'm dreaming, but you seem so real."

"I can't believe it either. It must be a miracle. I was yearning to be with you, remembering the promise of eternal love that we made to each other at the Alameda Central in Mexico City, imagining that I was walking the wedding march down a forest trail and that you awaited on the other side of a dense fog bank. Is it really you, Diego? Allow me to touch you to be sure."

She got close to me and caressed my face. I recognized her beautiful chestnut eyes, her curly, long eyelashes, thick eyebrows, aquiline nose, fleshy lips, and soft amber skin. She was seventeen, the age she was when we first met.

"Yes, Alma, it's me, but why do you call me Diego?"

"How else should I call you, *Cielito*?"

"You know better than anyone that my name is Uriel."

"Forgive me, my love. I must be dreaming. Anyhow, what difference does it make if your name is Diego or Uriel? Why should it matter whether I'm awake or asleep? What matters is that you are here in front of me. I don't want to break the spell."

"Why have you come, Alma? You and I know you are dead."

"I came to communicate the Holy Spirit to you. I've learned in the convent that erotic caresses seal the spiritual union of God's servants. Despite our doubts and sins, our souls still aspire to know the supreme good. The soul is the only human element that can be perfected, and it only gets perfected by climbing the stairway of love. United we can climb it. Let's go to your chamber and tear the veil of this sweet encounter once and for all."

She took me by the hand and led me to my bedroom. We sat at the edge of my pallet, and she said to me:

"Kiss me, darling. I want to savor your elixir; I want to soak up your warm essence."

My cell turned into a palatial chamber with marble columns, carved beams, high ceilings, and broad windows decorated with purple, embroidered silk curtains. It had lost its rancid smell thanks to the fragrance of the flowers and exotic plants that ornamented it and gave it a refined, naturalist touch. My pallet transformed into a majestic king-size canopy bed with a wrought iron headboard and frame covered with sheer curtains embroidered with gold thread and pearls. The mattress and the duvet were filled with feathers and covered with a lavender-colored silk cloth.

We lay down and kissed each other passionately. I felt the warmth of her breath diffuse all over my body. The cloth of her skirt was so light and fine that it seemed to float in the air. As soon as we embraced, her wedding gown, the veil, the crown, and other garments vanished. When I took off my habit, the rough sayal wool scratched her delicate skin. I looked at her face and saw that it belonged to a female that was barely seventeen years old.

I felt that night as if I had not only contemplated, touched, and enjoyed Alma's beautiful, tender body but also that I had glimpsed at the beauty and eternal unity of an infinite, resplendent, ethereal sun that vivifies, liberates, and perfects whatever its rays illumine. When we concluded that unforgettable coupling, I was so overjoyed that I couldn't bear the possibility of losing her again. I didn't want to wake up from that sweet dream, but I didn't know how to prolong it. I expressed to her my fears, and she replied:

"It is true that I have to leave now, but we will meet again on another occasion. God has united us, and nothing can separate us. We are one single body, Diego."

As soon as she left, my chamber turned into the same old rustic cell it was before. What the hell! I refused to trust my senses. I felt the scratchy sayal cloth of my habit, the cincture, my thighs, my belly, my chest. I touched my face and my head with both hands. I made a fist and punched the wood of the pallet and the adobe wall. I rubbed with the palm of my hand the rough surface of the hardened clay and mortar. I traced with my index finger a crack on the wall. Everything seemed so real that I had to accept I was no longer dreaming.

I sat up and lit a candle. I observed the flame carefully. It was small and vacillating. The inner flame was white and the outer flame was a pale and dull yellow. I looked up and noticed the details of the wood ceiling, the wavy grain of the rustic beams, the undulating veins of the cracked and water-stained planks of pine. I looked down and saw my small notebook with sweat-stained leather covers on the pallet. I decided to get up to write down my dream.

I titled the entry "The Night Upside Down," a reference I was sure nobody would understand. If Brother Antonio or another superior were to read it, they would think that it was about a night in which I slept in this forbidden position. I had fun writing some journal entries in "upside down" code, the name I gave to the stories in which everything I wrote meant the opposite. It was difficult to recount my dream with Alma in this code, but it was worth it. Unfortunately, when I finished it, it was time to get up to pray the matins. I was exhausted.

11

THE MONTH OF OCTOBER 1665 WAS ONE OF THE HARDEST ONES for me. I got sick with dysentery and felt weak both physically and emotionally. I asked myself, again and again, What can I do to awaken and free myself from this nightmare? I didn't have the slightest clue and couldn't hide my miserable state of mind. Several times, during the examination of conscience, Brother Antonio asked me why I looked dejected. He told me that the Devil liked to put in the mind of novices disturbing thoughts and wild dreams to make us return to the secular life, where he would be able to dominate us more easily. He tried to persuade me to reveal to him clearly and openly all the thoughts and temptations that the Devil and my natural inclination had put in my mind. He warned me that the Devil sometimes transfigured himself into an angel of light to deceive us, making us do things that would confuse and disturb us easily. He said that I shouldn't give credence to any revelation, vision, apparition, dream, or the like, that I should always be self-restrained and suspicious of my own self, my mind, and my will, and that I should always trust and follow his advice. He asked me to tell him all my secrets without omitting anything, because through him the Lord would disclose to me the truth and what was in my best interest.

Nonetheless, I locked myself up in my mental cell. In the confessional I resorted to all the available formulas to admit my numerous transgressions, but without revealing to him any of my secrets, or my memories as Uriel. "Brother, I accuse myself of not having the right disposition to deserve the highest sacrament; of not examining my conscience with the necessary diligence; of not atoning for my sins conscientiously; of the careless and negligent way in which I have received the love of God." "Brother, I accuse myself of lukewarmness, remission, lack of attention and reverence when praying the Divine Office and when fulfilling my holy service duties." "Brother, I accuse myself of having numerous flaws in holy obedience matters; of doing everything carelessly, apathetically, and sorrowfully; of my lack of humility and patience; of my inattention and discontent; of my arrogance, conceit, wrath, envy, laziness, and concupiscence; of being nosy and indiscreet; of being a glutton and eating without permission." I committed all the sins and was the worst of all. When he wanted me to tell him all the details of my wrongdoings, I told him anything that occurred to me. I was not afraid to contradict myself because I fully trusted both my extraordinary memory and Brother Antonio's benevolence and compassion.

Everything was going passably well. However, the abduction of several Apache children complicated my relationship with Brother Antonio and the custodio. A band of kidnappers marauded an Apache encampment in the Tularosa Basin, kidnapped some children, and locked them up in the shed of an hacienda owned by Juan González, one of the encomienda landowners of Las Humanas Pueblo. The kidnappers were going to transport the children to Parral to sell them in the local slave market. However, the wagon train that was going to transport them got delayed and Captain Chapo and other Apache from Seven Rivers rescued the children one night. In the operation they killed the *encomendador*, his wife, and six day laborers; then they plundered the hacienda and set it on fire.

As was usually done in these cases, the governor of New Mexico ordered the lieutenant governor and captain general of the Río Abajo jurisdiction to organize a punitive expedition to apprehend the Apache involved. However, according to rumor, the whole incident had been plotted by the governor and the lieutenant governor. On the one hand, the murdered encomendero had no children who could inherit the property and trust. Therefore, upon his death, the land and the Indian subjects of the encomienda had to be transferred to another Spanish landowner by law. As expected, the governor had already chosen the lieutenant governor to take over this vacant encomienda. On the other hand, these two officials had partnered in the lucrative slave trade. The war against the Apache favored their business because they obtained prisoners that they could legally sell in Parral.

Brother Antonio also informed me that the lieutenant governor was my uncle and my godfather, for he was the younger brother of my adoptive mother and had baptized me. This complicated my situation because my superiors suspected that my godfather had planned everything not only to increase his profits but also to ruin their plan to pacify and convert the Apache in the area. They also assumed that my godfather wanted to prevent me from being sent to this mission. I had recently returned from Mexico City, or so I was told, and my superiors conjectured that I had asked him to do something to keep me from doing my apostolate in Apache country. Both Brother Antonio and the father custodian interrogated me several times to try to get some information out of me. As much as they threatened to excommunicate me and report me to the Inquisition, they couldn't get anything out of me. Several times I was about to confess my situation to them, but fortunately I kept my composure and remained silent. They had no choice but to believe me and disassociate me from this intrigue.

The chieftains of the Piro, Tompiro, Jumano, Tiwa, and Acoma expressed dissatisfaction and disagreement with the order they received from the governor to recruit four hundred men from their communities to participate in the punitive expedition. The governor of the Piro, Don Mateo Vicente, and the cacique of Senecú, Don Roque Gualtoye, met in the office of the convent with Brother Antonio and the vice custodio, Brother García de San Francisco, to ask them to intercede for them before the governor and lieutenant governor of New Mexico. This expedition was going to further complicate the difficult economic situation they were in because of the loss of the cotton crop that year. They needed to obtain hides from the Apache, as there was not enough cotton cloth in the region to pay the biannual tribute in October to the encomenderos. Nor did they want to be at war with the Apache because they knew they were going to attack and loot their villages and kill many of them. With great difficulty they had been able to negotiate peace with this bellicose tribe ever since some Tegua accidentally killed a man from Seven Rivers in Cuarac. The armistice with the Apache of Seven Rivers had been going on for two years and this expedition was going to break it.

Although the vice custodio and Brother Antonio knew that the governor's order was going to cause serious trouble for everyone, they said that the custodio and the members of the Definitorio had already met with the governor and the lieutenant governor and had failed to dissuade them. They said they had their hands tied because the charges the Inquisition made against former governor López de Mendizábal had weakened not only the viceroy's deputy but also the custodio himself. Besides, Governor Villanueva had recently arrived in New Mexico and they didn't want to have any problems with him so soon. They knew that he had been manipulated by the lieutenant governor. Moreover, they didn't want to antagonize the person in charge of protecting all the peoples and missions of Río Abajo. Don Juan de Mendoza, although corrupt and greedy, was one of the most effective military leaders in all of New Mexico and no one better than him could defend them against the Apache.

Don Mateo Vicente and the chieftains of the peoples of Río Abajo had no choice but to accept the order of Governor Villanueva. They recruited the four hundred militiamen who were requested and placed them at the command of Captain General Don Juan de Mendoza. Apparently, the only one who struggled to gather his warriors was Don Roque Gualtoye. Several young men led by Tambulista did not show up to the draft and, to avoid being punished, they left the village. Gualtoye had to call an impromptu meeting in the Senecú plaza that same afternoon to try to resolve the situation. The captain general had threatened to imprison both him and the war leader, Don Pablo Tzitza, if by the next morning they did not recruit the militiamen required by the governor. Although Gualtoye and Tzitza said they were willing to be imprisoned if there were no more men willing to enlist, everyone in the community knew that this campaign was going to drag them into a war that would be as bloody as it was unwanted. An eloquent speech by Santiago Mutanama convinced two dozen Piro war veterans that it was useless to try to postpone the inevitable: the war of the end-of-the-world had been already prophesied, and they needed to fight it on the Lord's side.

The forty Piro militiamen left Senecú in early November under the command of Captain José Telles Jirón. Along with them were nine mounted arquebusiers and three hundred and sixty warriors.

They were on their way to the encampment of Captain Chapo's band. Since they found it abandoned, they continued to the Sierra Oscura and then proceeded to the Sierra de San Gregorio, where they believed the Apache community had taken refuge. They looked for them until the end of November. However, they had to return because the cold was already starting to bite and the supplies were running out.

12

DUE TO THE CONSTANT FIGHTS BETWEEN THE ECCLESIASTICAL and civil authorities of New Mexico, some Christian Indians in the province had become disappointed by Spanish institutions and were reverting to their ancient rites clandestinely. To replace these "profane and heinous" celebrations with more "honorable and holy" ones, Brother Antonio was planning a special festivity of the day of the Immaculate Conception with a solemn Mass followed by matachines and Moorish and Christian dances, as well as a procession, a religious drama, and a banquet. However, due to the events of the Day of San Lorenzo, Father Guerra wanted to cancel the dances, arguing that it was a surreptitious way of practicing the cult of the Kachinas.

Brother Antonio wrote a letter to the vice custodio arguing that these dances offered Christian Piro the opportunity to express their faith and loyalty to the Virgin Mary and that it would be counterproductive to cancel them. The incident on Día de San Lorenzo had caused mistrust and discontent among some Piro and, given that a good part of the annual harvest had been lost due to the drought,

Brother Antonio informed him that the political atmosphere in the village was becoming volatile.

The vice custodio agreed to proceed with the celebrations, but only on the condition that Brother Salvador Guerra officiated the Mass and presided over the procession. He said that it was important for everyone to know the serious consequences of committing another transgression such as the one that Tambulista and his companions perpetrated. He warned that Father Guerra's message would be abundantly clear: Anyone committing a similar act in the future would be executed.

The preparations for the December festivities broke the monotony of my daily routine and pulled me out of my state of depression. It also helped that Jesús Ignacio fractured his hand. Since the mission was going to be without an organist, Brother Antonio asked me to take over. At first I refused because as far as I knew I had never touched a portable organ. But Brother Antonio assured me that it had been part of my instruction at the Convent of San Diego and that I had obviously forgotten it, as was the case with so many other things about my past. He asked Jesús Ignacio to give me some lessons and, indeed, after a brief explanation of the particularities of the instrument and keyboard, I was able to reproduce the notes with relative competence and ease. Thanks to this charming instrument, my days at the convent became a little brighter and more colorful in December.

The portable organ also brought me closer to the members of the children's choir, who, with their laughter and spontaneity, contributed to my feeling a little more at home in the church. Every day we would gather to sing in the church several times, not only to participate in the liturgy of the hours and in the morning and evening Mass but also to pray the rosary before dinner. Since Our Lady of the Immaculate Conception was the patron saint of the children's choir, during the first days of December not just the members of the choir and the church staff but everyone in the convent were devoted entirely to the preparations and celebrations of this festivity.

The people of Senecú devoted themselves completely to the festivity as well. Dozens of volunteers cut and hauled logs to the village for the bonfires. They also smoothed and trimmed the logs that were used to make the comedy corral and the stage; they decorated the streets and the pueblo plaza; they manufactured the fireworks and erected the structures for the various pyrotechnic shows that were scheduled between the night of December 7 and January 6, the day of the Epiphany.

13

ON THE NIGHT OF DECEMBER 7, I HAD A DREAM THAT LEFT ME absolutely perplexed. I was fast asleep after having taken care of the children all day. I felt exhausted. Fortunately, I don't have to get up to pray the matins tomorrow, I said to myself. I'm going to be able to sleep peacefully until six in the morning. Then I began to realize that Brother Antonio was shaking me and saying:

"Why are you asleep? Wake up, Diego. This is your chance. Get up. You can liberate yourself tonight! You have got to get up. It is the eighth day of the twelfth lunar month and the Pleiades are shining at their zenith. The morning star will soon appear."

I woke up. Everything was spinning. I felt an intense headache. It was all so dark that I couldn't even see Brother Antonio's silhouette. From the echo of his voice, I knew we were in a cavern, and, because of its hardness and coldness, I inferred that my bed was a stone cavity. I got up, bewildered and stumbling. Brother Antonio held my hand and said, "Come on!"

Instead of walking, we flew. We rose gently and passed through the roof.

"Don't be afraid," he told me. "You are a specter, and I am an illusion. Your only limit is the sky. You can reach it if you get rid of the dead weight that your soul carries."

"What dead weight? I'm a luminous goshawk," I replied. And to prove it to him, I went to the towns of El Paso del Norte and San Felipe del Real; I flew to the Alamo; I contemplated the grandeur of Balbuena's Mexico City; I visited the Imperial Toledo, Agustín Lara's Madrid, and the cityscape of New York; I saw the twin towers and came back in a flash.

"You see?" I said proudly.

We were suspended over the Founder's plaza in front of the Mission de Guadalupe. Brother García de San Francisco was standing on the portico, welcoming the parishioners. Opposite, on the plinth, Benito Juárez gave a patriotic speech to the people, and in the Plaza de Armas, Francisco I. Madero commended his troops after taking the city. The presidential cars of Adolfo López Mateos and Lyndon B. Johnson were parading on the Sixteenth of September Avenue. Behind them a long line of cars full of young people were cruising along, obstructing the vehicular traffic from Juárez Avenue to Américas Avenue. My friends and I were riding in one of those cars. We drank beer and listened to "Danger Money" at full volume.

"Don't you realize you're stuck in the past?" Brother Antonio told me, looking me in the eye. A remote flame was lit inside his pupils. He added: "While you can relive each of the experiences that you and your late ancestors had, you cannot go beyond them. Try it and you will see that something keeps you from leaving this maze of dreams and memories." Then he said something to me that I'll never forget: "Listen attentively to what I'm going to tell you.

You will not be able to return to your spiritual homeland until you fulfill the mission that the Most High assigned to you when you migrated to the realm of mortals."

"To the realm of mortals? What mission?" I asked him naively. We were standing in front of the statue of Brother García de San Francisco. A gray dove was perched on his head.

"The day you get out of the haze that clouds your mind, you will remember your mission and fulfill it. Fortunately, tonight the stars have lined up in your favor. The Supreme God has given you the gift of contemplating, in one vision and for one single time, the whole of your story. If you comprehend it, you will discover your mission in life. And if you accomplish it before dawn, tomorrow you will be able to embark on your journey back home. Otherwise, you will continue to wander in the Kingdom of Illusion as a tormented soul."

Brother Antonio led me to a colossal ravine. When we found a mountain that had a wide opening on one side, he told me to enter there. In the entrails of that mountain was a complex maze of grottos covered with numerous mineral formations. The walls and ceilings of the grottoes were decorated with a myriad of tiny, star-like lights. When we entered a huge cave that had a deep illuminated pond in the center, he invited me to sit and contemplate it.

"Where are we?" I asked him.

"In the navel of your land."

I looked to the bottom. At that moment the pond turned into a giant screen. It was showing a film of my life.

"I filmed it myself," Brother Antonio told me proudly. "Interesting, eh?"

I didn't say a word. I couldn't believe my eyes. Starting with the bicycle accident and, at a vertiginous speed, all my experiences were being projected into the pond in reverse chronological order.

"Don't dwell on the details. Look for the hidden plot that guides your existence, the sap that has unconsciously nourished all your actions. Rebuild the family history and the social narrative to which you belonged; discover the ties that connect your actions to those of your relatives and friends. Reflect on who you transformed yourself into over the years and how you were formed at different stages of your life: in Ithaca, Albuquerque, Las Cruces, El Paso, and, above all, in Ciudad Juárez. Also think about who and what your friends, teachers, and neighbors were like. Keep in mind, especially, all your loved ones: your parents, siblings, grandparents, uncles, cousins, and Alma, of course. Remember the life trajectory, aspirations, fears, achievements, misfortunes, strengths, weaknesses, preferences, and dislikes that each of them had."

I tried hard to follow his instructions, but when Alma's suicide scene appeared on the screen, I couldn't stay calm and started to shake out of control. At that moment I heard Alma yell at me from inside a contiguous cave:

"Don't be afraid, Uriel. I'm here!"

I heard a noise that sounded like a flock of screeching bats and screamed at the top of my lungs. Then a powerful whirlwind pulled me in and shook me violently in all directions like I was a pile of leaves.

I woke up confused. It was still dark. It was about three in the morning. Bernardo still had not rung the bell to summon us to the prayer of lauds. I could sleep an hour and a half more, I thought. I was tired but felt uneasy. I tried to fall asleep but I couldn't. I'd gotten used to getting little sleep. Sleeping more than three hours in a row was a luxury I hadn't enjoyed since my arrival in Senecú. I couldn't stop thinking about my dream.

What did it mean? Why was Brother Antonio in many of my dreams? Who was this man? I wondered over and over again without finding an answer. Was he a product of my imagination, or was he an acquaintance? Could he be a divine messenger? They say that angels sometimes appear in dreams to communicate a divine message or to reveal some mystery to us. I didn't know what I was going to do when my training was over. I needed to make an exit plan.

But where and by what means? My only possible escape seemed to be going with the Apache. Maybe this was what Brother Antonio meant when he said that I wouldn't be able to return home until I fulfilled my mission. Was God testing me? What if I didn't fulfill this mission? Would I ever leave this purgatory? Obviously, I could get out of this place by going with the Apache. The idea of escaping with a *N'nee* woman and living in freedom in her community, living off hunting, gathering, trading, and looting, sounded romantic. But I did not idealize the harsh and precarious life of the Apache, nor did I identify myself with their culture. Nor did I speak their language, nor share their beliefs, nor their worldview. No matter how different I was from the Franciscans, and how much I had distanced myself from Catholicism, a strong linguistic, cultural, and historical tie still bound me to them. At the end of the day, if it was true that a confrontation with the Beast was inevitable, whether this was Satan or a xenophobic personification of Indigenous deities, I would not hesitate to side, and even fight, with the Christians, if necessary.

What if I really had a life mission and I didn't fulfill it? Or I hadn't fulfilled it yet, of course, if I was still alive? Because I may be dead. I could be a tormented soul, as Brother Antonio told me in my dream. Whatever it was, whether I was dead or alive or dreaming, I had no idea what this mission might be.

I lost myself in these thoughts and, without realizing it, I fell asleep until the church bell called us to Mass.

14

THE MASS OF THE DAY OF THE IMMACULATE WAS GOING TO BEGIN at eight o'clock. Since I was going to assist Fernando de Jesús, the school prefect, I got up to meet him in the hallway. He was already waiting for me. We went directly to the children's bedroom to wake up Marcos, the eldest.

The twelve children slept tightly in the same room, each in his own bed. Marcos was a tall, thin fourteen-year-old who played his role as the waker both seriously and effectively. He forced his peers to get up immediately. As they did every morning, the sleepy children began the day by making the sign of the cross and praying in chorus an Our Father, a Hail Mary, a Creed, and a Salve. Then they did their business, made their beds, washed, combed their hair, and put on a blue tunic and a white surplice. Those who were ready went out into the hallway of the cloister where they formed two rows. They waited for the rest of their relatively quiet companions until Marcos came out with the stragglers. All carried on their bosom the book of Hours of the Virgin, except the littlest one. Realizing this, the prefect grabbed the clueless *atsamé* by the left ear and, without telling him anything, led him to the room so that he would pick up his book. The boy, who was barely eight years old, returned teary but composed and willing to fulfill his duty.

Once ready, the twelve choir boys walked in a line to the temple. Upon entering the altar we genuflected, headed to the pews in the back, and prayed in choir the Prime of the Little Office, presided over by Brother Lorenzo. Then we went up to the triforium to wait for Mass.

The church bell summoned the residents of the region. Almost all the parishioners arrived clean and wearing the best clothes that their caste and condition allowed them. The first to arrive were the matachines who, after genuflecting and placing in front of the presbytery railing their flower crowns, rattles, bows, arrows, drums, cudgels, and other pieces of their costume, walked to the back of the temple, sat, and waited for the other parishioners. Gradually their relatives and the villagers began to arrive. The pews in the front were reserved for members of the region's most prominent families. The mayor sat in the front row on the left side. He was a tall, mustachioed, and stocky man named Matías López. Immediately next to him sat the two encomenderos Félix de Carvajal and Alonso Mondragón and, next to them, Don Bartolomé Romero López and Captain José Telles Jirón. On the opposite row sat their respective wives and the guest of honor, a maternal great-aunt of mine named Doña Ana Robledo de Gómez, who was the president of the Sisters of the Immaculate Conception in New Mexico.

Among the parishioners was the woman who supposedly was my biological mother. Her name was María Bandama Romero. She was the daughter of a merchant of Flemish origin and a criolla whose father was a well-to-do rancher of Portuguese origin. At the age of seventeen—a year after I was born—María married a compadre of her grandfather, a man in his sixties named Joseph Varela, with whom she had two children. The second died when he was little. The firstborn, Pepe, who was eighteen years old, had just married a fifteen-year-old mestiza from Sandía Pueblo. Because his father had died of a heart attack two years ago, he lived and managed the hacienda of El Cerralvo. María Bandama lived in the village of Santa Fe with her mother and half-sister, Teresa Romero, who was born from an extramarital relationship that her father had with a genízara maid. My grandmother raised her as her own daughter along with María and her son, Diego.

María and Teresa came to Senecú to participate in the public announcement—called *grito* in Spanish—and the procession. They stayed in the house of a cousin, Juana Romero, who was married to Diego Pérez Granillo, a man in his forties who made a living hauling salt and trafficking slaves. The Romeros were related to other prominent families of New Mexico and so it seemed that half of the landowners in the region were my relatives. Several of them lived in the vicinity of Senecú, including Juana's father, Don Bartolomé. He was María Bandama's maternal uncle and was married to Doña María Granillo, who was a paternal aunt of Diego, her son-in-law. Juana's parents lived in a ranch that was located on the outskirts of Senecú Pueblo, as did another first cousin of my mother, Catalina Romero, who was Captain Telles Jirón's wife.

Before Mass began the boys and I performed some Marían hymns, including my favorite one, the "Ave Maris Stella." The Mass began with an entry procession presided by Father Guerra, during which we sang the Lauretan litanies. After the father began Mass and pronounced the dogma of the Immaculate Conception, we sang the "Glory in Excelsis." For the first reading Brother Antonio read the passages of the Book of Kings that recount the story of the sacrifice at Mount Carmel. For the second one he read the verses of the Book of Revelation that describe the appearance of the woman and the dragon. For the reading of the Gospel, Brother Antonio read St. Luke's narration of the Annunciation of the Angel Gabriel to Mary.

The most devout ones expected Father Guerra to base his sermon on this story and to praise the virtues of the Virgin Mary. However, Father Guerra took the opportunity to address the issue of the Kachinas and associated the sacrifice at Mount Carmel with recent events. To the surprise of the parishioners, he claimed that some rebels led by a self-exiled healer were clandestinely promoting a return to the pagan traditions and beliefs of the Piro and other Pueblo Indians. According to him the apostates claimed that the Kachinas would bring beneficial rains to the region for which everyone had been praying. Father Guerra compared the rebels to the Israelites who believed the prophets of Baal, the Canaanite god. He said toward the end of the sermon:

"The four hundred and fifty prophets invoked Baal at Mount Carmel all morning. They prayed to him incessantly until the hour in the afternoon when sacrifices are offered: 'Answer us, Baal! Baal, answer us.'"

Father Guerra paused for Santiago Mutanama, the acolyte, to translate his homily. Today, more than ever, Father Guerra wanted everyone to hear and understand his message.

"They danced and danced," Father Guerra continued. "They cut each other with sharp knives until blood came out and they fell into a trance. But Baal gave no proof of his existence or his supposed might. The four hundred and fifty prophets could not persuade Baal to deliver the much-needed rain. The prophet Elijah, on the other hand, alone, prayed and invoked the true God by name, saying: 'Answer me, Yahweh. Answer me. Let all the people know that only you are God.' The prophet Elijah, alone, achieved the prodigy."

Mutanama did not simply translate the sermon; he dramatized it as if he himself had witnessed this event and was giving his own testimony. He modulated the cadence of his phrases and the volume of his baritone voice effectively. He made gestures and motions, pointed to the sky with an index finger, and waved his forearm with energy. Father Guerra looked at him from the pulpit and discreetly approved of his interpretation as if he understood the Piro language.

"Thanks to this veritable miracle," Father Guerra continued, "Ajab and all the unfaithful Israelites finally became convinced that only Yahweh is God and that only Yahweh hears our prayers. Then Elijah, vindicated and authorized by Him, was ordered to slit the throats of all the prophets of Baal. And, once this was done, he told Ajab that the beneficial rain would soon fall. And, indeed, it rained. From a small cloud that rose from the sea, from a cloud the size of the palm of the hand, a great rain fell. Brethren: Mary is like this little cloud. She announces the coming of the Savior that puts an end to the drought. Jesus is the rain that waters our fields!"

The parishioners understood why Father Guerra based his sermon on this biblical story. It had been five years since the then governor of New Mexico, Bernardo López de Mendizábal, authorized the mayor of Cuarac to allow the Indians to perform their traditional dance in which they personified and invoked the Kachinas to ask them for rain, health, and other boons. Although the governor had been removed from his post and prosecuted by the Inquisition in 1664 for allowing these dances in his province, during his administration there was a resurgence of these dances in several towns of New Mexico. Some villagers continued to practice them even after the commissioner of the Inquisition, Brother Alonso de Posadas, banned all local dances in 1661. Although no one openly performed these dances, one of their religious leaders, a healer named Tsikié Fayé, Firebird in Spanish, tried to persuade Senecú's leaders to revive them. However, both the Piro governor, Don Mateo Vicente, and the cacique of Senecú, Don Roque Gualtoye, strongly opposed this initiative. As a result, Tsikié Fayé left Senecú. His departure produced divisions in the village, as some Piro were eager to reenact the dances that the authorities had forbidden for four years.

At the end of the sermon, Father Guerra and Mutanama continued with the liturgy. The offering and communion were made in a somber environment. Father Guerra gave his farewell to the parishioners by saying, "Have faith and confidence. The Queen of Heaven, before whom the Enemy lies defeated, is with us."

At the conclusion of the religious services, the choir boys went to the refectory to enjoy the chocolate with pastries that we all had been craving since the first hours of the morning. In the atrium, Father Guerra and Brother Antonio were saying good-bye to the parishioners. Just as we were exiting, Brother Antonio began talking to María Bandama. As soon as he saw me, he asked me to come over and introduced me to her. She was a tall, elegant lady of sad countenance and abstracted gaze. She had long black hair, brown eyes, and well-marked features. She wore a long black dress and a mantilla. The only colored garment she carried was a blue scapular that distinguished the Sisters of Our Lady of the Immaculate Conception.

Since I was not allowed to touch anyone, I simply bowed when Brother Antonio introduced us. He explained to her that, at this stage of my novitiate, I was not allowed to talk except to praise God and confess my sins. María Bandama told me she was happy to meet me and that in Santa Fe I would always be welcome in her house. I smiled, nodded, bowed again, and left for the refectory to have breakfast.

15

AFTER EATING WE RETURNED TO THE CHURCH TO BEGIN OUR preparations for the procession. In front of the presbytery, members of the Congregation of Saint Joseph had placed the throne where they were going to parade the statue of the Virgin. The bier had Corinthian-style columns; the throne was richly decorated with copper oil lamps, candle chandeliers, white floral arrangements, poinsettias, braided garlands with fir and guaco branches, multicolor banners made of rice paper, and brightly colored ribbons. A blue, gold-threaded, embroidered tablecloth with a lace trim covered the base of the throne. After Father Guerra burned incense around the statue and sprayed it with holy water, the float carriers carefully lowered it from the pedestal and placed it on the throne. They wore wool indigo-blue robes with the emblem of the Congregation of Saint Joseph tied with a white sash. Guided by their leader and encouraged by the ringing of the bell and the Marian chants of the parishioners, the float carriers slowly removed Our Lady from the temple. They laid the throne on a table with carved, gold-painted edges that had been placed at the bottom of the bleachers of the church in front of the atrium.

The parishioners gathered in front of the church. At the opposite side of the square, women could be seen preparing the feast for the procession participants and attendees. The air was filled with the aroma of toasted chili peppers and freshly made bread that came out of the semispherical ovens that were built on the rooftops of the houses. Thanks to the rays of the New Mexico sun that illuminated a completely clear sky, it had ceased to be cold.

The matachines were ready to perform their dance. As soon as the arquebusiers fired a couple of shots into the air to start the festivities and the four drummers beat their cylindrical instruments forcefully, the dancers waved their rattles and began dancing. They wore white shirts and carmine-colored *naguilla* aprons richly embroidered with thin reed beads and adorned with feathers and wool pom-poms. They danced barefoot, wore bells tied to their ankles, and, on their heads, carried a scarlet miter adorned with multicolored slats that reached the back of their knees as if it were a cape. Their faces were painted white with black stripes and their mouths were covered with red kerchiefs. They held a *guaje*, a type of maraca, in their right hands, which they constantly waved, and in their left hands they held a bow and an arrow, indicating that they were soldiers of the Virgin Mary. They formed two rows of twelve dancers each. At both ends of each row was a captain, who helped coordinate the movements of the dancers. There were also two monarchs located on both flanks, Don Pablo Baxcajay and Don Pablo Tzitza, who yelled vigorously whenever the dancers had to make turns, crossings, streamers, and waves.

A large audience admired the matachines and the statue of the Virgin, which was about a meter high. Twelve stars crowned her face with classic features and a circle of golden rays radiated from her folded clothes. She wore a white robe knotted at the waist and a blue cloak with golden plant motifs. She was standing on a crescent moon, and she pressed the nape of a dragon with her right foot.

Diego's great-grandfather, a captain of the conqueror Don Juan de Oñate named Bartolomé Romero Andujo, brought the statue to New Mexico from a trip he made to Seville in 1597. Thirty years later, when Don Bartolomé and his wife, Doña Luisa

López Robledo, settled in Senecú with some of their children and their respective families, they presented it to Brothers Antonio de Arteaga and García de San Francisco to beautify and purify the kiva or "stove," as the Spaniards called it, that at the beginning of their missionary work these two friars used as a church. That kiva, which was built by members of the Clan of the Sun, the lineage of Don Pablo Tzitza, was once located in front of the church about ten meters behind where the matachines were dancing. Our Lady possibly realized that the semi-underground construction in which she had lived temporarily had already been demolished. Now the whole village of Senecú seemed to have converted to Christianity and this group of dancers worshipped her with unusual fervor. And since the statue hadn't left her house for thirty-five years, the Virgin Mary seemed to admire the matachines show as much or more than the viewers themselves.

Don Pablo Tzitza had not forgotten that in that kiva he had learned Spanish and catechism with Brother Antonio de Arteaga. Nor that his father, grandfather, and other ancestors had been initiated there into the rite of the shamans. It was also there that many of his relatives kept the masks that would facilitate their entrance into the spirit world when they died. It was precisely Don Bartolomé Romero Andujo's workers who demolished this kiva once the residents of Senecú finished building the Catholic temple. It was also Don Bartolomé who employed Pablito in one of his ranches when his parents died of smallpox. Since then, Don Pablo Tzitza had worked at the Hacienda de la Chupadera, which now belonged to the son of his former boss, Don Bartolomé Romero López.

No one among the Piro seemed to know or wanted to speculate what motivated Don Pablo to organize and participate in this foreign dance. Perhaps it was out of nostalgia for those years of his youth that he reportedly participated in some dances that the Franciscans had not yet forbidden to the Pueblo people of New Mexico. For example, there was the dance of the butterflies, and that of the antelope and the eagle. Or perhaps it was out of discreet rebellion, because apparently Don Pablo participated as a young man in clandestine dances organized by a shaman of Pilabó in Arroyo del Tajo: that of the winter solstice and that of the summer solstice, in which they give, respectively, their welcome and farewell to the Pueblo gods and the Pueblo people's deceased ancestors, those masked and ethereal figures whom they called Friends, or "Piyeé" in the Piro language, but which the Franciscans called "Demons"; that is, the Kachinas. Or perhaps Don Pablo never ceased to believe what his late father taught him: that the material and spiritual world are but two different faces of the same coin and that in order to enjoy good health and harvests, they had to pay tribute not only to Mother Earth and to Father Sun but to all the benefactors of Heaven and Earth, including those beings from another dimension who help us and visit us. What everyone knew for sure was that Don Pablo believed with fervor and passion that the best way to communicate with the spirits, praise them, implore them, thank them, and ask them for boons was to dance to the rhythm of the heart and the drums.

Don Bartolomé Romero López, his patron, a bald, bearded, burly man of medium height in his sixties, observed the dance, like me, from the stands of the atrium. He wore a black slouch hat adorned with a long feather, a buff coat, a black doublet, a *valona* collar shirt, baggy breeches, and high-top boots. When the matachines finished dancing, he approached me to say hello. Knowing that I was a newcomer, but that we were related, he started to talk to me about the family and the leading role his father played in the founding of Senecú's mission. He told me that several former officers and soldiers of Oñate, including his father, settled with their respective families in 1627 in the vicinity of Senecú, and that two years later the friars Antonio de Arteaga and García de San Francisco arrived from Mexico City to begin the conversion of the Piro. He explained that there were then fourteen Piro villages, but that now the vast majority of the Piro had become Christians and lived in four villages: Senecú, Socorro, Alamillo, and Sevilleta. Thanks to God and the Franciscans, he told me, the missions they had founded had paid off with good fruits and, with rare exceptions, the vast majority of the Piro were "faithful servants of God and loyal subjects of the king of Spain." He claimed that the matachines were a perfect example of this, and especially the veteran Don Pablo, whom he described as "an exemplary Piro."

He also told me that the Romeros were going to have the honor of leading the procession and that I was going to carry the banner. He observed with pride that he and Don Felix de Carvajal wore the insignia of the Congregation of San Joseph, which was founded in New Mexico by their respective parents. Then he lowered his voice and confided in me something momentous whose significance I didn't understand then. He revealed that they were all faithful Siervos de Dios, "like me." Later I learned that this was a shibboleth that Crypto-Jews, Christians who secretly followed the Law of Moses and who practiced some Jewish rites and customs, used to identify themselves with their co-religionaries. He seemed puzzled by my obvious cluelessness and quickly changed the subject. He started to talk about my brother Pepe and told me that he was his favorite nephew because he was the hardest working in the family. I was surprised to hear that he held my brother in such a high regard since Pepe had always considered work as unworthy of savvy people like him who knew how to make money quickly and easily. However, soon it dawned on me that he was referring to Diego's half-brother Pepe, the eldest son of María Bandama, Diego's biological mother. Don Bartolomé explained to me, I thought unnecessarily, that Pepe was unable to attend this event because he was dealing with some urgent matters in his ranch, but he assured me that he was "a devout Catholic," and that he and I would get along "very well" when we met each other. He said this nodding and with a big smile, clearly expecting my acquiescence, which I granted diplomatically but unconvincingly, still unaware of the key role that Pepe would later play in my life in Senecú.

16

THE SOUND OF THE BELL ANNOUNCED THAT IT WAS TIME TO form the procession. It was about ten in the morning. Don Bartolomé said good-bye and Santiago Mutanama approached me to give me the banner. He told me that I was going to lead the procession and said not to worry because he was going to come with me and tell me where to go. When we began to line up, Brother Lorenzo began to sing acapella the song to the Immaculate:

Everyone together,
Sing, Chosen Queen,
You were conceived
Without original sin.

Then the drummers, the boys' choir, and many other people joined the procession. Mutanama and I led the march. Gradually we advanced toward the plaza and, as we advanced, many residents gradually widened the ranks of the procession. Throughout our tour around the village, we alternated the song of the Immaculate with the prayer of the Salve Regina, the Angelus, and other Marían songs led by Brother Lorenzo.

It was the first time I had walked the streets of Senecú. They reminded me of Taos and the day I visited it with Alma. The night before we had attended a staging in Santa Fe of Gluck's opera *Orpheus and Eurydice*. That July morning we visited the Millicent Rogers Museum and, while we were seeing figures from the sculptor Patrocinio Barela, we had a conversation with a Tiwa language teacher named Adam. After chatting for a while in the museum's inner courtyard, Adam invited us to have lunch at his house. He lived with his wife and three daughters in an apartment in the so-called North House, Hlauuma, in the historic village of Taos. After having four delicious blue corn sopaipillas for lunch, we heard some cassette tapes with songs that he and other teachers recorded to teach and help preserve the Tiwa language. He also sang a prayer that lauded the importance of forgiveness. When we continued the conversation that we had started at the museum, he addressed the issue of the abuses that the Spaniards perpetrated against the Pueblo people in colonial times. He said that the Spaniards not only invaded their pueblos but they also stole their best lands, subjected them to forced labor and all kinds of abuse. They assaulted their consciences and hearts and imposed on them a language, an alien way of life, foreign beliefs, and forced them to think and publicly declare that all their stories, songs, dances, rites, ceremonies, and spiritual beings were diabolical. And, not yet satisfied, many of them, including some friars, entered their homes, penetrated their chambers, and raped their daughters, women, and even some male children, when their husbands, parents, or relatives were not home. He said that all of these thefts, abuses, and outrages had left deep wounds in his people that had not yet closed, and these ills had been perpetuated by a few of them and the cycle of physical, verbal, and sexual abuse continued within their own homes, schools, and other public and private spaces. He said it was a problem that affected many members of his community, but very few of them talked about it.

That conversation with Adam deeply affected Alma, for she herself had been sexually abused by her father and by the priest to whom she had entrusted these painful experiences of her childhood and adolescence. After this encounter she was not the same person anymore. Over the next few months, she had a series of confrontations with her father and with her entire family that plunged her into the deepest depression from which she never emerged.

These painful memories accompanied me on a good stretch of my walk through the village. The grave and resonant voice of Santiago

Mutanama intonating the chorus "without original sin," as well as his gesticulations and a slight push, took me out of my dream state and helped me rejoin the procession in mind, body, and soul. The rest of the way I was able to hold the banner vertically and with my arms forming right angles, as Mutanama instructed me to do.

Mutanama marched and sang through the streets of Senecú with the religious fervor of the convert who sees himself as a prophet in his land. He developed this fervor at a young age when he learned from his Franciscan tutors that everyone in his village, including his own parents, uncles, and grandparents, worshipped the Devil and would end up in Hell. Due to the teachings of Brother García de San Francisco, the little atsamé—who was baptized with the name of the legendary warrior apostle, the Moor-slayer Saint James—assimilated the Christian doctrine and assumed his name with exceptional religious zeal. He literally accepted Jesus's words that are quoted in Matthew 10:34–36: "Do not think that I came to send peace upon Earth: I came not to send peace, but the sword. For I came to set a man at variance against his father, and the daughter against her mother, and the daughter-in-law against her mother-in-law. And a man's enemies shall be they of his own household."

Little Santiago began the process of breaking with the family when, on his own initiative, he revealed to Brother García where his father kept the paraphernalia he used to perform the ceremony of the *Petsuntoyané*, or Snake, the totem of his clan. Little *Kuensilué*, the name meaning thunder, with which his paternal grandmother presented him to the sun when he was twenty-one days old, received from his father such a beating that he was almost sent to the roof of his maternal home, the place where the souls of dead children lay to rest until they are born again in another body, according to their traditional beliefs. As a reward for this courageous act, which helped Brother García free the Piro from the clutches of the Infernal Enemy, not only the members of Santiago's clan but the Piro people in general, Brother García adopted him and made him a leader in his crusade.

Mutanama's religious zeal was founded both on a hope of heavenly reward and on a vehement desire to eliminate the thorns and bramble from the Lord's vineyard. He believed that his land was spiritually barren, if not cursed, because the real vine had not been planted there yet. He believed that only when the Franciscans planted the true vine would his homeland begin to produce spiritual fruits that would be pleasing to the Lord; he assured me that only when the people of New Mexico acted righteously and faithfully, according to divine law, would the heavenly Father send them abundant rain and protect their crops from plagues and the fire with which dry vines and weed were burned. The time of the divine harvest was coming soon, he firmly believed. For this reason, Mutanama was devoted to the task of helping Franciscans to evangelize and Christianize his people and ensuring that they did not revert to their old beliefs. Those who did so, or who refused to abandon their old beliefs, deserved to be bound in sheaves and burned as was done to dried branches after pruning, according to Mutanama. Fortunately, the majority of the Piro people had planted the real vine in their fields, he said. Now all they needed was his assistance and vigilance so that the vine shoots the Piro people planted would yield an abundant spiritual fruit that would glorify the Heavenly Vinedresser.

Like Brother García, Brother Antonio, and many other Franciscans of the time, Mutanama believed in the imminent arrival of the Son of Man and the establishment of his Kingdom on Earth. He also believed that there was a single divine law, a single revealed text, a single spirituality, and a single righteous and correct social and cultural behavior, a belief that was closely linked to that ceremonious religiosity full of ancient, precise, and immutable rites, formulas, and gestures instilled in him by Brother García. In this he clashed visibly but quietly with Brother Antonio, who practiced a less formalized and more austere and critical religiosity of the rites and ceremonies of the Church which, he once told me, supplanted God with vicarious and idolatrous cults full of intolerable constrictions that led to rebellion or debauchery. Mutanama seemed to be uncomfortable, or perhaps secretly scandalized, by the way Brother Antonio taught me to pray and meditate silently, standing and not covering my head. At that time I wasn't aware that Church authorities considered these practices heretical. Mutanama was also aggravated by the fact that Brother Antonio allowed me to pray and meditate for a time that he considered excessive. Although Mutanama was discreet, it was obvious to me that he longed for Father Santa Cruz's return so that he could restore order on the mission. It also seemed clear that it was Mutanama who warned Father Guerra that Tambulista and his comrades were going to make a manda or offering to San Lorenzo on his day and that he also considered the punishment that the daring dancers received that day more than fair and necessary. It was obvious that Mutanama was pleased by the message that Father Guerra had conveyed to the Piro this morning on this mission before Mass.

Today was a day of singular personal importance for Mutanama. He had written a religious drama that was going to be staged in the late afternoon. He had set the scene of the Annunciation in the local milieu and in the present period so that everyone would understand his redeeming message. He was pleased and proud of his personal accomplishments. He marched, prayed, and sang with such passion and dedication that it seemed that he had just returned triumphant from a long campaign against the hosts of the Devil.

We concluded the procession with a festive ceremony of the Triumphal Rise of the Immaculate and finished the event with a brief Mass. When it ended, everyone was more than ready to partake in the feast that awaited us. Visitors from all over the region had come to enjoy the extraordinary banquet, including some Apache from Ojo Caliente and other nearby encampments and villages.

17

SENECÚ SPARED NO EXPENSES, AS IF THE WORLD WAS REALLY going to end at any moment. Brother Antonio ordered three cows from the mission's corrals be sacrificed and six dozen bushels of corn, wheat, chili peppers, and beans be taken from out of the warehouse so that there would be no lack of food during the celebrations.

It was impressive how the villagers organized themselves to feed so many people. Members of the Congregation of St. Joseph and other Pueblo men sacrificed the animals, cut the meat, hauled the firewood, and prepared the corn beer known locally as *tesgüino*. Their wives and daughters contributed to the effort by grinding the grain and preparing the dough for the tortillas, baking the bread, roasting the chili peppers and the tomatoes, and cooking the beans, the vegetables, and the meat.

When Mass ended, parishioners quickly vacated the church. The mayors, the encomenderos, and other leading figures who were part of the processional cortege, along with their respective families, exited the temple through the side door and went to the convent's refectory and courtyards to enjoy the feast. Brother Lorenzo, the prefect, the choir boys, and I followed them. We ate comfortably and away from the hustle and bustle that formed in the plaza. Those who did not attend Mass had to make way for the parishioners to be served first. This annoyed those who had been waiting in the plaza since the early hours of the day, to which they protested with a squeal. There was a multitude of people in the plaza, and several were so anxious not to lose their place that members of the village guard had to intervene to make way for the parishioners.

Despite this tense and noisy beginning, the banquet took place in a cheerful and fraternal atmosphere. Once they ate and did their obligatory reading, the choir boys enjoyed an hour of recreation and played with other children who had dined with their relatives at the convent. Brother Lorenzo went for a nap and Prefect Fernando and I went to the backyard to supervise the children. We talked for a while. I was happy because it was the first time that I had spoken with anyone other than Brother Antonio. Fernando knew that I was not allowed to talk to anyone until the beginning of spring, but, given the circumstances and that no one was watching us, he told me not to worry and that we could talk with confidence.

Before the two o'clock bell rang, we went with the children to church to pray vespers and compline of the Little Office of the Blessed Virgin Mary. Then we led them to their room so they could clean themselves and change. They were to participate in the religious drama by singing and representing the twelve virtues of the Virgin Mary. The twelve boys wore white robes and bands of different colors representing each of the virtues: faith, hope, charity, piety, obedience, prudence, mercy, chastity, devotion, humility, patience, and poverty.

We met Brother Lorenzo at the gate and went out to the plaza where they were going to perform the play. It was an hour early and they were still serving food in the plaza. In front of the gate of the convent, Brother Antonio chatted with a small group of Apache. Among them were Refugio and Francisquillo, the captain of the Ojo Caliente encampment, as well as Chilmo, the regional leader of the Gila. Judging by the enthusiasm with which Brother Antonio spoke to them, it was obvious that they were talking about something related to the baptism of children and our future mission in Ojo Caliente, a mountain spring located at the end of the Alamosa Glen, at the foot of the Sierra de San Mateo, where, as Refugio later told me, healers and Gila warriors of other groups and bands went to acquire a supernatural power that the Apache called *godih*.

We walked to the western plaza of the village where "The Most Beautiful Flower in the Valley" was going to be staged. The choir boys sat provisionally on the pews that had been reserved for the prominent people and their families. Soon after, the musicians arrived with their flutes, vihuelas, and drums. They sat next to the children to test their instruments and to converse with each other. Brother Lorenzo, Fernando, and I stood quietly behind the children as we awaited the arrival of the performers and the spectators.

Mutanama and his assistants were making the final adjustments to the scenic space. They placed it in the middle of a plaza so that spectators could see the play from the rooftops, standing around the stage, or sitting if they were from a prominent family. The plaza was spacious. It was located south of the mission's cemetery in the northwestern part of town. The housing block surrounding the plaza was semicircular and angled, like a cantaloupe slice. The houses were one and two stories high. The afternoon light slowly stretched its shadow. In the center of the stage was a quadrangular wooden platform that resembled the roof of a typical adobe house. Around it was a fenced area planted with corn and grape vines. A corral divided the scenic space from that of the spectators. Another space, about four meters wide, was created between the fence and the corral. One of its halves was divided into two sections. In the northwestern section was a high throne surrounded by stones depicting Hell. In the southwestern section was a circular space with a woodpile in the center representing a kiva. In the northeastern and southeastern sections were wooden panels painted with pines and trees that simulated a forest.

The first performer to arrive was Lupita Tzitza, Don Pablo's granddaughter. She arrived with several family members, including her parents and grandparents. Lupita was going to represent the Virgin Mary. She was thirteen years old, and her Christian parents had raised her carefully, making her into an exemplary girl. She possessed the qualities that everyone most admired and sought out in a young Christian woman. Besides being beautiful and diligent, she was kind, obedient, modest, and very Catholic. She was also eloquent, self-possessed, and endowed with a privileged memory and a beautiful treble voice. When Mutanama created the role of the protagonist in his play, he thought precisely of her and cautiously prepared her parents in advance so that, when it came time to ask them for permission, they would let her participate in the play with enthusiasm. However, it was not easy to convince them, especially the mother, because neither of them wanted Lupita to stand out in this way in the village. Mutanama had to ask Lupita's grandfather to intervene. Fortunately for him, Don Pablo saw nothing wrong with Lupita playing the role of the Virgin Mary in the play; quite the opposite. He told his daughter and son-in-law not to be afraid of what people would say. After all, the author and main promoter of the play was the prosecutor of Senecú Pueblo himself; the rehearsals would be carried out in the convent where she would be safe and where no one could bear false witness or make rumors against her without having to deal with Mutanama and Brother Antonio. To ease any lingering doubts or fears, Don Pablo and Mutanama gave their word to Lupita's parents that they would take care of her and always keep a close eye on her.

One thing that helped convince the mother was that the play would possibly help Lupita get distracted and heal her from the heartbreak she had recently suffered when her fiancé mysteriously disappeared from the village without a trace. The parents thought that perhaps the play would even help her find a better match, because they were aware that Don Pedro Carvajal, the encomendero's son, a good-natured, serious, hardworking, honest, and very Christian young man who courted Lupita, was going to have a starring role in the play. It was one of the reasons why at first they had hesitated to let her participate in this event, since they did not want to fan the flames of gossip. But Lupita's mother finally agreed when Mutanama commented that, in case Lupita did not participate in the play, he was going to ask Ana Luisa, a granddaughter of Don Bartolomé, who, as everyone knew, loved Pedro and harbored the desire to marry him.

The other performers and the spectators arrived gradually, and the performance began. The cast of characters included the Maiden or Virgin Mary, who was depicted as a humble peasant girl who lived with her siblings and their sick widower mother, for whom Mary cared. The antagonist was a sorcerer who had been expelled from the village. He was obsessed with taking revenge on his fellow villagers by kidnapping their most beloved neighbor, Maiden Mary, and forcing her to participate in the winter solstice ceremony that he and his henchmen were going to celebrate in a nearby cave.

Throughout the play the Sorcerer used his magical powers and the help of Lucifer and his servants to try to deceive and abduct the Maiden Mary. The Sorcerer's henchmen were embodiments of some figures of the mythology and folklore of the Pueblo people: Coyote, Spider Woman, and the Twin Warriors. Although Mary spent most of the day caring for her disabled mother while her brothers and sisters tilled the family plot, Mary was protected day and night by her faithful mastiffs, Care and Will, and her twelve guardian angels, the Virtues. The last act also included Mary's cousin Isabel and the archangels Gabriel, Michael, and Raphael.

In the first act the Sorcerer summoned Lucifer and asked him for help in kidnapping Mary. But Mary rejected him, and her guardian mastiffs attacked and dismembered him. In the second act Lucifer sent Spider Woman to trick Mary. However, the mastiffs attacked Spider Woman and a heavenly sparrow ate her in one bite. In the third act Lucifer sent his gallant sentries, Morning Star and Evening Star. Mounted respectively on an albino white and a jet-black stallion, they went to the village fully certain that they would be able to convince Mary to participate in the solstice dance. They went to her house and, after they serenaded her, she told them to leave, but they refused. Fortunately, several heavenly soldiers arrived and gunned them down with their arquebuses. In the fourth and final act, Lucifer, tired that none of his emissaries had succeeded, decided to carry out the mission himself. He left his underground shelter in the shape of the Flayed God. However, the angels Michael, Raphael, and Gabriel were already waiting for him, and before he could cross the Río del Norte, they subdued him. The drama concluded with Mary's speech at the end of the account of the Annunciation in the Gospel of Luke 1: 52–53: "He hath put down the mighty from their seat, and hath exalted the humble. He hath filled the hungry with good things: and the rich he hath sent empty away."

The play delighted many in the audience. Most of them applauded, whistled, and made a great bustle praising Lupita's voice and celebrating the good young actors' and actresses' performance. But not everyone enjoyed the show. Several guests of honor found Mary's final words subversive. Among them were the two mayors and the two encomenderos of Senecú. At the same time, some Marians were outraged that the play placed the Virgin in the local milieu and exposed her to "vile" folk characters. Others felt affronted because the play desecrated and ridiculed Mother Earth, the Lord of the Underworld, the Sons of the Sun, and the wise and generous Spider Woman.

Despite everything, Father Guerra commented the next day that the festivities had been "a marvel." It was the most bustling event in recent years in the area. According to Mutanama, there were about a thousand people in the village, almost twice the population of Senecú, and more than three hundred people had attended the play. In addition to convening hundreds of people to the festivities and the various religious, artistic, and civil events, Father Guerra and Brother Antonio baptized more than fifty children and adults and married nineteen couples. Both were pleased with the results and neither seemed to worry about the fact that the play had infuriated some people in the audience.

18

THE YEAR 1666 BEGAN FAVORABLY. HOWEVER, ON THE DAY OF the Epiphany, something happened that triggered a long series of misfortunes. When they unfolded in the summer, some in the village began to think that, indeed, the end of the world was coming.

The day of Epiphany passed normally at first. We celebrated the traditional morning Mass with cheerful songs and enjoyed the *rosca de Reyes* in the afternoon. Then we attended the annual ceremony of appointment of the Senecú pueblo officials that took place in the central plaza. As had happened during the last ten years, Matías López, the mayor of Senecú, gave to Don Mateo Vicente the staff of the local governor, which symbolized the power he held as head of the secular government of the Piro people. The first lieutenant, the second lieutenant, and the Pueblo constable, who had been part of his team for several years, were also reappointed. The only surprise was that Fiscal Mutanama was removed from office. He was replaced by Estebanico Quele, a nephew of Don Mateo Vicente, who did not share Mutanama's religious zeal and whom Matías López, the two encomenderos, Brother Antonio, and other influential figures considered a loyal Christian and a reliable Piro.

The dawn of January 7 was particularly beautiful. I got up about fifteen minutes before five o'clock to pray the lauds and do my Sunday morning chores. After hearing Mass and having breakfast, I asked Brother Antonio for permission to go for a walk. On the western horizon the waning moon shone over the mountains. Although it was very cold and the sky was partially covered with a thin layer of cirrostratus, as soon as the sun appeared, it illuminated the clouds with shades of yellow, orange, pink, and red.

I walked around town and enjoyed that splendid morning for about an hour. I returned to the convent before the nine o'clock bell rang to pray the terce in my bedroom. After meditating and praying, I began to read Ecclesiastes. But I felt tired due to the walk, the numerous celebrations, and the intense social life in recent weeks. Without realizing it, I fell asleep on the chair with the Bible on my lap.

Brother Antonio came by my room a little before noon, the time of the sext. I must have been snoring when he knocked on the door because he scolded me when he woke me up. He patted me on the shoulder and said:

"How come you are asleep at this hour of the day?"

I got up quickly and prostrated myself before him without saying anything.

"Brother Diego, holy prayer is the spiritual teacher of friars," he told me in a didactic but stern tone. "When I tell you to pray and study with the door of your bedroom closed, it is not so you can take a nap but for you to take better advantage of the divine lesson. As the Carmelite sage points out, 'To pray, one must choose a place where the senses and the spirit get the least impeded from going toward God.' He who interrupts the spiritual exercises and his prayers to sleep invites the Devil to be in his dreams."

"I'm sorry, Brother. I didn't realize I fell asleep."

"Don't apologize. Listen to my reprimand quietly."

He sat on the wooden trunk where I kept my personal items and invited me to sit down. I tried to cede him my chair, but he didn't accept.

"You must always remember that, although it is necessary to know the Holy Scriptures well to preach the Word of God in a dignified and appropriate manner, what you need most is to lead an exemplary religious life. Your studies should not consume your time nor lead you to sacrifice the practice of prayer. Hold in high regard mental prayer. To pray is to speak to God with one's heart. Praying is not only speaking to God with one's lips. Private, mental prayer is necessary for salvation and is more beneficial than the prayer we say publicly aloud. Mental prayer purifies us and presents us to God in an appropriate attire. He who seeks the Lord must have great stillness, peace, and tranquility. He must have an attentive heart and a concentrated mind, for God is not God of disorder but of peace, and when one prays in silence, one prays in peace."

He continued his sermon on the importance of mental prayer for a few minutes. Little did I know that Church authorities frowned upon silent prayer. As Brother Antonio revealed to me later during confession, they regarded it as quietist and individualistic, if not Judaizing and heretical. No wonder Mutanama seemed outraged when he saw me absorbed in silent meditation.

When Brother Antonio finished his reprimand, he said:

"From now on you will have to do two community hours of prayer, instead of just one. The first one shall be after the lauds and the second before the vespers. You must end your prayers with the sacramental blessing."

"As you wish, Brother."

"But do not think I came here to punish you. I am here to give you the good news that you've passed your novitiate's first test. Our statutes state that novices should be evaluated three times a year. Congratulations, Brother Diego. Despite your occasional oversights, in these four months you have shown that you can be one of the chosen ones. If you amend your faults and continue to fulfill your obligations, at the end of the summer I will send the custodian a final summary recommending that he approve your profession of vows."

I forced a smile on my lips, trying to seem appreciative. The idea of continuing the religious life for an indefinite period produced in me such a deep anguish that I could hardly convey satisfaction and gratitude.

"As you well know," he said, using the familiar "tú" form, which indicated that he had finished his reprimand, "next month you will complete the six months of your novitiate. You will no longer need to keep the obligatory vow of silence. This spring, toward the end of March, you will be able to begin the mission that the father custodio and the members of the Definitorio have assigned you in these provinces. I am also pleased to inform you that the health of Brother de la Cruz has continued to improve. It is possible that by then he will be able to take over the administration of the convent again. If this happens, God Our Lord willing, you and I will be able to go to the land of the Apache. Together we will live in the Ojo Caliente encampment where we will be able to catechize all those who wish to receive the sacrosanct water of baptism."

I didn't know what to say. I looked down and kept quiet for a few moments. The idea of being a missionary in Apache territory terrified me. Sometimes, however, I fantasized about the idea of running away. Life in the convent was suffocating me.

"And why that silence? Don't you realize that in this mission you can fulfill your pious will to suffer martyrdom for the salvation of pagan souls?" He asked me as if this news should actually fill me with joy.

"Martyrdom? I have never told you of this intention," I said, disconcerted and with unusual frankness.

"I know, Brother Diego. I know. But do you think I ignore the contents of your diary? As you know, I have to keep an eye on everything you do."

"Everything?" I asked, frankly annoyed. Annoyed with him for meddling with my things, and with myself for being so naive. Didn't he have enough milking my conscience twice a week in the confessional? Didn't I have the right to a crumb of mental or literary freedom in this place?

He got up and opened the trunk where he was sitting. He took out the notebook where I recorded my experiences and my thoughts in a veiled and cryptic way.

"Here," he told me. He showed me several entries that I did not recognize. They were written in my own handwriting. One dated Thursday, August 10 of 1665, said: "Blessed are the dead who die in the Lord." Another one, dated Monday, September 11 of the same year, stated: "Above all things, I want to reach God by saving the souls of heathens." In a Thursday, November 2 entry, I reflected: "If it is glorious for a soldier to die for the fatherland, how much more glorious will it be for a Christian to reach Paradise after beating Lucifer?" Also, there were several passages from the Bible demanding self-sacrifice to be admitted to the Kingdom of God, including John 12:25: "He that loveth his life shall lose it: and he that hateth his life in this world, keepeth it unto life eternal." And a recent annotation describing my hardships in the convent, closed with this passage from the Apocalypse: "Fear none of those things that thou shalt suffer. Behold, the devil will cast some of you into prison that you may be tried: and you shall have tribulation ten days. Be thou faithful until death: and I will give thee the crown of Life."

I thoroughly examined the calligraphy and verified that it was mine without a doubt. My tiny script floated slightly over the lines of the page; all capital letters were adorned with my characteristic hook; the *s* I had designed was faithfully reproduced; the *g*s looked like ducklings praying; the *a* did not close at all; the *i* had no dot; the *y* looked like the number four. All the details of my writing were faithfully reproduced in these spurious entries. I didn't know what to say. It was my writing, but they were not my writings, as if someone had perfectly imitated my handwriting to set me up.

Was it possible that Brother Antonio could have done this? Who else could have done it? Why and for what purpose? I was quiet and thoughtful for a few moments. I did not want to accuse him without being sure that he had been the author of these apocryphal annotations.

"Rejoice, Brother! The Lord has given you the occasion and the fate of the apostles. Rejoice that soon it will be your turn to obey the Most High and to sow and expand his holy faith in the Kingdom of New Mexico. Remember how many hardships and persecutions the apostles and the other saints endured imitating their master; remember the glory they have today for all that they suffered by converting the souls of the Gentiles who, because of the dearth of light and preaching in their world, did not know the true God, our Lord. At last you will be able to fulfill your desire to sacrifice yourself for the salvation of the souls of the infidels. Praise the Lord."

"Yes, Brother. God be praised," I answered mechanically, trying to hide my confusion and multiple doubts and fears.

"And now I will leave you alone to pray and thank God for granting you to follow the example of his son, Jesus Christ. He came into this world to serve and give his life for all of us. Spilling your blood for the conversion of the Apache you will also earn your entry to Heaven."

"No, Brother. I won't forget it. Go in peace."

19

THE NEXT DAY THERE WAS A GREAT COMMOTION IN THE VILLAGE. At about eight o'clock in the morning, Don Roque Gualtoye and Don Mateo Vicente came by the convent. When they arrived, Brother Antonio and I were in the desk room updating the convent's accounting records. He asked the doorman to let them in and asked me to stay. They came to inform us about the disappearance of Lupita Tzitza and Chayito Guilixigüe.

According to their account, on the morning of January 6, the women had gathered to prepare the roscas de Reyes of their clan. Lupita and Chayito were asked by their mothers to bring firewood because there was not enough to heat the oven. The two girls left the house at about six o'clock in the morning. They headed toward the communal lands where the goats graze. Unfortunately, they didn't come back. Realizing this, their mothers first expressed frustration; they complained that their daughters were always chatting, getting distracted, and neglecting their chores. However, after two hours passed, Chayito's mother asked her two eldest children to go look for them. They went to all the places where the villagers regularly searched for firewood but returned without a clue of the girls' possible whereabouts.

By then the women had finished making the roscas, and everyone needed to leave their chores to attend the Epiphany Mass that took place at ten in the morning. When it ended, the family and friends of Lupita and Chayito formed groups and went to look for them in the village and the surrounding area. They asked all the neighbors from house to house, but no one seemed to have seen them that morning. The last people who apparently saw them were their own mothers before they went out to get the firewood.

All their relatives and friends were concerned because they knew that Lupita and Chayito were obedient and responsible. They interrogated everyone who knew them well, especially their friends, but no one had any idea where they might have gone. Some contemplated the possibility that they escaped to meet with the rebels. Although this possibility was not ruled out, they judged it unlikely that the girls had made this decision without telling anyone. Chayito's fiancé was among them and was offended by insinuations that his betrothed had abandoned him.

In the afternoon some had to interrupt the search because they had to attend the annual ceremony of appointment of the village officials, including Lupita's grandfather Don Pablo Tzitza, who was the *opi,* or war leader, of the Senecú Piro. At the end of the ceremony, they reformed groups to go out and looked for the girls in the surrounding area. Unfortunately, they had to interrupt their search because it was pitch black and extremely cold.

They returned home to eat rosca de Reyes, but no one among Lupita's and Chayito's relatives and friends enjoyed it; the rosca tasted like *pan de muerto*. The Dia de Reyes's long-anticipated feast became a kind of wake. They all kneeled down to pray and ask God and all the saints to protect the girls from the cold and the danger and to bring them back home at once.

When Don Roque Gualtoye finished his account of the events, he said they were doing everything possible to find them. He noted that Lupita's grandfather and his subordinates had searched the entire village and the surrounding area to no avail. He added he was going to ask the chieftains and governors of the surrounding villages to help them. Given that his grandson Martín Gualtoye had allegedly joined the rebel group led by Tambulista, and that everyone knew that Lupita had been heartbroken since his departure, both Don Mateo and Don Roque wanted to reassure Brother Antonio that they did not approve of the rebels' actions and that they "in no way" supported them nor were going to do so in the future.

Don Roque politely asked Brother Antonio to warn all the ranchers in the county about the disappearance of the girls. He also asked him to accompany them to the Casa Real to talk to Mayor Lopez, to which Brother Antonio agreed.

Brother Antonio returned alarmed from the meeting with the mayor. He came directly to my cell to talk to me and let me know that he had decided to change his plans.

"Our sacred mission in Ojo Caliente is in danger," he said.

He told me what happened at the Casa Real. Apparently, Don Matías López was already aware of what had occurred on Saturday morning. After Don Mateo gave him his version of the events, the mayor asked Don Roque about his grandson Martín's relationship with Lupita. When the Senecú Pueblo leader replied that she had been his grandson's fiancée, the mayor claimed that the girls had "gotten together with the rebels just like the grandson." Hearing this, Don Roque "turned red out of shame or anger," said Brother Antonio. Despite this, he said that the leader kept his composure and acknowledged that this was not impossible. He assured the mayor that even if his grandson was with them, neither he nor his family nor his people supported the rebels. Don Roque said that the girls and their families were "very Catholic" and that many in the village feared that Lupita and Chayito had been abducted as had happened to the other two girls from Socorro.

Brother Antonio explained to me that last summer two girls from the neighboring village of Socorro had been abducted. They were said to have been taken to Mexico City, where they were interned in a cathouse disguised as a nuns' convent. Brother Antonio acknowledged that even though this was likely, it was impossible to prove it, let alone punish the culprits, for they were very powerful people. He said the band of kidnappers and slave smugglers was led by my godfather, Don Juan de Mendoza.

He added that, at the meeting, the mayor had claimed that he knew who the kidnappers were. He assured them they were members of the Chilmo band, whose territory includes the Magdalena Mountains. He was certain that Don Chilmo and his people were protecting and helping the rebels and Tsiké Fayé to carry out their plan to organize an uprising and expel the Spaniards from New Mexico.

Brother Antonio told me that he intervened to assure the mayor that there was no need to give credence to these rumors. He reminded him that Captain Chilmo and other Apache had attended the Feast of the Immaculate. He said that afternoon he had been invited again to go to Ojo Caliente to baptize some of them. The Apache, said Brother Antonio with a phrase he often used when talking about them, "although they are bellicose, are trustworthy and boast of always telling the truth." He noted that Captain Chilmo would not have attended the banquet nor invited us to his encampment if he were protecting the rebels. Don Mateo stepped in and said he agreed with him. He commented that in all the trade dealings he had had with the Apache, he had never been deceived or let down. He also stated that "the Apache are people of their word" and that some "hunter friends" had found tracks of the rebels "to the east of the village, over in the Arroyo del Tajo." Then Don Mateo added with some irony, "The Magdalena Mountains, as you know, Señor Don Matías, are located to the west of Senecú." According to Brother Antonio, Don Mateo's comment greatly angered the mayor. He got up from the chair, saying: "'Stop your sarcasm, Don Mateico. I know this territory perfectly well and I also know the place I occupy in this town. I don't need you or anyone else to explain to me what Apache are like. I know them very well and I don't trust them. I'll decide whether I give credence to the rumors I hear around. I'll take care of finding those rebel raccoons myself. I'm going to shoot them out of their burrows, wherever they are.' Adding that he had other important matters to attend to, he walked us to the door," Brother Antonio said.

He revealed to me his suspicion that Governor Villanueva and my godfather wanted to find a justification for continuing to capture Indians from the plains and sell them as slaves in Parral. Although the Audience of Guadalajara had declared the capture and enslavement of Indians illegal since 1660, this lucrative practice continued to be carried out clandestinely. He told me that Matías López and Juan García Holgado, Socorro's mayor, were part of the network of traffickers headed by Villanueva and my godfather. Several slaves were just about to be boarded on a caravan train. The provincial mayor of the Holy Brotherhood, Don Cristóbal de Anaya, was going to take them to Parral in a commercial caravan that same afternoon. Governor Villanueva had appointed precisely my godfather as the caravan inspector to make sure that Anaya and his crew had no mishaps.

"They want to blame Captain Chilmo for the disappearance of the girls so they can make war on the Gila Apache," Brother Antonio told me. "Our plans to catechize and pacify them are going to be ruined. Before it's too late, we need to save some Apache souls. You need to get to Ojo Caliente as soon as possible. This Sunday, if Refugio comes to hear Mass, I'm going to ask him if you can go with him. Get ready to depart right away."

20

EVERYTHING SEEMED TO BE BACK TO NORMAL THAT DAY. I WAS in my chamber doing my usual spiritual exercises and prayers of the sixth, trying not to think about my impending departure to Ojo Caliente. Suddenly I began to hear a strange, high-pitched, continuous noise. At first I thought it was a kettle boiling water, but I remembered that there were no such pots in the convent. I also thought of the screeches of the owl when I got lost on top of the San Mateo Mountain, that unforgettable night from my memories, but I remembered that owls make these noises only in the fall when they are looking for a partner, or in the spring when the males want to protect their partner or their chicks. For a minute I was alarmed because it sounded like women screaming; but I was relieved when I noticed that the screeches were following a regular, repetitive rhythm as if they came from a mill.

I decided to go outside to investigate. At the gate of the convent, I ran into Pedro and asked him if he knew where that noise came from. He laughed at me for being so concerned and explained that it was a wagon train approaching the Camino Real.

As I exited the convent, I noticed that several women were rushing toward the village's main road and that a group of men were running after them. To reach the road one had to go down a stony and zigzagging hill. The men were able to stop some of them at the top of this slope by grabbing them from where they could, but others slipped away and continued their race downhill. At first the scuffle unfolded as a silent theater scene; however, when the tussle intensified, some of the women started to give such loud screeches that it seemed they wanted to awaken all the dead buried within a three-league perimeter. They were dramatic, desperate howls that broke one's heart.

I ran toward them and saw that one of the women was Lupita's mother, whose husband was holding her. She was trying to get away, yelling at him things I didn't understand. She was tousled and disheveled. Her tears and face expressed pain, anger, hatred, and exasperation. Other women who had also been arrested joined the deafening and poignant clamor. The men who held on to them were both desperate and powerless to stop the irrepressible torrent of cries and howls that were coming from the depths of their souls like the violent surges of steam, stone, and ash that precede the eruption of a volcano.

In the background one could hear the raucous counterpoint of the wagon train pulled by a team of mules slowly approaching the Camino Real. It was followed by droves of sheep and cattle, and loaded with salt, pine nuts, furs, wool socks, and other goods produced in New Mexico. Inside the wagons were Indigenous children and adolescents who had recently been held up or kidnapped by abettors whose powerful bosses controlled the slave trade and sold them for fifty pesos, and the most select ones for more than a hundred—what ten horses were worth—to the owners of the mines, workshops, ranches, and estates of New Spain.

It didn't take long for a crowd to gather. Soon came the chieftain, the governor, and other members of the Council of Senecú Pueblo, as well as Brother Antonio, whom the onlookers allowed to pass through. I stood motionless at the epicenter of the conflict. Amid the screaming I was able to figure out that some of the women accused the Pueblo leaders of being cowards for allowing the white faces to humiliate and dishonor them. Soon after, the lieutenant governor of Río Abajo, Don Juan de Mendoza, Mayor Matías López, and several soldiers arrived well-armed, but the crowd blocked their way. They came from the Camino Real. They had been waiting for the wagon train to arrive in order to inspect its contents. When they heard the screeches, they came over to check what was happening. They had to fire their arquebuses a couple of times into the air to force the crowd to let them pass through.

The clamor almost completely gave way to the resounding voice of the lieutenant governor, who let us all know that he would not allow them to disrespect him or to disturb order in the village. But no matter how much the Pueblo men tried to silence the women they were holding, Lupita's mother and another woman yelled at him that they wanted the stolen girls back.

"You're to blame! Your men took my daughter! Give her back to me!" Lupita's mother yelled at Matías López, pointing her finger at him.

"Shut up or I'll lock you up!" the lieutenant governor yelled, incensed with anger.

"What nonsense is this woman talking about, Don Mateo Vicente?" he shouted at the governor of the Piro people, pretending to seem clueless of what was happening. Matías López was standing next to him. He had a grimace of disdain and held his arquebus firmly.

Don Mateo Vicente gave the order to shut her up and take her and the other women away immediately. Taking off his hat, he told the lieutenant general that he and his deputies would like to check the train wagons because they believed that Lupita and Chayito were kidnapped, and their abductors were transporting them there. My godfather replied that they were not authorized to inspect the caravan's contents. From his gown he drew a document signed by the governor of New Mexico showing that he alone was the appointed train wagon inspector, or *visita*. Wielding the rolled-up document and brandishing it as if it were a cudgel, he said that the position of visita commissioned him to personally inspect the contents of the wagon in Senecú and to ensure that nothing or anyone who did not have the proper license could leave the province. He claimed that if he were to find anyone who was not on the boarding list, it was his responsibility to forbid and prevent that person's departure. He observed that the owner of the fleet was the provincial mayor of the Holy Brotherhood, Don Cristóbal de Anaya, to whom Governor Villanueva had granted a license to transport goods and people to San José del Parral. Since the wagon train had just arrived, he said it was urgent for him to inspect it and that it would be better for them to give up attempting to usurp his duties. Otherwise, their presumptuousness and the public disturbance they were creating would cost them dearly. As he spoke, the women were gagged and tied up and forcibly escorted away.

Don Roque Gualtoye replied by saying that they were not there to usurp his duties or question his authority but that they were entitled to investigate the disappearance of the girls. His clear and calm voice expressed resolve, and his tranquil countenance expressed serenity and dignity. He was a stocky and short man in his sixties with long hair. His head was covered with a red kerchief, and his body with a red and black blanket with stripes. He added that it had not been their intention to complicate this delicate situation and gave the order that everyone should leave and return to their activities, except the leaders of the Piro people and representatives of the Church. He declared they would be in charge of solving this matter and told his people things in the Piro language that I did not understand. However, because of the tone, it was evident that he ordered everyone to leave immediately. The constable and his assistants executed the order quickly and no one resisted. The only ones left, besides the lieutenant governor, the mayor, and his men, were Don Roque Gualtoye, Don Mateo Vicente, Don Pablo Tzitza, Brother Antonio, and me. By then the wagon train had come to a complete halt and the loud squeaking had stopped.

Brother Antonio intervened in the dispute. He acknowledged that inspecting the fleet was the job and the responsibility of the visita, but he added that it was the lieutenant governor's obligation, as Río Abajo's highest authority, to ensure compliance with the laws in his jurisdiction. He said the disappearance of the girls was a serious matter that required the investigation and participation of the Senecú authorities and that it was his legal and moral duty to support them in this task.

My godfather reacted in a brusque and high-handed way. He told Brother Antonio this was none of his business and that we should go back to the cloister where we would better serve our souls and community. He said there was no evidence of any crime and that they were all suppositions based on rumors and speculations made by superstitious and bad-faith people who wanted to undermine his authority and disrupt order. He warned him that he should stop from inciting the Indians by giving credence to their unfounded assumptions. He said he knew exactly what his duty was and that if we didn't give up our intention to usurp his duties and leave immediately, they would arrest us all.

Brother Antonio reminded him that, since we enjoyed ecclesiastical immunity, he could not arrest us, but my godfather ignored him and asked me what I was doing there. He told me that even though he had baptized me as a child, he didn't have any kinship or obligations with me, and warned me to be more careful "from now on." He asked me to go back to the convent and advised me not to allow myself to be influenced or listen to "these halfwits," and added that all the Indians and Church officials were liars and fabricators.

I wanted to get out of there, but a strange force beyond my will kept me from leaving or saying anything. The scene seemed to take place in slow motion, as it happens in certain dreams when we find ourselves in a dangerous situation but can't do anything to protect or defend ourselves. On the one hand, I looked at the faces of Don Juan de Mendoza, Matías López, and their henchmen contorted by disgust and contempt. They were holding their arquebuses and pointing them at us with their index fingers placed on the trigger. On the other hand, I saw the undaunted faces of Don Roque Gualtoye, Don Pablo Tzitza, Don Mateo Vicente, and Brother Antonio. As much as I told myself, "Get the hell out of here, Diego. Don't be a dimwit," I was paralyzed and waited for us to be detained.

21

MATÍAS LÓPEZ AND HIS DEPUTIES TOOK US ALL TO THE DUNGEON of Senecú, which was located at the back of the Casa Real, next to the convent's courtyard. The cloister where the choir boys, the prefect, the organist, and the sacristans slept was on the other side of the wall, about fifty meters away. The dungeon was a dark, cold, stone-walled room. It had a small window with iron bars through which bursts of cold air and the rays of the afternoon sun infiltrated. It was identical to the rooms where the grain, beans, chili peppers, and other provisions were stored in the convent. The ceiling was made of wood, the dirt floor was covered with sharp pebbles, and there was nothing to sit or lie down on. Here they locked up violators of the law and Christian beliefs until they were transported to the Santa Fe dungeon where they were tried and sentenced.

In New Mexico there were no prisons. If someone was accused of committing a crime and was found guilty, they were given a lashing as punishment and then were released with the warning that, if they committed another crime, they would be given a much harsher punishment. This often consisted of sending convicted criminals to perform forced labor in a Nueva Vizcaya mine, ranch, workshop, or house for a period of ten years, depriving them entirely of their freedom and, de facto, enslaving them.

We all accepted with resignation our detention and confinement. This was partly because we knew it would be fruitless and counterproductive to resist, and partly because we did not want the conflict to escalate. When they locked us in the dungeon, none of us said anything. We just sat on the floor and waited for them to release us. We knew that the lieutenant governor was committing a grave injustice and was taking a huge risk by imprisoning the mission guardian and the three top political leaders of the Piro people. We couldn't be there for long. As soon as the villagers realized we were locked up there, they would rise up to rescue us.

Not even an hour had passed when we heard some voices and noises in the yard. We recognized the voice of the mayor and two of the men who imprisoned us. At first we thought they had come back to let us go, but soon we realized that they had detained someone and were tying him up to lash him.

We couldn't see out the window who it was, but we knew exactly what was happening. This kind of punishment was called the Law of Bayona. All of us who lived in the convent were used to hearing the crack of the whip and the wails of the detainees being punished in this compound.

The lashes and insults quickly began to fly. The torturer savagely flogged the detainee, and the mayor yelled at him insults like "bastard dog," "Indian shit," "whoreson," "good-for-nothing," "scumbag," and "swine." Occasionally, he would ask, "You thought we wouldn't get your gibes and innuendo, eh?" or "You think you are a phoenix of ingenuity, ha?" or exclaimed phrases like, "Your little theater has fallen down on you" and "Take this so you learn to respect your superiors!"

The victim was Santiago Mutanama. His theological drama had infuriated the political leaders of the region, who interpreted the play as a personal affront and attack on the political and economic system they represented. They suspected that the Franciscans wanted to get rid of the civil government and the encomienda system so they could establish in New Mexico a theocracy where they would be in charge not only of the government but also of the means of production of this remote and marginal province of New Spain. Although "The Most Beautiful Flower in the Valley" was primarily an attack on Indigenous beliefs and on some of its religious gods and heroes, the political leaders interpreted it as a rebuke and a threat to their interests, position, and privileges. According to this interpretation, the figure of the Sorcerer personified not only Tsiké Fayé, the spiritual leader of the Piro rebels, but also the leader of the Spanish anticlerical apostates, former governor López Mendizábal, who had been imprisoned and prosecuted by the Inquisition for being an alleged Crypto-Jew and with whom the political leaders of the region had forged an alliance against the Franciscans. The Warrior Twins were identified as Don Juan de Mendoza and his compadre, New Mexico's richest and most influential encomendero, Maestre de Campo Francisco Gómez Robledo, who was also arrested and prosecuted for being an alleged Crypto-Jew. The figure of the Coyote supposedly represented and mocked Matías López whom, later I learned, they nicknamed the "coyote mayor," because in New Mexico they called the children of Indians mixed with Africans coyotes.

No wonder the mayor was being so mercilessly brutal with Mutanama. It was a chastisement for him, a warning to the Piro leaders, and a torment for Brother Antonio, who was blamed by both civilian and Church leaders not only for having allowed the staging of this subversive theological drama but also for fanning the flames of rebellion among the Piro, who wanted to regain their economic and political autonomy.

As the tormentor lashed Mutanama and the mayor abused him verbally, Brother Antonio shouted at them not to flog him anymore. He kept saying, "For God's sake, have mercy! Don't hurt him anymore! Leave him now, you've hit him enough!" But it seemed that the more he begged them to stop, the more viciously they tormented the hapless Mutanama.

After they got tired of whipping him, they poured hot turpentine oil on his back. Although Mutanama had endured the lashes with fortitude, the torment of the living flesh scalded with the burning oil was too much. He let out a few horrific shrieks of pain that gave me a chill and drew tears in my eyes just to imagine the extreme agony he was suffering. Then they took him away, and we didn't learn more about him or where he was buried.

"This is how Brother Salvador Guerra punished and killed Juan Cuna in Orayvi ten years ago," the dismayed Franciscan remarked.

"Tragically, an ungodly one is now applying the Law of Bayona to a faithful and loyal Christian just because he wrote a drama in honor of the Virgin of the Immaculate that annoyed him. When are these injustices going to stop?" Then he stood up, got close to the window again, and continued to yell at the torturers: "You're a bunch of savages! Heartless! Wicked! Scoundrels! Impious! You're worse than the beasts! God is going to punish you!"

"For God's sake, Father Antonio, please calm down." Don Mateo Vicente begged him to stop insulting them. "You're going to upset them even more and they are going to punish us all."

Brother Antonio heeded his plea. He squatted, crestfallen, and remained quiet and reflective in a corner for a few moments.

"They're the worst. Those wicked Castillas have no heart. They are capable of anything," Paul Tzitza exclaimed disconsolately. "They have taken away my granddaughter and are going to sell her to a ruffian out of revenge and to dishonor and injure us where it hurts the most. She didn't do anything bad; all she did was play the role of the Virgin Mary. I'm the one to blame for persuading my daughter to allow Lupita to participate in the play. I deserve the same punishment. We should have listened to the women. We're cowards. We should have risen up and killed these tyrants. We let these scoundrels humiliate us, mistreat us, and destroy what's most sacred to us. We allow them to whip us, rob us, kill us, dishonor us, and steal, rape, and murder our daughters and our granddaughters. My granddaughter is such a good little girl. Why her? What did she do to them? It would have been better if they killed me."

"You don't deserve that punishment, compadre," Don Roque intervened. He approached him and sat next to him. He put his right hand on Don Pablo's left shoulder and, looking Brother Antonio in the eyes, said aloud and fervently: "He who lives by the sword perishes by the sword. Mutanama often used the whip to punish those who secretly practiced our ancestral ceremonies. He followed the orders of Fathers Arteaga, García de San Francisco, and de la

Cruz and continued even after you, Father Antonio, ordered him to stop doing so." Brother Antonio seemed surprised to hear this revelation. "Yes, Father, even if you don't believe me. He also used the whip to intimidate those who didn't obey him. Do you know how he found out that my grandson was the one who carved the Kachinas? Ramón and Licho, his assistants, interrogated Martín's brothers and, because they couldn't get anything out of them, they took the youngest one, Jorge, who is also a carver, so that Mutanama could interrogate him. Mutanama flogged him and threatened to accuse him of being the one who had made the Kachinas if he didn't denounce his brother. Jorge had no choice but to say that it had been Martín, even though he knew nothing about it." Don Roque paused briefly to fix his poncho. "We also know that Mutanama was the one who told Father Guerra that Martín and others had promised San Lorenzo a dance this past August 10. Father Guerra and the other Franciscans who have been in charge of this mission are not like you, Father Antonio. They are like the mayor. They apply the laws and rules to their benefit and will. They whip us whenever they want. We have no choice but to fulfill their whims and quietly accept their humiliations."

"I am aware of it, Don Roque," said Brother Antonio. He got up and sat next to him. "They believe they are the absolute and natural lords of this land. All they do is demand. They infect and corrupt everything. They're drones. They eat the honey that the others make. They give them excessive work. They demand tribute and service. They treat you worse than beasts. But God's justice is relentless, and the day of the Last Judgment is approaching. You will then be freed from your sufferings. When that day comes, you will be able to pronounce these words written in the book of Isaiah 14: 4–8: 'How is the oppressor come to nothing, the tribute hath ceased? The Lord hath broken the staff of the wicked, the rod of the rulers that struck the people in wrath with an incurable wound, that brought nations under in fury, that persecuted in a cruel manner.'"

"Father Antonio, what we want most is to cultivate our own fields and not be forced to work in the missions and the estates of the Spaniards," said Don Roque. "We want to go back to the life we had before. It was a better life. When we lived according to our customs and traditions, we harvested enough corn, beans, cotton, and squash and lived more happily. Now that we live under your laws and government, we harvest less and less and work more and more."

"Yes, but before you did not know or worship the true God; you worshipped the Devil," Brother Antonio replied. "You were going to condemn your souls for all eternity. When the day of Judgment comes and God punishes the serpent Leviathan and its idolaters with his sword, he will spread his spirit in this wilderness and turn it into a garden that will produce justice, peace, and welfare for all. Then the Lord will wipe away the tears in everyone's faces; he will restore the honor of his people, and of the entire world. And we will all say, 'This is our God, whom we expected to save us. This is Yahweh whom we trust. Now we are happy because He has saved us.'"

"I hope so, Father," Don Mateo Vicente intervened. "Without losing faith in God, we need to put our feet on the ground. Don Juan de Mendoza has locked us up here unfairly and we don't know what he intends to do with us. I do not agree that we have acted in a cowardly way, Don Pablo. We did what we could to check the contents of the wagon train, but we don't know for sure if the girls were on it or not, or if they were kidnapped, or if they joined Martín and the rebels. We must be cautious. Isn't that what we agreed upon during our meeting, Don Roque?"

"Yes, Don Mateo," the chieftain replied, "but the women accused us of cowardice and got all worked up."

"They were the ones who made the uproar and we're the ones paying for it because we did not stop them," Don Mateo continued. "We should not have allowed them to attend our meeting this afternoon. What do they know about weapons and avenging our lost honor against these tyrants? We put our head into the wolf's mouth because of the women. Now what we need to do is get out of here. We have to admit that we made a mistake, Don Roque. We blundered. I can talk to Don Matias, if you all agree."

"Alright, Don Mateo. I think you're right. We have no other choice. And you, compadre, do you agree?" Don Roque asked Don Pablo.

"As you wish, *Taikemtsaé*. The only lost fight is the abandoned one. Locked up here, we are useless and helpless."

"If that's what you all want, I have no objections," Brother Antonio said.

Although it was a smart move, I found it strange that Don Roque gave in so quickly and with such resignation to Don Mateo's conciliatory proposal. At the time there were still many things I did not understand. I was unaware of the many differences that existed between the chieftain and the governor and their distinct set of motivations. I also ignored how my godfather manipulated everything at his convenience and sowed discord between the Native inhabitants and the Franciscans. Thanks to this incident, which fortunately ended the way I hoped it would, I was able to better understand Brother Antonio. It taught me to trust him a little more and helped me gain a greater understanding of the complicated world in which I had been thrown.

Don Juan de Mendoza and Matías López came that same afternoon, escorted by several soldiers, to give us back our freedom. They just said we could leave and opened the door of the dungeon. The Piro leaders left immediately, but Brother Antonio tarried in the dungeon. He wanted to know what they'd done with Mutanama. My godfather stated that Mutanama had received the punishment he deserved. He said that Mutanama used to flog his people just because they danced and participated in their traditional ceremonies and warned us that anyone who allied himself and plotted with Father Salvador Guerra "would be shot and killed, even at the altar."

On our way back to the convent, Brother Antonio could not contain his anger and showed me a side of him that I had not seen before. He said a diatribe against our jailers as soon as we walked away:

"These men are the worst; they are evil and wicked. They treat with indifference and contempt the censorships of our Holy Mother the Church and are declared enemies of her sacraments and her ministers. Last year Matías López told one of his comadres, when he was making lascivious propositions to her, that fornication was neither a sin nor a transgression and that she would still go to heaven if she slept with him. Can you believe it? And Juan de Mendoza is even worse. He's an apostate, a blasphemer, a perfidious and evil being. As you may have noticed, he despises ecclesiastical immunity and rejects the legitimacy of the spiritual relationship that exists between the godparents and their godchildren and relatives. As a lieutenant of former governor López Mendizábal, whom the Inquisition condemned as a Jew, he wrongly accused many Franciscans of doing awful things and allowed the Natives to perform the Kachina dances where they committed satanic and depraved acts and in which the Devil himself participated."

Brother Antonio made a pause and looked at me as if I wanted to say something. Possibly he remembered that Juan de Mendoza was the brother of my late adoptive mother. Or perhaps he thought that I felt some affection or loyalty toward him. Then he added, using a more compassionate and conciliatory tone:

"Don't think I'm telling you all this because I hate your godfather, or out of wrath or spite. I say this because of the great pain it causes me to see the damnation of your godfather's soul."

"But of course, Brother." I broke my silence. I said in the most diplomatic way I could at the moment, "I know that you do not wish evil on anyone. If you say this, it is because you know them, and because the harm they do to others and to themselves afflicts you as well."

What mattered most to me was that I didn't have to spend the night in that filthy dungeon, tormented by the anguish of all that might have happened to me in the hands of those thugs. I promised myself never to be the prey of my own curiosity, or to meddle in other people's business again.

That incident shattered the hope I had previously entertained that it would be relatively easy for me to leave the convent when the time was right. My godfather's disdain and enmity toward all religious people and his comments made it abundantly clear that he felt no obligation toward me whatsoever, despite the family and spiritual ties that supposedly bound us together. I had fantasized about obtaining protection, shelter, and employment from him, and had clung to the hope that he was going to help me remake my life outside the convent and forever abandon the material and intellectual narrowness of religious life. But this brief and unfortunate encounter with him and his associates forced me to understand that life in the convent, at least under the protection and supervision of Brother Antonio, who, after all, claimed to be my father, was a better choice for me for the time being.

I felt relieved after we left the dungeon that afternoon. However, soon after returning to the convent, I began to worry again. I remembered that, in a few days, I was going to have to go to Apache country and begin my missionary work for which I was not at all prepared. What the hell was I going to do there?

22

IN THE DAYS LEADING UP TO MY DEPARTURE TO OJO CALIENTE, the search for the missing girls continued. A group of Christians from the village led by the mothers of Lupita and Chayito tried to meet with the mayor, but he evaded them. He did the same to Brother Antonio, who wanted to know Mutanama's whereabouts so that he could give him a Christian burial. The only ones with whom he met separately, accompanied by the lieutenant governor, were Don Mateo Vicente and Don Roque Gualtoye.

In his meeting with them, Don Mateo Vicente failed to quell his people's thirst for justice and their outrage over the girls' disappearance. What he did achieve, however, according to Brother Antonio, was to reestablish the business ties he had lost with the mayor, the lieutenant governor, and other encomenderos and merchants of the region about five years ago. They had broken all ties with him because he had signed and submitted to the Inquisition a false testimony penned by the vice custodio, Brother García de San Francisco, which claimed that former governor López Mendizábal had authorized the Native inhabitants of New Mexico to worship the Kachinas in their villages. To recover his lost business dealings with them, Don Mateo only had to give more credibility to a rumor that was circulating in the village. It claimed that some Apache had abducted Lupita and Chayito because the girls had seen the faces of the dancers who had personified some mountain spirits, which is a taboo severely punished by the Apache.

In his meeting with Don Roque Gualtoye, the lieutenant governor agreed to investigate the physical and labor abuses of several men and women from Senecú in recent years. He asked all the victims and witnesses of these abuses to present their depositions, and especially those who had complaints against Fathers Salvador Guerra, García de San Francisco, and Román de la Cruz. As a "gesture of goodwill," he also allowed them to practice their Indigenous dances.

Brother Antonio wrote a letter to the custodio in which he told him about the recent events. He denounced Don Juan de Mendoza for violating the immunity that religious men enjoy in the province and for "despising the censorships of Our Mother the Church." He accused him of blasphemy for questioning the legitimacy of spiritual relations between godparents and godchildren and of sacrilege for promoting "various idolatrous dances among the Natives." He also blamed him for being hostile to the clergy, for persecuting them, and for inviting the Piro people "to give sworn evidence" against several members of the clergy, including the vice custodio himself. He accused Matías López of "mercilessly giving a hundred and forty lashes" to the former Fiscal Mutanama and then disappearing him. He also charged him with committing "a great and grave sacrilege" by not allowing this "brave and faithful martyr of the Piro the Christian burial that his body requires for God to receive his soul in his glory." He noted that he could not call any witnesses because they were "terrified by Mutanama's murder and intimidated by the power that the lieutenant governor wields in the region." He signed the letter and made me sign it as a witness.

After drafting the letter and the necessary documents to initiate a legal process against my godfather and Matías López, Brother Antonio shared with me his frustration with the slowness with which all inquisitorial investigations were carried out in New Mexico. He told me that the trial against former governor López Mendizábal and other "dogmatists" related or associated with him had been prolonged for more than five years and that, "for various reasons," relations between the Holy Custodia of New Mexico and the Holy Office in Mexico City had deteriorated significantly. He told me that, for this reason, he doubted the inquisitors would call for the defendants to appear before the Holy Office's court. He added very seriously that "our struggle" in these lands was not only against "the rulers and corrupt authorities but, above all, against the dark and supernatural forces of evil that these apostates favor and magnify." Then he asked me to stand up and forced me to "solemnly" swear to him that I would always wear "the armor of God," "the belt of truth," "the armor of justice," "the sword of the spirit," "the shield of faith," "the helmet of salvation," and that my footsteps should at all times be fueled by "the zeal to spread the gospel of peace."

Taking advantage of the opportunity that he brought up the subject of the provisions that I needed to make my trip to Ojo Caliente, I expressed to him some of my concerns. I shared with him my worry that I did not know where I was going to sleep, or what I was going to eat, or how I was going to protect myself from the cold. Quite frankly and bluntly, I admitted that I didn't know how to fend for myself in the outdoors. Brother Antonio answered me sternly:

"And why are you so concerned? Where am I going to sleep? What am I going to eat? Didn't our Lord Jesus Christ criticize the apostles for these kinds of questions? And what was his answer? He said: 'Birds do not sow or harvest or store food in barns, and yet God feeds them.' Dear Brother Diego, are you not more valuable to the Lord than any bird? Just as Christ said to the apostles, I say to you: 'Don't worry about your bodily needs.' Those who live in the material world care about it. You must understand your Father knows what you need. He works for his kingdom, and he will give you all these things in addition to many others. Only one thing is necessary in life: the Word of God. Devote yourself to prayer and the ministry of the Word. Look for the things above, not for the things on Earth. Pray incessantly and always thank God for everything."

This answer bothered me. It made me want to ask him, Are you crazy? Do you want me to starve to death? All that praying does to me is open my appetite more. But I contained myself. I didn't mean to offend or disrespect him. Without giving it much thought, I offered an answer that I thought was more pertinent and reasonable.

"Brother, what Jesus says in the Gospel cannot be taken literally. He says it only figuratively."

I hadn't finished saying this when Brother Antonio blew up. He told me how I dared to make this "offensive proposition," that "with what authority I touched upon the affairs of Sacred Theology," that if I ignored all disciplines and had never studied "the Queen of the Sciences," I should not address these "sacred matters" whose body of knowledge was beyond the grasp of "ignorant" and "unworthy" people like me.

He gave a tirade in defense of the literal interpretation of the Gospel. He told me that I spoke like those fools who claim to be wise but who, with their false interpretations, "alter the glory of immortal God that is embodied in the Sacred Scriptures."

"You sound like certain people I know who, although they live far from the mysteries of our Lord Jesus Christ, offer others their sordid and bitter wine, assuring them that it is the pure and authentic truth that God Our Lord manifested to us in the Holy Scriptures. These Pharisees and false teachers of the law interpret the Word of God according to the laws of the flesh. Christ gave the Gospel its definitive form to God's law and clearly warned that only those who lead a more perfect life, unlike the ancient masters of the Law and the Pharisees, will enter the Kingdom of Heaven. You must be clear about this, Brother Diego. Not only must we believe in Christ: we must suffer like him to enter his kingdom. Those who care only about earthly matters and do not want to carry their cross are enemies of Christ. He who does not seek the cross of Christ does not seek the glory of Christ. Christ is the way, the truth, and the life, and the door through which the one who wants to be saved must enter."

After lecturing me and ordering me to fast and pray incessantly the rest of the day, he assured me that he would make sure that I would not lack anything during my journey. He told me that he would bring sufficient dried meats and fruits, pinole, and atole for three months and that, in addition to the horses and mules we would take with us on the trip, he would send another twenty with provisions at the beginning of the spring so that all members of "our band" could benefit from them in the way that best suited "us."

23

THE DISAPPEARANCE OF LUPITA, CHAYITO, AND MUTANAMA LEFT a void in the hearts of the Christians of Senecú. They tried to mitigate it with Masses and rosaries but gradually filled it instead with the anger and hatred they had already accumulated against the civil authorities. Adding insult to injury, Governor Villanueva authorized some villagers from Río Abajo, including Senecú, Socorro, and Ysleta, to resume their traditional dances. Apparently, this new development was masterminded by my godfather who, by exacerbating the conflicts between Christian and pagan Piro, believed the civil authorities would benefit and the Franciscans would be harmed by it.

What they may not have considered in this calculation was that the group of Piro rebels led by Tambulista had been coordinating a general Indigenous uprising in the region. This permission to practice their traditional dances gave greater impetus to the anti-Christian and anti-Spanish rebel movement in the following months. Because some Christian Piro alerted the mayor of Socorro of this conspiracy, my godfather and his soldiers were able to quell it. But it was at a high cost. The mayor of Socorro, five Spanish soldiers, and six Christian Piro lost their lives in the impromptu ambush they carried out in the Magdalena Mountains. My godfather then organized a punitive expedition against the Apache. However, before this happened, he either discovered or invented that Don Roque Gualtoye, Don Pablo Tzitza, and other Senecú Piro had been collaborating with them since the beginning.

Governor Villanueva and my godfather crushed the Piro rebellion with singular cruelty. They summoned all the inhabitants of the village to the main plaza and, after flogging the six alleged conspirators, including Don Roque Gualtoye, Don Pablo Tzitza, Tsiké Fayé, and Tambulista, they hung and burned them for being "traitors and sorcerers." The other rebels were taken in shackles and eventually transported to San José del Parral, where they were sold as slaves in the silver mines. This was the beginning of the end of the village of Senecú in New Mexico.

When I went to Apache country, I didn't suspect this was going to happen. Brother Antonio's apocalyptic prophecies seemed to me to be the absurd predictions of a fanatical, outdated, naive millenarist. The Kingdom of God was never established in New Mexico; neither the Piro nor anyone I knew were liberated by Yahweh and his army. But in 1680 a real catastrophe comparable to an apocalypse would wipe out New Mexico's "Spanish-style" life in the late seventeenth century.

24

THE EVE OF MY DEPARTURE TO OJO CALIENTE ARRIVED. IT HAD been sunny and relatively temperate. Although I was nervous about my impending journey, physically I felt healthy, except for a light headache that started to bother me that day. Concha the cook assured me this was due to the noticeable increase in the "bad air" circulating in the area.

After doing my midday work, I went to my cell to pray the sext and pack my luggage. When I was almost done, Brother Antonio came by to inform me that Refugio, who was going to be my guide and host, had been to the convent in the morning and brought me a gift: a pair of moccasin boots. They were brown and had adjustable leather laces. I loved them. To my surprise, Brother Antonio said that I should wear them both for the trip and throughout my visit.

"Moccasins are the traditional shoes of the Apache people. As you will surely remember, Jesus asked the apostles to wear ordinary shoes when preaching in foreign lands. Plus, they are more comfortable and appropriate than the pair of *cordobán* shoes you are intending to wear," he added with sarcasm.

He inspected the other belongings I had arranged neatly in the chest and exclaimed:

"Blessed God, you have so much stuff. Hat, shoes, sandals, bronze wash basin, lamp, knife, scissors, hand mirror, razor, the catechism of Friar Alonso Molina, *The Dark Night of the Soul*, *The Consolation of Philosophy*, two, four, six candles, two notebooks, three pens, three ink bottles, two towels, five bars of soap, two tunics, three braies, three pairs of socks, a scarf, two wool blankets. Where do you think you are going? To sojourn in the court of the Marquis of Mancera? For God's sake, Brother Diego."

I lowered my head and remained silent. I thought he was going to congratulate me on my frugality and packing skills.

"Jesus told the apostles not to carry anything for the trip other than staff, shoes, and blanket, and you want to take this heavy wooden chest full of luxuries? Do you think it is a small thing to carry the load of corn, dried meat, salt, and nuts on the horse and the two mules that you are going to bring as a gift to your hosts?"

He reminded me that the purpose of my visit to Ojo Caliente was to preach and convert the Apache. After scolding me for caring more about myself than about the evangelization of the Gila people, he lectured me about the importance of winning the trust and hearts of my hosts with good deeds and by respecting their customs, provided they were not "against God's commandments and our Christian beliefs."

"The best way to show them respect," he told me, "is to learn their language and adopt their ways."

Although Refugio had agreed to be my interpreter and teach me the rudiments of the Gila Apache language and customs, Brother Antonio took the opportunity to explain some basic social norms and made numerous recommendations on how not to offend them. He noted that it was very disrespectful to say the name of the people present and, much more, of the deceased. He told me that if I needed to address anyone, I should point at the person with my finger or lips, or use an epithet, descriptions, and sometimes a nickname. Only under very special circumstances did they address people by their name; for example, when they needed to ask a favor to a relative or friend, or when they wanted to confront a transgressor or an enemy. He also explained that I should be very restrained when speaking and looking because Apache disliked and distrusted indiscreet and prying people. A son-in-law, he pointed out, could not approach, see, or talk to his mother-in-law, even if she called him or asked him for something, because doing so would be an affront to her and her entire family. He explained that Apache did not abide in villages or houses but in camps and wickiups in the summer, and in buffalo-hide teepees in the winter. He said that they were constantly moving from mountain to mountain looking for animals to hunt. He warned me that a visitor should always announce his arrival by coughing or clearing his throat; when entering a dwelling he should sit near the entrance and not touch anyone, and, before leaving, he must notify the host. He also mentioned that, when a guest was visiting, he must express his agreement and interest in the conversation by nodding and saying "do'a" or "ji, ji" periodically. He warned me that, at the table, Apache served themselves with their hands directly from the pot, and with a wooden spoon if the food was liquidy. He said that, although one should not make noise when eating, it was acceptable to smack one's lips to indicate that the food was tasty. He also pointed out that some males liked to rub their arms, legs, and hair with animal fat because they believed it strengthened them and made them better runners. Finally, he advised me that, if my hosts did not welcome my redeeming message, I should shake the dust off my feet in protest as I left their home.

"If you follow my recommendations and obey the ten commandments, you will have no problems. You will earn their trust and goodwill. But be especially careful not to break the tenth commandment because Apache men are very jealous: If a wife betrays her husband, he mutilates her nose and kills the person with whom she slept. And now it is time for me to go to bed. I do not know why I have a pounding headache and an ache on my left side. It must be the pangs of old age."

"That's odd. I also feel a strange pressure on my forehead and temples, as if I am getting a cold."

"Let us hope not. According to Refugio, a blizzard is coming. But with this benign climate we have had these past few days, I am not so sure about it. At least not this weekend. You must know that Refugio, being a medicine man, is very superstitious. He claims he knows how to interpret the language of birds and the temperament of the wind. He told me it would be better for you and him to leave this afternoon, but I asked him to wait until tomorrow because I'm going to dedicate Sunday Mass to your mission."

He said good-bye and left me worried about the weather and wondering what to do with my luggage. I decided to borrow a large leather bag I saw hanging in the storage room. I went to get it and filled it with all the things I considered indispensable. I was able to fit in almost everything, except for the basin, the lamp, the shoes, the hat, and the two wool blankets. These last three things I decided to take with me separately. The other stuff I left in the chest along with other items for personal use.

25

THAT NIGHT THE WIND BEGAN TO ROAR AND MY HEADACHE intensified. I tormented myself by letting my imagination fly, thinking of all the bad things that could happen to me during my trip and my stay in Apache country. I thought about how difficult it would be for me to leave my life in the convent. Despite its oppressive restrictions and rules, I felt protected there and safe from the outside world, which I found intolerable and hostile. Apache country, especially, evoked in me everything that was opposite to the orderly, routine, and relatively predictable and safe life at the convent. I ruminated obsessively on the idea that the bad weather and my sudden illness would make my departure impossible. I resisted the urge to get up and awaken Brother Antonio to let him know that I was getting sick and to tell him that Refugio was right, that these were not mere superstitions, that the sudden change in temperature and the clash of a northern cold front with a warm southern front were unequivocal signs that a powerful storm was imminent, that this phenomenon had been well studied by modern climatologists. Too bad I couldn't tell him this. I had to keep to myself so many things.

I hoped again that I would soon wake up from this nightmare. I reasoned that none of what was happening was real, that it could not be, because it made no sense, that it was only a long dream from which I had to wake up sooner or later. And, if everything was a dream, nothing bad could happen to me. It was all a product of my imagination.

I fell asleep inadvertently. At about midnight someone knocked on my cell door. I got up and opened it. It was Pedro, the gatekeeper. He looked alarmed. He told me that Father Antonio was calling me; that he had suddenly gotten sick and was "going mad" in his room; that he kept saying "strange things" and was singing "hymns." I got up immediately, worried about Brother Antonio, but happy inside thinking that his illness implied the postponement of my trip. I felt vertigo when I got up. I saw my arms and hands expand and contract as if I were in front of a distorting mirror. I felt like I was in the cabin of a brig sunk at the bottom of the sea.

I walked down the corridor as if I were submerged in an aqueous environment. Everything was ebbing and flowing. When I entered Brother Antonio's cell, Concha and his son Pascual, the groom, were taking care of him. Brother Antonio lay on his wooden platform. A red mantle partially covered his body. He looked like a biblical character painted by El Greco. He had a cloth on his forehead and his elongated face was illuminated by the flickering flame of a candle that seemed like it was going to get extinguished at any moment. He was intoning some biblical verses in Latin.

I stood in front of him, waiting for him to acknowledge my presence. I didn't want to interrupt him or startle him. He was singing ecstatically and levitated slightly. When he finished chanting, his body descended gently on the platform. After pausing briefly, he continued his plaint, this time in Spanish. He was reciting chapter seven of the Book of Job:

"The life of man upon Earth is a warfare, and his days are like the days of a hireling. As a servant longeth for the shade, as the hireling looketh for the end of his work. So I also have had empty months, and have numbered to myself wearisome nights. If I lie down to sleep, I shall say: When shall I arise? And again I shall look for the evening and shall be filled with sorrows even till darkness."

Suddenly, it seemed to me that Brother Antonio began to change consistency. He melted, sublimed away, and then liquefied and solidified again, as if he were made of wax. At times I could see his muscles, veins, bones, and organs. But he continued his plaint as if nothing was happening to him.

"My flesh is clothed with rottenness and the filth of dust, my skin is withered and drawn together. My days have passed more swiftly than the web is cut by the weaver and are consumed without any hope. Remember that my life is but wind, and my eye shall not return to see good things. Nor shall the sight of man behold me: thy eyes are upon me, and I shall be no more. As a cloud is consumed and passeth away: so he that shall go down to hell shall not come up. Nor shall he return any more into his house, neither shall his place know him anymore. Wherefore I will not spare my mouth, I will talk with the bitterness of my soul."

Mysteriously, his eyes began to shine as if they were luminous organs. His face also expanded, contracted, extended itself again, and shrunk like the umbrella of a jellyfish. His hair and beard waved like the tentacles of sea anemones.

"Am I a sea, or a sea monster, that thou hast enclosed me in a prison? If I say, my bed shall comfort me, and I shall be relieved speaking with myself on my couch: Thou wilt frighten me with dreams and terrify me with visions. So that my soul rather chooseth hanging, and my bones death. I have done with hope, I shall now live no longer: spare me, for my days are nothing. What is a man that thou shouldest magnify him? Or why dost thou set thy heart upon him? . . . How long wilt thou not spare me, nor suffer me to swallow down my spittle? I have sinned, what shall I do to thee, O keeper of men? Why hast thou set me opposite to thee, and I am become burdensome to myself? Why dost thou not remove my sin, and why dost thou not take away my iniquity? Behold now I shall sleep in the dust, and if thou seek me in the morning, I shall not be."

Concha came up to me and told me:

"*Pobrecito!* He's got a high fever and he's complaining of aches on his head and left side. He has foamy diarrhea. I think he has bad air."

"What is that?

"It's a disease. People get it in heavy places where there is much evil. They say you get it when you go through a crossroads or pass by a place where someone has been killed."

"Really?" I replied in a tone of condescending incredulity, waiting for Brother Antonio to finish his plaint. I wanted to ask him if he needed anything.

"In such places the Ciuapitlis wander around," Concha continued her explanation. "These are the souls of women who die when giving birth for the first time. They say they're the ones who produce the bad air and that it gets into the body of those who pass through these ill-omened places. Be careful, young Brother Diego. You've been with him. Maybe you also got this illness. They say that tobacco smoke cuts it off. You should take some tobacco with you, just in case. I'm also going to give you some twigs of St. John's weed to protect you from evil spirits and wild animals."

Suddenly, Brother Antonio came out of his dream state.

"What am I doing here?" he said, bewildered. "Where is the choir of angels? Where is my flock, my mountain, my river, my land? My son!" he exclaimed when he saw me by his side. "What are you doing here?" He looked at me strangely and surprised, as if he hadn't seen me in a long time. "He's my son, the prodigal one," he told Concha, pointing at me. "He was dead and he has come back to life. He was lost and I found him."

"Brother Antonio, I'm going to call my comadre," Concha told him, leaning over his ear so that he could listen to her better. "She will be able to cure you. You're burning with fever."

"And what do you want to call her for, woman?" he replied angrily. "So that she gives me a cleansing? What I really need is to return to my homeland. That is all. I want to talk to my son alone. Everybody, please get out. Get out, right away!"

Concha and Pascual left the room immediately. As soon as they left, more stunning things started to happen. Brother Antonio had lost a lot of hair and the tufts he had left looked like withered, faded seaweed. The skin of his face was cracked like drought land, and he became bony and wrinkled like a mummy. He sat up with difficulty on the edge of the bed. He was wearing a white robe with a fleur-de-lis red cross on his chest. He stared at me and said in a metallic, sententious voice:

"Listen carefully to what I'm going to tell you, Uriel." He addressed me using my real name for the first and only time. He uttered it clearly and emphatically: "Urieeel. For a long time, your spirit has been wandering through the world of shadows. You have sailed the sea of life in the dark and without sextant. Up to now, you have been content with living a nocturnal life. But you must understand that you are not the son of night or darkness. You are the son of day and light. The eyes of the spirit are not like those of the body. You must not fear the light of truth; it is not a blinding light; it is life giving and liberating. You need to look up at the light, like a sunflower. You must awaken. God is the supreme good. He is light itself. Follow His light and you will awaken from the dream of life."

As he was speaking, his figure was gradually blurring, as if it were a luminous body that was losing intensity. However, his voice remained emphatic.

"Esteem heavenly things; despise the material world. Everything here is an illusion, a dream. God does not rule in this world. Satan does. You have come into this world to discover and follow the path of salvation of your soul. Do not waste the little time you have looking for and following paths that will lead you to your doom. You must only love God; you must love God with all your heart, mind, and spirit; everything else you must shun. Only love brings us closer and unites us with God. Virtue is the way that leads to God; it is the perfect love for God. And Jesus Christ is the virtue and wisdom of God. No one reaches God, except through His son. It is Jesus Christ and his Spirit who bring us inseparably into God. Let nothing separate you from Him: neither affliction, nor fear, nor persecution, nor hunger, nor cold, nor danger. For His love you must suffer every day; for His love you are like the sheep destined for slaughter."

His figure continued to become pale and opaque, but his words acquired greater intensity and vehemence.

"In the name of the Most Holy Trinity, and for its greatest glory, honor, and reverence, go to Ojo Caliente and preach to the Gila people the Holy Gospel of our Lord Jesus Christ; preach them the evangelical word so they admit it in their catechism and so they allow us to build a convent and a church. Take away from the Infernal Enemy his tyrannical possession of their souls; snatch away from the Devil his dominion of those brave and gentle souls that he subjugates without opposition. Depart at once. Hurry. Do not worry about the presents you were going to take with you. Captain Chilmo and other members of his band will pick them up later. Blessed is the one who made his servant travel at night."

When he finished speaking, his dim, ethereal silhouette collapsed and extinguished itself like a flame without fuel. I was stunned and speechless when I contemplated his hallucinating transformation and dissipation. Although I felt as if I was submerged in an aqueous medium and everything I saw was deformed as if I were in a house of mirrors, physically I didn't feel bad. I figured it was a dream and let myself go with the flow.

I went to my cell to pick up my bag and leave. I reflected that now that Brother Antonio was gone, perhaps I should go to Santa Fe and seek refuge and help from María Bandama, my supposed birth mother. But I remembered Father Guerra's threat that the Holy Office would be watching me and that I needed to comply with my apostolate. Fearing that disobedience could lead me to jail or the stake, I decided to comply despite the adverse weather conditions and my strange state of mind.

At that moment I realized that I didn't know where Refugio was and that I had no clue where to find him. I put on my moccasin boots and hat, wrapped myself in a blanket, grabbed my bag, and left my cell looking for someone who could tell me where I could find him. In the ambulatory I ran into Pedro, who seemed surprised and worried when he saw me. I asked him about Refugio. He told me that he was probably in La Chupadera, Don Bartolomé

Romero's ranch, where he sojourned when the weather was bad. He reminded me that Apache were not allowed to stay overnight in the pueblos nor even to visit them at night. The ranch was located at the intersection of the Senecú Road and the Camino Real, and it was easy to get there. He asked me if I felt well, and I said yes. Actually, I was horrified to see that his head was covered in worms but decided not to say anything because I wanted to leave immediately. Brother Antonio had told me the trip to Ojo Caliente would take me a full day on horseback and I didn't want the blizzard to catch me by surprise along the way.

I went to the corral looking for the animals I was going to take with me. Pascual was just about finished loading them. They were a dapple-gray mare called La Mora and two brown mules. Lucius, a horse mule, seemed as anxious to leave as I was. His assertiveness let me know that he was the leader of the team. Pascual told me that he was the smartest and most perceptive hinny he had ever known, and the most stubborn too. Lucius neighed with joy when he heard him say that. Then he scraped the ground with his hoof as if telling me it was time to go. He was a hardened mule and full of zest. His body emanated a faint opal glow and a resinous fragrance that contrasted with the oily shine and acrid odor of the other two animals. Lucius and La Mora were saddled and La Castaña was carrying most of the supplies.

Pascual tied my bag to Lucius's saddle and helped me mount. He untied the animals and, taking the reins, led us out. He commented that although it was dark, I would have no problem getting to La Chupadera because Lucius made this trip with my brother Pepe every day and knew how to get there without any guidance.

Concha caught up with us when we were about to leave. She gave me a bag of food and a water canteen and told me she had added a pouch with tobacco, St. John's and jimson weed, and white deer grass with which I should make a medicinal tea. To get rid of the "bad air," she recommended that I drink this tea and pray the Blessed One three times a day, three days in a row. As we were departing, she stood in front of me and, closing her eyes, bowing her head, and joining her hands in front of her chest, she recited the following supplication:

> If you suffer from bad air,
> May St. Claire expel the air,
> If it entered through your nose, St. Ambrose,
> Through an ear, St. Casimir,
> Through your chin, St. Catherine,
> Through your view, St. Bartholomew,
> Through your memory, St. Gregory,
> And if caused by a mistral,
> God, be merciful.

Then she signed us with the cross. I wondered at the idea of a disease that could be transmitted by the northwesterly wind. I thanked both Concha and Pascual for their help and good wishes and said good-bye. It was pitch dark as it was still the middle of the night, and it was cloudy with a new moon. Although the conditions were inauspicious, I decided to set off since the wind was not yet cold.

26

I HAD BARELY LEFT THE VILLAGE WHEN I STARTED TO HEAR SOME strange noises. At first I thought it was the whistling of the wind, but I noticed that Lucius raised his ears and uttered a neigh to alert me. The noises turned out to be the weak and intermittent sobs of a woman. She was crying as if her strength to continue living was collapsing. Every now and then she would repeat, "*El am'euisuné! El am'euisuné!* My little girl, what happened to you? Where are you?"

Because of the darkness I could not locate her precisely. However, Lucius, following his compassionate instinct and fine senses, began to walk toward her. We got off the road and entered a rugged, pebbly terrain teeming with *lechuguillas*. When the woman realized we were heading her way, she exclaimed with feeble fury: "Go away! Leave! I want to be alone! Let me cry in peace! Stay away!" Then she let out a pitiful howl.

I recognized the voice of María Tzitza, Lupita's mother. Lucius stopped, but I told him to keep moving. He obeyed me and we approached her slowly and carefully. María was sitting on a sandbank surrounded by spiky bushes that pinched us as we passed through them. By then my eyes had adjusted to the darkness of that moonless and starless night. When we got to the sandbank, I dismounted and approached María, who was hugging her legs. She neither spoke nor moved; she kept sobbing and was shaking. She was wearing the same black dress she wore the day she went out to protest over the kidnapping and disappearance of Lupita and Chayito. But now her dress was in rags and showed parts of her back and arms. I took off the blanket I was wearing, covered her with it, and squatted in front of her. Her face was filthy and covered in tears and snot. Her hair was a mesh of tangled wool. Although she was not old, sadness had aged her so much that she looked like a specter.

"Can I help you in any way?"

She looked at me as if she had never seen me before and said:

"My womb was barren. Day after day, night and day, for twenty-one years, my husband and I prayed to God to bless us with an am'euié. Fifteen years ago, God Our Lord granted us our wish. He gave us an am'euisuné whom we raised with love and care. She was a virtuous Christian girl. She didn't wrong anyone. She was our pride and joy, the apple of our eyes. People said she was the most beautiful flower of the Piro. She was about to turn fourteen and dreamed of marrying a good Christian and starting a family as God commands. A few days ago she went out with a friend early in the morning, but they never came back. The two disappeared as if they were swallowed by the earth, leaving no trace. Some of Satan's children stole them. My husband, my whole family, and my clan members have tried to comfort me, but I can't take it anymore. I need to see my daughter. I need her back! I've been looking for her day and night. I'm not going to return home until I find her. I'll stop drinking water and eating. I'll die of cold looking for her."

When she finished her account, she burst into sobs again. I didn't know what to say. I knew I couldn't do anything to help her, so I just put my hand on her shoulder, but she shoved it away. She told me to leave and said she wanted to be and die alone. The wind began to howl like a chorus of wailers and suddenly a thunderous voice, coming from who knew where, exclaimed:

"This woman is the mother of this land. The children of the *Naayéé* are desecrating her shrines, destroying her temples and relics, forbidding her rituals and celebrations, silencing her songs and prayers, taking away her lands, stealing the fruit of the labor of her children, enslaving them, abusing them, burning her nation's sages at the stake, raping her daughters, flogging and murdering her sons, corrupting her nation's leaders and warriors. Go to the mountain where there are no foundations or buildings because not one stone will be left upon another. Mother Earth is furious and will wipe out this entire kingdom invaded by the heirs of the Naayéé. And you, María, you will no longer suffer in this valley of tears. I will take you with me where you will enjoy eternal life in the Milky Way next to the righteous and the pious."

Then a pillar of light shone down and lifted her luminous body to the sky. My blanket lay spread on the sandbank. I stood speechless and paralyzed by terror, but the animals remained still and calm as if nothing was happening. At that point I heard someone with a hoarse and twangy voice say to me:

"What's the matter with you? What are you doing standing there? Didn't you hear we should take refuge on the mountain? Pick up your blanket and the amulet that the woman left you under it. We'll need it to get back to our homeland."

I couldn't believe my eyes and ears. The one talking to me was Lucius. Bewildered, though aware that he was right, for now the wind was beginning to blow furiously, I lifted my blanket and saw that, indeed, beneath it was a dream catcher. The hoop was made of intertwined willow twigs, and the net was woven with ultrafine hemp thread in the shape of a spiderweb. A pair of cotton thread braids were tied around the bottom of the hoop; each braid had an eagle feather entwined at the tip. When I took it, a passage I knew, God knew from where, came to mind. I repeated it aloud:

"Is my mind deceived and my soul dreaming? Speak, my Lord, but do not forsake me. I don't want to die before my time. For I have seen what I did not know, and I have heard what I do not understand."

"Don't be scared," Lucius replied. "You have heard what the Most High will do to those who dwell on Earth in the last days. Now let's go. Refugio is waiting for us."

27

I HAD A MEMORY LAPSE OF WHAT HAPPENED AFTERWARD. IT WAS possible that I lost consciousness, or maybe I fell asleep without realizing it; I didn't know. All I knew was that suddenly I found myself in the midst of a powerful blizzard in a snow-covered wooded area, facing a headwind and walking without a sense of direction. A hurricane-force wind made me stagger, and sleet particles stung me in the face. I was in a semi-unconscious state and was walking aimlessly, knowing that if I stopped to rest, I'd freeze to death. I was exhausted, dazed, disoriented, and terrified. At some point I began to pray. I asked God to save me or awake me from this unbearable nightmare. That's when I started to get back to my senses. I realized I needed to find a lair. I tried in vain to recognize the terrain. A snow whirlwind whipped me and blinded me. I wondered, Why am I walking? What happened to Lucius and the other animals? Where's Refugio? Is he traveling with me? Did he steal the goods and abandon me? Am I badly hurt? No, I wasn't, I checked. I thought Refugio might be near me. I screamed with all my might, but the hissing wind smothered my faint voice. I ran desperately all around me, trying to find a nook where I could protect myself from the blizzard and the cold, but I could hardly see anything. Afraid I'd fall off some cliff, I sank into the deepest despair. I fell on my knees and started to sob. When I couldn't take it anymore, I fell flat on my face and waited, defeated, for death.

Moments later, someone was pushing me, as if trying to wake me up. I opened my eyes and turned to see who it was. It was Refugio. I recognized the medicine wheel necklace that he was wearing when I first met him. I sat up, dumbfounded. The wind had calmed down suddenly and mysteriously.

I wiped the snow off my eyes and face. I noticed that I was wearing a suede fringe jacket and leather pants with fringes like Refugio's, and the moccasins he had given me.

"*Jat'enaá ansí?*" he asked me.

I stared at him, not knowing what to answer.

He pointed toward a bearded phantom with long gray hair that was standing in front of a cave and said in a defiant tone: "Are you gonna let yourself die just like that, without fightin' the Enemy Ghost? Look, there!"

The phantom wore a majestic black cape embroidered with hermetic symbols. He was looking up at the sky and invoking the elements with his arms raised, his hands opened, and his fingers curled. On a rock between the Sorcerer and me perched a spotted owl who was looking at me impassively with its big, black, marble eyes.

"And what can I do?" I answered in a despondent and desperate tone.

"Tell him he's just a ghost, that he can't vanquish you."

Fear and confusion paralyzed me momentarily.

"Come on. Tell him you're protected," he insisted. "Show him the amulet." He put in my hand the dream catcher that María left under my blanket when she departed.

"Don't be afraid. Look him in the eye and show him the amulet. Repeat four times: 'You're just a ghost. Leave me alone!'"

I summoned all my courage and, brandishing the dream catcher in a menacing way, repeated four times in a faint voice: "You're just a ghost. Leave me alone!"

Refugio had a tobacco-lit pipe in his right hand. He stood up, gave it a puff, and blew the smoke in the direction where the owl was. The falling snowflakes, mixed with the smoke, blurred the owl's fright-inducing image.

Refugio turned and faced the east. Then he said: "Holy Wind, don't let anyone come to hurt him." Pointing at the owl, he yelled: "You did this. Don't do it again!"[3]

The spotted owl looked at him impassively.

Refugio gave another puff to the pipe. He turned southward and blew smoke in that direction. Then he pointed at the owl and yelled again:

"*Búh*, don't harm this *Nakaiyé* again. Stay away from him!"

The spotted owl ignored him, and the Sorcerer continued his invocation. Then Refugio faced westward and, after inhaling and exhaling smoke from his pipe several times, he said:

"This Nakaiyé is sick. It's your fault. Stay away from him!"

Then he looked up at the sky and exclaimed, "Protect him from his enemies. Cure him!"

Refugio turned and faced in a northward direction. Then he said, "Give him health and a long life."

He turned eastward and, raising his arms high, repeated four times: "East, listen to me!" He did the same when he turned and faced in the direction of the other cardinal points. Each time, he shouted four times: "South, listen to me!" "West, listen to me!" "North, listen to me!" When he finished, he chanted a song to the Great Spirit of the mountain. Then he declared:

"Send away his illness to the east. Blow the bad air to the west."

By the time he finished his exhortations, the owl and the Sorcerer were already gone. It had stopped snowing and there was absolute silence and quietude in the forest.

I got up with difficulty because my legs were stiff, and a massive snow blanket covered the ground. Refugio approached me and said:

"*Łanohwile*, the Enemy has power."

"Who?" I asked him, still without understanding what had happened to me.

"The Enemy Ghost," he told me, making a face of distress.

He wiped the remaining snow off my face, gave the pipe one last puff, and blew the smoke at me. Then he put out the pipe by dipping it into the snow. He took a pinch of ash from the bowl of the pipe and marked a cross on my forehead with his index finger.

Refugio's face was covered in snow but, up until that point, he had done nothing to wipe it off.

"You need to rest," he told me in a stern tone. He picked up my blanket from the ground, dusted off the snow, and said: "We have to build a *chagoch'o*. Soon it will be dark. Follow me!"

I walked leaning on him. We entered a wooded area and, to my surprise, Lucius, Mora, and Pardo were there tied to some trees. The three animals had plainer and more worn-out saddles than the ones I remember them wearing when we left Senecú. They were eating white pine needles. Lucius stopped eating as soon as he saw me. He raised his head and ears and whinnied effusively several times.

"*Dant'éé?*" Refugio asked the mule, as if it were a person. Lucius answered with even louder neighs.

"*Ha'a shii nzhǫǫ?*" he asked, laughing.

"Lucius says he likes you. He's glad you're feeling better," Refugio told me, as if he was translating his neighs. "He's so smart! You must be grateful for it."

There was a ledge near us. Next to it some items I did not recognize were lying on the ground: a drum, two bows, two quivers with arrows, two knives, two mallets, a basket for water, a large bag made of untanned leather painted with black, yellow, blue, and white geometric figures, and several large palm-leaf baskets. Refugio took the baskets and tied them to the horses. He asked me to help him pack and secure everything well.

As I was loading the animals, I started to get back to my senses. What has happened to me? Where am I? How long has it been since I left Senecú? Where is all the food I was carrying? Why am I dressed like an Apache? Are these items mine? I had no idea, but I concluded it wasn't the right time to ask Refugio anything.

When we finished loading, we untied and mounted the animals and left. We wandered in the forest for a while. Lucius galloped happily through the snow despite his heavy burden. When we reached a clearing that was located at the foot of a hill, Refugio indicated that we had found the ideal place to build a quinzee. I had no idea what these snow huts looked like or how to make one. Although I was dead tired and was making a huge effort not to fall asleep, I told him I was ready to help.

We dismounted, unloaded our belongings, and placed them under some trees. Refugio unsheathed his spear and walked toward the center of the clearing to measure the depth of the snow at various points on the ground. He confirmed that it was the perfect place and asked me to bring him the two shovels that were rolled up inside the blankets that were tied to the back of Lucius's and Mora's saddles. I untied the strings, unrolled the blankets, and put on one of them, for mine was wet and stiff due to the cold and the snow. I grabbed the shovels and took them to Refugio, who was now tamping down the snow with his feet. He asked me to help him shovel snow. I was overtired, but I did what I could. We shoveled and shoveled and, when we finished flattening an area of approximately six square meters, he drew an ellipse around it and told me that we now had to shovel the perimeter to create a high mound. I don't know where I got the strength to continue shoveling. Then we compressed the snow and, when we finished it, he said, panting:

"We just need to dig the entrance. The snow needs to harden first. I'm gonna get some water. I'm thirsty. Wanna come?"

He didn't wait for an answer and headed to the place where we left our stuff. I was dying of thirst too, but I was so exhausted and weak that I remained standing there without saying anything. I felt dizzy and had a pounding headache. My heart was beating fast.

I'm out of shape, I thought.

I would have liked to find a dry place to lie down, but I felt unable to walk. I decided to use the shovel to support myself, as I didn't want to sit on the snow. I put my head on the back of my hands to get some rest. I didn't know if I fell asleep or if I fainted, or how long this lasted, but in that time span I had such a vivid, horrendous dream that I was scared to death when I woke up.

I was running for my life in the dark, down a stony road. I was barefoot and felt an agonizing pain, as if the bottom of my feet had been burned or sliced. But my fear was even greater. Someone was chasing me, and I was deathly afraid to see who it was. I kept on running despite the torturing pain. My pursuer yelled at me, "And you thought you were going to escape? Not anymore! Not anymore!" Then he said, "Miserable thing, why do you run away? I will tear you to pieces, or let you go if I please." I was screaming like a coward, "No! Please, God, help me!" My pursuer then burst into laughter and uttered some gruesome squawks. Then a gigantic eagle attacked me. It grabbed me and tried to lift me up with its talons. I resisted and made a futile effort to free myself. It started pecking my crown and cracked my skull. My face was covered in blood. I was screaming like a madman, but the eagle wouldn't let go of me. I didn't understand how I was able to withstand such agony and, in a moment of lucidity, when I felt a stabbing under my left shoulder blade and felt that the tip of an arrow had pierced my heart, I deduced that it was a nightmare, for I kept running as if nothing had happened to me. I decided to stop, and both my pain and the eagle vanished instantly.

I felt the sharp point of the arrow and the warm density of my blood flowing from my pierced heart. There was absolute silence for a moment. Then a crow cawed, and the sky lit up. The corvid was perched on the upper branch of a leafless oak under a partially cloudy sky. Its intermittent cawing made a counterpoint to the morning song of the birds. I experienced an unexpected peace of mind for a moment. I thought the nightmare was over, but I soon heard the footsteps of my attacker approach me stealthily. I decided to confront him and turned. Though I couldn't see him, I felt his presence in front of me. I looked up and his skeletal face gave me such terror that my heart stopped beating. Then I woke up.

Refugio was squatting next to me, trying to help me wake up.

"Dant'éé? Are you well?" he asked me repeatedly, patting my cheek.

I tried to get up but couldn't. Although I could see and hear him, for some reason I was paralyzed. Maybe it was just for a minute, but it seemed like an eternity to me. At that interval I had another incredible vision.

I felt like I started to float and rise slowly. I contemplated the sky. It was resplendent in the extreme. Strangely, the sky was not blue: it radiated a myriad of yellow, orange, pink, and red hues of unimaginable variety, intensity, and beauty. Instead of blinding me, the light amplified and sharpened my vision. But the most wonderful and amazing thing was not what I saw but what I heard. Initially, I noticed something that I thought was the sound of a creek or a fountain whose murmur was mixed at first with the sound of Refugio's voice, the cawing of the crow, and the singing of the birds of my previous nightmare. However, gradually this mysterious murmur eclipsed the other sounds and gained musical intensity and richness. It was a heavenly symphony whose exuberant variety of frequencies, timbres, and melodic lines gradually displayed a lush Eden where all creatures danced, sang, and enjoyed life fully and in perfect harmony. And the most wonderful thing of all was when I heard an angelic voice call me and tell me that there was a place reserved for me in this Paradise.

> O day of tearful joy! O grateful day!
> O thou, my maker's day![4]

I was in bliss, but Refugio snatched me out of it. I regained consciousness and mobility and sat up.

28

"WHAT HAPPENED TO YOU, *SHIBEHÉ*?" REFUGIO ASKED ME, PUTTING his hand on my shoulder. It was the first time he called me nephew.

"I don't know," I replied, still stunned. I tried to disguise my bewilderment, but Refugio seemed to know what had happened to me.

"You had a dream, right?"

I nodded.

"A nightmare?"

I nodded again.

"With Skeleton?"

I looked at him, surprised by his uncanny perception.

"Did a crow appear?"

"Yes."

"Was the sky clear or dark?"

"Partly cloudy."

"Ah, good sign! You've got an Enemy Ghost inside. I'm healin' you. It can make you sleepy, give you nightmares, and immobilize you for a while. You must be tired. Deadly fight with Enemy Ghost is exhaustin'. Tomorrow we'll continue. And now, back to work. We must finish chagoch'o. Soon Father Sun will set."

Refugio had collected some sticks and inserted them at different points on the mound to make sure the walls of the quinzhee would be thick enough. Satisfied with what he saw, he took his shovel and started digging a hole to make the entrance and carve the interior. He asked me to remove the snow that piled up. After shoveling hard for a while, our snow hut was ready. He invited me in and showed it to me with pride. It was amazing to me how cozy and temperate its interior was. But it still seemed unbelievable to find myself in that snow hut, dressed like an Apache, and with Refugio. It was all so very strange. What had happened to me?

Until then I hadn't found the right time to ask him. As I was shoveling snow, I was reflecting and wondering. I thought it was too strange that the wind had calmed down so suddenly when Refugio found me. I started to doubt if, in fact, it had been windy at all. Everything that was happening to me was too weird. I decided to be honest with him and clear up my doubts.

"What happened to me? I don't know where I am or what I'm doing here."

"Shibehé has an Enemy Ghost inside. You suffer from delirium. I'm performing a healin' ceremony. We're in *Dziłcho*. It means 'large mountain' in N'nee. Our ancestors dwell here, but also *gą́hé*, *dadilzní*, *ch'iin*, and other friendly and enemy spirits. There's muuuuuucho godih here," said Refugio, raising his eyebrows and making a gesture of astonished excitement when he uttered this word, which means "power." And, changing the subject, he added: "Let's make a fire and have dinner. I'm hungry."

He asked me to follow him by turning his face and pointing his lips toward the exit. We crawled out of the quinzhee and went looking for the gear and materials we needed to light the campfire. From a saddlebag he pulled out a stick of mullein and a white pine tablet with which he was going to light the campfire. From a basket he pulled out a handful of hay and moss and made a bird nest with them. Then he pulled out some birch bark, spread it out, and asked me to grab the basket with branches and wood that was on the ground and follow him. He carried with him the saddlebag with the food and the jug of water with two mugs. We walked toward a nearby ledge that would offer us protection against the wind.

There he began to arrange the firewood. He built a small teepee with several layers of branches and logs of different thicknesses. Inside it he placed hay, moss, and a small piece of pine trunk covered in resin. At another spot he placed the sheet of birch bark and, on top of it, the tinder nest he had previously made. He pulled a knife out of the saddlebag and with its tip made a small hole in the white pine tablet. He then took the mullein stick, smoothed it out with the knife, and covered it with a layer of pine resin. Once the stick was ready, he placed the white pine tablet on the birch sheet and sat down. Resting the bottom of his left foot on the tablet, he inserted the stick into the incision of the tablet and, putting it between his hands, began to turn it by rubbing the palms of his hands as if he were whipping hot chocolate with a *molinillo*. The friction produced both heat and sawdust inside the hole of the tablet. Within a few minutes it also started to produce smoke. Once there was enough sawdust inside the tablet, he stopped the drilling-like motion. He put the tinder nest close to the burning sawdust to ignite it and blew a couple of times until the tinder caught fire. With a branch, he rolled the burning tinder and placed it inside the pile of logs, where there was more tinder. This was how he lit the campfire, as our remote ancestors had done for millennia.

Once the firewood was burning and we made sure there was enough fuel to feed the campfire, he pulled a couple of baskets out of the saddlebag. One of them contained meatballs made of crushed, dry deer meat mixed with pulverized acorn, dried berries, and animal fat. The other basket had pecan and pinyon nuts. He offered me food from both baskets, but I didn't accept because I had a migraine and felt nauseated.

"You haven't eaten since you got lost in the Camino Real. The wise feed the body and empty the mind."

"Thank you, but I'm not hungry." I was more concerned with understanding what had happened to me than with eating. I could no longer contain my confusion and anguish and added, "I don't know what happened to me or how long it's been. Can you tell me?"

Refugio, by contrast, was more interested in eating than in talking. He took a bite of a meatball and started chewing with gusto. I was very thirsty, so I got up to get the water jug and the mugs. I filled them up, gave one to Refugio, and sat on the opposite side of the campfire to drink and rest.

Refugio ate avidly and silently. He fixed his gaze on the flames and entered a kind of trance, as if he were in communion with the elements and the material world. His face reflected the glowing colors of the campfire. The whimsical flames started to produce phantasmagoric tricks with his image. Suddenly, he seemed to turn into an arboriform numen, and the fire began to consume him. His head looked like a treetop on fire and his body resembled the contorted trunk of a century-old juniper. He irradiated a strange energy that dazzled me.

I wondered if the water was actually a hallucinogenic potion. I took the mug and carefully observed its contents. I gave it a little sip, verified that it was plain water, and put the mug back on the ground. I concluded that maybe I was still sick. Since I was cold, I put my arms on my chest and started blowing my hands to warm them up, which made him laugh.

"What are you doin'?"

"I'm warming up my hands."

"You're cold?"

"Yes, very much."

"If you don't eat, you're not gonna get better. Your illness is in the nose." He continued to chew and focus his gaze on the campfire.

I found his diagnosis strange. However, later I learned that, according to the Apache, the nasal cavity was the seat of the mind.

"Today was very windy, right?" I asked.

"Not really," he answered while chewing and making a derogatory gesture. "Today the four winds hardly said anything; they just murmured. Some bad air is trapped inside you. Your enemy spirit blew it in there."

"My enemy spirit? As far as I know, I have no enemies here," I said with both skepticism and naivety.

"I'm sure it's a ch'ii, a harmful evil ghost. Łanohwile! Ch'ii have muuucho bigodih. They chase their enemies even in their dreams. Sometimes they turn into owls. Only a special ceremony can get rid of them. The ceremony I did to you I learned from my *shiwoyé hastiin*, my mother's father. Sanaba was his name. He was a very wise healer. He taught me the ceremony here. Many ch'ii and other spirits live here, both good and evil. Only mountain spirits and Child of Water can defeat the ch'ii. Mountain spirits cure aaaaaaaaalll illnesses. They'll cure you too. You'll see."

He reached for the basket with nuts. He took two pecans with one hand, cracked them together, and shelled them with skill. The two halves of the cotyledon came out in one piece. Before eating them, he watched the nut meat as if he had never seen it before. He looked at it from different angles and then placed it in his mouth and savored it as if it were a divine delicacy.

After watching him eat for a few minutes, I couldn't wait any longer. I was dying to know what had happened to me after I ran into María Tzitza on my way to Ojo Caliente. I decided to tell him about my encounter with her. Refugio listened attentively as he savored his meal. When I finished my account, he commented:

"Holy Wind spoke to you because you helped the woman in distress. Holy Wind revealed to you the calamity that will fall on the children and servants of Big Giant."

I had never heard of Big Giant and asked him who he was.

"Big Giant is a child of Father Sun and one of his concubines. Big Giant is selfish and arrogant. He doesn't like White Painted Woman's children. He thinks he's the lord and master of everythin'. In another world, Mother Earth's holy children, the Warrior Twins, Child of Water and Killer-of-Enemies, eliminated the bastard children of the Sun. Now, the children of Big Giant, the Nakaiyé, have come to avenge their father's death. But Holy Mother will return from her home in the west. She will send the Nakaiyé a plague and pestilence. Father Sun will burn their fields and crops and bring a drought with extreme heat and cold. And with the help of the Warrior Twins, our people will kill the children and servants of the Big Giant. We will destroy their temples, plunder their haciendas, and hunt the Nakaiyé like wild boars. This is the Holy Wind's revelation."

Although I was intrigued by this prophecy, what most interested me was knowing what had happened to me.

"I don't remember anything after I saw María ascend to heaven. Do you know?"

"You got lost on the Camino Real. Nant'an Chilmo found you and asked you, 'What's going on? Do you have a problem? Where's *Diyin* Refugio?' You said you didn't know. Then you told him about María's vision and asked him for protection. You assured him your name is Uriel and that you are not Christian. You also said that Lucius the mule is the true Brother Diego, that a seductress witch cast a spell on him, and that he's lookin' for the Promised Land where he'll regain his human form."

"Did I tell him that?"

"Yes, you did. You also told him that you're lookin' for Alma and that you got lost in the mountain chasing an owl. Nant'an Chilmo realized the owl had bewitched you. You said other things in some foreign tongue he had never heard. You were only wearin' a habit. Nant'an Chilmo gave you these clothes so that you wouldn't freeze to death."

"And then what happened?"

"Nant'an Chilmo didn't know what to do. If he took you back to Senecú, he knew the Nakaiyé would accuse him of bewitchin' you. Nant'an Chilmo had made a deal with Brother Antonio, so he decided to take you to Ojo Caliente."

"And where were you?"

"In Senecú."

"And where are they? What am I doing here with you?"

"They're in Ojo Caliente. Diyin Baltasar confirmed that an owl had made you sick. Owls are evil. They lurk in the darkness, in crossroads, and in places where people have been murdered. Diyin Baltasar burned your belongings and consulted with his power. It revealed to him that he would be able to heal the animal, but not you. So he cured your horse with a special ceremony. But you have Enemy Ghost sickness; only a mountain spirit can cure you."

After he said this, Refugio changed the subject and asked me to recount him my dream.

"Which dream?"

"The one that scared you to death."

I wondered how he knew about it but decided not to ask and simply complied. He listened with apparent carelessness as he continued to contemplate and savor the nuts. When I concluded, he didn't say anything but remained absorbed in that peculiar ritual.

After a while I got impatient and asked him, full of curiosity and anxiety, what he thought of my dream.

"You Nakaiyé don't like silence," he said, frowning, and using a term that means both Mexican and Spaniard. "You love talkin' and fret when N'nee don't answer right away. You Nakaiyé love to hear opinions and pretty words. But these don't express the truth. He who speaks much knows little. You need to learn to understand silence and be patient."

He took his mug, showed it to me, and said:

"This *idee* is made of clay, but the hole inside it is what makes it useful. Without the hole, an idee is worthless. The same is true for words. Without silence, words are meaningless. I don't know much; that's why I think before I talk."

"I'm sorry. You're right," I replied embarrassedly.

We watched the fire for a while. He heated water, prepared mugwort tea for me, and said it was going to help me sleep and not have nightmares. I drank it quietly while he sang a N'nee prayer.

After an extended moment of silence, he said to me:

"Ever since we found you on the Camino Real, you've been full of fear of Skeleton. You dream of *Dá'its'inzhá* and feel persecuted by Dá'its'inzhá. This is a bad sign. The arrow in the heart means that you're sufferin' and in danger. But the presence of a crow and the half-clear sky is a good sign. Your decision to confront the Enemy Ghost is also a good sign. The homin' eagle of *Binaideeł* wants to take you to its nest, to its abode, but you resist. You're afraid of life in Binaideeł's homeland."

"Who's Binaideeł?"

"The Giver of Life."

"And Datsinchá?"

"Da'its'inszhá," he said, correcting my pronunciation. "Skeleton Man. The Flayed One. The Nant'an of the Underworld. Here in the mountain there are also netherworld shadows, guardians of the kingdom of Skeleton Man. We call these shadows *bichagoch'o*. In the winter solstice they get out to take part in the ceremony of the Kachinas' homecomin' in the Pueblo villages, which is presided by Skeleton Man. It's veeeeery dangerous to bump into the bichagoch'o. Like the ch'ii, they give bad air sickness to their enemies. Shibehé is gonna have to make a great offerin' to calm down Skeleton Man. Believe me. There's no worse enemy than him. Tomorrow I'll tell you what you need to do to appease Skeleton Man's anger. Now it's time to sleep. I'm tired and I need to sleep to cure your illness. Dreams give me revelations and power."

"Alright," I replied. I also was dying for sleep. We put out the campfire and went into the quinzhee.

Before lying down, he scattered romerillo leaves inside the quinzhee and put a black knife under the blanket that I was using as a pillow. He told me the romerillo would take away my fear, and the knife would keep the Enemy Ghost away. Then he put the dream catcher on his chest, started vocalizing, and asked me to imitate him.

"Aaaaaaaaaaaah."

As we vocalized, first he made a circle with both hands on his chest. Then he put the dream catcher on his heart and, pointing at it with his right index finger, he instructed me to visualize the dream catcher over my heart while I was asleep. It was the same strange gesture that he made when I met him for the first time. I should have asked him about it at that point, but I was dead tired and needed some sleep desperately.

"It's veeeery important to do this while you sleep. It helps you stay alert and, if you have a nightmare, it will catch it and make it a sweet dream. Then you will be the king and not the slave of dreams. Do you still have a head and belly ache?"

"Yes, I do."

He made a grimace of disappointment. "Tomorrow we will visit the Mountain People to make an offering to Da'its'inszhá."

As soon as he lay down and closed his eyes, he fell asleep. I was so exhausted that I also fell asleep immediately while vocalizing the "aaaaaaaaaaah," trying to visualize the dream catcher and not to think about Skeleton Man, friendly and enemy spirits, owls, and all the other strange things that happened to me that day.

29

I HAD A HARD TIME WAKING UP. MY BODY HURT AND FELT HEAVY as if I had a high fever. I was shivering and wanted to go back to sleep, but the pounding of a drum and a choir of voices did not let me. I had no choice but to get up.

I came out of the quinzhee and was dazzled by the auroral light reflected in the limpid snow. Dazed, sleepy, and very cold, I walked toward a juniper at the center of the clearing to relieve myself. It was a century-old tree that seemed strangely familiar. It was planted on the bedrock. Its intricate trunk and twisted branches and roots made me think of a fervent orans kneeling and praising the polar star with her arms wide open. As I tainted the snow yellow, I listened to the group of singers welcoming the sunrise. I figured I couldn't see them because the juniper was blocking them. The golden sky offered a majestic panoramic view of the same mountain valley that Brother Antonio had shown me a few months ago. Suddenly, I heard a hoarse, twangy voice that said to me:

"Beware of the Lord of Dreams, Uriel."

I turned to see who it was and realized it was Lucius the mule. He was tied to the juniper, grazing with Mora and Pardo.

"He is a malevolent genius who will deceive you and prevent you from reaching your spiritual homeland."

"Who are you? Why are you talking if you're a mule?"

"Don't be fooled by the tricks of the Lord of Dreams. I am not a mule, nor do I talk, nor do I exist. I'm just an illusion, like you."

"What are you doing here?"

"The same as you. I want to get out of here. I'm just as lost."

"And how do you know?"

"Because I am you."

"What do you mean?"

"I know you're an impostor who wants to pass as me."

"I do it against my will. This identity was imposed on me."

"My body and my story too."

"Are you Diego Romero?"

"I am. Or, rather, I was Diego Romero in another dream. In this one I have the body of a mule and the name of a famous equine of Latin literature. But that doesn't matter. Even though I have the body of a mule, my mind is still Diego's."

"What are you saying?"

"You are reliving my life in this dream. Everything you're living I've already lived in another dream. That's why I'm telling you, beware of the Lord of Dreams. He's going to try to divert you from your journey to your place of origin, your spiritual homeland. He's a powerful lord who's going to offer you this kingdom, and Heaven too, if you submit to him and serve him."

"And what interest does this lord have in my service?"

"He wants you to believe in him and give credence to his fabrications. He is like all powerful earthly gods. He suffers from narcissism and needs humans for self-affirmation."

At that moment I heard the voice of Refugio. He was calling me to join him in his morning rite.

"Go, go with Refugio. Listen to him and trust him. And remember, don't be fooled by the Lord of Dreams. Otherwise, it will cost us dearly."

"What do you mean?"

"My destiny depends on yours. I won't be able to get to my place of origin if you don't get to yours. Our destinies are intertwined."

Refugio approached me. I wanted to get more information out of Lucius, but he started to bray. I had no choice but to follow Refugio. He was singing, dancing, and beating the drum. Without stopping, he asked me to participate in the celebration through facial gestures and jovial body movements.

I thought I was going to join a small group of singers and dancers, but Refugio was singing and dancing alone. For some odd reason I continued to hear a large group of singers. Maybe I was hallucinating because of the fever.

Refugio was wearing a white leather cloak decorated with geometric figures painted with bright colors, depicting natural and supernatural beings and phenomena. These included mountain deities, an eagle, a sun, several rainbows, lightning flashes, clouds, and a cross of the four winds. He was also wearing a skirt-like breechcloth fastened with a leather belt, as well as moccasin boots adorned with *ayoyotes* that jingled when he danced.

He was singing "We Are Here," a cheerful chant that invited us to appreciate and enjoy the beauty around us. Although Refugio articulated clearly and repeated the chorus numerous times, which simply said, "*koon-ky-he-ee*," I was still drowsy and did not feel like joining the chant. He insisted with patience and, seeing that I was not giving in, handed me the drum and asked me to play it. He started dancing and continued to sing cheerfully and inspired. It was a simple dance in which he thumped his feet on the ground to the rhythm of the drum and moved his body as if he were running. His energy seemed inexhaustible. After dancing and singing for a while, he asked me to hand him the drum and the drumstick. Still singing, smiling, jumping, and now beating the drum, he urged me to dance. I had to comply, which gave him great joy, especially when I joined the singing of the chorus:

koon-ky-he-ee, koon-ky-he-ee
koon-ky-he-ee, koon-ky-he-ee

When we concluded that morning rite, we were both sweating profusely. I was panting as if I'd participated in a marathon. Refugio patted me on the back and congratulated me, saying: "*Nzhǫǫ, nzhǫǫ*. Well done, well done." Then he opened the leather pouch he carried on his belt, took a pinch of cattail pollen, and put it on my lips. He told me that it was going to invigorate me. I reluctantly tasted the turmeric-yellow and slightly sweet powder, which did revitalize me as if by magic. When I finally stopped panting, he told me we needed to go to the Coyote Witch Falls. For my healing, he said, it was essential that I bathed in the waters of this sacred canyon. But first we needed to go to the spring of San Mateo to fetch water and firewood for our journey.

After drinking water we fastened the baskets and jugs to Lucius, Mora, and Pardo. We headed to a nearby pond and followed a downhill trail that offered a beautiful view of the canyon and mountains. I had woken up with a voracious appetite and longed for breakfast, but I decided to endure hunger out of decorum or shame. As we approached the pond, we tied the animals and went down a natural staircase formed in a ravine slit. As soon as we descended, Refugio undressed and went into the pond in just a loincloth. He assured me it wasn't that cold and invited me to take a bath too. I just smiled and waved to indicate to him I was going to sit on a rock and wait for him.

After drying and dressing he meditated for a while, standing silently by the pond and facing the sun. When he finished, he filled the jug with water and asked me to come over to fill mine. I did, and as I filled it, he said:

"We N'nee make a prayer to Mother Earth when we wake up and to Father Sun at sunbreak. If a river or a stream are nearby, we pray after bathin'; if not, we wash anywhere we can praise Mother Earth and Father Sun in peace. Every N'nee has a special ceremony. My shiwoyé hastiin taught me to pray My Mother and Our Father. Of course," he added, slightly changing his tone and staring at me, "not all people fulfill their sacred obligation." Although he did not say it in an accusatory tone, it seemed clear to me that he disapproved of the fact that I did not bathe or praise any deity that frosty morning.

"We the N'nee respect the beliefs of others. We don't force anyone to believe anythin'. We think that good people go to another world and that bad people become ghosts in this world."

Refugio paused briefly, waiting for me to say something, but I remained quiet. I was starting to feel a little liberated being with him. It was the first time in a long time that I didn't have to pretend anything to anyone. With him I didn't feel obligated to perform any religious act or say anything I didn't think or believe.

"Our beliefs are not written anywhere. We don't preach or convert. If you believe other things, we won't punish, condemn, or curse you. We don't have temples or shrines because we revere Mother Earth and Father Sun everywhere. Giver of Life has many shapes: a star, a mountain, a spider, an eagle, a man, a woman. *Ussen* is present everywhere: at night, during the day, in the mountains, the rivers, the flowers, the desert, the rocks, the water, the air, the sky. Ussen is equally generous with N'nee and Nakaiyé, women and men, plants, animals, and rocks. Giver of Life created and embraces everyone. Just like the sun illuminates everythin' and just like the wind blows everywhere without leavin' out anythin', Ussen loves everyone and everythin' the same way."

Having filled our jugs with water, we returned to the place where the animals were grazing. We ascended the ravine with difficulty. Refugio's container was full, but mine arrived half empty.

"At least it didn't break," I said, a bit embarrassed.

"Don't worry, shibehé. I got water for the two of us," he replied as we were tying the jugs to the animals.

Then we gathered enough firewood for the day. Refugio was delighted when he saw a bush of mugwort. He squatted in front of it, sang a prayer, and carefully cut a few branches and put them in the saddlebags with the firewood. Finally, we rode back to camp. It was time for breakfast.

30

BY THEN THE SUN'S RAYS WERE MELTING THE SNOW AND SMALL icicles began to form on the trees. I was so hungry and thirsty that I tore a handful of juniper berries covered in snow. They tasted bitter but calmed down my hunger for a few moments. Refugio did not seem to be hungry or in any hurry when we unloaded, cut, and stacked the firewood, nor when we set up the campfire. Even when he performed the most trivial tasks, in the mountain he acted in the same way that Brother Antonio acted in the church: all his movements and actions seemed to follow a pre-established, sacred order.

Finally, Refugio lit the campfire. He heated water in a clay pot and pulled out of a saddlebag a sack with ground mesquite flour, a bag with dried agave stalk pieces, and the small basket with pecans and pinyon nuts from the night before. He mixed the mesquite flour with water to make a slightly sweet hot cereal that tasted delicious. The steamed and sundried agave flower stems were not as tasty, but I devoured them happily, nonetheless. I would have eaten the pinyon nuts without shelling them, but my carious teeth wouldn't have withstood such abuse.

After enjoying our meal in silence, he asked me:

"How is your dreamin' goin', shibehé?"

I hesitated to tell him the truth. However, reflecting that maybe this was all a dream, I decided to confess to him who I really was. I had nothing to lose, and he could even help me, I thought.

Refugio listened, fascinated. When I finished my story, he told me something that surprised me.

"All diyin are brothers and sisters."

"I don't understand."

"To know our secrets, you must become a brother. Do you promise to be my brother always if I tell you this secret?"

The candidness with which he asked me this question completely dispelled the last vestige of mistrust that still tarnished my lethargic conscience.

"Yes, I promise," I replied, without giving it much thought, perhaps out of curiosity and convenience. Certainly, I didn't know what it meant to become his "brother."

"*Ha'a shiá hnzhǫ*," he said, smiling. "I like that. From now on you are my *shidizé*, my younger brother, and I'm your *shidee*, your big brother." Then he said in a solemn and confessional tone:

"I'm a diyin."

"I beg your pardon?"

"Diyin means spiritualist and medicine man. I have a sacred endowment. My gift is dreamin'. Dreams guide me and give me knowledge and wisdom. Dreams give me power and truth. Almost nobody knows about this power of mine; only fellow diyin. Like you, I also dream of another life. I dream of people in other villages in another time, people who die and reincarnate in another body. I've also dreamed of Uriel. I've seen his life, his world, his future."

"Do you know who I really am, then, Don Refugio?" I told him with a mixture of enthusiasm, disbelief, and fear.

"Shidee," he corrected me.

"Shidee," I repeated to please him.

"You're not Uriel, shidizé. You're Diego."

"No," I contradicted him, certain that I was having a lucid dream. "I'm dreaming I'm Diego, but I'm actually Uriel."

"Your mind is deceiving you. You're sick, shidizé. You have an Enemy Ghost in your nose. I'm going to exorcize you with the help of the Mountain People. We're gonna cure the illness that the owl gave you."

"I'm neither sick nor crazy nor possessed," I said, irritated, though trying to control myself. "I'm dreaming."

"And how do you know?"

"I know because I know. I know who I am. I know my life perfectly and in detail. I only know about Diego what others have told me. Diego is someone completely strange to me."

"Then why do you have Diego's body, face, voice, and story? Why do you walk, eat, and behave like Diego?"

"Because I'm dreaming!"

"And how do you know? Show me you're not Diego," he said, unconvinced and crossing his arms.

I hesitated for a moment, wondering if I should ask Lucius to tell Refugio who Diego really was. But I feared this would convince Refugio even more that I was sick, if not crazy, and I gave up.

"You and I know we're always dreaming, day and night," he told me. "But wide-awake dreams are different. If I pinch my hand, it hurts; if I put my hand in fire, it burns; if I cut with a knife, blood comes out; if I want to fly and throw myself into an abyss, I kill myself."

I did a test to see if I was dreaming or not. I put my hand close to the fire and removed it instantly, making a grimace of pain. Refugio laughed and said, mocking me:

"*Adíídí yá' át'é?* What is this?"

I remained silent with my pride and my pain.

"Put your hand in the snow," he advised me.

I did, to my relief. Although the feeling of the snow intensified my pain at first, it gradually diminished it. Refugio got up to bring more firewood and I started to ponder.

What if it was true that I was not dreaming? What if I was actually Diego and not Uriel? What was I going to do? Give myself in to the missionary work? Try to convert the Apache into a religion I didn't believe in? Continue this masquerade? Why was I letting the Franciscans push me around like a sheep to the slaughterhouse without resisting and without fighting for my survival? Did I have an alternative? What if I asked my mother, or one of my relatives, for help? Would Brother Antonio accept my renunciation of the religious life? Would the custodio, the members of the Definitorio, the bishop, the archbishop? What if they found out that all my belongings had been burned, including my habit, the crucifix, the scapular, and the psalter? What if they discovered that Refugio performed a ceremony on me and now he considered me his spiritual brother? What if they realized I was an agnostic and I had all kinds of heterodox beliefs? They'd burn me at the stake like a necromancer! Didn't Brother Antonio and Father Guerra warn me from the beginning?

I had to do something radical, I thought to myself. Escape, yes. Run away. But where and how if I didn't have a single real on me? Moreover, I was completely unable to fend for myself or survive in the woods and, much less, in the desert. What was worse? Dying at the stake without fighting, or dying of thirst, or getting devoured by wolves, looking for a new life and chasing my ideals? Which ideals? What did I believe in? What did I want? What did I aspire to in life? That I knew regardless of who I was. My dream was to write, to live an examined life, to cultivate wisdom. I wanted to reunite with Alma, if she was still alive. And that I couldn't do in New Mexico. I had to leave no matter what. I'd go to Mexico City on Lucius's back, just like how I got here. I'd ask Refugio for help. Yes, that's it! I would beg him to teach me how to survive by hunting with bow and arrow and collecting food and herbs in the desert. I'd go to Parral, then to Mexico City. Would he help me?

Refugio returned with more firewood, added a few logs to the fire, sat near me, and started to eat some nuts quietly. I mustered courage and asked him:

"Why am I here, Shidee? Why are you helping me? Why do you want to cure me?"

Refugio became pensive. He took a stick and started to dig the ground with it. After a while, without saying anything, he got up and went to grab something from the leather sack where he kept his belongings. He came back with a rolled leather canvas. He stood in front of me and spread it out.

"This painting announces the destruction of my people," he told me, and approached me so I could see the canvas closely.

It was a richly illustrated pictorial catechism colored with natural pigments. It was about sixty centimeters wide and ninety in length. It had a painted Catholic scale that instructed how to go to Heaven on it. The left side summarized the biblical history and, the right side, Native American history. Both accounts had two different versions that followed different courses and destinations that were represented by two separate, winding paths. A straight ladder representing the life of Christ crossed and divided them.

In the biblical account the path on the left was called the Way of Doom. It was painted dark gray and illustrated Old Testament passages associated with idolatry. The path on the right, called the Way of Salvation, was painted yellow and traced the path followed by the most pious Old Testament prophets and New Testament apostles. At the base of the ladder, painted in the middle of the two paths, there was an old, long-haired, white-bearded man wrapped in a purple robe. His arms and hands were open wide; he showed and contemplated his creation. Beneath him were nine images representing nothingness and initial darkness along with the seven days of Creation and the Fall. Below the images was drawn a large square explaining the mystery of the Trinity. Inside the square was a circle. Within it was an equilateral triangle that covered almost the entire circle. It was surrounded by straight lines that represented rays of light. The number one was drawn at the center of the triangle; a bearded, white, old man was drawn at the top vertex. At the lower left corner appeared the face of a bearded Semite who represented Christ; and at the right corner, the silhouette of a white dove flapping its wings represented the Holy Spirit. At the other end of the central ladder, on the upper rung, was an image of Christ crucified. The Virgin Mary prayed standing next to him. Next to her was Mary

Magdalene. She sobbed and was prostrate under the feet of Jesus with her hands on her face. In this scene an image of Christ the King was suspended in the sky. He radiated light as if he were the sun.

In the historical account the left path was called the Sinister Way and was painted dark gray. It illustrated the great episodes of the continent's political, economic, and military history, from the founding of Mesoamerican civilization to the present Novo Hispanic viceroyalty and the reign of Charles II, the Bewitched. This path led to a region called Apocalypsi, where the archangels slit the throats of the Beast and his dragons. The path on the right was called the Right Way and was painted yellow. It recounted the great events of New Spain's ecclesiastical history, from the arrival of the twelve Franciscan apostles in Central Mexico to the founding of New Mexico's missions. The two paths were connected by trails that represented the journey that converts made as they went from the Sinister to the Right Way, and the apostates as they went from the Right to the Sinister Way. These trails were depicted as the uneven steps of a twisted staircase. In the middle of it was a solid, straight ladder that had a church at the base, which functioned as the ladder's underpinning. At the same time, the church was the first rung of the historical account and connected the Right and the Sinister Ways. Beneath this temple was another image of Christ the King suspended in heaven and radiating light. It was almost identical to the image that crowned the biblical history, except that, beneath Christ, there were some friars and nuns prostrate and looking up to the sky, some of them with their arms raised, and others with their hands joined in prayer. Christ the King was on the top of the ladder. He sat open-armed on the top rung. His left index pointed toward Hell, a dark region covered in flames and smoke. It was populated with demons who administered punishments to idolatrous Natives and sinners of all kinds. His right index pointed toward Paradise, where Christ the King was on his throne hugging a kneeling child dressed as an altar boy as the Virgin Mary and the angels watched them with a pious look and posture. Beneath them was an angel holding another blessed man, who waited his turn to be received in the Kingdom of Christ in the postapocalyptic millennium.

"The painting tells the story of the destruction of the N'nee," Refugio said again after a long period of silence.

"Where?"

"On the Bright Way, all people wear robes and habits," he told me, pointing to the figures of those who ascended to Heaven by the Way of Salvation and the Right Way. "N'nee go here with bad Nakaiyé," he told me, pointing to the Sinister Way. "Look, the N'nee go to Hell and get destroyed by demons."

"Your interpretation seems accurate to me."

"It's not mine. Diyin Sanaba, my maternal grandfather, taught it to me."

"Is the canvas yours?"

"Yes. Abuelo gave it to me."

"And who painted it?"

"Blue Lady."

"Blue Lady?"

"A missionary who visited Ojo Caliente in Abuelo's time. She left the canvas in his teepee."

"And why are you showing it to me?"

"I want to protect my people from the Christian prophecy."

"But what can I do?"

"Teach the catechism to me."

"What for?"

"To understand the Christian prophecy."

"Alright, Shidee, I'm going to teach the catechism and the Bible to you."

"Thanks, Shidizé."

"But on one condition."

"What condition?"

"That you teach me to hunt with bow and arrow and to survive in the mountain and in the desert."

"And why do you want to learn that?"

"Because I want to escape. I want to leave the mission. I want to leave New Mexico."

"You wanna go back to Mexico City?"

"Yes."

"And why not go by wagon? It's much easier."

"Because the Nakaiyé will want to kill me when they find out I've become your brother."

"I understand. Alright. I'm gonna teach you to survive."

"And to hunt?"

"And to hunt."

I extended my arm to shake his hand.

"But first, I need to take out the Enemy Ghost. Do you agree, Shidizé?"

"Alright, Shidee. I agree."

"Then, from now on, you're *Dikohe*, which means novice in the Nakaiyé language. It implies you can't disobey me," he warned me and shook my hand.

31

REFUGIO WENT IMMEDIATELY FOR HIS SADDLEBAG AND PULLED out a sharp stick and a short reed tube attached to another with a long leather string. He told me I had to scratch myself and drink water with them because N'nee novices were not allowed to scratch themselves or drink anything without the help of these utensils. Moreover, I had to tie them on my belt and take them with me everywhere. He also handed me a knife, a bow, and a quiver with arrows.

"You must always have them close to you in case of an ambush. Also your moccasins. You must always be alert. The enemy can attack any time. Don't sleep too much. Wake up with the Morning Star. Don't let her get up first."

Then he handed me a small leather pouch with cattail pollen and said:

"The first thing you gotta do when you get up is to blow *hadndin* at dawn. As soon as the sun rises," he explained, taking a pinch of pollen from the pouch, "spread hadndin to the east and repeat: '*gozhó ńłt'ee leegunyule, ch'ígoná'áí, sichizi, gunyule hayołkaałyú ijanale.*' This means, 'I beg you, sunshine, be good with me. I beg you, dawn, be good with me. Let me live long.' And then, after sayin' this prayer," he said, emulating the movements of a fast runner, "Dikohe runs one league fast and without stoppin'. Strong legs are your best friend in the mountain and in the desert." When he finished his explanation, he added:

"Now, Dikohe. Time to run. Go!" he yelled and stared at me.

I don't know why I thought he was waiting for me to say something. Since I needed to do my business, I took the opportunity to ask him to excuse me for a moment. I indicated it to him with a hand sign.

"No. You need to run, now."

I thought he was joking and waited for him to smile. However, the opposite happened. Very seriously, he took a pinch of pollen, blew it in the direction of the sun, and pronounced the prayer again:

"Gozhǫǫ ch'ígoná'áí, gozhǫǫ hadá. Hagodizyaa nzaad' shi ni' doleeł. Now it's your turn. Repeat the prayer," he said sternly.

I stood there without doing or saying anything. Seeing that I didn't obey him, he lost his patience. He grabbed a stick from the ground and threatened to hit me with it if I didn't follow his orders.

Incredulous but fearful, I took my pollen pouch, opened it, took a pinch, and blew the hadndin toward dawn. I asked him to repeat the prayer again.

He articulated each syllable slowly and carefully. His face and lips were slightly stained with turmeric yellow.

I repeated the prayer as best as I could.

"Now run!" he ordered me, making a fierce gesture and hitting his own hand with the stick.

I started to run fast down the trail toward the pond. Even though I was going downhill, I soon realized that I wouldn't be able to run far at this pace. I remembered the saying in Spanish, "A slow pace that lasts is better than a trot that tires you out." So, as soon as I saw that I had strayed far enough from his sight, I began to jog as slowly as possible. After a while, when I arrived at the place where we had left the animals to descend into the pond, I decided to stop to do my business. I looked for a place to relieve myself and get a second wind. I had barely pulled my pants down when I heard a horse's distant trot. I rushed to finish. But Refugio, being a veteran in the art of surprise onslaught, arrived in a flash. Suddenly, I found myself lying on the ground bellowing with pain, for he had hit me hard on the back with a reed stick.

"What did I tell you? Dikohe always obeys. If not, whack."

I pulled up my pants, tied them up, and got up immediately because he threatened to give me another thwack. I started jogging at a moderate pace, but he ordered me to run faster. And to make sure I didn't slow down, he followed me closely.

In that stretch the trail was relatively flat. However, after I crossed a meadow, the slope began to tilt uphill gradually. Every time I slowed down, he yelled at me, "Run faster, or Cuco will get you." Later he told me that Cuco was an evil owl, an adversary of the Warrior Twins, who appeared in many N'nee creation stories and children's tales. When I finished a stretch full of sharp curves, the slope of the terrain and my exhaustion made it impossible for me to continue the race. I could not even walk for my life, so I began to walk no matter the consequences. Then Refugio began to unnerve me by imitating the hoot of an owl:

"Aeúúúúúúú, aeúúúúúúúú, aeúúúúúúú."

I went as far as I could down the slope until, finally, I couldn't run anymore. I fell on my knees and threw up. Refugio got off the horse and told me:

"Enough for now."

He waited for me to recover. When I started to feel better, he said:

"Now we need to hunt some rabbits to eat," and he helped me get on La Mora.

Although La Mora had been snorting like me, by then she had already taken a second wind. Guided by Refugio, who walked ahead of us with reins in hand, we ascended the mountain until we reached the top.

When we reached the ridgeline, Refugio pointed to the precise place where I appeared in one of his dreams, but I didn't understand the allusion then. He reminded me of the time when Brother Antonio found me when I supposedly strayed away from the Camino Real while traveling alongside the wagon train. In this stretch the path was covered with junipers and bent in the shape of a hairpin. It gave the impression that it disappeared when we reached the ridge.

"Shidizé went down this path on a horse with your father, remember?"

"Of course I remember. How could I forget?"

I immersed myself in silence while Refugio proudly showed me a fraction of the immense territory that the N'nee band of the Łíhéne controlled and considered their nation and their domain. It was the same valley that Brother Antonio showed me the day I ran into him, when my nightmare started.

Minutes later we descended. It was still morning. We returned to camp to have lunch, pick up Lucius and Pardo and all our paraphernalia. We needed to depart as soon as possible to the Coyote Witch Falls, where we were going to camp for a few days. There he was going to continue the curing ceremony with the help of the spirits he called the Mountain People, for it was taboo to mention their name, the Gáhé, explicitly.

I was distracted and angry, reflecting on how unfair Refugio had been by forcing me to run and then beating me just as I had a strong urge to defecate. Meanwhile, as we crossed a hill with a broad meadow, Refugio spotted some rabbits among the bushes and quickly arrowed one of them. I barely noticed it. I just heard a violent whoosh that ripped the silence enveloping the mountain. When I looked back to see Refugio, he was pulling the bow and was already aiming at another rabbit.

"What are you doing there?" He scolded me after he arrowed the second rabbit. "Fetch the rabbits!"

"What rabbits?" I asked cluelessly.

"The hunted rabbits!"

"Where?"

"Over there. Where else? Run now!"

Being a novice, I didn't just have to obey him. I soon discovered that it was also my duty to fetch and cut the firewood; light the campfires; carry the heavy loads and the stones; bring water; dig holes; climb trees; collect fruits, seeds, roots, and edible plants; retrieve, skin, and gut the animals we hunted; prepare and cook our food; clean up and guard the camp; clean, condition, and repair the gear; build and dismantle the teepees; care for and saddle the animals, in addition to many other things. From that day on I didn't have a single moment to rest, and I would sleep only when my body and mind completely gave in.

That distant afternoon, realizing that Refugio was treating me like his servant, I reproached him. I emphasized that I had only asked him to teach me how to hunt and survive in the wild.

"Mother Earth produces everythin', but she doesn't cook or take care of us. We need to fend for ourselves. If not, we die. If Shidizé doesn't learn, you'll die like an innocent bunny. Shidizé doesn't know anythin'. When Shidizé learns a woman's work, I'll teach you hunting. Hunting is for men. You're not a man yet; you're a dikohe. Dikohe obeys and shuts up."

He ordered me to remain silent from that moment on. I could only speak when I explained to him the pictorial catechism and when I taught him Nakaiyé history and culture. He also allowed me to use my voice to sing, pray, and repeat the various words and phrases of the language of war that he taught me daily. This was a secret, figurative language that every dikohe must learn in his training. N'nee men used it only when they were on "the war path." For example, a lightning bolt, *hách'íłgich*, they called "friend of thunder," *ididii'ach*, and fire, *kó*, was "the one who tells stories," *nagoni'i'na'godi'*, perhaps because of the custom of telling stories in front of the campfire at night. He also told me that I had to learn to listen to Mother Earth; that plants, trees, and all animals had their languages; that I had to learn it to dialogue with them; that all the children of Mother Earth were a source of indispensable knowledge for surviving in the mountain and in the desert.

"If we speak their language, plants tell us their goodness, trees help us find our way, animals reveal to us if there is danger and where to find water."

That day I also learned that winds were the source of life, both natural and supernatural, and that winds gave thought, speech, and understanding to all living beings.

"The Holy Wind gives us life and guidance. Animals and plants speak and think like us. Sometimes they know what we're thinkin', thanks to the Holy Wind. If you have bad thoughts, it's because a bad wind put it inside you. If you're sick, it's because your *niyi' siziiní*, the air inside you that holds your body, is weak. And if your niyi' siziiní is weak, a bad air can attack you and make you ill. To cure you we're gonna have to make an offerin' to the Holy Wind. We'll ask it to give strength to your niyi' siziiní. Here in the mountain there is muuuuuucho godih, lots of power. Mountains are alive. They are the source of our well-being. Thanks to the mountains, N'nee are strong. Here Shidizé is gonna gain strength and heal."

He told me about the sacred mountains of the N'nee: the Three Sisters, Sierra Oscura, Sierra de Guadalupe and, above all, Sierra Blanca. He told me the story when White Painted Woman gave birth, in the midst of a great storm, to Killer of Enemies and Child of the Water—the Warrior Twins—and the story when they defeated the Naayéé. He told me again the prophecy that some white-eyed beings, children of the Great Sorcerer, would come to seize all their territories and desecrate and harm Mother Earth. But he assured me that the Warrior Twins would return and defeat them and that White Painted Woman, their Holy Mother, would take the N'nee people to another place where she would found a new world. He assured me that something similar had already happened at another time when the Anasazi were destroyed by a wind of fire sent by Father Sun at the request of the Warrior Twins for defiling all sacred things. According to Refugio, these ancestral enemies of the N'nee and Navajo lived in adobe houses built inside caves and refuges formed on the cliffs of the ravine. They were very ingenious and powerful beings who learned to control the elements and even fly, he claimed. They had large areas of cultivated land and enslaved people from surrounding villages to use them as loaders, including many N'nee. However, greed and disrespect for the sacred ended with them. They were so disrespectful and abusive that they even wanted to force Killer of Enemies to work. But he got angry and turned them into fish.

"That's why we N'nee don't eat fish," he told me at the conclusion of his story.

32

AT AROUND NOON WE RETURNED TO THE CAMP. SOON AFTER, Refugio taught me how to make campfires and roast meat. Once the embers burned, I put one of the rabbits in the fire. When it was partially roasted, I skinned it, gutted it, and finished roasting it. As we ate Refugio said:

"The Mountain People live in a bottomless cave. They're gonna cure you."

He told me that, first, we were going to make an offering to Skeleton Man.

"There's lots of power and danger in caves. They are the entrance to the Kingdom of Dá'its'inzhá."

Then I naively asked him if Dá'its'inzhá was a figure of death. Refugio panicked as if I had summoned the Devil himself. He started to choke and cough, desperately trying to spit out a piece of meat that got stuck in his throat. I got up and slapped him on the back, which helped him. When he finally recomposed himself, he sat down to eat again. He warned me that it was ill-omened to say that word—the word death—and begged me not to say it again. He explained that Dá'its'inzhá was the Lord of the Underworld and that he demanded tribute whenever someone stepped on his territory. He asserted that Dá'its'inzhá was an arrogant god who claimed to govern not only the Underworld but also the entire surface of the Earth, including the territories of the N'nee. When the Nakaiyé set foot in his dominion, and especially the Christian missionaries, Dá'its'inzhá got furious because they disrespected him and belittled him. He told me that Dá'its'inzhá, taking advantage of the fact that my *shiyi' siziiní* was weak, had commanded a bichagoch'o to get inside me and make me sick. But he told me not to worry because the Mountain People were going to help heal me.

Then he told me a story of two disabled young men who were cured by them.[5] One was born without eyes and the other without legs. Their family and friends took care of them until they grew up. But, because it was difficult to be on the move with them, one day they got fed up and left them on the mountain. The boys had no choice but to try to survive by helping each other. The blind one helped the legless one climb up his back and asked him to tell him where they should go. They spent many hours searching for water and food without any luck. Before night fell they found a cave and took refuge there. They were so hungry, thirsty, and sleepy that they thought they were going to fall asleep in that dark chamber and never wake up ever again. Around midnight strange noises woke them up. The boys felt great terror, but they were so weak that they could not even move. Suddenly, the cave lit up and five men covered in ash appeared. They wore loincloths, moccasins, and deer-skin caps with deer antler crowns. One of them wielded a flaming sword. As soon as they saw the boys, they approached them, lifted them up, and put them on their shoulders. They walked with them through a narrow passage until they reached a chamber covered with petroglyphs and pictograms. The leader of the group approached a huge rock embedded in one of the walls. He touched it with his fire sword, and the rock moved. It disclosed another passageway, only darker and narrower. The leader went in and the others followed him, forming a line. The passage gradually became less dark and wider. Until, finally, it lit up as they approached the exit. They entered a forest and followed the course of a stream until they reached a vast green valley where there were several camps with people like them. There they held a lavish ceremony to help the boys. They danced, sang, and prayed for them for several days. At the end of the ceremony, the blind boy had healthy eyes and vision as sharp as that of an eagle, and the legless boy had grown limbs as strong and as fast as those of a deer. Once they were cured and rehabilitated, the Mountain People asked the boys if they wanted to go back to their people. They said yes and the mountaineers revealed to them where they were camping and gave them directions. They recommended them to climb to the top of a mountain next to the camp and, from there, to call their band members. Once they heard them they had to reveal who they were. However, four days had to pass before they could get near them. That's what they did. On the fifth day the boys' parents went up to the top for them, apologized, and the two boys returned with them to the camp. Thanks to the knowledge they received from the Mountain People, the boys became diyin. They cured many diseases and saved all members of their tribe from epidemics and countless dangers.

At the conclusion of this account Refugio told me that my mind and spirit were like the legless boy and the blind boy before the Mountain People rescued them. He affirmed that my spirit and mind were weak because I did not fulfill my sacred obligations. I asked him what these were, and he said:

"Your sacred obligations are four: to have a strong body, a clear mind, a clean spirit, and to serve your tribe. Shidizé has a weak body, a cloudy mind, a sullied spirit, and, worse still, is selfish."

He told me this with a critical tone that was unusual for him. Perhaps to justify himself and give it a positive twist, he added:

"But don't worry, Shidizé, I'm gonna cure and help you."

I understood why he spoke this way about my physical, mental, and spiritual state. But I didn't know what my supposed "sacred obligation to my tribe" was, or why he was accusing me of being selfish. I asked him with gestures.

"We don't dream for our benefit but to help our tribe. Dreams protect our tribe against misfortune and enemies. Diyin tell their dreams to the members of their tribe. Our dreams guide them on their journeys and during difficult times. Dreams reveal the truth and the future. Diyin reveal their dreams and record them on rock. Rock writing protects the tribe from misfortune and enemies, in the present and the future."

This made me think of my most precious belonging, my dream diary, which I missed. I thought I'd ask him about it, but I knew it wasn't the right time. I was going to keep the question for another time, but Refugio seemed to have read my thoughts, for he said:

"Shidizé does not share his dream with his tribe or write them on rocks. Shidizé writes on paper book for himself. Shidizé is selfish."

"Me, selfish for keeping a dream journal?" I replied to him with my eyes, for I dared not violate his order to remain silent. "Don't you understand how risky and helpful it has been for me to record my dreams behind Brother Antonio's back?"

He didn't reply. Then I asked him again, with gestures and hand signals, where my diary was.

"We will offer your notebook to the Mountain People. It's necessary for your healing. Time to go. It's gettin' late." He stood up suddenly.

33

WE PUT OUT THE CAMPFIRE AND PACKED EVERYTHING TO HEAD out to the Coyote Witch Falls, which were about thirty kilometers away. We went down a hill until we reached a canyon populated with firs and pine trees. I realized we were in the Apache Kid Wilderness, the place where I got lost following an owl when I was camping with Alma. The Apache Kid Mountain peak was located northeast on the path we were traversing, except that we were moving in the opposite direction. We descended through the forest until we reached a place populated by ponderosa pines. Then we passed near a rocky picacho where we saw a herd of deer. When we got to the base of a canyon, I knew we were at the place where I camped with Alma. There we rested for a few moments. The animals drank water and grazed for a while. I had to quench my thirst using the reed tube, because my lips couldn't touch anything else when I drank water. While Refugio set out to look for some herb he was going to use for that night's ceremony, he left me there sharpening his knife.

I sat on a rock. It was a slate blade knife with a wooden handle secured with a sisal string. As I was sharpening it, I remembered that ill-fated morning when Alma left me right here on our way to Truth or Consequences. This time, however, everything was different. Interestingly, my means of transport was a mule who claimed to be me. I was accompanied by my tutor and "brother," a shaman of dreams, and was heading to some falls where I was going to be cured of a rare disease caused by an owl. If all went well, I was not only going to be cured but, according to Lucius, I was going to be able to get to my place of origin. My return home depended in part on Refugio's help and, above all, on my ability to defeat my ghostly enemy. I wondered what would have happened if, on that distant afternoon, I hadn't gone out looking for a spotted owl in the Apache Kid Wilderness. I came to the obvious conclusion, which at the time seemed like a divine revelation to me, that I would never have had this dream. My life would have followed a very different course. I wouldn't have had a bad night lost in the woods, nor would I have awakened Alma the next morning. She wouldn't have gotten up in a bad mood. On the way to Truth or Consequences, I would have calmly explained everything to her and would have admitted my own transgression. Maybe she would have forgiven me for reading her diaries without her permission, and then she wouldn't have left me nor killed herself. Everything would have been so different, and I wouldn't have had this nightmare.

Refugio returned pleased that he had found the herb he was looking for and we continued our expedition. We walked part of the winding trail I took with Alma in Goldfinch, my Toyota pickup. We passed by La Questa de Trujillo and continued our descent along the path of the Red Rock Arroyo Canyon. However, before crossing the boundary of Cíbola National Park, we turned right and ascended again in a northeasterly direction along the path of the Placitas Creek Canyon. We crossed the Calvario Draw, whose stream flowed near Monticello. We skirted the source of the Arroyo del Cedro and crossed its canyon until, finally, we saw the Coyote Witch Falls, whose perennial waters flowed into the stream of the Cañada Alamosa. The latter, Refugio told me, channeled the sacred waters of the Ojo Caliente spring and poured them into the Río del Norte, the cardinal vein of the N'nee Nation.

As we approached the falls, he told me the story of the Coyote Witch and the bats.[6]

A pack of coyotes had been partying for several days. Tired of reveling, they arrived and camped near Standing Rock, he told me, pointing at Vick's Peak. In this place lived one of the party-animal coyotes who had a beautiful wife and mother-in-law. Every time the coyotes visited Standing Rock, they challenged one another to climb it and, when one of them did, it would grow so much it touched the sky. Then they would ask the rock to become small again so that the daring coyote that had climbed it could come down. One day one of the coyotes who wanted to sleep with his fellow coyote's wife dared him to climb the rock. He accepted the challenge not only to prove his fearlessness but also to increase his reputation as a witch, because his friends knew that he had slept with his mother-in-law. Refugio explained to me that those who slept with their mother-in-law were surely witches. However, for some reason, once the rock rose, it did not shrink back and left the coyote witch up there. Several days passed and the Coyote Witch remained trapped at the top of the mountain. The pack of coyotes couldn't wait for him any longer because the entire band of coyotes needed to move on. Meanwhile, the Coyote Witch's party friend took advantage of his absence to seduce his wife. The Coyote Witch had almost given up trying to go down the mountain when a flock of bats flew past him. The Coyote Witch yelled at them, "Hey, bat friends, I need help." They didn't hear him until he called them four times. Then one of them answered his call and, flying in spirals above him, asked him how he could help him. The Coyote Witch begged him, "Old friend, can you carry me and get me out of here?" He replied, "You are very heavy. Besides, what if we fall?" But the Coyote Witch begged him and implored with such fervor that the bat agreed to help him. He went for help and returned with three fellow bats. They brought with them a basket which they were carrying with a very fine thread. The coyote inspected the basket and, observing that the thread was just a filament, said to them, "What kind of thread is this? It's going to break and I'm going to fall." But the leading bat assured him, "This thread never breaks."

Then the coyote asked them to do a test with some rocks. They accepted and put four big ones in the basket. The bats lifted the heavy basket and, when the coyote verified that the thread didn't break, he said, "Alright. I'm going to get in." He removed the rocks from the basket and, when he got in, the leading bat warned him, "You need to close your eyes when you're inside the basket and must keep them closed until we get you down. If you open them, we'll fall down and crash." The coyote said, "Okay." He climbed, closed his eyes, and the bats lifted the basket with the coyote inside. The coyote began to shout, "Rock, stick, stick, stick. Rock, stick, stick, stick." He kept repeating this all the way, and when they were getting closer to the bottom, he exclaimed, "I can't take it anymore. I have to look." The bat said, "Don't open your eyes. We'll crash to smithereens." However, the coyote insisted, "I have to." The four bats begged him not to open his eyes, but the coyote did not listen to them, so all five collided against the rocks. "With the impact," Refugio concluded, pointing toward the falls, "they made that slit in the canyon and are buried forever deep in earth."

"Later we're gonna enter the cave through the canyon slit. You'll see," he ended his tale.

Refugio explained to me that his band spent the winters in Sonora and told lots of stories at night by the fire. He confessed he would have preferred to be with his people, but he said he had agreed with Nant'an Chilmo to cure me away from Ojo Caliente because some band members believed that I was a witch. Not only did they not trust me because I was a Nakaiyé and an alleged witch but also because I was Don Juan de Mendoza's godson. They feared that my godfather wanted to enslave them, as former governor Felipe Sotelo Ossorio did to their Navajo brothers shortly after Refugio was born. He explained that his father, Captain Don Bartolomé Romero—that is, my paternal great-grandfather—persuaded some members of the Navajo Nation to go to Santa Fe to see a statue of the Virgin Mary because they thought she might be Changing Woman. However, when this group of Navajo people arrived in Santa Fe, Christian Tewa, associated with Governor Ossorio and his gang of slave traffickers, attacked them. Several Navajo brothers were killed; the others were kidnapped by the governor's gang and sold in Parral. He told me that some of them didn't want me around because I wanted to change their language, customs, and beliefs and force them to live in villages. But now that he had made me his brother, he assured me I was no longer going to serve the Nakaiyé. From now on I was going to learn to love, respect, and serve Mother Earth and all her children equally. That's why we had come to Coyote Witch Canyon.

He told me that in this place he received his power when he was a dikohe. He came with his maternal grandfather, who was from Dinétah, the country of the Navajo. He brought him here to dream and learn to write his dreams on rocks. Here he spent ten days without eating and learned to listen to Mother Earth and her creatures. He said that this mountain was his school for a period of four years. Here he learned everything he knew. Plants, trees, and animals told him many secrets.

"There's lots of power and mystery here, and also danger. The mountains give health and strength. Thanks to them, N'nee and Diné people prosper. Dziłcho, this mountain, takes care of Łíhéne people. When I was a dikohe, I came here with Shiwóyé Hastiin, my maternal grandfather. *Dziłntsa* is the house of the Mountain People. Here is also an entrance to the Kingdom of Dá'its'inzhá. One night I went down the Coyote Witch's cave to Dá'its'inzhá's house. A Mountain Spirit took me there. He said to me: 'Nant'an of the Underworld is very dangerous and powerful. Don't show him any fear if you want his help. Fear can be your worst enemy or your best ally. Treat fear like an ally, not like an enemy. Fear has power, both good and bad. It depends on how you use it. Never show fear to the Nant'an of the Underworld.' The Mountain Spirit also told me: 'When Nant'an of the Underworld asks you how you got there, reply, "I came with a Mountain Spirit." When he asks you, "Who are you?" answer him, "I'm a child of Father Son and

Mother Earth." And, this is very important, when he asks, "What do you want?" respond, "Health and happiness for my people."' That night, when I went to the Underworld"—Refugio continued his story—"I followed the advice of the Mountain Spirit. When he asked me, 'Whose ceremony do you wish to receive to help your people?' I replied, 'The Mountain People's ceremony.' He said, 'Good choice. Mountain People are benevolent and powerful. Mountain People will help you bring health and happiness to your tribe.'"

34

WE ARRIVED AT COYOTE WITCH FALLS WELL BEFORE DUSK. FORTUnately, it was neither snowy nor as cold there. As soon as we unloaded, Refugio asked me to gather plenty of oak branches to build our chagoch'o, as well as juniper and spruce branches—"not pine!"—to make a barrier around the hut. He told me where to find them to speed up my task, as the sun was going to set soon. I was starving and would have preferred to have dinner first, but I had to shut up and obey. Meanwhile, Refugio made all the preparations for the healing ceremony.

The hut was going to serve us both as a tent and as a sweathouse. Before starting the ceremony, it was essential to cleanse myself by taking a sweat bath first and a cold bath afterward. Once I gathered the necessary materials, we built the hut, covered it with buffalo hides, and surrounded it with branches. Then he asked me to bring big rocks and pile them near the entrance to the hut. When I asked him, using signs, how many, he retorted, "*Doo ałch'í-dé!*" which meant, "Not a few, but many!" Worst of all, he ordered me not to drink any water until I was finished.

I had a hard time finding and hauling the rocks. The good thing was that I discovered a collapsed bluff close to the creek. Thanks to it, I was able to drink enough water surreptitiously.

Once I finished this task, I was more than ready to eat roasted rabbit. However, Refugio told me it was time for my sweat bath and asked me to undress. He put a band of braided sage on my head, covered me from head to toe with the smoke of a rosemary bouquet, daubed me all over with crushed juniper needles, and spit on me mesquite bean water. After the cleansing he gave me a mug of mesquite water, a jug full of water, my reed tube, and my stick. He reminded me that I had to use them if I wanted to drink water or scratch myself and ordered me to enter the hut.

He had already lit a campfire and had put some stones in it to heat them up. While Refugio sang a prayer, I put the reed tube in the mug, drank some mesquite water, and waited. Once one of the rocks was burning hot, he rolled it into the hut using a stick. He told me I had to pour water from the jar on all the rocks he would bring inside. Then he closed the curtain. After pouring water on several rocks, the hut filled with steam, and I began to sweat profusely. I drank all the mesquite water and drank all the remaining water from the jug and scratched myself with the dikohe stick until I drew blood.

After half an hour the heat became unbearable. I couldn't wait any longer and tried to get out of the hut, but Refugio was guarding the exit and told me I had to stay inside longer. Every second that passed by was a torment. I knew I couldn't disobey or disappoint Refugio. I did my absolute best to stay there until he allowed me to exit. But when I felt nauseous and realized I would pass out if I stayed there a minute longer, I ran out straight to the fall's pond and dove into the icy cold water.

My heart was pounding as if I were going to have a heart attack. To avoid it, and to vent out my shock, I issued a Mexican grito that came out from the bottom of my being:

"UUUIYAAAAAAYAAAAAHAAAAAHAAAAEEEEEEEEE!!!!!!"

The treatment produced an unexpected cathartic joy in me. Refugio was standing by the pond and, through jovial signs, prompted me to frolic for a while in those healing waters. He walked away and, soon after, returned to the pond beating the drum and singing.

By then I was hungry like a famished coyote. I longed for Refugio to tell me it was time to roast the other rabbit he had hunted that morning. To my disappointment and heartbreak, that plump delicacy, a symbol of fertility and innocence, was going to be our offering to the Coyote Witch. At the time it was not very comforting to hear that it was part of my training to learn to live intimately and prolongedly with hunger and thirst. It also didn't do me much good to know that the sacrificial rabbit was going to try to persuade the Coyote Witch to intercede for me before the Lord of the Underworld to persuade him to placate his wrath against me for being one of those hooded religious men who had come from yonder to seize his dominions. As Brother Antonio had warned me, the Prince of Darkness especially hated the religious people who dismissed the carnal, hierarchical, and legalistic Catholic Church, who embraced Discalced Franciscan practices, who wished to lead the itinerant life of Jesus and the first apostles, who aspired to found an authentic Franciscan utopia in New Mexico, and who longed for the arrival of the Third Age of the Holy Spirit in which the survivors of the Apocalypse were to regain their lost angelic nature after the Fall.

The offering to the Coyote Witch was simple and brief. After covering ourselves completely with cedar ash to make ourselves invisible and protect ourselves from evil spirits, we got dressed. He handed me the rabbit and took a forked branch with a bracket fungus on the tip covered in pine resin, which served as a torch. He lit it and we headed for the slot that the Coyote Witch made in the canyon when he fell with the bats. We entered the canyon through the slot and walked until we got to a narrow, deep hole where, Refugio assured me, there was a deep cavern that reached the Coyote Witch's lair in the Kingdom of Dá'its'inzhá. After briefly asking Coyote Witch to persuade the Great Lord to leave me alone,

I threw the rabbit into the hole. Then he pulled my cherished diary out of the inside of his cloak. He threw it into the hole without saying anything and we went deeper into the canyon. He told me he was going to show me a "very important place" for the novice diyin who went there to learn their "craft."

He led me through a narrow, zigzagging passageway that descended and got narrower and more impenetrable. I was terrified that at any moment we were going to run into a coyote den, or afraid that maybe Refugio had brought me to that place to kill me. When it seemed that we had reached the end of the passageway, Refugio crouched down and entered a nook. I contemplated the possibility of returning, but that labyrinthine canyon was so dark and so intricate that I decided to follow Refugio. We went through and walked on our knees through a tunnel that was even narrower than the passageway we had just crossed. The smoke from the torch was making our breathing difficult. I began to suffocate and feel claustrophobic when we finally reached the chamber of a cavern.

Refugio got up and walked to the center of the cave chamber. He raised the torch to better illuminate the walls.

"Cave walls are the notebook of the diyin," he declared as I was standing up, stunned by that exhibition of pictorial art.

There were printed hands, spiral labyrinths, anthropomorphic figures, animals, fantastical beings, hunting scenes and weapons, war scenes, celestial bodies, geometric figures, and a variety of hieroglyphs.

"Look." He approached one of the walls and asked me to get close to where he was standing. He illuminated one of the pictograms with the torch and said, "You wrote this, Shidizé."

I didn't quite understand what he was telling me. I was confused and uneasy. The pictogram consisted of a series of rectangular blocks of various sizes arranged at irregular intervals that made me think of the capricious merlons of a Moorish mansion.

"Dziłcho," he told me with the expression of someone who spoke with full knowledge of some arcane mystery.

The name sounded familiar, but I didn't recognize it. I got close to examine the pictogram. It traced the contour of a cityscape. On the contour of the irregular rectangles of the buildings was a curved, trembling line, the meaning of which I did not understand. I drew the length of this line with the index finger and looked at it by making a grimace of interrogation.

"Sierra Sandía," he told me.

I looked at the line carefully and saw that, indeed, the pictogram traced the outline of the Albuquerque skyline.

"Shidizé wrote down this dream in another time."

"Have I been here already?" I asked using gestures.

"Shidizé has come back here to solve a personal matter."

"What personal matter?" I asked, again with gestures.

"That's what you must discover, Dhidizé. Let's go. Soon the torch will go out."

As soon as we got back, he prepared the instruments for the ceremony in which he was going to summon the Mountain Spirits and ask them to exorcise my Enemy Ghost. The main implements were the campfire, the dream catcher, Refugio's black knife, and a rattle stick he made with a cedar branch, a snake's rattle, and eagle and falcon feathers. He rubbed the rattle with scorched medicinal herbs and red ochre mixed with grease. The rattle stick and the knife embodied the qualities and powers of the Warrior Twins, and the dream catcher deterred nightmares and stimulated auroral dreams. In these kinds of dreams, he explained, we received or found something valuable; for example, information about how to cure an illness, or when and where the enemy planned to attack.

"In these dreams we understand and speak foreign languages. Sometimes we travel to another world and live another life. We can also meet our killer. In a *hayołkaałyú* dream we can receive a ceremony as well. I received the Enemy Ghost ceremony in a hayołkaałyú dream here in this mountain."

When we entered the hut, Refugio consecrated the knife and the dream catcher with songs. He hung the dream catcher by the door, and he put the knife under the blanket that I was using as a pillow. He asked me to take off my moccasins, and he anointed my feet, hands, forehead, eyelids, nose, lips, ears, and other points on my head and body with cattail pollen. He told me he was going to sing and play the drum all night long. If the Mountain People came to his invocation and accepted his request, he stressed that it was vitally important that I not leave the hut nor attempt to see them under any circumstances. This would infuriate them and would cause us both a terrible misfortune, he warned me. And if the spirits agreed to help me, they would give me precise instructions in one of my dreams. He gave me the rattle stick and asked me to shake it to the rhythm of the drum and to use it as a cudgel to kill my ghostly enemy. He warned me that the Dream Sorcerer was going to resort to all kinds of tricks to prevent my healing. But he assured me that I had the power to defeat him no matter how powerful and cunning he was. He served me a strong, pungent tea that made me nauseous and, as soon as I finished it, he asked me to go to sleep. He told me I was probably going to have some terrible visions. To avoid them, he recommended that I think of prickly pears, plums, and melons.

35

I SLEPT DEEPLY ALL NIGHT LONG. AT LEAST, I THOUGHT SO. BEFORE dawn, the beating of a drum awakened me. It was marking the rhythm of a martial dance. I was still exhausted and had a migraine, so I closed my eyes again. Despite the drumbeats, I fell asleep immediately. At some point I had one of my usual nightmares.

"Diego, wake up," Brother Antonio urged me. "The time has come! Your godfather and all your relatives are waiting for you in the Field of Truth."

I was sleeping in an outdoor military camp on a desert plain. I was a pikeman of a Spanish *tercio* commanded by my godfather, Maestre de Campo Don Juan de Mendoza, and formed by all my Old World ancestors. I had been assigned a position on the very last line of the rear guard due to my lethargy and incompetence. I had not been discharged and sent to the Holy Brotherhood dungeon only because my great-grandfather, Captain Don Bartolomé Romero, Refugio's father, was convinced that I would not let them down. The enemy front was formed by all my Native American ancestors and relatives. We were about to start the attack, but I hadn't joined my unit yet. My morion, my short sword, and my pike were lying next to me. I had my armor on, and, under the rusty breastplate, I wore a frayed and dirty white shirt with a fleur-de-lis red cross on the front. My yellow breeches were smudged; my red tights, faded; my cordobán shoes, unpolished.

Brother Antonio was shaking and telling me that the maestre de campo had given him permission to try to persuade me to join my unit. I got up and contemplated the battlefield. Both armies were almost ready for combat on the endless desert plain. The north wind began to blow.

"Brother," I said, "when I see all my relatives and ancestors here on this battlefield, my mind is in a quandary, and I am paralyzed by horror. I feel unease and infinite sorrow."

"Abandon that ungodly timidity and join your company. Don't give in to that pernicious impotence. Cowards don't conquer eternal goods. I am also sorry for making war on them, but it is for the salvation of their souls since they do not want to accept Jesus in their hearts. Even if it is by the force of arms, God will forgive us if we convert just one of them. After all our sacrifices and efforts, they have been very foolish and unwilling to convert. And now, on top of it, several of them have revolted and killed many of our brothers and sisters. Behold yourself," he said, looking at me from head to toe as if I were a specter. "They have finished you off too. We will only kill those who resist and refuse to swear allegiance to the king and the pope and fidelity to our Holy Faith and the Holy Mother Church. To the meek of spirit, we will offer mercy and eternal life in the Kingdom of God."

"I'm not capable of killing anyone," I replied. "I don't want to punish or force anyone to convert. I don't want to be received in any kingdom founded on injustice, in this world or in any other."

"A war that opens the gates of Heaven to the unbelievers is worth making. It is a holy war that God sees with good eyes, for the power of Christ will heal the soul of these idolaters. When they accept Christ's medicine and are welcome to his eternal kingdom, they will understand why we converted them. They'll be like the sick that we take to the doctor by force to cure them."

"No war can be called holy or just. A righteous God cannot tolerate the conquest or forced conversion of anyone."

"The war against the servers of the Infernal Enemy is both holy and just. It's a battle for their own good and ours. To renounce this battle is cowardice and disloyalty to God and the fatherland."

At that precise moment, my godfather approached us, galloping on his white stallion. He interrupted us with blunt severity:

"So, this weakling does not want to do his duty? Captain Romero!" he yelled, demanding the presence of my great-grandfather.

"Yes, Maestre." He arrived on the scene immediately.

"Impale this coward!"

My great-grandfather obeyed dutifully and, like a lancer in a bullfight, he charged at me. Without mercy and without looking me in the eye, he thrust a spear right into my heart.

The earth swallowed me. I descended through a dark tunnel and fell on a mound of sand. I palpated my body. To my surprise, I didn't have a single scratch. I touched the spear wound with my fingertips and noticed I wasn't bleeding. That's weird, I thought. I looked around and noticed that I was in an immense cavern.

Toward the north end there was an exit. I crawled on my butt down the mound, stood up, ran down toward the exit, crossed a threshold, and ascended through a dark, labyrinthine corridor. After a grueling and distressing ascent, the passageway brightened up and, finally, I saw the exit.

I found myself at the bottom of a huge, arid canyon. The sky was gray, as if leaden with overcast, but there were neither clouds nor fog. It was a sunless, moonless, starless, dull sky. Near me was a huge granite tower that looked like a Gothic cathedral. I walked toward it. At the base of this tower was a gap from which smoke was coming out. I got closer and noticed that there was a four-rung ladder that led to an underground dwelling, and I decided to go down.

"Come in, come in, Son," a tender female voice said to me as I was descending the ladder. She was sitting by the edge of a chair, warming her hands in front of the fireplace. She was a thin old lady with a sad look and a fragile but healthy appearance. She had long hair and wore a flowery pink blouse with wide sleeves, a long, red cotton skirt, and a black wool shawl. Her neck and chest were adorned with various turquoise bead necklaces and a human-shaped, wooden amulet.

"We've been waiting for you. You're finally back. I thought you'd forgotten us."

I didn't know what to say to her, of course. I'd never seen this woman before.

"You look at me like you don't remember me, Diego. I'm Flora, your wetnurse. I raised you until you became a young man. When your mother died, you went to the City of Palaces with your father. Why are you blowing on your hands?" she asked me, looking puzzled.

"I'm cold," I replied and kept blowing on my knuckles.

"Did you bring the tobacco and the food?"

"No, I wasn't aware I needed to bring anything. I am sorry."

"What? Didn't Concha tell you?"

"Concha?"

"Yes, Concha. Didn't she give you tobacco and food for the trip?"

"Oh, yes, she did." I remembered the pouch and the bag that Concha Baxcajay gave me when I departed from Senecú. "I'm sorry, I forgot them."

"Don't worry. Those things happen."

"I just had an accident. Look."

I unbuttoned my shirt to show her my wound and justify my forgetfulness.

"Let me see. Yes, it is a mortal wound. I see why you've come," she said, putting her warm, trembling right hand on my wound. "What happened to you?"

"They impaled me with a spear."

"Who?"

"My great-grandfather."

"Don Bartolomé?"

"Yes, him."

"Oh, gosh. Don Bartolomé. Always so zealous about his duty. He was always afraid they'd find out he was a Crypto-Jew. Like many other Siervos de Dios, he came to these lands seeking his tribe, the descendants of a certain Manasseh. According to him, Manasseh is our patriarch too, and that of all Athapascan people. Can you believe that?"

At that point a tall and heavyset man in his sixties with long hair came out from another chamber. He was wearing a loose red shirt and a white, cotton, skirt-like breechcloth fastened with a leather belt.

"Demetrio, look who's here," she said.

He examined me from the back of the room with a piercing look and an expression of mistrust, though without hostility.

"Who is it? Do I know him?"

"Come closer. It's Diego."

"Don Valerio's son?"

"He's grown so much, but he's still the same old *ich-kiín*. Isn't he?"

He grabbed me by the forearms and, shaking me slightly, said to me mockingly, "What wind brought you here? It must have been a spinning one, one of those sinister winds that blow where the world ends. Just look at you. You're unrecognizable. You look like a feeble whirlwind. We're going to have to ask the Holy Wind to send us a gentle, calm wind to invigorate you."

I just smiled.

"Are you sure this is Diego?"

"How can I not know if I breastfed him myself?"

"Then what are you waiting for? Bring him the soup."

Flora got up and went to the kitchen. She immediately brought a steaming hot pot. She put it on a palm leaf rug in front of me.

"Do you have any good wishes for your family members?" Demetrio asked me as I looked at the tantalizing soup.

I just stared at him without knowing what to answer.

"Do you have a request?" he insisted.

"No," I said cluelessly. All I wanted was to eat soup. It looked delicious and I had a voracious appetite.

"He came ill-prepared," Demetrio told Flora.

She shrugged and gestured incomprehension. I didn't care. I grabbed the spoon, dolloped some soup, blew on it, and slurped it with gusto.

"Why are you blowing this time, Diego?" Flora asked me, puzzled again.

"Because it's too hot."

She made a grimace of disapproval and Demetrio frowned.

"But it's delicious," I added to justify myself.

After a tense pause, exacerbated by my blowing and slurping, Flora remarked to Demetrio in disbelief:

"He blows cold and hot with the same breath."

"That's his problem, no?"

"One proposes, Ussen disposes."

I didn't worry and kept eating until I was full. When I finished, I said, rubbing my tummy:

"Thank you very much. It's the most delicious soup I've ever had. What is it made of?"

"Hope, Diego. What else?" Flora said.

"It's obvious he doesn't know where he is," said Demetrio.

"Do you know where you are, Son?"

"No, I really don't know. I came here by accident. I'm lost."

"You're on the Edge of the World," Flora said. "You came ill-prepared. It's not your destiny to cross to the other side yet. You'll first need to learn your sacred obligations and fulfill them."

"What sacred obligations?"

"You don't know what your sacred obligations are? What did they teach you in school?" Demetrio asked.

"Sadly, we're going to have to send you back to the River, *mijito*," said Flora.

At this juncture a group of elders came into the chamber. They behaved as if they were members of a commission. They looked at me as if I were an alien and started interrogating me.

"Who is this white face, dressed like us?" asked an old man with a twangy voice.

"He came from far away," Flora replied.

"Could he be the Great Gambler? Has he returned from the Other Side to enslave our children?" the old man asked.

"We don't want him here," an old woman with a hoarse voice said. "He must leave."

"He's not the Gambler," a man who sounded exactly like Refugio intervened in my defense. "Is he wearing a turquoise talisman on his chest or a blue feather in his hair? Do you see him chewing devil's gum? Has he invited anyone to gamble or to play a competitive game with anyone? Have you seen him throw the bow, or play with hoops, or burn kneecaps and make holes to hide them?"

"No, but they say he was struck by lightning," an old man with a weak voice said.

"And his eyelid and jaw tremble when he speaks," another man said.

"I heard him speak in a strange language that sounds like coyote barks," the woman with the hoarse voice added.

"He has the mark of Caesar," the twangy-voiced man said. "He speaks Spanish and was baptized; he must believe that the leader of his people is a god."

"He is not like the other Nakaiyé," asserted the man who sounded like Refugio. "Now he only believes in man. He also confessed to me that he comes from the future, from a powerful country called the United States of America. That is why he also speaks English, the language of its inhabitants, the *Magáání*, but in his veins runs *Chichimeca* blood. He revealed to me that the Magáání, some white-eyed beings from the north that are far more powerful than the Nakaiyé, will invade our territory and steal our movement. They will cram us in villages and arrest our movement and lifestyle."

"This Nakaiyé must be a messenger of the wind," said the old man with the weak voice.

"I consulted with my power, and it informed me that he also has a few drops of Diné blood and that he was born in Na'nízhoozhí, in Dinétah, the land of the Navajo," said the man who sounded like Refugio.

"Was he born in Bridge?" asked the man with the weak voice.

"Yes," said Flora.

"Then this Nakaiyé was shaped by good winds," stated the man with the weak voice.

"He was born with a calm but firm inner wind. The Dark Wind of the East instilled in him knowledge of the good. The Southern Blue Wind gave him the power of movement. The Yellow Wind of the West gave him moral reasoning. The Northern White Wind gave him courage and resolve. Mother Earth has given him good health and Father Sun has regulated his habits well," Flora explained.

"I wonder what happened to him," said Demetrio.

"Harmful winds disoriented and weakened him," said the man who sounded like Refugio. "It must have been Striped Wind and Coiled Wind. They blew foreign ideas up his nose; he is an avid reader and has inhaled too much humanistic dust. He's among those who think that Mother Nature has nothing to teach him and believes all wisdom is stored in libraries. Although he stopped believing in what the Bible says, he still believes he can find wisdom and truth in books. He's wasted the best of his adult life inhaling the dust of moldy paper. By seeking wisdom in books, he has not fulfilled his sacred obligations. His body is weak, his mind cloudy, his spirit fatigued, and he does nothing for the welfare of his people."

"Just look at the poor guy. Both his body and his spirit are debilitated. He probably never breathes fresh air, and he hardly ever absorbs the sun's rays," said Demetrio.

"He had great literary ambitions," stated the man who sounded like Refugio. "He wanted to write the great border novel. But writing it, he wanted at the same time to achieve liberation. Writing his novel was for him a process of knowing himself and reconciling with the history of his people. And the worst part is he didn't even get to know himself. He wanted to know everything, but he never wanted to know his own history, nor his origins, nor his own nature. Like a hummingbird, he went from flower to flower, picking a little knowledge here and a little knowledge there, but never arrived at any conclusion about anything. Ever since he got here, he's been more lost than ever."

"Let's ask him some questions to see what he knows," said the old woman with the hoarse voice.

"Yes, let's examine him," stated the twangy-voiced old man.

"Let's see, Dreamer. Tell us who you are and what the path to well-being and beauty are."

I would have wanted to try to answer, but I was paralyzed and drawing a blank.

"What is or who are your creators?"

"Ussen and Mother Earth?"

"Other deities?"

"Why are you here?"

"Who or what brought you here?"

"What is your origin and your destiny?"

"How can you get out of your dream state?"

"You see. I told you," the man who spoke like Refugio interrupted the interrogation. "He ignores the most basic elements of his condition and existence. And the worst part is someone stole his speech."

"Who was it?"

"Well, who else can it be?" said the woman with the hoarse voice. "It must have been his Catholic conscience. He got deathly afraid when his lucid mind was searching for his ulterior abode."

"Yes, that's what happens to all the cowardly apostates," said the man with the twangy voice. "When their time comes, they're deathly afraid to cross the River. A Christian sentinel appeared to him on his way to the other side and persuaded him to bathe in the waters of the Id. Since then the Catholic Spirit has once again taken over his conscience."

"At least he didn't allow the Franciscan to brainwash him," said Flora.

"Yes, but he came here to try to brand our children with the mark of Caesar," said the twangy-voiced man.

"We don't want him here," said the woman with the hoarse voice.

"Let's send him back to the River so that the gods of his ancestors judge him," said the twangy-voiced man.

"Duty compels us to help the needy, even if he is the son of our enemies," said the man who sounded like Refugio. "Besides, although he's an unbeliever and a consummate skeptic, he seems to understand us. Let's help him first before sending him off."

"I agree with All Covered With Pollen. Let's help him first."

"Alright. And how about you, Woman Who Always Walks Straight. Do you agree?"

"If that's what you want, I don't object," said the woman with the hoarse voice.

"Alright. Let's give him a ceremony to perform in the world of the sleepy ones," said the man with the twangy voice.

"Let's offer him a simple ceremony of the Song of the Holy Winds," said the man with the weak voice.

"Great idea!" the man who spoke as Refugio exclaimed.

"Agreed," they all said.

"You dictate it to him, All Covered With Pollen."

"Alright. I'll do it," said the man who sounded like Refugio.

"Let's see, Stranger. Pay attention. Don't forget my instructions, as this will cure you."

All Covered With Pollen must be Refugio, I thought to myself. Why did he call me stranger if we were spiritual brothers? "Don't you remember me, Shidizé?" I tried to protest, but I was muted and paralyzed.

"When you return to the Other Side, tell Refugio your dream and ask him to help you make the following offering to the four Beneficial Winds," All Covered With Pollen instructed me. "Spread the hide of a newly sacrificed fallow deer on the ground and place prayer sticks in all four directions: one pointing eastward, with an elm stick painted black and adorned with a crow feather; another pointing south, made of oak, painted blue, and adorned with a Mexican jay feather; another pointing west, made with a cattail stalk, painted yellow, and adorned with a goldfinch feather; and another pointing north, with a birch stick, painted white, and adorned with a white-tailed kite feather. Drill the top of each stick and daub tobacco into each hole. Spread cattail pollen in all four directions. First, take the oak stick, light the tobacco, and, looking east, utter the following words with all devotion: 'Dark Wind, you who travel the earth's surface, I make this offering to you. Today you must strengthen my body, clear my mind, purify my spirit, and restore my speech. Let me be at peace wherever I go. Take me down the path of beauty and happiness. Don't leave me.' Pray the same prayer to the South Blue Wind, the Yellow West Wind, and the Northern White Wind. When you're finished, sing to the rhythm of the drum this sacred song:

"The Dark Wind is here,
the Son of Jet is here.
The Blue Wind is here,
the Son of Turquoise is here.
The Yellow Wind is here,
The Son of Amber is here.
The White Wind is here,
the Son of Quartz is here.
Blessed be the Holy Winds."

After giving me these instructions, they kept talking to each other. In the meantime, I did a mental review of the prayers and song to make sure I would not forget them.

"Then the prophecy of the *Natagé* is going to be fulfilled," the old man with the weak voice said. "They say that before the end of the world, white-eyed beings will invade our territory and the N'nee survivors will adopt their ways and customs. They will cut their hair and dress like the white eyes and will not be distinguished from the Nakaiyé. No one will scatter pollen in rivers anymore or collect sacred soil from the mountains. The mountains will no longer give them health and strength. The Holy People will abandon them. They will become Christians and forget all the songs and ceremonies that help keep Mother Earth healthy and beautiful. The children of the Naayéé will poison the rivers with their waste and desecrate all our sacred sites. Winds in all four directions will no longer be able to drive away the Revolving Wind, or the Wind of the Wild Beasts. All enemy and dangerous winds will be loose and will do a lot of damage to everyone."

After verifying that I perfectly remembered the prayers and song I had been given, I began to worry if I would be able to remember them when I woke up. I knew I had enjoyed a privileged memory until then, but I wasn't sure I was going to remember my dreams as accurately as I did in Senecú.

"What if I forget the ceremony?"

"The Natagé sages did not speak incorrectly," All Covered With Pollen interjected. "I once had a dream in which the N'nee lived with the white eyed in villages with houses so high that they reached the sky. We were all traveling in cars pulled by tin horses and fed with blood drawn from the bowels of our Mother Earth. Silver giants capable of reaching the moon and the stars flew the skies. Their weapons were more powerful than lightning and more destructive than tornadoes. The children of the Naayéé had stolen and invaded our territory. They had learned to control the Wind of Wild Beasts and caused great harm to Mother Earth and all of her creatures."

"What happened to our people in the past will be repeated," said one of the elders. "Their enemies also lived in houses located in the heights. They allied themselves with the Naayéé, who taught them to fly like birds and travel on the back of lightning. They enslaved our children. They forced them to haul wood, water, and stones on their backs for long distances and to perform all kinds of heavy labor without paying them and forcing them to endure thirst and hunger. They were proud, arrogant, and greedy like the Nakaiyé; they had large herds of animals enclosed in their land; they sowed and stored corn, beans, pumpkins, and cotton; they built large houses located on cliffs that protected them from their enemies and the elements. They were very ingenious. They learned to control the winds and to harness power from the mountains, caves, rivers, and seas. They became as numerous as ants. But the richer and more powerful they grew, the more disrespectful they became. They altered the traditional symbols. They redesigned their ceramics, baskets, and fabrics. They painted inverted rays and rainbows, twisted winds, and all sorts of sinister figures in their household items and clothing. They forgot who they were; they neglected their parents and their creators; they stopped caring for the sick and the elderly and warred with one another. They defiled all that is sacred. They found their demise when they disrespected Killer of Enemies and Child of Water. Just as they did in another time when they defeated the Naayéé, the Warrior Twins traveled to the house of Father Sun to request his help to get rid of their enemies. Father Sun granted them their wish and began to burn more than ever. The entire Holy Family helped him. They denied their enemies all their pleas. They sent drought, famine, and all kinds of pestilence and disasters that slowly decimated them. Until, finally, Father Sun sent a great fire storm that ravaged the canyons and the cliffs where our ancestral enemies lived. The Oscura Mountains, White Sands, all the Badlands, and the black stripes that cover the gorges and rocks of our territory are traces of that cataclysm."

Then I started to worry about how the hell I was going to find the materials for the ceremony. I knew I would have no problem getting tobacco and cattail pollen, as Refugio carried them with him all the time as if his life depended on it. Elm, oak, and birch sticks and cattail stalks wouldn't be hard to gather either. But the exotic feathers. Where was I going to obtain them?

36

THE SOUND OF A DRUM INTERRUPTED MY DREAM AND WOKE ME up. I kept my eyes closed to try to fall back asleep and the same old questions began to bug me: Why was this happening to me? Why was I suffering from these nightmares and misfortunes? It was as if I had been looking for these dreadful things. Sometimes I felt like someone was testing me. Suddenly, I heard a voice that said into my ear:

"Do you really want to know who's testing you?"

I opened my eyes to find out who said this. For an instant I thought it was Refugio, but I was alone in the hut. Moreover, the sound of the drum came from afar. If Refugio had been playing it, it couldn't have been his voice.

Although I felt afraid, I mustered my courage, got up, and took a cautious peek. But there was no one outside. I laughed and told myself it was just my imagination. I came out of the hut and briefly explored the surroundings. But I couldn't locate Refugio. I decided to go back to the hut and try to fall asleep again. I was dead tired.

When I was almost asleep, I heard the same voice again. It whispered in my ear like it was telling me a secret.

"Listen, Uriel."

But this time, for some reason, I couldn't get up. I couldn't open my eyes or move either. I was paralyzed again, as had happened to me in my previous dream.

Soon I began to hear a cacophony of unintelligible sounds, as happens in an auditorium when the lights have just been turned off and a performance is about to start. Gradually the murmurs diminished, and a strange colloquy began to gain clarity and volume.

". . . due to changes in the penal code, the whole process is long delayed. I doubt we'll be able to bring your lawsuit to court any time soon."

"The truth is everybody's afraid of him."

"We want justice, Your Honor."

"Give us back our lands!"

The voices sounded like normal human beings. A group of people argued with an official. What was weird were their names, their titles, and the formality with which they spoke to each other, as if they were high dignitaries.

"Honorable Lord Skeleton, Honorable Deities of New Mexico, I understand you are frustrated because we have not resolved your lawsuit, but in this supreme court you must act respectfully. We have a tremendous workload. We can't keep up with all the lawsuits of land invasion and dispossession, and so much crime."

"We're tired of your excuses and pretexts. We need our territories back."

"Honorable Deities of the Native Peoples of New Mexico, I recommend that you file a civil lawsuit. If you request vindicatory action, it is possible that you will get back both the territories and the souls of the subjects they took away from you. Seek the advice of an actuary. If you win the lawsuit, they should be able to help you get rid of the goods and the buildings you don't wish to keep. The actuary can also help you request troops of the Confederation to expel the invaders."

At that moment someone with a deep voice arrived and said in an arrogant tone:

"Good evening, Your Honor. I have been called to appear again before this supreme court of justice. Are these wretches still trying to take away what I've obtained legitimately through my own merit, as dictated by the supreme law of the cosmos?"

"Your Majesty, kindly be more respectful in this court. The law of the strongest does not rule in our sacred Confederation."

"Perhaps not in our Confederation, Your Honor, but in my dominions it does. These savages aim to reduce the size of my possessions, which are duly executed in title deeds. Let's see, Honorable Deities of New Mexico, do you have any documents proving that you are the rightful owners of the land in dispute?"

"We are entitled to these lands by the natural right of antiquity. We have been here for millennia. We are the aboriginal gods of the Pueblo people. Your Majesty and all the members of your royal court are outsiders."

"What does that have to do with anything, Honorable Lord Skeleton? We're working the land to produce. There are mines to explore and exploit. Isn't it written in our constitution that we all have the right to fill the earth and subdue it? You're squandering its resources. You want to take care of Mother Earth as if she hadn't died."

"She's alive, Your Majesty."

"Yes, she's alive."

"Don't make me laugh. If so, why isn't she active in this Confederacy then?"

"You know better than I do."

"And then why don't the stars help her?"

"Because they don't take care of our affairs. They're busy governing their own systems. They live locked up in their inner world, defending their own interests. They are as avid of power and veneration as the Unnamable and are subject to the same Axis that governs Him, you, and all of us. The only one who really cares about human welfare is Mother Earth."

"We are civilizing her aboriginals. What did she do when she was the queen and guardian of her progeny? She had her children immersed in barbarity, as if they were beasts. Instead, we are imbuing them with the classical spirit. We are infusing them with the spirit of romanitas and, indirectly, the wisdom of the Greeks and the Egyptians."

"You are right, Your Majesty. We taught almost everything to the Greeks and to you Romans, even if your subjects ignore it or pretend to ignore it."

"Under the tutelage of Mother Earth, her children could not even read or write. Now they have even come to know the Holy Scriptures."

"We know that Your Majesty fancies yourself pious, but under the cloak you're wearing armor, and your staff turns into a spear when you awaken the warrior spirit that always burns in your heart."

"And what do you want me to do, Honorable Spider Woman? I'm the most powerful war god on this planet. In my empire the sun never sets."

"That is true now, Your Majesty, but someone more powerful than you, a white-eyed giant, will vanquish and humiliate you as you are humiliating us."

"That remains to be seen. No one can beat our army and Invincible Armada. Now that you mention it, why don't you and your troops get into a skirmish with us? We'll crush you with our itsy-bitsy pinkies."

At that point, someone knocked on the door.

"Who is it?"

"Seshat, Your Honor," replied a feminine voice.

"Come in, Your Highness."

"Good evening, Your Majesty, Your Honor, Honorable New Mexican Deities. Please excuse the interruption."

"You're not interrupting us, Princess. Our meeting is over."

"Your Majesty, it's Honorable Princess Seshat, Mistress of the House of Books, even if you have a hard time saying it."

"Whatever you say, wise and honorable Princess, not for nothing you are goddess of charm and destiny."

"Your Honor, leader of the Ogdoad and supreme judge of this divine court: On the other side of the River there is a miserable mortal who is bent on returning to his place of origin. Nobody pities him or listens to him. The wind of karma dragged him to the origins of his hometown and is treating him rather harshly. To top it off, a malevolent genius is playing with his mind and tormenting him. He wants to know if any of us are testing him."

"Who is it, Honorable Princess Seshat?"

"He has no name, Your Honor. He's a commoner. He never published or created anything. He died without a testimony or trace of his existence."

I heard this with no small amount of shame. Did they know that I was listening to them?

"If no one hears his prayers, it must be for a reason. He who doesn't sow doesn't reap."

"He is an apostate Roman Catholic, Your Honor."

"Ah. So, it's settled. He's an unbeliever."

"Not necessarily, Your Honor. He suffers delusions of persecution by the gods. As we know, whoever suffers from this relentless torment has not really stopped believing in us. Moreover, on his desk he had a statuette of His Honor and a rubber stamp with an image of our sacred bird."

"If I may, Honorable Lady of Books, I can clear up this question."

"Please, Honorable Skeleton Lord. You do not need to ask for permission. We're peers. Enlighten us with your knowledge."

"Thank you, Your Highness. Honorable Princess Seshat, the mortal you're talking about stepped on my territory and remained in it without paying any tribute or making the smallest offering."

"Your former territory, that is."

"Your Majesty, Honorable Lord Mars, I beg you not to interrupt Lord Skeleton."

"As I was saying, Honorable Princess Seshat, I am the one who has been pestering this impious and disrespectful individual. But I'm satisfied. If he leaves my territory, I promise I'll never torture him again."

"Honorable Lady of Books, was this individual a subject of the Honorable Lord Skeleton?"

"Yes, Your Majesty, he is a member of the cosmic race. Like most members of this bronze lineage, a part of his soul served and worshipped different manifestations of his Divine Flayed Figure and many other deities of pre-Hispanic Mexico and New Mexico as well. The other part of his soul venerated and reverenced many of the deities of the Old World, especially Yahweh and Allah."

"Honorable Princess, in such a case, my scribes must have in their files the summation of all his good and evil deeds and intentions. They should be able to give you a report of his net worth. Have they weighed his heart yet?"

"Yes, Your Majesty. That's why I'm here. They need to decide whether to let him cross the River or throw him into the Netherworld. This individual's heart weighs a picogram more than the feather of truth."

"And what are his merits, Honorable Princess?"

"According to the report I received, he was only a dilettante, a lover of letters and wisdom who never produced or published anything of value. He devoted endless hours to writing a novel that remains unfinished. His entire legacy is a box of confusing, unpublishable notes of zero literary, humanistic, or scientific value, signed under the pretentious pseudonym of Neferkaphtah."

Her account only intensified my embarrassment and my desire to wake up so I could finish my novel and, hopefully, earn some merit worthy of their attention and consideration.

"Honorable Lady of Books, please don't waste our time. You know perfectly well what the fate of this wretched soul is. To be admitted to Limbo, it is necessary to have published or exhibited at least one artistic, literary, scientific, or humanistic work of value. Dabblers go straight to the Netherworld, unless one of us is willing to intercede for them."

"I do not want in my domain that soul contaminated by the spirit of the Invader."

"Don't worry, Honorable Lord Skeleton. If the Netherworld is his destiny, we will send him to the Kingdom of Lucifer."

"Send him at once, Your Honor. Get him out of there and give him to Lucifer. He needs amalgamators for his silver mines. I know whom you're talking about. We have sent one of our agents to try to persuade him to return to the Church, but he does not want to submit; he's stubborn and proud. He does not want to give himself to his Lord and is paying dearly for his pride and rebellion. I doubt there's anyone among us who wants to advocate for that poor bastard. And now it's time for me to leave. I don't want to waste any more time on these trivial matters. Good-bye, Honorable Lords. Next time you request my presence, it'll be on the battlefield. I haven't turned you into dust yet only because of my loyalty to the Confederacy. With your permission, Honorable Lord Three Times Great. Lady of Books, Goddess of Charm, see you next time."

"We, too, are leaving, Honorable Lord Sun of the Night," said the Indigenous Deities of New Mexico.

At the conclusion of this meeting, there was a prolonged silence. I was still motionless and deprived of most of my senses, attentive to what I might hear. After a few moments the judge and Seshat had a conversation.

"Lord of Time, my father, Supreme Judge. If this were an impious man, his sentence would be more than fair, but my heart breaks for Uriel. He's far from his city and his time. He suffers from all sorts of misery without knowing why. An evil genius has taken ahold of his mind and manipulates him like a puppet, making him believe that the objects he perceives with his senses actually exist. The miserable ignores that they only exist in his mind and for his mind. But he aspires to awaken from his permanent dream state. He feels persecuted by the gods. Dear Father, god of wisdom, writing, memory, and great master of dreams, my father, is your heart insensitive to the suffering of a man who is hungry for metaphysical knowledge? Wasn't there a time when the seekers of your eternal wisdom were pleasing to you? Oh, Sun of the Night, why is this adept of yours indifferent to you? Just because he has writer's block and couldn't finish his novel? Are you going to condemn him before you give him a chance to fulfill his mission in the world of mortals?"

"My child, don't speak nonsense. Do you think that I, the author of the biographical index of all mortals, ignore the fate of Uriel Romero, the author of the novel *1666*, which pays literary homage to the story of Neferkaphtah? I'm the one who saved him. The prosecutor wanted to blame him for Alma's suicide, but I acquitted him. Although Uriel acted unscrupulously by reading and plagiarizing her diary, he didn't do it so Alma would commit suicide, but to know and reveal the truth of Juárez's femicides. Moreover, if Uriel had made known in his novel the content of the pseudo Book of Thoth that Hermes García Sánchez wrote, he would have died as a brave martyr of truth, which would have secured him a place in Paradise. So, let's both think about how to help Uriel get home. The Lord Father of the Romans and Lord Skeleton will not be able to oppose our will if we act in coalition."

"My Father, supreme among the wise and the powerful, if you please, let us immediately send a Gáhé to teach Uriel the way home. I'll fly to his chamber to give him the kiss that will wake him up."

"So be it, Daughter. I know how you get when you're on a mission."

When this conversation ended, I was still motionless and speechless. Mysteriously, I no longer felt pain or discomfort. Nor did I feel hunger, thirst, cold, warmth, fear, or anguish. I was neither sad nor happy. I was suspended in a silent, dark void. Was I dead? Alive? Asleep? In a coma? Crazy? I knew nothing with certainty at the time. All I knew, or thought I knew, was that my mind and memory were still active. I reflected on the strange conversation I had overheard and found it obvious that it had been another dream. It was both ridiculous and implausible, a work of my imagination and the product of my poor emotional and physical state. If I was alive, if I was not a mere illusion, or a soul in a state of dream or transition to something unknown, I would soon discover it.

I interpreted this absurd dream as a divine message. The Supreme Judge exonerated me of Alma's accusation in her posthumous letter of inciting her to commit suicide. I paid, or was paying, a dear price for this accusation. I interpreted my present state as a kind of purgatory because of my many faults and flaws. However, this dream gave me hope that I was not dead and that I would not be condemned eternally for Alma's suicide.

37

WHERE WAS I? ON A MOUNTAIN IN NEW MEXICO IN THE SEVENteenth century? In Senecú? In Ithaca, in the twentieth century, in my apartment? Somewhere else and in some other time of my earthly existence? In some timeless space? Or in some spaceless time? In the realm of dreams? Had I cheated death, or maybe life itself?

I had no clue being in that strange state of mind. I had a myriad of thoughts and memories. That was it. I remembered with the same blurriness the strange conversation I had overheard in my other lifetime dreams and experiences. I was able to think and recall many things, but not everything. There were parts of my past that were inaccessible to me. The images I had of all things, including those I had known intimately and with detail, mixed in my mind like chimeras. There were things whose names I remembered, but whose image, texture, smell, and taste I could not bring to the surface of consciousness. I remembered vaguely certain sound impressions: certain vibrations, timbres, tones, rhythms, and fragments of melodies. I remembered more precisely the sounds I had heard most recently: the voices I had just heard, the sound of the drum, the voice of Refugio, the blowing of the wind, the cracking of the wood when consumed by the fire, Lucius's neighs and brays, his twangy voice, the ghost or spirit who spoke to me when María Tzitza ascended to the sky, her ethereal voice. I remembered Brother Antonio's diction, and that of all the people I had met in Senecú with the same inaccuracy and uncertainty that I remembered my own voice and that of all the people with whom I had interacted in my previous life.

My memories seemed to me to be data devoid of tangible reality, images that I could evoke with the mind but which I was unable to corroborate with the senses. I didn't remember the taste or smell of anything I'd supposedly eaten or drank in Senecú, or in my other life. Without a cup of freshly roasted coffee in front of me, it was impossible for me to evoke the subtle aromas and flavors of this delightful drink, let alone the most intimate moments from my other life that a cup of coffee would help me retrieve from my memory bank. The music I remembered was just what I had heard and played in Senecú. I was not able to remember a single song or piece of music I had heard or played in my other life when I occupied Uriel's body, which gave me nostalgia, but not pain or sadness, despite how much music had meant to me, like when we remember the things that we used to enjoy as children but that have ceased to interest us.

What caused me concern was thinking about my loved ones, those in my previous life, my true and only life? Had my parents, siblings, relatives, friends, neighbors, classmates, coworkers, teachers, other acquaintances, and the love of my life, Alma, existed or were they inventions of my imagination, as was the conversation I had just heard? What might have happened to them? Were they looking for me? Were they missing me? Had I lost all agency or any kind of say in how the events I experienced were to unfold, or, as Brother Antonio would surely have me believe, had I never had any say in them in the first place?

In Senecú I had developed an ambiguous affection for Brother Antonio, and I wondered what had become of him. Had I dreamed my last encounter with him? I didn't know. I remembered the day I met him and told myself that this encounter could also have been a dream, as could all my other experiences in Senecú and on the mountain with Refugio. There was nothing to help me verify their possible existence. The sound of the drum was gone. The material world was out of my reach, and I found it impossible to evoke it.

How long did I remain in that cataplexy? I had no idea. They say that before dying we observe our entire life in an instant. My mind traversed all the moments I could remember from my stay in

Senecú and on the mountain until that moment, which I was able to record in these pages. I was also able to remember other events in my other life which you, reader, will soon discover if you continue reading the rest of this story. I remembered many things I wasn't able to write down here due to lack of space and time. My mind extracted everything I could from that unfathomable and unconscious repository that stored like seeds each and every one of my past actions and thoughts no matter how banal and trivial they were. I remembered my previous life, not as a film narrated chronologically from birth to death but as a succession of fragmented images that I retrieved from my memory in a capricious and disorderly way at times, and voluntarily and orderly at other times when I experienced some lucidity. I had fantasies and thoughts of all kinds, and I came up with numerous stories I would have liked to write down at the time but that I forgot, as happens with dreams and so many other things we think about in our lives.

I thought, remembered, imagined, invented, fantasized, dreamed, and mixed countless times and in infinite ways everything that my mind was able to extract from its most remote and intimate corners. It was as if I had lived several lives, except that they were lives in an immaterial world, outside of space and time. I imagined many lives in a complete and absolute solitude, without deficiencies or material desires.

I wondered countless times when I was going to wake up from this incredible dream. I had previously been able to wake up from dreams, voluntarily or unintentionally, and return to the same place where I had fallen asleep, a place in a world full of things and people that I could see, touch, smell, listen to. However, in my current state, I had no idea how to wake up, or if I was ever going to awaken again. Was I in limbo? I asked myself infinite times.

38

A FAMILIAR VOICE SUDDENLY PULLED ME OUT OF THAT CATAPLEXY. It was Yes singer Jon Anderson. I thought I was hallucinating. I opened my eyes and saw that I was still in the chagoch'o. But Refugio was not by my side. I figured he'd risen to welcome the first light. Steve Howe's electric guitar notes started to vibrate in my head and, soon after, Chris Squire's bass picking, his voice, and Alan White's cymbals joined the melody. When Rick Wakeman's mini-Moog made its triumphant entry into that hymn to dawn, which set to music "The Revealing Science of God," it was impossible for me to continue lying down. I got up, bewildered, wondering where I was. I was still wearing Apache clothes. Except for Yes's music and the glow of dawn that lit the interior of the quinzhee, everything seemed to be just like the night before.

I went out to find Refugio and found him sitting in the snow about ten meters from the quinzhee. He was just wearing a loincloth and was looking at the light of dawn, chanting with his arms raised. I approached him and was surprised that he was intonating an Apache song in English. His voice was ethereal and feminine.

I had a hard time understanding his chant, for Yes's music kept playing in my head. I didn't want to interrupt him, so I looked up at the horizon. I noticed that the sky had an unusual range of colors: dark blue, red, and orange; purple, magenta, indigo, and fog blue. The latter came from a strange cloudiness that appeared to be the edge of a galaxy's nebula. Refugio continued his chant to dawn.

The sky brightened and the galaxy's disks slowly unfolded. Refugio kept repeating the same chant and Yes's music continued to play in my head. After a while a column of light and a halo of splendid brilliance announced the imminent appearance of the galactic bulb. The sky seemed to have burst into flames. When "The Revealing Science of God" concluded, the center of the galaxy shone.

Refugio finished chanting. He stood up and turned to see me.

"Where are we?" I asked.

"Where else? The Land of Enchantment."

Physically, Refugio had not changed, but his facial expressions, bearing, manners, and voice had softened and acquired feminine qualities.

"I didn't know you spoke English."

"Are you forgetting I was born in America?"

"Aren't you Apache?"

"Apache? Me? Don't be fooled by appearances. I'm Dr. Hogan."

"Dr. Hogan?" The voice and name sounded familiar, but I could not place them in space or in time.

"How are your dreams going?"

"My dreams?"

"Yes, your dreams."

"So-so," I replied with disappointment.

"Remember the magic word Refugio taught you last night before you went to sleep?"

"Aren't you Refugio?"

"I'm telling you, I'm Dr. Hogan. Don't you remember me anymore? I am your guide in this astral field."

I finally realized that she was my psychotherapist who had been teaching me dream yoga in Albuquerque.

"Dr. Hogan. Long time no see." I was surprised and happy to see her. "And what are you doing here?"

"Before I can answer, you have to give me the signal," she said.

"What signal?"

"The mantra and the sign that I taught you in our previous session."

"Sorry, I don't remember them."

"Try to remember them, Uriel. Otherwise, you won't be able to advance in your training."

I was making a huge effort to concentrate because in my head I kept listening to Yes's music.

"Please concentrate, Uriel."

"I'm sorry, Doctor. I find it hard with the music that is sounding in my head. I don't know why."

"Don't you remember the *nada* yoga I taught you?"

"Nada yoga?"

"Yes. The kind of meditation that consists of noticing without judging all the noises and sounds we hear."

"I'm afraid I forgot that too. I'm sorry."

"No problem, Uriel. Let's try again."

Dr. Hogan stood in front of me, put her hands on my shoulders with her arms outstretched and, looking me in the eye, said:

"Focus your mind on the music without judging whether it's pleasant or unpleasant and let it fill your consciousness. Once you steady your mind by focusing on the music, you will begin to hear the sound of nothingness spontaneously, and the music will gradually move to the background of your consciousness."

"Ah, yes, of course," I responded enthusiastically and enlightened by her deep eyes that made me think of a fathomless wellspring.

I closed my eyes and focused on the music. While listening to Jon Anderson sing "The Remembrance," I recalled the sound that Refugio taught me and repeated it, singing:

"Aaaaaaaaaaaaaaaaaaaaaaah."

Dr. Hogan drew a smile on her lips and nodded. Then she requested the visual signal. I immediately remembered the circle Refugio taught me to do with both hands on my chest. I signaled it with pride and relief.

"What does the circle represent?" she asked me.

"The dream catcher María gave me."

"And what is it for?"

"To transform negative mental formations into positive ones, right?"

"That's correct. And what does it symbolize?"

"The circle of the spirit."

"Yes. I see that you're lucid in this dream," she told me condescendingly.

"Am I dreaming?"

"Have you ever stopped dreaming?"

"No, I don't think so."

"The only thing is that, in this dream, you have acquired some lucidity."

"What do you mean?"

"There are varying degrees of lucidity. Even though you realize you're dreaming, your karma is in control, not your mind."

A gong and two cymbals clanged. "The Ancient: Giants Under the Sun" began. The synthesizer and vibraphone chimed into the overture and filled the air with sparks.

The music induced a terrible vision in me. In the firmament appeared Utu, Ra, Shapash, Suria, Xihe, Amaterasu, Tonatiuh, Kinich Ahau, Taandoco, Inti, Mitra, Helios, Sol, Belenus, Shams, Mawu-Lisa, Tawa, Pautiwa, Awonawilona, Oshach Paiyatiuma, Jóhonaa'éí, and other solar deities. Suddenly, I perceived the smell of gunpowder and smoke. Then a nauseating stench of rotting corpses struck me. It's the smell of war, I thought.

An unexpected roar and a rapid succession of notes produced by a vibraphone, an electric bass, and drums marked the start of the race against time for world domination. Baal and Anat, Mars and Minerva, Yahweh and Christ, and then Huitzilopochtli, Tohil, Copijcha, and the Twin Warriors appeared on the scene. The latter threw me on the battlefield. The weeping and the howls of an electric guitar intensified the dread and anguish I felt throughout this horrific odyssey. I participated in the wars of the Hispanic peoples against Carthaginian, Roman, Germanic, and Muslim invaders; I fought against the Teotihuacan, the Toltec, the Zapotec, the Mixtec, the Aztec, the Itzae, the Xiue, and the Cocome. I fought in the wars between the Moors and Christians, in the Crusades, in the battles of the Reconquest of Spain and the Conquest and conversion of

Indigenous peoples in the Americas; in the countless rebellions and the numerous civil and international wars against empire and tyranny; in the wars of the Counter-Reformation, Independence, Liberal Reform, and the Mexican Revolution.

"Did you hear what I said, Uriel?"

"Sorry, I just had a terrifying vision. What did you say?"

"I said that your karma is in control."

"My karma? I don't know what or who that is."

"The chain of causes and effects produced by all your past actions. Its effects manifest and materialize in karmic dreams. Your karma is the creator of this and most other dreams you've had and endured so far. It has brought you here and manipulates you as if you were a puppet. It's a malevolent genius who has taken control of your mind and uses all sorts of tricks to deceive you. Everything: the sky, the wind, the earth, colors, figures, sounds, celestial bodies, yourself, and I are its creation."

"And why am I here? What do I have to do with a Franciscan friar from the seventeenth century?"

"That's what you need to discover and understand."

Could I never get a straight answer to a direct question anymore? I longed for a New York City answer. Instead, a long and useless explanation followed.

"In the life of every individual there must be a key to some mystery that concerns your existence and impedes your transcendence. You must understand that your life is not a beginning but the continuation of other lives that preceded it. You must discover your existential plot, which has governed your existence since time immemorial. Until you do, you won't be able to continue your journey to the House of Light, your spiritual homeland, that luminous light you see there," she told me, pointing toward the center of the lenticular galaxy that illuminated the firmament like a morning sun. "If you were aware of your existential plot, assumed your ancestral responsibilities, and resolved the conflicts that have lagged and remained unresolved from your past, you would be able to reach your spiritual homeland. Remember that only by serving the heavenly homeland will you have a reserved place in it. And if you manage to break the chains of karma that binds you to the cycle of transmigration, the cycle that attaches all beings to mortality through ignorance and thirst for sensual and mental pleasures, you will finally reach the House of Light, your eternal abode."

I didn't know what to say and remained quiet for a while. By then the music had changed to the soothing chords of a Spanish guitar and Jon Anderson's melodious voice reflecting on the meaning of history and human cruelty.

"But, as you well know," Dr. Hogan continued, "the road to the homeland is arduous and labyrinthine. It is full of dangers and hostile forces will try to block and detour you. Take this dream catcher and use it judiciously," she told me, and handed me the amulet María Tzitza left me.

"Your greatest challenge is to not let yourself be manipulated by karma. You need to be the helmsman of your dreams."

"And how do I overcome karma?

"You'll need to attain mental clarity and presence first. Have you been practicing *trekchö*?"

"What's that?"

"The relaxation technique I taught you that helps you remain aware of the fundamental reality of existence at all times. With this technique we eliminate our ignorance and our thirst for sensual and mental pleasures. When we attain quietude and presence of mind, we free ourselves from attachments and aversions. This allows us to root out karma and, eventually, helps us break the cycle of transmigration."

"I think I forgot the trekchö."

"I see."

"Can you teach it to me again?"

"This is neither the place nor the time. We need to take advantage of your state of lucidity to combat the mental rigidity that has you trapped at this stage of your dream journey. When novice dream travelers get stuck in a dream, it is due to lack of strength and nimbleness. Yesterday Refugio taught you a valuable lesson to help you overcome fear and strengthen your spirit. Fear can become an energy source if you know how to channel it effectively. Now that you have gained enough lucidity and strength to explore another stage of your personal history, you need to develop nimbleness, which is essential to reducing karma's fierce control over you."

"And how can I get out of here? I can't take it anymore."

"It's easier than you think. It's all a matter of being willing to do it."

"Believe me, it's not due to lack of will. I've tried many times, all in vain."

"The first step is to tell yourself you can do it. When dream travelers get stuck somewhere it is because they don't know they have the power to overcome any situation. They don't know or don't believe that everything is possible in dreams. We can re-create and transform them at our whim at any time. Part of your training is learning to recognize, combat, and transform whatever your mind considers an obstacle, a limitation, or an impossibility. Nimbleness loosens the cognitive knots that constrict our mind. Have you dreamed again that you are an auroral bird of prey and that you can fly to other worlds and times?"

"And how do you know I had this dream?" I asked her, intrigued and surprised that she knew I once dreamed I was a luminous goshawk. I remembered that Refugio could also divine my dreams. I was going to ask her if he was her avatar or emissary in my dreamworld. However, she showed no interest in answering my questions.

"That's irrelevant. The important thing is that you know that this dream shows that you have not only the ability to imagine and visit other worlds but also the ability to pilot your own dreams and go wherever you wish at any time. Remember what stopped you that time from embarking on the journey home?"

"I think I had a panic attack when I saw the scene of Alma's suicide."

"Indeed. Since then you have not had a dream again in which you fly freely to other worlds and epochs."

"Yes, it's true. Most of my dreams are distressing or terrible nightmares."

"Except yesterday."

"Yesterday?"

"Yes. Yesterday you had an extraordinary auroral dream. You dreamed you were traveling to the heavenly homeland."

"Yes, it's true. It was a wonderful dream. Why do I linger in the realm of false appearances?"

"You need to free yourself from the cycle of transmigration that souls go through due to desire and ignorance. To do this you need to serve the heavenly homeland. A soul dedicated to acquiring greater virtue and to improving the welfare of the heavenly homeland will fly more quickly there. By contrast, those who devote themselves to attaining earthly goods and who succumb to the desire for bodily and mental pleasures violate divine law. Their souls, attached to existence, earthly goods, and beings, get stuck revolving around Earth and never reach the heavenly homeland, or arrive only after many centuries and torments. You run into this danger, Uriel, if you neglect your dream yoga practice and keep thinking only about yourself and your well-being. If you were to remember the previous lives you've had, you'd be the most studious disciple ever. Your nightmares will last several eons if you don't practice and improve."

"Suffering this nightmare is enough for me. I promise to be a better student."

"Let's see if it's true. I'll remind you when we meet again. I'll tell you, 'Those who cannot remember the past are condemned to repeat it.' I hope you'll remember this conversation next time we meet."

"I'll remember it, Doctor. Although my understanding and my will have been weak lately, my memory has been stronger than ever."

"I know, I know, but don't be overconfident, Uriel. Remember that in the dream world we have extraordinary powers. Conversely, in the material realm the soul is trapped in its bodily prison and forgets many things, especially its divine origin. Hence the importance of these dream exercises. For, as you know, the goal of dream yoga is to recognize and follow the limpid light of dawn, which is the way to the true homeland. Do this at all times and in any state or realm in which you are, be it in wakefulness, dream, meditation, death, Hell, Limbo, or Paradise."

"How can I be guided by this light if I don't even know what you're talking about?"

"In dreams your mind is like a projector that illuminates the shadows of your past that your karma revives and re-creates. All you perceive is your karma's invention. What you need to do is become the creator of your own movie. Once you create and direct your own movie, you will learn to recognize the limpid light of dawn that will lead you to the House of Light."

"And what do I need to do to achieve that? Help me, please."

"It's very easy. Think of somewhere you'd like to go."

By this time Steve Howe's electric guitar had entered a meditative trance. I closed my eyes to visualize the place where I wanted to go, aided by the music that was so intimately associated with my youth and, especially, with my life in New Mexico with Alma. When Jon Anderson's voice sang "Ritual (*Nous sommes du soleil*)," I recalled the trip I made with Alma to this same mountain shortly before she committed suicide. I imagined a wonderful sunrise like this on a summer's day and remembered the morning when I woke up at Vic's Peak after I got lost chasing a spotted owl. I clearly visualized that majestic view of the landscape and the surroundings of Río Abajo.

"Do you know where you want to go?" Dr. Hogan asked me.

"Yes. I'm seeing it very clearly."

39

A TORRENT OF PIANO NOTES STARTLED ME AND WOKE ME UP. I couldn't believe it. I was lying down, in the open, on top of Vick's Peak. It was daybreak. It was neither cold nor hot and everything was very green. I was wearing my red raincoat, a white T-shirt, blue jeans, and hiking boots. Next to me was my backpack with supplies and a map of the San Mateo Mountains displaying trail #50, named Shipman Trail. Was I still dreaming?

The whole scene reminded me of the day I got lost chasing the spotted owl. I had woken up on this same spot then. I was wearing these same clothes and was carrying this backpack with me. The sun was peeking out. I admired the view around me and remembered my first encounter with Brother Antonio when he showed me this landscape. Had I finally woken up and returned to my previous life? Had I dreamed Alma committed suicide? Where was she? Was she looking for me? How long had it been since I was asleep and lost? One night? Two? An eternity?

I opened my backpack and found the same supplies I had packed for the hike: a fourteen-ounce bottle of vanilla latte; five bars of Oats 'N Honey granola; a bag of dried mangoes; one of trail mix with peanuts, almonds, cashews, raisins, and M&M's; a six-pack of purified water in twenty-ounce plastic bottles; the brown wool sweater with a white stripe and a reindeer figure that Alma gave me for my birthday; a whistle; a map of New Mexico; a Walkman with headphones; and the notebook where I was scribbling for my novel.

I opened the bottle of latte and took a sip, but I spit it out immediately.

"What's this repugnant drink?"

I opened a bottle of water and took a big sip to rinse my mouth and quench my thirst. I was starving and unwrapped a granola bar, took a bite, and opened my notebook on the first entry, dated April 15. "Patricia, a young widow and a member of a prominent Juárez family was kidnapped and disappeared. Her abductors collected a large ransom, fled without freeing her, and disappeared. Nothing is known about their whereabouts. There are many speculations about what happened. Authorities claim the abductors are in their custody. They are members of a Juárez gang called Los Azules. However, Patricia's attorney claims that they were forced to sign their confession through torture. Also, her parents assert her lover is the real kidnapper, as she was shot dead six times inside her vehicle while traveling to southern Mexico the day after her father and brother paid the ransom money to the kidnappers. Other versions blame Patricia herself for planning her abduction with her lover and for subsequently murdering him so that she could escape alone and remake her life under a new identity. But an anonymous letter recently published in a local newspaper rejects these hypotheses: It blames Patricia's father and younger brother for the kidnap and murder of Patricia and her lover. It is based on the alleged existence of diaries that she left, in which she accuses her father and brother of having committed several murders, including that of her ex-husband and several girls. My novel is based on Patricia's diaries in which she recounts the sexual abuse she suffered as a child and details the results of her investigations into the clandestine, dissolute, and criminal life that her father and brother have led in complicity with a circle of friends belonging to the highest circles of Juárez society."

I got up with difficulty. My body felt strange, as if it didn't belong to me. I longed to see Alma, hug her, kiss her, tell her how much I loved and missed her. I wanted to apologize for reading her diaries, for abusing the trust she had placed in me when she confessed the traumatic experiences she suffered as a child and as an adolescent, and for using her tragic story as a basis for my novel.

I promised myself that I would get rid of all the notes I had taken in preparation for it, and that I would start another novel in which I would tell the story I had just dreamed of. I was confident that, with this recent set of dreams, I was finally going to overcome my writer's block.

Yes continued playing another song in my head, this time about a sculptor whose beloved dies and whom he resurrects with his art.

A wooden sign confirmed that I was at Vick's Peak at 10,256 feet high. I consulted my map and decided to take the fastest route. The campsite was about five miles away. The return was rough. Along a stretch I had to slide down a scree. I was so exhausted at some point that I had to rest for a few moments in a place called Turkey Spring. Then I walked down a stony trail until I reached the campsite. Alma was still in the tent asleep when I arrived. I couldn't contain my happiness at seeing her. I lay next to her and woke her up giving her an effusive hug.

"Love of my life, soul of my soul. Oh, my darling, I missed you so much. I thought I'd lost you forever." I kissed her numerous times.

"Let me sleep, please. Move away. You've got bad breath," she said. Then she pushed me away, and added: "What's the matter with you? Are you stoned? You know I haven't been able to sleep much over the past few weeks. It's the first night I've been able to sleep peacefully. Don't be inconsiderate."

"I'm sorry, Cielito, I'm sorry. Please, forgive me," I said, pressing my palms together in supplication. "I got lost last night and fell asleep in the woods. I had some amazing dreams, really amazing. I think I had my first lucid auroral dream. I dreamed I was a Franciscan friar and that I lived in the seventeenth century. I reincarnated in one of my remote ancestors."

"Oh my gosh, Uriel. You're going to bother me with that New Age bullshit right now? I beg you to let me sleep. I'm not in the mood. I have a bad headache."

"Alright, Alma, no problem. Sleep, sleep, Cielito. I'm in no hurry. Would you mind if I stay right next to you?"

She didn't answer me. She turned her back on me and fell asleep quickly. She was obviously exhausted and in a bad mood. I hugged her and spooned her.

"I promise I'll stay still and quiet. I need to feel your warmth, enjoy your lovely presence and existence. I swear I had a bad night; I thought I'd lost you forever."

As she slept I began to reflect and tried to remember what had happened recently in our lives. Everything seemed very strange and familiar at the same time, as if I were reliving moments from my past. It was like a film I had seen a long time ago and whose story I had almost completely forgotten, except for its tragic ending, Alma's suicide.

At that moment I couldn't remember what had happened, or, in this case, what was going to happen after our hike to the Apache Kid Wilderness. I knew Alma was preparing for her doctoral qualifying exams and that she had been stressed out and depressed in recent months because of her family problems. I also remembered the contents of her diaries, which I had accidentally discovered a few months ago. I felt bad about reading and photocopying them behind her back. I couldn't remember if I had already confessed it to her and if I had asked her to forgive me. However, judging by her behavior, she gave me the impression that she hadn't forgiven me. It wasn't just the fact that she wasn't happy to see me when I came back after being lost last night. What worried me the most was her body language of rejection and aversion. She was not the same Alma I remembered; she was distant and seemed angry with me. Wasn't she ever going to forgive me? I promised myself to be patient and understanding, no matter what. I shouldn't allow my temperament, pride, or self-esteem to ruin my relationship with her and sink her deeper into depression. If her anger and contempt were the price I had to pay for my impertinence and opportunism, so be it. It would be a minimal sacrifice I could make to perhaps save her from committing suicide. I loved her too much and knew how much I was going to suffer being without her. The burden I was going to carry with me for the rest of my days if she killed herself would be unbearable.

As soon as she woke up, we disassembled the tent and packed all our stuff to head back to Albuquerque. I still wanted to tell her about my dreams, but she wasn't interested. I decided to leave that for later. She had woken up in a bad mood and I knew it was better to give her some space. I hoped she was in a bad mood only because she was hungry. I proposed that we have breakfast at a diner in Truth or Consequences, which she accepted.

We walked to the parking lot of the Cíbola National Forest, where we had left Goldfinch the other day. When we arrived I was thrilled to see the five-speed, four-wheel drive, 1981 Toyota Trekker I'd had since I was a freshman at NMSU. It was bright yellow. I had added black, gray, and white wings on the sides and black stripes on the hood to magnify its gringo goldfinch look. I felt sorry to see it all muddy. I kept it in top shape because I wanted it to last another five or ten years. In the parking lot I saw the remains of an old wagon that reminded me of the animal-drawn carts that were common in Senecú. I found it wonderful, almost miraculous, that a vehicle could ascend the steep and stony mountain road without being pulled by a team of mules. Excited, I opened Goldfinch's hood to admire its inner anatomy. Its steel viscera and rubber veins evoked in me the image of an alicanto, a nocturnal mythological bird of the Atacama Desert.

"Don't you agree my *troquita* is a marvel, Alma? If only it could fly, it would rival the alicantos."

"Don't exaggerate. You're acting like a peacock mama." Alma seemed to be in a better mood.

"Hey, Uriel, you're sounding a bit weird. Are you alright?"

"I've never felt better in my life. It's as if time has gone back and I have the golden opportunity to correct my mistakes and correct the course of my life and destiny."

"You well know that every moment of our lives offers us that opportunity. I don't see how a simple dream could have changed you so much."

"You're wrong. A dream can completely transform you overnight. I read in a book that lucid dreams . . ."

"Are you going to talk about that subject again? Let's go. I'm starving." She got in the Goldfinch and left me standing there, talking to myself.

I closed the hood and got in too, without saying anything, telling myself I had to be patient and understanding and that she wouldn't believe me anyway. I was pleasantly surprised to find *Yessongs* inserted in the cassette player. I rewound it to enjoy the "Firebird Suite" overture. I put in the key and turned on the 22R SOHC four-cylinder engine. Immediately, I felt the roar of Goldfinch's ninety-seven horsepower and was both thrilled and proud to be the pilot of such a magnificent machine. I grabbed the steering wheel with both hands and pushed the accelerator several times as if it were a race car.

"Stop clowning, Uriel. I'm telling you, I'm very hungry and I need to get back home and start studying for my quals as soon as possible."

"No problem, Cielito. We're flying right now."

"I'm not sure it was such a good idea to spend the weekend here," she said, stressed out and irritated. "My exams begin next month, and I still haven't reviewed Renaissance and Enlightenment philosophy."

"Don't worry. You're going to do very well. You'll see."

"It's easy for you to say that. You don't know my advisor. He can be such an asshole, especially toward women."

"What I know is that you've been studying nonstop since the year started and you've hardly slept over the past few months," I said. "You need to rest. At that work pace you can get sick. You'll see that the mountain air and contact with nature have been beneficial to you. You'll be able to concentrate and sleep much better from now on."

We headed out toward the road to Albuquerque in search of a place to eat breakfast. I couldn't contain the urge to return to the subject of dreams.

"As I was telling you, dreams can transform you and even cure you of psychosomatic ills. A psychiatrist documented the case of one of his patients who was cured of chronic pain after experiencing a lucid dream. Overnight he stopped needing his levorphanol pills."

"Oh, really? Where did you read this? In a scientific journal or in one of your New Age books?

"I read it in one of my books, but my dreams last night have convinced me that this is possible."

"What illness healed in your lucid dream last night? I see it was neither your naivety nor your gullibility."

"You're going to laugh at me, but I think it cured my writer's block."

"I didn't know indecisiveness and cowardice were a disease."

"Don't be mean, Alma. I'm serious. I don't know why, but I feel as if I'm going to finally write my first novel. The dreams I had last night were fascinating and incredibly detailed. I have it all in my memory and I will write my novel nonstop and without hesitation this summer."

"Seeing is believing. If last night's dreams cured you of your chronic indecision, then I'll believe they can be miraculous. But I'm afraid writing your novel requires more than lucid dreams. You need a good dose of honesty and self-confidence."

"My dream happened here in New Mexico in the seventeenth century," I continued, trying to ignore her innuendo. "I have decided to abandon my previous project. I'm going to write a historical novel based on this lucid dream."

"Oh, Uriel. This sounds like another one of your failed projects to me. I don't know how many times you've said and done the same thing. You get excited about a new project. But after a few weeks, you abandon it."

"Believe me, this time it's going to be different. I've got half the novel written in my head. It's just a matter of sitting down and writing it. I'm sure I have enough material to write the whole thing. You'll see."

"What about the stuff you've written in the last six months? Are you going to throw it overboard? It's the first time I've seen you work long hours. You usually just read and scratch your belly button."

"Yes, but I've decided to forget about drug dealers, corrupt politicians, Richie Riches, and femicides. I'm tired of these commonplaces. As Milan Kundera says, 'A novel that does not discover a hitherto unknown segment of existence is immoral.'"

"I thought your novel was about a community of radical environmentalists who founded an experimental community in the Biscay Desert imitating the nomadic life of the Cochimíes. I didn't know you were writing about femicides," she said in a tone that I found too ironic and emphatic.

"It's actually a secondary topic," I replied, knowing that I had screwed up. "You know one can't write anything about northern Mexico without bumping into the subject of drug trafficking and femicides."

"What does your experimental community of environmentalists have to do with drug trafficking and the Juárez femicides, then?"

"I didn't say it was about the Juárez femicides."

"Then from where? Tijuana? Mexicali?" she asked me, visibly irate.

"From Canada," I replied, shrewdly, I thought. "In recent years more than fifty Indigenous Canadian women have been murdered or disappeared, and their cases have not been resolved to date either."

"Oh, really? Where did you read this? Also in one of your New Age books?"

"Where else? On the Internet."

"On the Internet? I didn't know you were so interested in these issues. You've always said that you aspire to write novels in which the main characters cultivate virtue and seek happiness, wisdom, and utopia. Did a killer of Canadian Indigenous women infiltrate your community of environmental nomads?"

I didn't know how to reply. Alma had me cornered with her questions, and I was not sure if I should bring up the subject of her diaries. If she didn't know I'd read them behind her back, why reveal it to her now? I was overwhelmed by everything I had dreamed last night and felt ecstatic at having her back in my life again. I wanted to do everything possible to prevent her from leaving me, even though I knew she was going to leave me anyway. Regardless, I started to have some doubts. What if she already knew? She'd accuse me of dishonesty, justifiably. I thought it would be better to wait and tell her at a more opportune time, but she asked me point-blank and I reacted in a stupid and cowardly manner. I evaded the truth to avoid ruining that bright July morning.

"Answer me, Uriel. Tell me the truth. Have you been nosing into my personal affairs?"

"What personal affairs? Femicides concern all people from Juárez, don't they?"

"Don't play dumb. You know exactly what I mean."

"Are you surprised that I'm worried about what's going on in Juárez and the world too?"

"Very much so. You've never bothered to learn much about Juárez's political and social problems. You have always said that you find that unworthy of your attention and reflection; that you don't want to know anything about drug traffickers, murderers, corrupt politicians, or families and people motivated by self-interest and money; that you want to focus all your intellectual and literary energies on noble and uplifting projects. Have you changed so much overnight?"

"I'm telling you, I'm not the same person anymore. My dream has transformed me more than you're willing to accept and more than you've allowed me to explain. It's been a transformative experience. It's as if I have resurrected and as if you've come back from the afterlife. I have so many things to tell you and share with you. After last night's dream I have promised myself not to continue to make the same mistakes that will inevitably lead us to the abyss. I promise to make amends for my mistakes, to repair the damage I've done to you."

"You think I'm a dumbass, don't you?" she said, infuriated. "You think your hollow words and banal dreams are going to move me? You think I don't know you've been prying into my stuff and reading my intimate diaries? I never imagined you could be such a scumbag!"

"I beg you to forgive me, *Almita mía*. I can explain everything, if I may."

"I've given you enough chances. I thought you were going to have the decency to confess your intrusion, but I see you're even more dishonest than I thought."

"Please, Alma. Don't judge me without first listening to me."

"You're the one who has to listen to me!" she yelled.

After a long silence that I dared not break, she continued after collecting herself:

"A few months ago I did not find one of my diaries in the place where I usually keep them. I suspected it was you who took them, but I decided to keep trusting you. Last week I read one of the notebooks you left on the dining room table. That's when I realized not only that you had read my diaries but also that you are plagiarizing them. What shame and boldness! You want to publish, disguised as fiction, the inquiries I did about my brother and my corrupt father. You know better than anyone that I risked my life and sacrificed everything investigating and confronting them."

"Forgive me, Alma. I admit I've been stupid and selfish."

"Do you know what it's like to be the sister of a murderous psychopath and the daughter of a physician who claims to be an exemplar of respectability and moral integrity, but who is actually one of the most corrupt and despicable beings on the planet?"

". . ."

"Do you know what it's like to be married to a selfish jerk who thinks it's okay to plagiarize my story and exploit my suffering to satisfy his vanity and realize his literary fantasies?"

". . ."

"And now you claim a lucid dream has transformed you overnight and that you want to repair the damage you've done to me? What harm are you talking about, Uriel? The irreparable damage you've done to me and our relationship?"

"Please listen to me now. I have so much to tell you and explain. I was planning on telling you everything, but I wanted to find the right moment."

"Liar! You could have admitted everything a few moments ago, but you kept on trying to hide the truth and deceive me with your false pretensions and hypocritical assertions. Besides, the damage is done. I don't want to be with you anymore. I'm sick of you! Stop right now! I don't want to spend another minute with you! Stop or I'll get out even if the truck is moving!"

I had no choice and pulled over. She got out, took her backpack, and walked down the mountain's dirt road. I followed her until we got to the village of Monticello. There I got out to try to convince her to come with me, but she ran away. Since I didn't want to make a scene, I got in Goldfinch and followed her until she went into the post office. I waited for her for a while. Given that she didn't come out, I decided to go in and talk to her. To my surprise, she had slipped through a side door. I looked for her all over town but I didn't find her. I went down North Street toward I-25, hoping to find her on the road.

As I was driving I reflected on what was happening to me. I had a feeling I'd lived through all this before, but I wasn't sure if they were forebodings based on a real knowledge of what was going to happen in the future, or if my fears and my dreams had fabricated this story. I admitted to myself that I was always imagining tragic scenarios that never happened and told myself that I shouldn't give so much credit to my dreams and my imagination; that I should put my feet on the ground. I needed to be more optimistic and disregard my catastrophic thoughts. My obsessive-compulsive disorder was ruining my life, and I needed to overcome it.

40

I ARRIVED AT THE APARTMENT TWO HOURS LATER WITH NO IDEA where Alma had gone and not knowing if she would come back or not. I walked into the apartment. Everything seemed familiar and strange at the same time. I got the impression that I hadn't been in my apartment in a long time, as if time had regressed. I recognized all the furniture and objects, but they seemed to belong to a distant time in my life: the sofa, the ornaments, the shelves with books, the LPs, the CDs, the display case with my stereo. My stereo. It gave me immense joy to see my Marantz amplifier, my Onkyo CD player, my Technics turntable, my Polk speakers. I looked at the alarm clock and saw it was 9:45 a.m. I wondered what date it was and realized I had no clue. I checked the calendar and saw it was Memorial Day: Monday, May 29, 1995. That was weird. I thought it was 1996. I didn't know if I was dreaming, or if the memories I had of the future were my confabulations. Was I going crazy? I tried to remember what I had done the day before, but I couldn't remember anything. It must be because of the strange nightmares I've had, I thought.

Even though I had a serious headache, I felt like I had been resurrected, as if I had miraculously returned from the afterlife. Everything seemed wonderful and happily familiar, as it happens when we find lost memorabilia after an intense search, and we enjoy these prized objects with renewed enthusiasm. I felt an intense urge to pee and went to the bathroom. The sound of my urine hitting the water and wall of the toilet bowl produced in me a childish joy. I began to think about how little I appreciated and valued the facilities of my modest apartment: the toilet whose simple but ingenious mechanism drained the polluted water in a few seconds;

the sink with running water available in abundance twenty-four hours a day; electric light; the air conditioner that turned on and off automatically. I washed and dried my hands; the towel felt so soft.

I came out of the bathroom and on the dining table I found a Yes CD: *Tales from Topographic Oceans*. I didn't know how it had shown up there. As far as I could remember, I never had it on CD; I had it on vinyl. Maybe I bought it and forgot. I never found out. At that moment what I most wanted was to prepare myself a cup of coffee and breakfast. I turned on the stereo, played the CD, and headed to the kitchen.

I opened the cupboard and was glad to find a bag of coffee beans half full. I put water in the kettle and turned on the burner to the highest setting. I measured four and a half tablespoons of coffee and emptied them in the Krups grinder. As I pressed the button, the grinder gave off a sweet aroma that produced a soft and delicate delight in me I thought I'd never enjoy again. Then I took a cup from the shelf and placed it on the countertop. I pulled out a paper filter from its box, placed it inside the plastic cone. and put it on top of the cup. Since the water wasn't boiling yet, I opened the fridge, took out a plastic bag with sliced whole wheat bread, and an egg. I grabbed the Teflon pan, turned on another burner, added a teaspoon of vegetable oil, and waited for the pan to heat up. Meanwhile, I took two slices of bread, put them in the toaster, checked that it was calibrated at three, and lowered the toaster chamber. As soon as the pan warmed up enough, I broke and fried the egg and turned off the burner. When the water was about to start boiling, I turned off the heat. I counted to thirty, grasped the handle of the kettle with a folded towel, reached the cone with the filter, held it above the sink, and filled it with boiling water. I waited for it to stop dripping and put it back on top of the cup, emptied the ground coffee into the filter, and gently swirled the cone to impregnate the filter walls with ground coffee. I grabbed the kettle again and emptied some water into the cone, enough to cover the ground coffee. I waited forty seconds for the grains to flourish, as this crucial moment of the brewing process was called when hot water released the gases trapped in the grains. I observed the bubbles and inhaled the delicate aroma that this magical process released. Then I gradually poured water into the cone until the cup was filled to the rim. I put the fried egg and the two toasted bread slices on a plate, grabbed the cup, and sat down by the table to enjoy my breakfast.

I savored my coffee as if it were a bring-back-to-life elixir. I took the cup with both hands and placed it in front of me. I inhaled its sweet, warm aroma, closed my eyes, and let the vapor saturate my olfactory receptors. Slowly, I put the cup on my lips and imbibed the bitter liquid. I examined the cup Qin Keqing, a pottery friend from Beijing, gave me as a present when I turned thirty. It was grayish white and had the Chen zodiac symbol painted in indigo blue, which was associated with the dragon, my spiritual animal. I observed the arabesque swirls of coffee vapor that emanated from the cup and noticed the tiny drops of oil floating on the surface. I imagined they were stars and that the light bulb reflected on the dark liquid surface was the moon.

I put the cup of coffee back on the table and dug in to my fried egg with toast. To entertain myself, I took the case from Yes's CD and observed the front cover. It struck me that a Mayan pyramid was painted in the center and that, behind it, the light of dawn and the morning sun shone. Although the sun had already risen, the sky was still dark and starry, as if day and night coexisted in this strange earthly landscape. On the left was a rocky mountain from whose hillside a spring emanated and descended, forming a stream and a pond that possibly drained into a cenote. On the right side appeared the foot of another rocky mount that was partially covered with moss. A sand dune blanketed the earth's surface. The landscape reminded me of the path of the moon mentioned in the *Bhagavad Gita*. The souls who traveled this dark path, the way of the ancestors, returned to this dusty and suffering-filled world. By contrast, the souls who traversed the path of the sun did not return to this world. They were liberated. I inferred that the picture represented the path to light. That's where I'd like to go, I thought.

Until then, I had never believed in reincarnation. The belief that we have a soul that has been transmigrating for centuries or millennia from being to being always seemed ridiculous to me. However, the Hindu belief that the soul has four conditions—the awakened life of the consciousness that traverses the outside world; the dreamworld in which consciousness travels to other dimensions; the life of quietude when consciousness neither thinks nor dreams; and the awakened life of the supreme consciousness, in which the soul reaches its pure state beyond all distinction between the subjective and the objective, in complete unity and harmony with being and becoming—seemed to me not only coherent but an inspiring yet insurmountable existential goal.

I finished breakfast and got lost in my thoughts listening to Yes. Then I felt sleepy and went to my bedroom to take a nap. I fell fast asleep until about 8:00 p.m. I was dead tired and probably would have slept until the next day. However, some door knocks woke me up. I got up quickly, hoping it was Alma. But it was Lisa, her best friend. She brought two empty suitcases with her. Without even saying hello, she informed me that Alma was going to stay at her place for the rest of the summer and that she had come to get her computer, some books, and other materials she needed to prepare for her exams. I let her in and helped her pack up and load Alma's belongings in her car. Lisa was upset, as if I had done something to her. When we finished loading everything, she told me that Alma had asked her to tell me to please don't bother her, or call her, or anything; that she needed to focus on her studies. She also mentioned that Alma was going to pick up the rest of her belongings once she found a new apartment and warned me to be prepared because Alma was going to initiate the divorce process; that her decision was final and unappealable.

I accepted Alma's request and decision with resignation and set out to do everything I could to not be overwhelmed by sadness. I thought maybe it would be best for her. Also, I had many reasons to be happy. I was thrilled to be back in my apartment and had woken up from that long and bizarre set of nightmares. I went to sleep again, sad to find myself alone in the apartment but happy to be back in Albuquerque.

41

I DREAMED I WAS DEAD. MY FAMILY WAS KEEPING VIGIL OVER MY body at a funeral home in Ciudad Juárez. My eldest brother, Virgilio, was talking to Sergio Mendoza, one of my best childhood friends whom I hadn't seen since 1988, the year I left Juárez. Sergio was a professor of Latin American literature at the University of Juárez. My brother was telling him I had been working on a novel about the Juárez femicides and had left many binders full of drafts. Virgilio was interested in knowing if there was anything publishable in those drafts and asked him if he could possibly sort them out and edit them. Sergio answered he was going to be quite busy over the next few months, but that maybe he would find time to do so next year. I wanted none of that and said to myself:

"I don't need help. I can put together the novel myself. I will show them."

I pushed the casket lid, sat up, gave an acrobatic leap to the floor, and started to dance and sing "El hombre vivo." However, nobody seemed to notice or hear me. They continued to keep vigil as if I were truly dead. I told them: "Here I am. Here I am. Are you people deaf or blind? Cheer up. Go home. You are keeping watch over a ghost." But nobody paid attention.

42

THE NEXT DAY, WHEN I WOKE UP, I WENT BACK TO MY USUAL routine. I worked in the library of the University of New Mexico shelving books from eight to five and the rest of the day I devoted to doing domestic chores and to reading and writing. Despite the sadness of losing Alma, I felt fortunate to have a secure job that allowed me to live modestly and dedicate myself to pursuing my literary dreams.

Alma and I rented a small apartment in a modest house in the Barelas neighborhood. Although my wages were low, I had no debts and led an austere life. With some adjustments to my budget, I figured I would be able to afford the rent and most of my other expenses. In one or two years, I was hoping to receive an inheritance from the possible sale of El Porvenir and other land that my mother's family owned in the San Agustin area. A real estate company wanted to purchase the estate to build an industrial park. I was entitled to a small part of this valuable property that my maternal grandfather bequeathed to all his children and grandchildren before he started to suffer from senile dementia. With this inheritance I was hoping to live without any financial worries for some time in the future.

That Tuesday morning I got up happy to go to work, though eager to come back to write. To my great disappointment, I remembered very few details of my dream in Senecú. My fantasy that the muse of dreams was going to inspire me, and that I was going to write my novel nonstop, quickly vanished. The goddess of memory, who had pampered me in Senecú, treated me with disdain in Albuquerque. Alma's prediction that my new novel project was going to last six months was not fulfilled, as I discarded it in a couple of weeks. I realized that I would need to do a lot of historical research on

New Mexico seventeenth-century missions and, frankly, I wasn't that interested in the subject.

The breakup with Alma hurt me more than expected and I sank into depression. All I would do was go to work, lock myself in the apartment, listen to music, and agonize over all the terrible things that had been happening to me lately. I was afraid I was going crazy. I was certain that I had lived it all before and I also remembered things that were going to happen to me in the future. What was happening to me? I researched my symptoms online and read about a condition called confabulation, in which the mind invents, distorts, or modifies memories. I made an appointment with my psychotherapist and waited impatiently for the day to see her.

"Come in, come in, Uriel. How are you?"

"I'm fine, thank you. Well, not so well, actually. I think I suffer from confabulation."

"Let me see. I got your message, but I didn't quite understand what you told me. Tell me what's wrong."

"I have a feeling that everything I'm experiencing I've lived through already. And, worse, I have memories of the future. I remember things that haven't happened yet. For example, the day Alma left me, I knew she was going to leave me."

"Did Alma leave you?"

"Yes."

"I'm sorry to hear that."

I couldn't contain my sadness and started to sob. Dr. Hogan reached for the box of Kleenex and put it in front of me.

"Thank you, Doctor. I appreciate it."

I paused to wipe my tears and snot and calm down.

"But, as I said, it wasn't a surprise. I already knew it."

"Did you know Alma was going to leave you?"

"Yes, and it wasn't just a fear. I knew it for sure. I had forgotten all the details of how it was going to happen, but I knew it ahead of time with absolute certainty. I did my best to avoid having the argument that I knew was going to break the camel's back, but it was useless. It happened. Later I remembered the details of that other argument. It was identical to the one Alma and I had last week, in the same place, and under the exact same circumstances. And she also reacted the same way: leaving me."

"Let's take it one step at a time, Uriel. Tell me what happened."

"Last week Alma and I went camping in the Apache Kid Wilderness, in the San Mateo Mountains. The evening before we returned to Albuquerque, I decided to take a hike to look for a spotted owl, as I have never seen one in its natural habitat. Alma did not want to accompany me; she stayed in the tent because she wanted to rest and sleep peacefully. I left at about eight o'clock and very soon I found an owl. I didn't know if it was spotted or not, so I wanted to make sure. I tried to observe it closely, but it wouldn't let me and, little by little, it went deep into the mountain forest. Unfortunately, I got lost chasing it. That night I had to sleep in the open air."

"Oh, I'm sorry. That must have been frustrating. Did anything happen to you?"

"Nothing. I woke up perfectly well. But I had some incredibly realistic dreams that night. I dreamed I was lost in a mountain forest. There I met a strange man who offered to show me the way home. However, along the way he transformed himself into a Franciscan friar and took me to his mission. He told me he was my father and that I had come from Mexico City to help him convert the Apache. It was the summer of 1665. When I went to fulfill my alleged mission, I met a mysterious Apache, who turned out to be my relative."

"How interesting." She was the master of understatement, or so I liked to believe.

"He was healing me from an evil produced by an owl. By the way, he wore a medicine wheel necklace just like yours, and he had an uncanny resemblance to you."

"Is that right?"

"Yes. His face resembled yours. He even made the same expression you make with your lips."

"What do you mean?"

"He would protrude his lips in a sulky pout when he was pensive and listened attentively, just as you're doing right now." I imitated her expression, which made her laugh.

"Is that what I do?"

"Yes. Didn't you know?"

"Actually, yes. It's a characteristic expression of my family on my mother's side. Also, the angular jaw and cleft chin are theirs."

"Refugio looked a lot like you. Of course, you're much prettier than him," I said, laughing. She celebrated my joke with jovial laughter.

"Refugio had lost an eye and had a large scar on the left side."

"Is that why I'm prettier than him?" she told me, laughing, but in a tone that hinted I had offended her vanity.

"You are much younger and more elegant and distinguished," I replied in a flattering tone, which caused her to blush.

"And then what happened in your dream?"

"A lot of things happened that I don't remember anymore. What I do remember very well is that I was aware that I was dreaming. However, no matter how hard I tried, I couldn't wake up. I even started to think that I was actually Diego."

"Diego?"

"Brother Diego Romero. That's who I was in this dream. I lived Diego's life for a period that seemed like an eternity to me. In Diego's body I had many realistic experiences and numerous equally vivid dreams, as if I had traveled through time to a myriad of possible worlds. Until I finally woke up."

"How fascinating!"

"And the weirdest thing of all is that I was hoping to wake up in Ithaca."

"In Homer's Ithaca?"

"No, in New York."

"Why over there?"

"Because that's where I moved after Alma killed herself."

"Alma killed herself?"

"Well, not yet, but she is going to."

"And how do you know?"

"I'm not sure how I know it. I even know how it's going to happen. She'll fail her exams and then will commit suicide."

"What exams?"

"Her PhD qualifying exams."

"Aren't you being too pessimistic? Aren't you having the usual catastrophic thoughts?"

"I ask myself the same question, but I'm not speculating. I'm sure I've experienced all of this before. I'm telling you, everything I'm going through I've experienced already, including this conversation you and I are having."

"We already had this conversation?"

"Yes, it happened on this very date, in this same place. You were wearing the same flowery dress, and you were equally incredulous with me. I'm telling you, I've lost all sense of reality."

"Existence is an illusion, a dream, Uriel. Human beings are unconscious fabulists, dreamers who don't realize they are only dreaming. You are not crazy, Uriel. You are simply a dreamer who has acquired a certain degree of lucidity about illusory existence."

"So, am I having another lucid dream?"

"That's right."

"How do you know?"

"I'm just your invention. You're the one who knows."

"That's what I suspect, but everything seems so real to me."

"The dreams of wakefulness are as illusory as nocturnal dreams. Both the real world and the dream world are creations of the mind produced by the mental habits you have acquired throughout your existence. Most of our dreams are born of our mental obfuscation, which is the product of our lack of understanding of reality. However, there are dreams that arise from clairvoyance."

"Like this one."

"I doubt it. Your mind is still as obfuscated as ever."

"But I'm having a lucid dream. I know I'm dreaming."

"It's a very weak lucid dream because you're not in control. There are varying degrees of lucidity. In truly lucid dreams it is you who control your dreams. So far you have let the inertia of your dreams push you around, like dry leaves tossed by the wind. Moreover, your dreams are the product of your lack of self-awareness. The dreams of obliviousness keep you bound to the illusory existence in which your soul has lived since time immemorial. They are produced by your ignorance, desires, and fears. These kinds of dreams reveal your lack of understanding of reality and your weak spiritual condition. Instead, the dreams of clairvoyance allow you to glimpse other possible worlds and higher forms of existence. They give you teachings that allow you to overcome the challenges we face in this life. They help us reach the stillness of the serene consciousness, an existence in which we have neither desires nor dreams."

"And how can I avoid obfuscation?"

"Free yourself from all attachments that bond you to this illusory world. When you have nothing to hold on to, you will put an end to obfuscation like the healed lunatic who finally escapes from his imaginary prison."

43

MY MEETING WITH DR. HOGAN TURNED OUT TO BE ANOTHER dream. Maybe it was a clairvoyant dream, I thought when I woke up, because in it the doctor communicated to me something that I found vitally important. I decided to write it down in a notebook. From that day on I promised myself to stop clinging to Alma and everything that tied me to her, telling myself that all my attachments were the shackles preventing me from leaving the mental cage in which I had locked myself. Every time I felt sadness about what happened, or nostalgia and longing for what I had lost, I was going to repeat my new mantra: Existence is an illusion.

When I finally had my appointment with Dr. Hogan, I told her my dream. She recommended that I write all my dreams in a diary as soon as I got up. In addition to being a source of literary creativity and helping me combat writer's block, she assured me that dreams were the key to my recovery. She pointed out the importance of journaling my daily experiences for these were not fundamentally different from dreams. Additionally, just as it was important to achieve lucidity in dreams, it was important to keep awareness when awake. I was not sure if this was an insinuation. Nonetheless, she discarded my fear that I was going crazy or that I had some kind of memory disease. She recommended that I continue to practice meditation and mindfulness to relax and harmonize body and mind, which would not only help me fight depression but also mitigate my personal crisis.

To this end, and to be with others who meditate, I decided to visit a Buddhist temple. My visit coincided with the celebration of the festival of hungry ghosts, *pretas*. Its purpose was to remember the dead, undo our karmic bonds with them, and, in general, detach ourselves from anything that obstructed and made our spiritual journey difficult. It was a week of daily meditation sessions that culminated in a weekend retreat and a festival on Sunday. Hungry ghosts were the lost souls of all those who did not find eternal rest because they devoted their lives to satisfying their material desires or carnal appetites. They suffered from perpetual starvation and thirst. They prowled the places that display an abundance of all the things they craved but couldn't have. The festival was partly made to help them. People meditated, offered prayers, mantras, songs, music, and food to the ghosts, and invited them to learn Buddhist doctrine to find peace and achieve liberation. Another important purpose of the festival was to help the living break the bonds that tied them to their deceased loved ones, as well as to solve karmic issues that were preventing or impeding their spiritual progress.

At the end of the ceremony, held on Sunday evening, the monks lit a fire in the chimney. They handed out sheets of paper and asked us to write down the names of our loved ones who had died in the past year, as well as the karmic problems we wanted to solve and our spiritual achievements during this period. Finally, we were invited to put in the fire what we wrote down to transfer our merits to our deceased loved ones and to purify our spirit. On my sheet I simply wrote *alma*, which means soul in Spanish.

During the months of July and August, I continued to go to the temple weekly and saw Dr. Hogan every other week. I practiced meditation and did yoga and exercised daily; I ate healthily; I took frequent Epsom salt baths; I did aromatherapy with a variety of essential oils; I read Buddhist and Hindu books; I studied a voluminous treatise on mindfulness; I wrote down in my journal my experiences, my thoughts, and my dreams. In sum, I did everything I could to clear and calm my mind, to strengthen my body and spirit, and to forget Alma.

I remembered how hard it had been to do it. However, the fact that I knew that I was going to overcome the pain of losing her and that I would be able to remake my life filled me with optimism. I promised myself to resist the temptation to look for her and beg her to come back, for I knew how harmful this would be for both of us. She needed to focus on her studies and I to free myself from all the attachments and negative emotions that prevented me from seeking Nirvana. But one September afternoon, when I saw Alma riding a Harley Davidson and hugging a Hell's Angel, I fell from that cloud castle and sank into the abyss.

I didn't do it for me; I did it for her. I knew the guy would lead her to doom so I couldn't remain a passive bystander. I wrote her emails alerting her of the danger; I called her at different times; I put letters in her mailbox at the university and at Lisa's house; I sent her flowers; I asked her friends to convey my messages to her; I looked everywhere for her and waited for her for long hours day and night. I didn't find her, and she did not answer any of my calls or messages. She disappeared. She left with that fiend, I don't know where, and she abandoned her studies. Inexplicably, she showed up for her exams and, as happened the other time, she failed them. I remembered that soon she was to go on a motorcycle trip with her lover on the Devil's Road and flew to Gallup to wait for her on the corner where Route 666 began. I waited for her in the Goldfinch for more than twenty-four hours without sleeping. But I didn't see her pass by, and I never saw her again. As I knew would happen, Alma turned up dead from a levorphanol overdose at a service station in Monticello, Utah, right where that cursed road ended. It was the night of Saturday, September 23, 1995.

Alma's tragic end happened again in a place called "mound" in Italian, which alluded to Thomas Jefferson's plantation, whose mansion was engraved on the back of the nickel. On the morning of Monday, September 25, I received a call from the Monticello police informing me of the event and notifying me that Alma's body was in the Utah Medical Examiner's Office. The agent informed me that Alma's body had been taken there because the circumstances of her death were suspicious, and because they had occurred within their jurisdiction. She informed me that the MEO investigated all violent or sudden unexpected deaths from unnatural causes, as well as suspicious ones. She told me that an investigator would visit me in the coming days to ask me a few questions and that as soon as the exact causes and circumstances of her death were determined, they would be able to issue the death certificate. She asked me to contact a funeral home to begin the paperwork for her burial.

As soon as I hung up, a cascade of painful memories engulfed and dragged me to bed, where I spent three days mourning Alma. That same afternoon I got a parcel from Alma with a letter addressed "To whom it may concern," stating that no one should be blamed for her suicide. Inside the legal-size manila envelope was a certificate she had obtained herself, attesting she had donated her body to the University of Utah's anatomy lab. It also contained her will in which she made me the universal heir of all her assets and belongings. "The dead impart teachings to the living (*MORTUI VIVOS DOCENT*)," Alma wrote cryptically under her signature.

44

OUR FAMILY AND FRIENDS IN JUÁREZ AND EL PASO SOON FOUND out about her death; I don't know how. Alma and I had made a pact to break with the past, give up everything that united us to it, and start a new life dedicated to philosophy (her) and literature (me). For this and other personal reasons, both of us had broken ties with most of our relatives and friends from Juárez–El Paso; so much so that almost nobody knew our phone number or address. Within two days, however, they filled my voicemail and inbox with personal and religious messages that I listened to with listlessness and never answered.

The phone rang incessantly until I unplugged it. I didn't feel like talking to anyone, much less with Alma's relatives, who considered me unworthy of being part of their prominent family. The fact that Pepe, one of my siblings, was a small-time drug dealer sealed their disdain toward me and my family. They would have accepted me a little more if I had at least done something with the master's degree in agricultural economics that I obtained in Las Cruces, and, above all, if I had saved from bankruptcy El Porvenir and the other idle lands that survived from the agricultural emporium built by one of my maternal great-great-grandparents in the Juárez Valley during the time of Don Porfirio.

When I married Alma, one of her maternal uncles offered that I manage one of his ranches in Villa Ahumada, but I didn't accept. Alma was about to finish her bachelor's in philosophy at UTEP within a year, and she was planning to apply for doctoral programs at various universities in the United States. In the meantime, I was looking for a part-time job in El Paso that would help us cover our expenses and allow me to devote myself to writing. Neither Alma's family, nor mine, nor my friends could understand how I had rejected this offer that would allow me to work with Rafael Falcón, who was one of the richest men on the US-Mexico border. They commented behind my back that what I really wanted was to live the good life at the expense of my in-laws. Anyone with a university degree who aspired to be a writer and who did not mind having a minimum-wage job seemed like an imbecile to them. My parents, who also lamented the fact that I renounced Mexican citizenship when I married Alma and Catholicism after reading Nietzsche, agreed on this.

On Thursday, September 28, five days after Alma's death, her mother showed up at my apartment accompanied by Lisa at about eleven in the morning. Alma's mother was an attractive and elegant woman. She had a certain resemblance to the Venezuelan designer Carolina Herrera and scrupulously aped her style and demeanor. She arrived in her Mercedes-Benz W140 followed by a Falcon Trucking van to haul Alma's belongings. Neither Lisa nor she knew about Alma's posthumous letter. I suspected that Alma's mother was mostly interested in getting ahold of her diaries. I showed her the letter, the certificate, and Alma's will and pointed out the paragraph where Alma said that she had bequeathed all her assets and belongings to me. She asked me why I wanted her clothes and personal items, and I replied that it was my business. She begged and tried to convince me with crocodile tears. She claimed that Alma's personal articles meant the world to her because she hadn't been able to say good-bye to her. She pulled her checkbook out of her Gucci purse and offered to write me a check for $25,000 to help me with my personal expenses. When I refused, she offered me $100,000 so that I could buy myself a house, but as soon as she realized she wasn't going to persuade me with her money, she lost control and went into a rage. She jumped at me and tried to snatch the letter from me. Luckily, Lisa intervened, and I was able to get away from her without pushing or touching her. Lisa had an expression of horror and disbelief. I also found it implausible to see Alma's mother, who was a conceited and distant woman, transform herself in this way. Her smoothed-back hairstyle and designer brooch popped loose; her mascara was dripping; her blouse had become unbuttoned. One of her earrings fell to the floor and she bent down to pick it up. It was a pathetic scene. Lisa helped her get up and tried to calm her down, but I asked them to leave. On her way out, Lidia Falcón de Mengel assured me that I would not get a nickel from Alma's inheritance and that I would pay dearly for my daring and insolence.

As soon as her Mercedes and the van left, I put Alma's diaries in my backpack and rushed to the library to put them in my locker, where they'd be safer. I assumed Alma's father and Luisfer would also come to Albuquerque and feared they could drop in at any moment. I went out the side door on my bike so I could go down the alley that ran by the house. Before getting on my bike, I made sure no one was lurking and, when I was certain nobody was, I pedaled in a hurry and looked back numerous times to verify that no one was following me. I checked into the library and put the diaries away in my locker. After I talked to my supervisor and explained to her why I had missed work all these days, I went to the supermarket to buy groceries. Then I went back to the apartment stealthily, locked the two doors, and made sure all the windows and blinds were fully closed. I knew that the members of the Holy Brotherhood, as Alma called the international network of child pornographers to which her father and brother belonged, were capable of anything. I was afraid someone might sneak through a window to kidnap and then kill me.

I was starving and made myself a couple of bean and cheese *molletes* and some coffee. I played *Into the Labyrinth*, a Dead Can Dance CD that Alma liked, and sat on the living room couch to eat. I began to reflect on the incident and realized that the facts did not correspond to what I remembered of my last meeting with my ex-mother-in-law. Had I foreseen this encounter in a dream? Had it actually happened?

The morning she came to my apartment with Lisa, I behaved differently, I recalled. I was courteous and accommodating. Not only did I allow her to take all of Alma's belongings but I told her that I did not intend to collect the inheritance Alma had bequeathed me. In addition, I gave her the envelope with the letter, the certificate, Alma's will, and wrote a letter stating that I renounced all her daughter's assets and belongings, without exception. She was moved by my acquiescence and wrote me a $25,000 check for my personal expenses, but I did not accept it. Then I helped the movers pack Alma's things and gave each one of them a twenty-dollar tip. I tried to give my ex-mother-in-law a farewell hug, but she stepped back and offered me her hand instead. When I extended mine, she shook it with both hands and, with tears in her eyes, wished me the best and departed with Lisa and the movers.

On that occasion I acted in a prudent way. I immediately realized that Alma wanted to set me up by bequeathing everything, including her diaries. I inferred this was going to offer me an insoluble ethical dilemma. From a legal standpoint, I had the obligation to give the Mexican authorities Alma's diaries and file a report. However, given the Mexican authorities' corruption and the enormous power and influence that Alma's father and uncles had in Juárez, it was obvious that following the legal channels would not only be a waste of time but extremely dangerous. Dr. Mengel or another member of the Holy Brotherhood would surely make me disappear for being a snitch and a meddler. Another option was to hand over the papers to some brave journalist willing to risk their life by publishing the results of Alma's investigations. An alternative was to give them to the *El Paso Post* journalist who was writing a book about the international network of child pornographers operating in Juárez and El Paso. The problem with both options was that I knew from experience that the powerful political allies of the Holy Brotherhood would intervene publicly to defend the accused and to question the validity of the investigations, as had already happened with the work done by several Mexican journalists. Worse, not only the journalist and I would be in grave danger but also our respective families, for the Holy Brothers would unleash their fury and quench their thirst for revenge against us all. The last resort was to edit the diaries and publish them as fiction, which would perhaps be overlooked by the Holy Brotherhood. However, it would show not only that I had no word, for I had promised Alma to abandon this literary project, but also that I was an unscrupulous opportunist willing to exploit and profit from her tragedy. That's why I decided to let my ex-mother-in-law take Alma's letter, diaries, and belongings, and that's why I also wrote that letter renouncing the inheritance Alma had left me.

Why did I act this way today? Wasn't I repeating what I had lived already? Wasn't I dreaming?

Then I remembered Lupita Gualtoye's savage killing. I felt guilt and remorse for having acted so cowardly when I decided not to fulfill my civic duty to report the horrific crime committed against her. The six-year-old girl was kidnapped, raped, tortured, killed, and mutilated by Luisfer and Damián Elizondo in front of a video camera in June 1984 in a warehouse owned by Alma's father near the airport. Alma discovered her brother watching this video and masturbating in their father's man cave in the basement of their house, located in Rincones de Senecú. Luisfer saw her and ignored her. He didn't even bother to hide the VHS cassette and left it inside the VCR.

The next day Alma saw the horrifying video and hid it without knowing what to do. When Luisfer could not find the video, he barged into her bedroom, where she was changing after taking a shower. He demanded that she return the video cassette to him. She tried to kick him out, but Luisfer beat her savagely until she was unconscious. She was taken in an ambulance and remained in the hospital under observation for a couple of days until she recovered from the concussion, which fortunately did not produce any brain damage. When asked by her relatives and friends why Luisfer had beaten her, Alma remained silent. Nobody bothered or dared to inquire what happened. They knew Luisfer had been traumatized by the six-month abduction he had suffered when he was thirteen; ever since, he had occasional fits of rage for no apparent reason. The only one who insisted that she reveal the truth was her mother.

According to one of Alma's diaries, shortly before she was discharged from the hospital, her mother questioned her. In the hospital room Alma confessed that she caught Luisfer watching a snuff film and that he beat her because she refused to give it back to him or tell him where she had hidden it. Alma wrote down in her diary the argument she had with her mother that day. I remembered clearly what she wrote in that entry:

> "You know very well that your brother is very irritable and doesn't like anybody to pry into his stuff, let alone his videos."
>
> "They're no ordinary videos, Mom," I replied, exasperated and tormented by inner pain but holding back tears. "It was a pornographic video in which a little girl was raped, tortured, and killed."
>
> "And how do you know?"
>
> "Because I saw it with my own eyes. I found it in the VCR, in my father's man cave."
>
> "And what were you doing there? You know your father has strictly forbidden you to enter that room."
>
> "Oh, Mom. You are always justifying Dad and defending Luisfer."
>
> "And you are always disobeying and doing whatever you want."

"What does that have to do with this?"

"Everything. You wouldn't be here if you hadn't entered your father's man cave."

"I went down to the basement because I was looking for Encarna."

"If you were looking for one of the maids, why did you turn on the VCR? Did you think you were going to find her there? You know your father watches movies that aren't appropriate for minors."

"Luisfer is younger than me and you don't say anything to him when he locks himself in the cave to watch those movies."

"Because he's a boy."

"Why does that matter? Besides, it wasn't one of my dad's movies. It was a video filmed by Luisfer and Damián."

"What the hell are you saying?"

"What you're hearing. Luisfer and Damián shot that video. They filmed themselves raping and strangling Lupita, the missing daughter of Elizondo's maid. Then, after choking her to death, they continued to rape and desecrate her inert body as if she were a rag doll. Afterward, they had fun hitting her with a tube and mutilating her with Luisfer's Swiss knife."

When she heard this, my mother remained silent and lost in her thoughts for a few moments. She didn't seem to be shocked or alarmed. I wasn't at all surprised by her reaction. I knew Luisfer was my mother's favorite child. She forgave everything he did and scolded me for anything. She justified her unfairness by saying that he had been tortured by his kidnappers and that I was a rebellious and spoiled daughter. Claudia, my younger sister, by contrast, according to her, was the model child. If she knew the things Claudia did behind her back! She's a two-face! But Claudia was submissive, sweet, and discreet. She took meticulous care of her personal image and belongings and never questioned my parents' authority. She accepted without protest the preferential treatment our brothers received and never meddled in their affairs or questioned their behavior. She accepted the place each of us occupied in the family. Boys were given all kinds of freedoms by our parents, including collecting porn magazines and films and decorating their bedrooms with posters of naked women. They were not required to clean or tidy up their rooms or help in the household chores; that's what the maids were for. They were allowed to use profanities in the house and be rude and high-handed with the employees; they were taught to shoot and were taken to the firing range and hunting in the wilderness from a young age and, if by the age of fifteen they had not lost their virginity, one of our father's friends would sponsor and take them to a brothel "so that they become men."

"Don't tell anyone about this. You hear me?" This was my mother's response. "I'm going to investigate this matter myself." She asked me to tell her where I hid the video, and I did.

When I got back to the house, it was no longer where I had left it. My mom took it. I don't know what she did with it. Nobody in our family ever said a word about what Luisfer did to me, much less mention the video. The only thing my parents did was to transfer Luisfer to Roswell's military academy. That was his punishment. They sent him hoping he would reform and become more disciplined there.

But whoever is born a fiend dies a fiend. Ten years later, news started circulating in local newspapers that some "juniors"—children of well-to-do parents—were the perpetrators of similar femicides. My brother's name was not on the list of suspects, but my parents soon learned that the FBI was investigating him. To protect him, and hoping to treat his alcoholism and drug addiction, they sent him to a rehabilitation center located in Spain's Costa Brava, where he was treated like a prince in a luxurious room with a sea view, hypnotherapy sessions, equine therapy, yoga, massages, sauna, and sun baths. At the same time, the Holy Brotherhood commissioned one of its members to infiltrate the FBI, which was investigating this international network of child traffickers and pornographers. This individual was hired by the FBI as a translator. As such, he had access to the computer files where Luisfer's case was being recorded, and he deleted them. Although he was caught and imprisoned for this and other crimes, he fulfilled his mission and, although an El Paso journalist has accused my brother of being the material and intellectual author of dozens of femicides, for lack of evidence and for the enormous influence exerted by the Holy Brotherhood at the border, neither my brother nor my father have ever been questioned or charged for the crimes they allegedly committed.

45

I FINISHED MY REMEMBRANCE OF THAT INCIDENT WITH MY EX-mother-in-law, whose outcome had been so different from the one I'd had with her recently. What should I do with Alma's diaries now that the day had gone so differently? Burn them? Notify the police? Contact a journalist? Give them to my ex-mother-in-law? Keep them and use them for my novel?

I was pondering what to do when someone knocked. The three strong, firm knocks startled me. I walked to the door, took a careful peek through the peephole, and saw a bald, pot-bellied, middle-aged Anglo man holding a binder. He was wearing a blue, button-down, short-sleeved shirt and brown slacks. I could only guess that he was the agent from the Utah Medical Examiner's Office, so I opened the door and, indeed, he handed me one of his cards, and I asked him to come in. He was sweating profusely so I offered him a glass of water. After finishing it and complaining about Albuquerque's summer heat, he pulled out a form and started asking me questions.

He wanted to know where I had been on the day of Alma's death and who had prescribed her the levorphanol pills. I replied that chances were that she was with the biker and that perhaps it was he who had given her the pills since she did not suffer from any illness or chronic pain. He asked me to describe him. I told him that I hadn't really seen him up close, but that he was a blond, tall, muscular man with a padlock beard and long hair and that he was wearing a black leather vest with Hell's Angels emblems sewn on the back. As he was taking notes, I realized that he suspected that I had something to do with Alma's death and assumed that he did not know about her posthumous letter.

I got up, went to my bedroom to grab it, and handed it to him. He read it closely and asked me how I had obtained it. I showed him the stamped envelope, which contained the certificate and Alma's will. Without asking, he seized all the documents and told me they were important pieces of evidence. He promised he would mail them back as soon as they solved the case. He gave me some instructions, verified all my personal information, and said goodbye cordially, if curtly.

I went to lie down to try to take a nap. I needed to rest because, although I felt indisposed, I had to go to work the next day. Even though it was roasting hot, I turned off the AC to save money. I was on a tight budget and didn't want to overspend. I had gone to Albuquerque to support Alma in her studies and to pursue my dream of writing works of fiction and to live an examined life. Now that Alma was gone, I didn't know if I should stay or move. But where? I contemplated but immediately discarded the possibility of returning to Juárez, where I had free food and housing at my parents'. In addition to being unwilling to let them see me as a spoiled sluggard, I feared that the Holy Brotherhood would disappear me while in Juárez. In Albuquerque I had a modest but stable job. However, now that my ex-mother-in-law knew where I lived, I began to worry, as the Holy Brotherhood could potentially send some of its agents to kidnap and disappear me as they did to Hermes, the trusted employee of the Falcons who betrayed them by giving Alma information about the Holy Brotherhood.

On the bedside table was an anthology of sacred texts from ancient Egypt that I had checked out from the library. I opened it to chapter eight, which contained the story of the Book of Thoth. I started reading it to distract myself and fall asleep. It took a huge effort to concentrate, both because of my worries and the intense heat. I had to reread the first paragraph numerous times to enjoy the story about Naneferkaptah, the son of the pharaoh who loved wisdom about all things and who did not care about the worldly affairs of the kingdom. When the story finally absorbed me, sleep also overcame me, and I started to dream that I was Neferkaptah.

I was shelving some books in the history of philosophy section, and I got distracted reading a few pages of a book titled *The Quest for Truth* when Bill, one of the library custodians, approached and asked:

"Are you interested in the subject of truth? I know where the Book of Thoth is."

"The Book of Thoth?"

"Yes, the book that compiles the whole and absolute truth of all that is, was, and will be. There you can find everything related to the femicides of your city: how, where, and when these horrendous crimes occurred; who the victims, the killers, the accomplices, and the abettors are."

"I don't want to know anything about it, because whoever knows the truth either shuts up or gets killed, and I'm a coward."

"There you can also find out what your destiny is and, if you read your biography, you will be able to return to the world of the living when you die or get killed."

"I'm not interested in resurrecting in this Hell."

"How about in Paradise?"

"It all depends. If Paradise is a place where everyone praises God day and night without questioning anything, I'd prefer to die and dissolve into Mother Earth's bosom."

"Aren't you interested in acquiring wisdom? Don't you want to know the origin and purpose of your existence?"

"Of course I do."

"Then follow me. I'm going to show you where the Book of Thoth is. It's in the catacombs of this library."

"There are no catacombs here."

"That's what you think, but every library that is worthy of the name has secret catacombs."

"Alright. Let's go."

He led me to the elevator. In one of the left-side loops of his trousers he had a bulky retractable keychain. He inserted and rotated one of the keys on the control board and we descended to the CC level. It was a series of hexagonal galleries on whose stone walls were vertically aligned the skeletons of its dwellers. Inside each gallery there were shelves with books and rolls of all kinds and sizes.

We walked through the corridors until we found the mummy of a guy named Hermes García Sánchez. He was perfectly preserved and had an uncanny resemblance to a high school acquaintance, who was his namesake. He was wearing a black, felt, ten-gallon hat, a black cowboy suit, a scarlet-red vest, a white linen shirt, a bolo tie, and a large silver buckle engraved with a triple golden cross. He was also wearing a pair of perfectly polished, black, alligator-leather boots.

Bill patted the mummy on the cheek, and Hermes woke up. Then Bill unfastened the belts that secured him to the wall. Once untied, Hermes stretched out to come to life.

"Hermes?" I asked.

He looked at me like a total stranger and asked Bill:

"What's this guy doing in the House of Life?"

"This man professes to be a lover of truth and wants to read your very erudite book, *The True History of the Femicides of Juárez*."

I protested. I explained that Bill promised me he was going to show me the Book of Thoth.

"Thoth is my secret name. Who revealed it to you? Was it you, Bill?"

"No, Hermes. I just told him I knew where the Book of Thoth was."

Suddenly I realized that this was Hermes, the trusted employee of Rafael Falcón who Luisfer tortured and killed for having disclosed to Alma the secrets of the Holy Brotherhood.

"Are you Hermes, Rafa Falcón's employee?"

"I am. And who are *you*?"

"Don't you remember me? I'm Uriel Romero. We both went to Park Middle School."

"No, I don't remember you."

"Do you remember Alma Mengel?"

"How can I forget her; it's her fault I'm here. She was the first and only reader of my book. To my misfortune, I allowed her to take notes."

"I have her diaries."

When I told him this, he pulled a coin purse out of his pocket and paid Bill with a gold coin.

"Here you go. Thank you very much, Bill. Good job."

"You betcha," Bill replied and left without saying good-bye.

"So you already know some of the contents of my book," Hermes said. "My whole book is at your disposal."

"I really don't want to know more about the Juárez femicides."

"And why not? If you've read Alma's diaries, your fate is already decided. My ex-boss will find out sooner or later and his henchmen will disappear you."

"I do not aspire to be a martyr for truth."

"Didn't Bill say you consider yourself a lover of truth?"

"I am, but not of historical truth. What interests me is the absolute truth, metaphysical truth, the truth of being and existence, not the relative and temporal truths of mortals."

"Do you ignore that the wisdom of the gods is not made for mortals?"

"That's what they say, but they also say that we don't discover the truth of our existence and our ultimate destiny until we die."

"Then why are you afraid to know the truth of the femicides? Only the dead know the ultimate truth."

"Do they? Even if you do, or you think you do, I'm not sure I'm ready for it yet."

"You are, Uriel. Believe me, you are, otherwise you wouldn't be here talking to me. So sit in that cubicle and listen carefully to what I have to reveal to you."

"Where is the Book of Thoth?"

"Don't be naive. They burned it before they killed me, but I know it by heart."

I sat by a desk where there was a bronze tray with a stack of authentic Egyptian papyrus sheets and a fountain pen. I wrote down all the information that Hermes slowly retrieved from his portentous memory. I wrote nonstop and, when I ran out of paper, he told me that I had finished my heroic task and that it was time to celebrate.

From an ebony bar cabinet, he pulled out a bottle of dark beer and uncorked it. To my surprise, he poured the sparkling liquid into the tray where I had placed my notes. He explained that, once the beer dissolved all the ink, I had to drink it to the last drop to leave no trace of what I had written.

"This is the method of learning of wise wizards since time immemorial," he remarked.

Once all the ink was completely dissolved, I drank the bitter concoction. When I finished it, he asked me to kneel and, with my head bowed and my eyes closed, to repeat the prayers to the goddess Isis and Harpocrates, the Greek deity of silence and discretion, that he was going to utter. I did so with both reverence and faith. Then he asked me to get up and led me down a hallway into a dining room where a feast with delicacies of all kinds was awaiting me.

As I was dining, Hermes took the opportunity to explain to me the seven principles of absolute truth, whose knowledge, he assured me, opens all the doors of the Temple of Wisdom. I listened to him, astonished, and told myself that this was undoubtedly the most important day in my entire life and that, having attained that eternal and liberating knowledge, I was ready to die.

46

I FELT A DEEP SATISFACTION AT FINALLY ACQUIRING THE WISDOM I had longed for since I first read Plato. But I soon realized it had been just a dream. Nevertheless, even though I did not fulfill my philosophical fantasy, I realized this dream was a premonition of what could happen to me if I did not leave Albuquerque. The Holy Brotherhood knew where I lived, and they would come to get me any day. I had to leave as soon as possible. But where? If I stayed in Albuquerque and kept my job at the library, it wouldn't be long before they found me. I needed to get as far away from there as possible to a place they wouldn't suspect. I immediately thought of Ithaca. If my memory of the future didn't betray me, I knew I was going to be able to remake my life there. They would never suspect that I would go to a town in upstate New York.

However, I didn't know anyone there yet, and without money or employment, it would be reckless to leave. I decided to call my brother Pepe for help. Despite being the black sheep of the family, of all my siblings he was the only one I could fully trust. I searched for his information in my address book and dialed his number. It was four o'clock in the afternoon.

"Hello."

"Bro?"

"Who's talking?"

"It's Uriel, Pepe."

"Uriel? What's up! How are you?"

"Not so great."

"It's been so long. Where are you?"

"In Albuquerque."

"Hey, bro, can you wait a minute? I can't hear you very well. Let me find a better place to talk."

"Where are you? I hear music."

"At La Rueda Bar. I'm having some drinks with my buddies."

"No problem, Pepe. I can call you back some other time."

"It's no biggie, bro. I just need to go outside. Hold on."

"Okay. I'll wait for you."

After a couple of minutes, we resumed our conversation.

"I'm so glad you called, Uriel. We've been worried about you. We heard about Alma. I'm so sorry about what happened. My deepest condolences, bro. We've been trying to reach you."

"Thanks so much, Pepe. Yes, I know. It's been really hard. I'm sorry I didn't call you back."

"No worries, Uriel. I just wanted to say hi and tell you I'm here for whatever you need. We haven't spoken in a long time. You must be having a hard time being all alone. Why don't you come over here for a while? All your family is here."

"I'd like to, Pepe, but you know how Mom and Dad are."

"I understand. They get on my case too. They're obsessed with what people would say."

"They still want to treat me like I'm a kid who doesn't know what he's doing."

"Same here, you know, but what can I say. That's how they are. You can stay at my place, if you'd prefer."

"Thank you very much, Pepe, I appreciate it, but I won't be able to go to Juárez for quite some time."

"And why not?"

"It's a long story. I'd rather not talk about it. You know it's better not to say certain things by phone."

"Yeah, I get it. Is there anything I can do for you, Uriel? Are you in trouble?"

"Actually, yes. I want to leave Albuquerque, but I don't have enough money for the move."

"How much do you need?"

"Two thousand dollars."

"No problem. I can lend you more if you want."

"Two thousand is enough. I can pay for the moving van, the deposit, and the first month's rent with that money."

"And where are you going to move to? If you don't mind telling me."

"I'd rather not."

"You can trust me."

"I know, Pepe. Don't take me wrong, but it's better that you don't know. In fact, this conversation must remain between you and me."

"You sound very mysterious, Uriel. What kind of trouble are you in? Does it have to do with Alma's death?"

"None at all. Don't think badly of me. Alma committed suicide and the police aren't looking for me."

"No?"

"Man, are you suspicious of me? How little you know me."

"No, it's not that, but it just seems like you have something to hide."

"To dispel your doubts, and so you can see that I trust you, I'm going to tell you what happened. Alma left me mid-May and went to live at a friend's house."

"Gee, man. I'm sorry."

"She had long been depressed, and her self-esteem was in the pits. All because of her family problems."

"Yeah. To tell you the truth, that was pretty obvious."

"The thing is, she got involved with a Hell's Angel. Alma died of an overdose while traveling with this guy on a motorcycle. She died in Utah."

"I'll be fucking damned. Sorry, bro, but what a motherfucker! And her family knows this?"

"I think so, but I'm not sure. You know Alma had broken ties with them, and her parents never liked me. They always thought I was unworthy of their daughter."

"I know. They think they're better than everybody else. They're filthy rich and they're rotten to the core. Regardless, you'd better clear the matter with them. You don't want them as your enemies. You know the Falcons are very powerful and influential. They're capable of anything. Be careful, Uriel, especially with what has happened. You don't want them to blame you for Alma's death. Have you talked to them?"

"Yes, with her mom. She came to Albuquerque."

"Everything went well?"

"Well, no, not really, but, as I say, it's better not to get into details."

"Does this have anything to do with Doctor Death's and Luisfer's foul play?"

"Yep."

"Fuck."

"Do you know anything?"

"Well, of course. Everyone knows but no one dares to say anything."

"That's why I don't want you to tell anyone we talked. Tread carefully, bro. They believe I'm not in touch with my family. It's better that they keep believing it."

"Don't worry about me. I can take care of myself; they can suck my dick. And where do you want me to send you the dough?"

"To my bank account. Please send me an electronic transfer tomorrow first thing, as I'd like to leave as soon as possible. I'm going to give you my account number. Do you have something on which to write?"

"Yes, I have my address book. Wait a sec."

"It's the Bank of Albuquerque. Thank you very much, Pepe. I really appreciate it."

"That's what brothers are for, right? If you need more, let me know. And don't get lost. Call me once in a while."

"Sure thing, Pepe. I'll call you when I settle down. Take care and say hi to everyone. Please don't tell them anything I told you."

"Of course. Loose lips sink ships."

As soon as I hung up, I started preparing for the move. I regretted having to leave my job at the library. I didn't know how my supervisor was going to take it and I was worried she wouldn't write me a good letter of recommendation. I was also worried that I would damage my credit and lose the deposit I had paid to the landlady, as I was going to have to break the lease. Either way, this mattered little compared with the risk I was taking staying in my apartment and in Albuquerque. I had to leave as soon as possible; tomorrow if I could. I needed to pack and book a U-Haul.

I called all the offices nearby and other moving companies, but no one had a van available for another eight days, which seemed like an eternity to me. I had no choice but to wait. It was the sensible thing to do. Besides, I still hadn't received my brother's transfer. Although I was confident he was going to send it to me, I knew Pepe well and knew that, once he started the drinking bout with his buddies, it would turn into a marathon, and it would be hard to get ahold of him for days.

It was almost five o'clock in the afternoon when the postal carrier arrived. In the correspondence there was a letter from the Utah Medical Examiner's Office. It notified me that they had completed their investigations and that the University of Utah was going to mail me the amended death certificate soon. They attached a provisional death certificate. It gave me a sigh of relief to know that the cause of Alma's death had been cleared. I reread the letter and noticed that it was dated Tuesday, September 26, which surprised me, as the MEO agent had just visited me. I pulled out the card the agent gave me and saw it didn't look authentic: it had been made cheaply with a photocopier or an inkjet printer. I freaked out and called the office to ask if John D. Lewis worked there. Unfortunately, they had closed already. I decided to dial John, but the cell phone number on the card was someone else's. I dialed again to double check. Fuck. It dawned on me that the Holy Brotherhood had sent someone claiming to be a MEO agent to get ahold of Alma's letter and will. Fuck. My ex-mother-in-law had gotten away with it.

And why the fuck did I let him seize them from me! What a dimwit! I repeated this to myself I don't know how many times. I was comforted for a few moments by my assumption that, now that my ex-mother-in-law had in her possession these documents, I could be calmer. No way, I reconsidered. As long as I had Alma's diaries, the Holy Brotherhood would not rest until it seized them and disappeared me.

What was I going to do? What if they were outside spying on me and waiting for me to come out? I thought I'd call the police, but I knew it was absurd to ask them for protection. They'd take me for a madman. What if the Holy Brotherhood had tapped my phone? How come I didn't think about this before I called my brother? There was no way to verify it. Besides, if this was the case, the damage was done. I feared for my brother and myself. I had to find an escape. I made sure again that all the doors and windows of the apartment were closed and locked.

I decided to stay in my apartment until the next morning. I was going to hide in the library starting tomorrow. I knew where to hide and sleep without anyone suspecting anything. I filled my backpack with everything I needed to stay a couple of days in the library. Once I received the transfer from Pepe, I'd decide what I was going to do with all my stuff. At worst, I'd run away without taking anything. I set out to search everything and destroy all the papers that could give a clue to the Holy Brotherhood where I was going to escape.

I couldn't sleep that night. At 3:30 a.m. I left the apartment as stealthily as possible. I was willing to scream and ask the entire neighborhood for help in case someone tried to stop me or kidnap me. Fortunately, it wasn't necessary. I walked out the alley and through the neighborhood until I reached downtown. I took refuge at a diner. I had breakfast and waited there until it was time to go to work.

That day was a normal workday. During lunchtime I went to the bank, but I hadn't received the money yet. When I finished my day's work, I said good-bye to all my coworkers as usual and had dinner at a Wendy's. Then I went back to the library and started reading at a table near the room where I planned to lock myself up before they closed the library.

I repeated this routine until I got the money five days later. It was Monday, October 2. In three more days the van I had booked was going to be available. I made the decision to return home that afternoon to start packing. I was exhausted from sleeping on the floor and desperately wanted to take a shower.

When I got to the apartment, everything seemed normal. However, when I checked my phone messages, I received the terrible news: my brother Pepe had been gunned down the day before. I received several calls and messages from my mother and my siblings. They were asking me to go to Juárez to join them and say good-bye to Pepe.

I felt terrible. My suspicion that the Holy Brotherhood had tapped my phone was confirmed in the most resounding way. I figured they had killed him to get back at me and because I knew too much about their operations. I had long feared that something was going to happen to my brother for engaging in drug trafficking, but I never imagined he was going to be killed because of me. I was about to dial my parents' number, but I was held back by the fear that the Holy Brotherhood would intercept my call and reach me. All my recent efforts to hide wouldn't have been worth anything. They'd come looking for me right away. I contemplated the possibility of going to Juárez for the funeral, but I discarded it for obvious reasons. They'd kill me like a sitting duck. Pepe wasn't going to be resurrected by anyone, and, if dead, I wasn't going to be able to do anything for him, for me, or for anyone. My only possible salvation was to get out of Albuquerque as soon as possible and start a new life somewhere else with a new identity.

I got to work. Thanks to Alma, we had kept the boxes from the old move and had few things. My most precious belongings were my books, my records, and my stereo, and Goldfinch, of course. In memory of my brother, I put on "Cruz de madera" by Ramón Ayala, Pepe's favorite singer, and toasted in his honor listening to this and other songs.

Even though I was exhausted, sad, and a bit drunk, I decided to pack that same night. I put Alma's clothes and other nonessential items in plastic bags to take them to the Salvation Army. I did the same with everything that wasn't indispensable. I packed my belongings in boxes and stacked them near the entrance to speed up the truck's loading. Even though I felt weak and a little dizzy because I hadn't had dinner, I started cleaning the apartment. I saw that I had a bottle of ammonia that was almost full. I had recently read an article that extoled its cleansing qualities, so I decided to apply it liberally to clean the tub and the bathroom tiles. The fumes must have been too much for my fragile condition. The last thing I remembered was that I felt vertigo and went to the bedroom.

47

MOUTH THAT EXHALES THE STIFLING VAPOR OF MEMORIES STUCK in the gaps of the wings of the unconscious; pupils that dilate when wounded by the evening ray, ripping the veil of remembrance; nose that inhales the pestilence of the remains of an apostate who wrests the innocence of an indigent with moon eyes; fists that squeeze the delicate smoothness of the silk padding the coffin of a dead assassin; hand that caresses his pale face made up with the pulverized cuticle of his penultimate victim who lays claim to the denouement of his most unfathomable dreams; iron legs that support the quivering volition of his thoughts and beliefs and that bend when the white misery of his sky opens up and sprays on his feet the delicate drizzle that heralds the arrival of daisies and the sellers of perfumes and refractories; flame that illuminates the face compressed by the hardships and disillusions laden in the delicate burden of the soul maculated by the shadow of his ignominious desires and pursued by the butterflies of his dead ancestors under the oppressive hecatomb of his petty greed; hope that remains trapped in the interstices of a metallic basket that protects the legacy of a specter desecrated by rats who gnaw at the foundation of the murderous saints' temple unsettled by the shit of dogs accompanying their impeccable tutors; skeleton that safeguards the revered memory of a distant relative who left his fortune buried for the exhumers of his respectable craft exonerated by civil and ecclesiastical authorities.

I sink into a dark river. Everything loses shape and volition. Neither the pebble wants to be a pebble nor the tree to be a tree. The snake does not long to have wings, and the magma no longer wishes to be the sea. Nothing is what it looks like nor what it used to be. I immerse myself in oblivion, into the unnamable. I'm looking for unity, the source of my being. I fear being dragged into that marsh where the current petrifies, or into the swamp where the dead rest. My liquid hands burn. A radula of fire licks and embraces me. Its thin membrane folds, consumes itself, and rolls down a cliff of bubbling tar. The line that divides the landscape dims and fades. I rise to the surface searching for light, but the current submerges me. A faint fluorescence trembles and shakes furiously trying to survive. Fluid quietude. A beam of light falls like a curtain and goes extinct. Time moves in segments. A night rider rejoices in his own death. His remains flow, roll, and precipitate into the void. I fall into a pit. I try to escape, but I'm scattered in a river of lava. There is a pristine darkness. Lava flows into its meridional quietude. A quartz flower emerges, rises, and defoliates. My mind errs, wanders, and fragments; seeks rest. I see traces of the sun, distant, and ephemeral; the traces sink, melt, condense, rise, and disappear. There is neither up nor down, only the vertigo of the moment, the materiality of nothingness. My voice crumbles and dissolves. I let myself be carried by the current. A vortex pulls me in and sinks me to the bottom of the abyss. A globule of light rises from the depths and bursts. I try to hold myself onto its melted fire. The viscous mass drags fragments of what used to be my skin, my guts, my veins, my nerves, my bones. Magma flows and absorbs me, but it petrifies before I melt into it. I look inward at the cave where I am. I observe the sedimented matter at the threshold that traces my contour. It makes me feel tangible, substantial, rock solid, albeit with gaps and fissures. It is motionless motion, a stratum of inert matter; residue of the past; materialized time. I cross the threshold but don't find the exit. The same images from before haunt and torment me in this grotto. A strong air current drags me and shakes me. Its terrible force pulls everything. It throws me into a gallery immersed in its impassive, asymmetrical solitude, beautiful in its own way. It smiles at me, welcomes me with its stone smile and shows me the scars of its granitic existence. Amber-gray clouds cover the darkness with a viscous veil.

The reverberating drone of a tanpura and the plucking of a sitar interrupt my visions. I open my eyes. The music comes from four speakers that are bolted to the ceiling, one in each corner. I'm lying cross-legged on a purple velvet couch. My arms rest on my stomach and several cushions support my back. The room is decorated with tapestries of mandalas and Tibetan deities. The carpets and the cushions are woven with Navajo designs. Sandalwood incense perfumes the air. At first I don't know where I am, but slowly I realize that I am in Dr. Hogan's office. It takes me a moment to recognize her voice.

"This is a morning raga performed by Nikhil Banerjee," she tells me from another room where the stereo is. "It's called *Bilaskhani todi*. Its healing properties are exceptional, especially to combat self-consciousness and its main afflictions."

She exits the room and walks toward me. She wears a yellow Tibetan chuba, a turquoise blouse, and Haflinger sandals. Her long salt-and-pepper hair is styled in the traditional Navajo way: folded four times into a bun and tied with white yarn. She sits on the edge of a chair next to the couch and tells me:

"Close your eyes. Breathe twenty-one times deeply and slowly. Focus your mind on the *Sahasrara Chakra*, the lotus of a thousand petals located in the cerebral cortex."

I follow her directions and, little by little, I relax.

"Fuse yourself with the melody, absorb its medicinal vibrations. This music is a path to enlightenment and the supreme consciousness," she tells me with her usual conviction in a sweet and soothing tone. "Dissolve the ego in the music and elevate the mind to the infinite."

The intense, and sometimes repetitive, plucking of the sitar and the hypnotic hum of the bourdon cover the room like a morning-fog blanket.

"Ragas are a journey home, a journey to the origin. Their notes are physical manifestations of the Supreme Reality. This raga, in particular, can help you tune your mind. Just as the tanpura's drone illuminates the path of the sitarist and keeps him from going astray by holding the tonal axis, so this morning raga can help you tune your untempered mind in accordance with the primordial music of the cosmos."

The opening section of the raga has a grave tempo and a solemn tone that gradually becomes somber. It goes through my conscience like leaves carried by the wind, evoking a rapid succession of episodes of my childhood and youth: the joyful Christmas Eves when all the children in the family sang the traditional carols before opening the gifts; the board games with my siblings and nephews when they visited my parents and me at the Nogales' house; the soccer matches I had with my friends in the neighborhood on the street, or in a vacant lot, under the incandescent sun of Ciudad Juárez; the dull afternoons when I had to interrupt a street game with my friends in order to take my private guitar lessons; the mornings when my father took me to school before he went to work; the afternoons when a street vendor of sweets, slushies, or corn on the cob would pass by the house on his bicycle and I would run to ask my mom for money; the weekends swimming and hanging out with my friends at the country club; the summers in my abuelito's ranch working in the corrals, riding horses and tractors, or shopping in the villages of San Agustin or Guadalupe; the long hours I spent with friends listening to music and chatting, first in a house and, later on, inside a car, or at the street corner of our neighborhood where we hung out and where we learned to smoke and started to drink beer; our Sunday walks in the mall during early adolescence and our car rides down Sixteenth of September Avenue in my late teens; the street fights; the adult movies at the Montana drive-in theater; my first rock concerts at the El Paso Coliseum; my first nights of revelry at Chaplin's and then at Chihuahua Charlie's; the dance parties at the country club and the Flamboyant; the disco nights at the Alive and the Electric Q; the nights of hunting when my high school friends and I would drive down the city at night, pick up women from the *maquila* factories, take them to the outdoor bar La Arboleda, or around the city, and sometimes park in a dark street or at a motel; the all-nighters at cantina joints and at the brothels of Tavo's godfather, which were in the domain of the Holy Brotherhood. The Garden of Eden was my ex-father-in-law's favorite cathouse. There, my friends and I had a beer with Luisfer and Damián, his crony and partner in crime. That night Luisfer had turned fifteen and his godfather took them both to the brothel, supposedly so that they could lose their virginity. It was 1981. I was seventeen. I was a freshman at the Escobar Brothers High School, the formerly prestigious and already dying College of Agriculture where one of my great-grandparents taught during the time of Don Porfirio Díaz and the Revolution, more than fifty years earlier. The institution remained open against all odds, despite the deep crisis in which Mexico and Mexican agriculture were plunged. Although the school did not close that year, it had earned a bad reputation because we were always partying and sometimes rioting and creating social chaos and political instability in the city along with other allied or enemy groups. It was the time of my youth when I started down the crooked path. Fortunately, around that time, I began dating Alma and, to spend more time with her and with the idea of attending New Mexico State University, I decided to enroll in the El Paso Community College to study English as a second language.

Then came to mind, like a sailboat that is ravaged by a sudden and ferocious storm, my wedding with Alma, our departure to Albuquerque, our relatively happy first years of marriage, and, finally, the abrupt end of our relationship and Alma's tragic end.

"What are you thinking, Uriel? You look distracted."

I briefly shared my memories with Dr. Hogan. She listened attentively and, when I finished, she said to me:

"All our actions and those of our ancestors produce karmic seeds that our unconscious stores. You're the depository of a burdensome legacy, Uriel. Something that started in a distant age is unfolding and concluding in you. This is why there are certain actions that aren't easy for you to understand, because they are pregnant with meaning. This is what you have to unravel. By being aware of this past and facing it, you can at the same time break free from this atavistic burden that so overwhelms and incapacitates you. Every rupture is a step toward rebirth."

"I think I understand what you're telling me, Doctor. I've been reflecting on this in my diary."

"I'm glad you have. Writing will help you know yourself better and cultivate lucidity."

"I hope so, although I must acknowledge that I keep having anxiety dreams for the most part."

"Have you been practicing trekchö?"

"Pardon me?"

"Those who cannot remember the past are condemned to repeat it."

"I don't understand, Doctor."

"Have you had the same recurring dream you told me about the other day?"

"Yes. I recently dreamed that I had become an apprentice Apache warrior. My mentor was that Apache relative who I told you resembles you."

"It's probably a karmic dream. Almost all of our dreams are of this kind. Your actions, your words, and your past thoughts haunt you in dreams, and they will continue to haunt you like a shadow if you don't awake. If you want to truly waken and reach the other side of existence, you need to uproot karma by developing supra-world consciousness. To do this you must combat self-consciousness and the restless mind along with all their afflictions and causes: desire, illusion, pride, self-love, opinions, doubt, and all conceptualizations."

"Believe me, I'm trying, but I don't seem to be making any progress."

"That's why it's important that you continue to practice meditation, mindfulness, and sleep yoga. What other kinds of dreams have you had lately?"

I recounted as best as I could the hallucinating visions that I had a few moments ago.

"Dreams are full of teachings, Uriel. They help us understand the illusory nature of existence. Once we understand this we can begin to govern our own future and destiny."

"I understand, but no matter how much I try to achieve lucidity in dreams, I immerse myself deeper and deeper in the dark."

"Dreams can be a practice and a vital training in this quest for the Supreme Light. In our dreams we walk blindly. To find our way we need to learn to distinguish and follow the light of dawn in the dark night. We need to learn to recognize and remain in the limpid light of dawn to escape the darkness. To distinguish the auroral glow we need to open the eyes of the spirit. We need to train the intellectual eye, for we are used to wandering through existence like bats, without the knowledge or guidance of the true light. To awaken you need to learn to recognize and follow the limpid light of dawn. The limpid light of dawn is the lighthouse that the dreamer needs to avoid going astray in the nocturnal journey. Only the knowledge of the Supreme Light awakens us from the dream of earthly existence. When you discover the auroral light in your dreams, that's when your awakening will begin."

"I understand everything you say. However, when it comes to putting it into practice, theory doesn't help me."

"If you practice sleep yoga regularly, you will become familiar with the different manifestations of auroral dreams. And if you persevere, it will get increasingly easy for you to acquire lucidity in dreams. Lucidity helps you not only to advance on the spiritual path but also to uproot karma."

"Sometimes, when I wake up and realize that I've had a lucid dream, I rush to write it down in my journal. If you read it, you would think I'm making progress, but the truth is that the wind of karma keeps whirling my mind around like a kite in a storm."

"If you have a lucid dream, rejoice and aim to maintain your lucidity the next night. You must persist and not give up. If you fail in your attempt, don't get discouraged. Remember that everything is a dream. Doing so will help you attain lucidity in both daytime and nighttime."

48

I OPEN MY EYES. I'M BACK IN ITHACA. FINALLY. WHAT VIVID AND strange dreams! I slept with my headphones on and a *tabla tarparan* is playing on the WinPlay3. It's already 12:23 p.m. What day is today? Did I miss work? I get alarmed and get up. Accidentally, I drop the headphones to the floor, pick them up, and put them on the desk. I look for my planner and find it under my dream journal. It's April 7, 1996. Easter Sunday. I calm down. It's my day off. Today is daylight savings. Too bad it means one less hour of sleep. While adjusting the digital alarm clock, I observe the black cloth cover of my journal and remember I left it open on purpose. I left something in the inkwell last night before I went to bed. It was a reminder to write something down as soon as I got up. I try to recall for a few moments, but I give up. There's so much to remember from the night before. It was an odyssey. I don't even know where I'm going to start when I try to write my report of this amazing journey. Better have breakfast and a cup of coffee before starting this arduous task. I doubt I'll forget them. My dreams have been so real that I remember them as if I lived and suffered them in my own flesh.

I recognize my loft. It's in the attic of an old gable-roof house on Aurora Street near the Commons. I take a peek through the window blinds and observe the houses across the street: a small, white, one-story, poorly maintained house with an old oak tree in front, and a gray, two-story house that was renovated and converted into rental apartments, graced by two young maple trees in the curb lawn. It's cloudy but it's neither snowing nor raining. What a relief. Although theoretically it is spring, it still snows in April and freezing rain is not uncommon.

I recognize the interior of my apartment. The heat that comes off the radiator is comforting. I watch my nocturnal travel station: the frameless futon covered with my black wool blanket. It lies on the floor, on top of a tatami mat. Above the futon, on the ceiling, I have installed a wooden frame where I periodically insert a different poster or image so that I get inspired to make a premeditated and lucid night trip. On the opposite side is my desk. It is a Japanese-style nook or *tsukechoin* with a rectangular cushion, *zabuton*, that I use for both writing and meditation. A statuette of Thoth, an image of my guardian spirit, Seshat, and a rubber stamp of an ibis dignify the scribbles I produce.

My apartment is small and modest but cozy since it is decorated in the traditional Japanese style. The apartment is almost entirely covered with tatami mats. Although it is a studio loft, a six-panel shoji screen separates the area that I have reserved for sleeping, writing, and meditating from the rest of the apartment. In the living room there is a coffee table and several cushions that function as a dining room. It is where my occasional guests sit down. On the northern wall there are two large shelves full of books and, on the southern wall, a bookshelf with my stereo, speakers, CDs, cassettes, and various decorative objects. Another six-panel shoji screen divides the living room from the kitchenette, which has white pressed-wood cabinetry, a small electric stove with oven, a refrigerator, and, on the lemon-green Formica countertop, there is a microwave. In the lobby there are two Ikea wardrobes: one modular made of wood with reed baskets and the other one covered with a canvas where I store winter clothes, shoes, and other belongings.

After having breakfast and taking a shower, I sit down to write in my diary. I move the mouse to clear the desktop and deactivate my computer's screen saver. An El Greco painting titled *St. Peter and St. Paul* appears on the monitor. I observe it and realize that Brother Antonio is identical to St. Paul. I smile when I recall that his religious name is, indeed, Fray Antonio de San Pablo. I asked myself so many times in my dreams: Where have I seen this man? I take a close look at the painting and wonder what is the meaning of the half-hearted, discourteous salute that the two saints are exchanging. Instead of shaking their hands, they're interlocking their wrists. Then I remember I left this investigation pending last night. That's why I left my journal open. I consult the Internet and discover that the painting illustrates the disagreement that St. Peter and St. Paul had in Antioch, where the latter was running the first mixed community of Christians and pagans in history. Their disagreement was on the question of whether it was obligatory for new Christians to comply with the Law of Moses. St. Paul's position was that pagans should be evangelized and that Christians should not follow the Law of Moses because only Jesus Christ saves. However, St. Peter does not accept his intolerant stance and rebukes him. Thus, the discourteous gesture. After this disagreement, St. Paul leaves Antioch to undertake a new mission. That is why St. Paul has a defiant look and that is why he holds a battle sword with his left hand. In the end, St. Paul's viewpoint became the norm for the whole Church. The sword, as is known, is the symbol of Imperial Rome and especially of Emperor Julius Caesar. St. Paul is called the Apostle of the Gentiles precisely for his continuous journeys and missions to spread Christianity through the world in the manner of a Roman legionnaire. He is depicted with a sword not only for being the weapon that killed him but also for being the symbol of his militant proselytizing. Not for nothing the territory conquered by Don Juan de Oñate was named the Holy Custodia of the Conversion of Saint Paul of the Province of New Mexico. What I don't understand and would like to know is the possible relevance that this dispute between St. Peter and St. Paul has in my family history. Or in the life I've been living in my dreams.

49

THE MOON AND THE SUN ARE ETERNAL TRAVELERS; WIND, WATER, and dust are too. So are we when we dream.

Before moving into this apartment more than six months ago, I set out to follow Matsuo Basho's example of making my life a permanent journey to the interior. However, since I do not write in verse and suffer from writer's block every time I intend to compose a literary work, I decided to look for another Zen master to learn the art of writing. A treatise on archery, written by a German philosophy professor named Eugen Herrigel, has become my new guide. There I have learned that every art has a spiritual aim and that the writer, like the archer, becomes his own goal: to perfect himself.

The purpose of my writings has since been not to produce literary art, as I intended, but to train the mind: to strengthen it, temper it, and purge it of emotions, attachments, intentions, ideas, and concepts until it is emptied and put into its primordial state. I aspire to write a noctambulist novel in which the writer's hand and the keyboardist's fingers are guided by the unconscious; a writing that writes itself; a writing without an aim; an artless writing in which the writer and writing are one and the same.

Who am I really? Why am I here? Why did I come into this world? Who and where am I when I dream? Who or where was I before I was born? Who or where will I be after I die? Does my supposed existence or my alleged and eventual nonexistence have any meaning at all? What is my mission in this world?

I'm writing a dream diary because I have asked myself these questions since I was a child. I've concluded that dreams are a mirror of reality that helps us better know ourselves and inquire and question the ultimate nature of the material world and reality. Dreams are experiences as authentic and meaningful as everyday events and more revealing than these.

My dream journal has been helping me in my intellectual and spiritual development and in my quest to get to know myself better. It is also helping me combat writer's block, particularly after Alma's suicide. I can't believe that more than ten months have passed since that happened. It feels as if it were yesterday. It must be because of the nightmares and distressing dreams I still have about that fateful event. I wonder if I've written down my most recent dreams.

I open my diary and see that in yesterday's entry there is a drawing of the Albuquerque cityscape that is identical to the pictogram that Refugio showed me in my dream. It is odd that Refugio described the writing of a journal as an intrinsically selfish act. I suppose it is because a diary is private and only in exceptional cases is published. Did Alma behave selfishly in writing her diaries and not making their content available to the public? Yes, in so far as they reveal a horrible crime committed by her brother and covered up by her parents. The public needs to know about it so that the police investigate him, in case it is still possible to find evidence and probe the crime after so long. Even if this were to happen, however, we know that in Mexico the rich and powerful don't go to jail.

I keep wondering if I should grant the interview to the *El Paso Post* journalist who is writing a book about the international child pornography network operating in Juárez and El Paso, but I'm afraid.

He has sent me several emails and I haven't answered them. I am almost certain that Luisfer will never go to jail or be investigated and that the members of the Holy Brotherhood will retaliate against my family if I denounce them. The dream I had last night about my brother's murder could come true. It would not be fair of me to endanger my loved ones simply because I want to clear my conscience by fulfilling my civic duty, especially when I am here safe and far from the violence. After all, I have already begun a new life away from all that.

I have so much to write in my diary, but I don't even know where to start. I get distracted by checking my email. I read the message my mother sent me yesterday. The lawsuit against my Uncle Alberto for fraud, dispossession, and breach of faith made by my mother and her two sisters did not proceed. My uncle denied the charges and the trial judge stated that the prosecutor did not prove that the claimant, my mother, had the right to make the claim, since my uncle Alberto possessed a power of attorney appointing him as abuelito's legal representative before the authorities. According to my mother, my uncle obtained this power of attorney illegally because abuelito signed it when he was no longer compos mentis.

Previously, my grandfather had divided El Porvenir equally to all his grandchildren, but, according to my uncle, he later changed his mind, asked him to modify the will, and bequeathed the property to him. Now that an American real estate company has expressed interest in buying the ranch to build an industrial park, my mother and sisters have realized, perhaps too late, the crimes committed by their brother. They want to invalidate the power of attorney and the deed of the ranch. But this will be extremely difficult since my grandfather suffers from senile dementia. My mother tells me she's going to send me some documents via National Express tomorrow and asks me to sign and return them right away.

I take a pen and write the date on a blank page in my diary. I attempt to record my recent dreams, but I can't. I'm blocked. I do what Dr. Hogan recommended to me in these cases: I sit down to meditate. When I finish, I get up and select Mahler's Second on my WinPlay3; I put on the headphones, grab my portable recorder, and lie down to try to get into a dream state so I can elicit and record my dreams from the night before.

I close my eyes and the coveted feat occurs. I turn on the tape recorder and start recounting my dream. I see myself marching in a funeral procession at night. I sport a black tailcoat and brown moccasins and walk along a winding path on a wooded mountain. The images reappear just as I dreamed them, and my words flow like spring water. I'm ecstatic. My fantasy of being able to accurately recount my dreams is being fulfilled to the letter. I see my dreams like a movie and hear my own words as if someone else were dictating them to me. I watch my movie and listen to the soundtrack dumbfounded. The story and the dream correspond; they are the same reality. There is no distinction or separation between what I see and what I narrate. Incredibly, I relive, one by one, each of the dreams I had the night before, and I narrate them as I perceive them. I narrate without thinking about anything but what I'm witnessing. I let myself be taken by the river of images and don't worry if what I'm narrating makes sense or not. I abandon myself. I am an empty circle, a purposeless tension, an aimless narrator, an artless artist. I remain in this state until the dream candle goes out twelve hours later. Exhausted but happy to have performed this feat, I fall fast asleep.

50

I OPEN MY EYES. I'M IN THE HOLLOW OF A VALLEY OF ROLLING hills surrounded by countless people. The sky is clear and the aurora borealis paints a rainbow on the horizon. Although it is night, I can perfectly scan the contour of the valley thanks to the blanket of flickering candles that cover it. The atmosphere is festive yet placid.

Next to me Refugio, Dr. Hogan, Aurobindo, Herman Hesse, Little Alice, Ibn Arabi, Sor Juana Inés de la Cruz, María Zambrano, and the Dalai Lama are sitting in a circle. Behind them, Lucius, La Mora, and Pardo graze quietly. Inside the circle, on a raw cotton tablecloth, there are jute baskets and terracotta dishes with sweet and savory breads, fruits, and nuts, vegetarian tapas, and assorted cheeses. We eat in silence as Kokopelli plays on his flute a song to creation. I'm naked.

"Are we celebrating Diwali?" I ask Dr. Hogan. Refugio looks at me with a gesture of disapproval by covering his mouth with the index finger, reminding me that novices cannot speak yet.

"Who in the world am I? Ah, that's the great puzzle!" says Alice and laughs. Then she takes a few apple slices, gets up, and goes with Lucius to comfort and talk to him.

"You've been accepted into the League, Diego. We're going to Morning Land," says Herman Hesse, glancing at me obliquely. He's wearing an explorer suit, a wide-brimmed Panama hat, and golden spectacles.

All nod in approval and congratulate me with a smile. Refugio gets up, puts a brimless suede cap adorned with a plume of eagle feathers on me, and asks me to declare that I will fulfill my sacred obligations from now on, which I do solemnly by closing my eyes and visualizing the iridescent path. Then the Dalai Lama approaches me. He gives me water in a conch shell and, with his fingertips, rubs my crown, throat, and heart. After I return the empty conch to him, he recites a prayer and urges me to always maintain a calm, composed, and detached disposition.

After this ceremony, I am pleased to have been accepted into the League and honored to be accompanied by such illustrious characters. However, I feel uneasy because Herman called me Diego. I would like to clarify that my name is Uriel, but I hesitate to say anything, partly because I don't want to make him look bad, partly to avoid another unpleasant discussion on the subject like the one I had with Refugio, and mostly because I am too shy to argue with Herman Hesse. I decide to remain silent when I recall the passage of the Dhammapada that says: "He who never identifies with name and form, and does not grieve over what is no more, he is indeed called an initiate."[7]

Little Alice comes for another handful of apple slices. Lucius walks behind her and forces Aurobindo and Dr. Hogan to step aside.

"I could tell you about my adventures, starting with this morning's," says Alice to Lucius as she puts the apple slices in front of him, "but there's no point in going back to yesterday because then I was a different person."

"That's alright with me, Alice. While you're at it, could you kindly serve me a plate of carob beans from that basket?" Lucius asks Alice, pointing his muzzle at a jute basket behind me.

"Of course," says Alice, just before a firefly distracts her.

"Are we interrupting you?" Lucius asks. Alice runs after the firefly and disappears.

"Not at all, equine brother," Herman says. "We are silently enjoying this magical night and the divine performance of Kokopelli."

The flautist is playing with incomparable virtuosity "Prelude to the Afternoon of a Faun."

"Mind if I join you? Next to carob beans, what I most enjoy is chatting."

"Of course not, Brother," I reply.

"Then, ladies and gentlemen, share with me your colloquy, not because I am curious about your speech, but because I want to know all things, or at least many," says Lucius.

"I would like to ask a question to the initiate," Herman says. "Brother Diego, as I think you know, not all members of the League have the same goal in mind. What are you looking for on the iridescent path?"

"I seek the perfect and complete awakening," I respond.

"Jeez! Are you sure, Diego?" Lucius asks me, visibly alarmed.

"What I want the most is to awaken from the dream of life," I add.

"The privileged awakening does not necessarily take place in dreams," says María.

"Maybe you should adjust your high expectations," says Dr. Hogan. "As I've pointed out before, to awaken you'll need to root out karma."

"With your immense ignorance and the insatiable thirst for worldly pleasures you manifest at every moment, that will take you eons," Lucius warns me. "Why don't we look together for the Promised Land? They say it's north of the Río Grande."

"A long life and happiness for you and your fellow beings is enough, Diego," Refugio intervenes, reminding me of what First Man asks for in his ascent to the Great Mountain.

"The thought of awakening includes the resolve to obtain awakening for the good of all beings," says the Dalai Lama. "It is a noble and irreproachable ideal."

"The ultimate and most admirable aim is the quest for Divine Life," says Aurobindo.

"Everything is true and not true. That is the teaching of the Buddha," the Dalai Lama adds.

"God has granted you a love of beauty and wisdom. To reach them you'll need to climb up the ladder of the human sciences and the arts," says Sister Juana.

"The greatest lesson I have learned in my wandering through glades is that we must neither look for them nor look for anything in them," says María. "But if nothing is sought, the discovery could be bountiful."

"This advice is helpful, María," says Herman. "As we all know, to join the League it is not necessary to have a specific goal in mind. Sense of wonder suffices."

"Diego, for your own sake and mine," Lucius insists, "let's look for the Promised Land. You are but a being of flesh and blood subject to passions like me. You are not made to spend your life in the wilderness fasting, praying, meditating, and making sacrifices of all kinds to attain liberation."

"I agree with you, Brother Lucius. I don't have a religious or an ascetic vocation. I only want to remedy my lack of wisdom and temper my mind and body. My ultimate aspiration is to live the awakened life of the supreme consciousness. I recognize that it is an arduous and perhaps unattainable goal in my present state, but I agree with Aurobindo that spiritual transcendence is the most fundamental and decisive human aspiration."

"If you persevere, you will reach your goal," Aurobindo tells me.

"Aren't you a Siervo de Dios? Open your eyes, Diego, for God's sake. You're going to regret it."

"I've got them open, Brother," I reply, "but I know I'm asleep."

"That's not what I'm talking about."

"What do you mean, then?"

"Know yourself! If you ignore the fundamentals of yourself and your origins, how do you expect to attain wisdom and liberation?"

"One who attains self-knowledge knows God," says Ibn Arabi.

"But I'm an agnostic."

"Your mother and all her relatives are Crypto-Jews," says Lucius. "Your adoptive parents were too. Right, Refugio?"

"We are all children of Mother Earth and Father Sun," Refugio replies.

"For the Spirit there is no birth or death at any time," Aurobindo adds.

"If one attains true knowledge through self-knowledge, one realizes that one's being exists neither by one's own existence nor by the existence of anything but oneself," Ibn Arabi says.

"I only know that existence is an illusion," I say emphatically.

"The wise should rely neither on existence nor on nonexistence," says the Dalai Lama.

"What is not real never exists; the real always exists," says Aurobindo. "The Spirit is everywhere; it is everlasting, immutable, motionless, and eternally itself."

"Everything you say may be true," I reply. "However, I believe that life is a dream."

"In dreams, being is one, Diego, self-identical, without pores and subtracted at the same time," says María.

"Everyone is confusing me," I say, exasperated. "My name isn't Diego. It's Uriel. Right, Dr. Hogan?"

"You know well that from now on, you should neither identify with names nor with appearances," she replies.

"So what do we call you?" the Dalai Lama asks. "No one can claim to be self-free."

"Let us say you are dreaming, and you believe your name is Uriel," Ibn Arabi intervenes. "But in your dream you discover that your name is Diego. Even though you realize you are not Uriel, you are still who you are. Changing your name does not take anything away from your true being since you were never Uriel."

"Sisters and brothers," says the Dalai Lama, standing up. "I'm sorry to interrupt this pleasant colloquium, but it's getting late. Having already concluded our annual Time Wheel Ceremony, and having welcomed Brother Romero in our League, it is time to say good-bye to him. He needs to return to the realm of wakefulness where he can begin to put into practice the teachings he has received in his training."

After giving a brief lesson on the Wheel of Time and giving me some tips on how to keep night practice both pristine and effective and how to integrate it into daytime practice, he tells me:

"Brother Romero, close your eyes and follow my instructions. Silently sing the 'Ave Maris Stella' and visualize the Mother of Liberation with an eight-spoke wheel on her chest playing the veena. She and the Spirits of the Mountain have been tasked with restoring vitality and balance to your mind and body, which this arduous and painful period of training has diminished temporarily. Don't forget to thank them and make an offering when you return to the earthly realm for the favor they have granted you. And don't forget to perform the ceremony that the Mountain Spirits taught you."

"No problem. I dictated it to him myself. Didn't I, Shidizé?" Refugio says, winking at me. "I will administer him the ceremony as soon as he emerges from dormancy."

Hearing this, I remember that Refugio appeared in one of my dreams as All Covered With Pollen and recall the canticle he taught me when I collapsed, exhausted, at the end of the Enemy Ghost ceremony:

> Dark Wind is here
> Black amber's son is here...

It's an important detail I shouldn't forget. I write it down mentally and promise to add it to my novel as soon as I wake up. I'm exhausted. I visualize the white-painted divinity and hum its Christian canticle. Gradually I sink into a sweet stupor.

> *Ave, Maris stella,*
> *Dei mater alma . . .*

51

I OPEN MY EYES AND I'M BACK IN COYOTE WITCH CANYON. I HAVE that strange feeling we experience when we awaken in an unexpected, if familiar, place after having had a bad night. I am also frustrated that I did not wake up in my apartment. It is Monday and I have to go to work. I don't want to dream anymore. I want to record the dream I just had.

Refugio is outside singing and playing the drum. I remember he's been healing me. I guess I'm still convalescing. I have no idea how long I've been inside the hut. I resist the urge to get up to urinate, for I remember that I must not leave for any reason until the Mountain People leave. I recognize the piece I'm listening to. It's on an Apache music CD that I checked out of the library and recently recorded on the WinPlay3. Indeed, I'm dreaming. I can still sleep a bit more. Surely it's not yet time to get up for work.

I close my eyes and try to rest a little longer, but I have doubts if I set the alarm. I'm betting that I didn't. I try to fall asleep, but restlessness and the drumming prevent me. I ruminate, toss, and turn for a while until finally, unable to contain my desire to urinate, I get up and leave the hut.

Refugio is semi-asleep, sitting on the ground beating the drum near the campfire embers. The sun is rising and the Mountain People have left. I look toward the waterfall and get to see the crown of one of them just before he crosses the threshold of the slit of the canyon. It is a dazzling crown of light in the form of a hand fan. After hiding behind a bush for a moment, I approach Refugio and say good morning. He keeps hitting the drum and humming but he is nearly asleep. When I touch his shoulder, he startles and asks me, alarmed, if I saw the dancers. Through signs and gestures, I reply that everything was normal when I exited the hut. Hearing this, he erases the alarmed expression and asks me how I feel. I tell him tired and hungry. He puts the drum on the ground and gets up with the countenance of someone who just witnessed a prodigy. He tells me that all night the Holy Black Spirit of the East, the Holy Blue Spirit of the South, the Holy Yellow Spirit of the West, and the Holy White Spirit of the North danced around the campfire. Overjoyed, he describes their dance moves and pirouettes, their moon faces, cypress trunks, mantles of stars, golden rattles, and crowns and swords of fire. Despite his obvious exhaustion, made evident by his poor balance, he holds my hand and leads me to the waterfall where we freshen up and purify ourselves. He then invites me to meditate and thank the Spirits of the Mountain and Mother Moon for their help and healing. When we conclude our act of gratitude, we have breakfast in silence. At the end, Refugio asks me:

"Shidizé, don't you know that visitors to Tierra Abajo shouldn't eat anythin'?"

The question surprises me. I know Río Abajo is the southern part of New Mexico, but I'm not sure what he means by Tierra Abajo. I wince to convey my lack of understanding.

"Why did you eat the soup at Flora and Demetrio's house?"

I want to tell him, "Because I was hungry!" and, also, because in my culture it is rude to reject the food that your hosts offer you. However, given my vow of silence, I have no choice but to shrug my shoulders both to express my ignorance in these matters and to show contrition for having transgressed the rules of the Underworld.

"Thanks to Mountain People I was able to intercede on your behalf before the Council of Elders."

I nod to express understanding and deep gratitude.

"Tonight, I'll do the ceremony that All Covered With Pollen gave you last night."

I nod again, this time smiling and expressing my full agreement.

"But first we must go to Coyote Witch Cave. Shidizé needs to write down your dreams there."

When he tells me this, he grabs a pouch he's carrying on his belt. It is similar to the one he uses to keep the hadndin. He opens it, shows me its contents, and simply says:

"Red earth."

It's red ochre, a crimson-red powder. He takes a pinch and paints with it a symbol of the sun on the back of his left hand and explains that it contains a mixture of red earth and pine resin and that, moistened with saliva, diyin write down their dreams on canyons with this paint.

"Shidizé is in Coyote Witch Canyon to gain strength and have visions. All diyin must write in rock the divine knowledge they learn from the Mountain People. This knowledge helps, protects, and saves their tribe against disease and enemies."

He asks me to put out the campfire, pick up the breakfast utensils and leftovers, and pack because we're going on a field trip. After recording my dreams in the Cave of the Coyote Witch, he says that we need to go and find the materials to perform the ceremony that All Covered With Pollen dictated to me in the dream.

Refugio leads me to the cave. After giving me a few brief instructions on how to apply the painting, he orders me to write down the dreams I had last night before noon because he will return at that time. The idea of recording my dreams on the walls of a cave seems to me original and full of symbolism. The task, however, leaves me overwhelmed because I ignore the secret language of shamans and the esoteric grammar of pictograms.

What I most want at that moment is to wake up as soon as possible to record my dreams on a tape player before I go to work. I would also like to transcribe them, but I know that this task will take me several months to complete. I wonder if the account of my dreams that I recorded yesterday was coherent. Maybe it was just a dream. Maybe I haven't really returned to Ithaca yet. I feel anxious and uncertain. As soon as I wake up, I'm going to write an email to my supervisor telling her that I'm not going to be able to go to work, that I got sick to my stomach or something. I feel exhausted and want to sleep and rest some more.

Having no idea how to complete the task that Refugio assigned me, I study the figures and techniques of the pictograms that cover the walls of the cave. As I'm contemplating, fascinated, an enigmatic hunting scene, I hear some mocking laughter that rumbles and resonates in the adjoining chamber. It's a low, scratchy male voice. Terrified, I turn everywhere around me, but there's no one. I'm paralyzed without knowing what to say or where to hide.

"Fear not, Nakaiyé, I will not hurt you," the voice tells me with a tad of insincerity.

"Who's talking to me?"

"A couple of hours ago you had the insolence of seeing a part of my divine figure as I was leaving Tierra Arriba. I am the Spirit of the North."

"I didn't mean to see you. It was an accident."

"Don't you know that outsiders aren't worthy of seeing us?

"Please forgive me."

"I forgive you only because you show a genuine interest in deciphering the mysteries that these pictograms and petroglyphs enclose."

"Then why are you making fun of me?"

"Because you waste your time trying to understand them."

"I know."

"You who boast of being a lover of wisdom, wouldn't you like to go directly to the original source from which come all the esoteric teachings that these rudimentary marks on the wall childishly babble?"

"Of course I'd like to."

"And what would you be willing to give in return?"

"It all depends."

"Depends on what?"

"On the value of the teachings."

"What if I told you that the wisdom I'm talking about will give you unlimited healing and communicative powers? Those who read the codices of Skeleton Man learn all the existing magical and medicinal formulas and can cure any disease as well as communicate with any being or spirit."

"Is there a mortal who would not want to have these powers?"

"Most people lack the will to know and the will to power that are indispensable for this arduous task."

"And why would a Nakaiyé like me have access to this privileged knowledge?"

"For the same reasons that Refugio and the Council of Elders have agreed to help you."

"But you know better than I do that Skeleton Man hates Nakaiyé, especially religious ones."

"It's true. He hates Christians and especially priests. But you are neither a priest nor a Christian. You should know that Skeleton Man is an enemy of all followers of the Light. For this and other reasons I need not dwell upon, he and I aren't friends. But Skeleton Man doesn't have to know that I'm going to share the contents of his codices with a member of the League."

"And what do you expect to receive from me in return? I'm just a fickle, timid neophyte."

"You're too hard on yourself. If I didn't consider you capable of accomplishing the mission I have for you, I'd entrust it to another member of the League. I know perfectly well your abilities and potential and that of the other members of the League who reside in these territories. No one will understand better than you the importance of the mission I want to give you."

"In that case, please tell me what this mission is all about."

"A group of enthusiastic League bibliophiles is organizing an expedition to the House of Life in Heliopolis. I want you to go with them and sprinkle hadndin on the altar to the Polar Star that is built there. You will also donate the codices of Skeleton Man to the House's special collections' repository. In so doing, you will not only honor and help disseminate your nemesis's wisdom but you will also placate his anger by nourishing his vanity and increasing his worldly fame and prestige."

The proposal of the Spirit of the North seems to me not only fanciful and odd but also extremely dangerous. Refugio has already warned me that there is no worse enemy than the Flayed God. Besides, I'm not sure I can trust this Mountain Spirit because I know I've committed a transgression. However, it seems clear to me that he is also motivated by vanity: he wishes to be honored vicariously in a city where the Polar Star is regarded as a divinity, albeit a minor one. And since I know I'm having a lucid dream and I don't want to miss the opportunity to put into practice Dr. Hogan's teachings, I decide to accept the mission. Nonetheless, remembering that only Hercules has been able to go to the Underworld twice, and considering Neferkaptah's story and my time constraints, I express to him my qualms.

"As you know, I just got back from the Underworld. My ignorance made me break a rule of cardinal importance that every visitor to this territory must know and respect. Still, thanks to Refugio's intervention and the mercy and goodwill that you and your fellow Spirits of the Mountain displayed toward me last night during the ceremony, I was able to return to the world of the living after having visited the country where the sun does not rise. I'm guessing that the codices of Skeleton Man are hidden in a remote place of the Underworld inside several indestructible coffers and that flocks of immortal soldiers and beasts guard them."

"I understand your apprehension, Diego, but I've got it all figured out. You won't have to go on a dangerous journey or accomplish any feat to get hold of the codices. Nor will you have to learn an arcane language or spend long periods of your limited time copying its contents and assimilating their knowledge."

"If that is so, then I'm all ears."

"I know that you are familiar with the old method that I have utilized to distill the essence of the codices to put them at your disposal. Please go to the chamber that is across the threshold where those hands are painted. There you will find a bowl of clay in a niche. Drink its concoction to the last drop. It's all you have to do to make yours the knowledge that the codices of Skeleton Man contain."

"Is that all?"

"That's all. That's how easy it is."

I do as instructed. I cross the threshold and, groping in the dark, search for the bowl. As soon as I locate the niche, I take the bowl carefully with both hands and sip the concoction. Even though it tastes and smells like blood, I go ahead and gulp the dense liquid. I clean the bowl with my tongue so as not to waste a single drop of the elixir. Inspired and in a trance-like state, I go back to the other chamber. I take the dish with the red ochre paint to start my work of art, but the Spirit of the North interrupts me.

"What are you doing?"

"I'm going to write down my dreams."

"Don't you realize this is the novice's workshop? This room is not worthy of your art."

I look at the pictograms and the petroglyphs and realize that, indeed, they are nothing but apprentices' scribbles.

"Master scribes display and disseminate their knowledge in more magnificent and sublime places: in grottos, caves, and caverns that are more majestic and accessible than this godforsaken hole in the ground. You must display your art on the surfaces of cliffs, canyons, picachos, rock formations, crags, and ledges that protect and adorn the riverbanks, streams, and springs. All the excellent sculptures and marvelous constructions of Mother Nature that abound in this valley are at your disposal for you to decorate and spread the wisdom of Skeleton Man with your art."

"Really? The problem is I don't know how to get out of here and it's getting late. I need to finish this work as soon as possible because Refugio and I are going out to look for the materials to do the healing ceremony you Mountain Spirits taught me."

"It is obvious that you have not yet assimilated the implications of the powerful gift I've given you. Take off your servile novice mentality. You can become the owner and lord of the world by leveraging the knowledge contained in Skeleton Man's codices. With them you can tame the wind, clouds, beasts, and all creatures that fly and move on the surface and in the bowels of the earth."

Then I remember Dr. Hogan's teachings. Indeed, she had told me that when we master the yoga of dreams, we can accomplish anything while dreaming. Instead of being subject to the whims of the wind of karma, we can manipulate dreams at our will and harness them to perfect ourselves and eventually attain liberation.

"I don't really have great ambitions in this world or any other. My greatest ambition is to achieve the perfect and complete awakening."

"You will succeed if you persevere and know how to take advantage of the teachings you have just received. Now get to work. Follow your instincts and you will find your way out of this maze."

I reflect and realize that, right now, all I want is to wake up from *this* dream. I close my eyes and visualize my apartment in Ithaca, but nothing happens. I visualize the Commons, the waterfalls, the Cascadilla Creek Trail, the Cornell campus, Olin Library, Minh's apartment in College Town, Cayuga Lake, but, again, nothing happens. Then I evoke different places in Albuquerque, Santa Fe, Las Cruces, El Paso, Juárez, Chihuahua City, Mexico City, Guadalajara, Monterrey, but nothing happens. I visualize the tree branch hut, the Coyote Witch waterfalls, the pool, the stream, the mountain trail, the mission, and the village of Senecú. All in vain.

Although I'm ashamed to admit it, I ask the Spirit of the North why my powers don't work. However, he doesn't answer me. I beg him to answer me, but he ignores me. Since I no longer trust my senses and I'm afraid I'll get lost if I try to get out of the cave, I decide to stay there until Refugio gets back. Then an inner voice begins to give me precise instructions on how to record the dream I had on the battlefield and in Flora and Demetrio's house. I write a detailed account of my dreams with pictographs and petroglyphs. When I finish the mural, I contemplate it, satisfied and proud. I sit on the floor and wait for Refugio, eager to show him my artwork.

I'm as exhausted as when I finished recording my dreams on the micro recorder. I decide to lie on the floor to sleep. Even if the bed and the pillow are made of stone, when one is tired, there is no such thing as a lousy bed. The WinPlay3 is currently playing a song from the album *Into the Labyrinth*. I'd like to get some more rest, but I know it's time to get up and go to work. The anguish of thinking that I will never wake up from this dream induces me to open my eyes wide. I look at the alarm clock and see it's 7:06 a.m. What a relief. I can sleep for five more minutes. I'm almost falling asleep again when a cavernous voice awakens me brusquely:

"Someone stole the marrow of my wisdom, and you drank it. Miserable fool! Don't you know that the wisdom of the gods is not made for humans? Give it back to me! I'll suck every last drop of your blood!"

The Flayed God jumps at me, but as soon as I open my eyes, he vanishes. I sit up, terrified. My heart is pounding. I think I'm going to have a heart attack. I try to recover from the scare. However, I freak out when I find out I'm no longer in the cave. I'm lying on the floor of a cell. My hands and forearms are still stained with red paint and I'm totally naked. Outside the cell someone is yelling insults and whipping a lash with fury. My terror increases when I discover that I am in the dungeon of Senecú and that they are applying the Law of Bayona to Refugio in the backyard. His executioner is Brother Salvador Guerra. He's whipping and insulting him viciously. He calls him "traitor witch," "sorcerer," "minister of Lucifer," "spawn of the Devil," "Satan's lapdog," "offspring of the Infernal Enemy," "accomplice of all the enemies of the Holy Faith." He also asks him where the rebels are hiding; who is the leader; when are they going to attack; what he has done to make me one of them; what he has used to bewitch me; who else is involved in the rebellion; who's the owner of the pictorial catechism they found in our saddlebags; if it belongs to Brother Antonio; if he is our accomplice; where has he hidden.

Refugio endures the whipping with fortitude. He doesn't say anything. He doesn't even whimper or groan. This infuriates Brother Guerra and he lashes him even more viciously. After he gets tired of whipping him, he pours turpentine oil or some other burning substance on his wounds. After a while, frustrated and incensed by Refugio's absolute silence, he threatens to burn him alive if he does not confess his "culpability" and his "dealings with the Devil and the enemies of Jesus Christ." He orders someone to bring him some firewood and continues to whip, insult, and question him until he gets fed up. Subsequently, he demands a lit torch and offers him one last chance to save his soul by declaring that "Only Jesus Christ is Lord and Savior." Refugio remains silent until then. But when Brother Salvador lights the pyre, Refugio emits a spine-chilling screech that gives me a nervous shock. I scream like a madman until I lose consciousness.

52

I OPEN MY EYES. IT'S NIGHT AND I'M STILL IN THE DUNGEON lying on the floor. A burlap sack covers my body. I'm handcuffed and I'm wearing a shackle on my left ankle. A migraine and nausea torment me. The disgusting concoction I drank in the cave comes to mind and I feel like throwing up. My stomach muscles contract but I have nothing to expel. Not even saliva. Crying and my intense thirst have completely dried my throat and mouth. I want to ask for water but can't. I try to stand up but I'm unable to move. I lie on the floor and start pondering.

Brother Salvador Guerra is the secretary of the Holy Office of the Inquisition in New Mexico. I'm sure I've been captured by the Holy Brotherhood. They'll keep me locked up and isolated until the last day of the trial. They will sentence me to death. They will accuse me of heresy, apostasy, and I don't know what else. They will give me a choice between death at the stake or, if I publicly declare my faith in Jesus Christ, by garrote. I don't know how long I'm going to stay in New Mexico, but I'll be transported sometime to 'the secret prison' in Mexico City, where I'll spend several years in solitary confinement. My only interlocutors will be my interrogators and the defense attorney assigned to me by the Holy Office. Until the day of the trial, I won't know the charges against me and will be presumed guilty. I will not be able to devoid or cross out any witnesses, even if their statement is patently unfounded and motivated by animosity. I will be questioned again and again for months, if not years, until I confess all my alleged sins and crimes. Then they'll torture me until they squeeze out of me any information that they couldn't obtain from me through interrogation. I will not have access to any books or reading or writing material. My only recourse will be to keep an absolute silence as Refugio did, but I know that my weakness and cowardice will urge me to confess everything. This will only ensure my downfall in the bottomless abyss into which I will be thrown.

53

"DO YOU KNOW OR PRESUME TO KNOW THE REASON THAT YOU have been imprisoned?" Father Custodio Friar Juan de Paz asks me. He is the commissioner of the Holy Office of the Inquisition in New Mexico. He's about forty years old. He is thin and inexpressive, but his large, bulging eyes and premature wrinkles betray his relentless religious zeal. He has a reputation of being uncompromising, intolerant, and of using the Holy Office to crush his enemies and anyone who questions his authority and that of the Church. As soon as he took office in 1665, he asked the archbishop of Mexico City to send an agent of the Holy Office to investigate Brother Antonio. He did so at the request of Brother Guerra, who accused him of being an Illuminatus and a Judaizer. He also filed a case against my godfather, Don Juan de Mendoza, at the request of Brother Antonio. The only ingratiating act he has performed in his brief tenure, for which he earned the respect of Brother Antonio and other friars who disagree with his methods, is to have started an investigation into the abuses committed by some friars against the Indians. Among those investigated is the secretary of the Holy Office himself, Brother Guerra.

I am determined not to answer any of his questions. I focus on a tiny cloud that I find in the fragment of the blue sky that is visible through the bars of the dungeon's window.

"Anyone who wanders outside the Christian religion is mistaken and walks inevitably to the precipice. Our Christian obligation is to take them away from the wrong path by any means, and even against their will. If not, we are not fulfilling our sacred duty, which is to drive the heathen away from their false beliefs and bring them to the knowledge of the truth and the true God."

". . ."

"Relieve your burden, Diego. Confess your sins and crimes."

". . ."

"Confess at once everything you have done, said, and committed in contravention of the holy sacrament of baptism's profession of faith and anything that goes against what our Holy Catholic religion and evangelical law believes, preaches, follows, and teaches."

". . ."

"Did you not make a vow and an oath to devote yourself entirely to God, to the edification of the Church, to the salvation of the world, to serve Our Lord in this Holy Religion, and to persevere until your death?"

". . ."

"Let's get to the point, Friar Diego. When were you circumcised?"

". . ."

"Since when do you secretly profess the Law of Moses?"

". . ."

"For what purpose have you befriended Refugio?"

". . ."

"We know that Refugio was a master of giving and casting spells and had a covenant with the Devil. He followed the Infernal Enemy's instructions and followed his counsel in the many evils and sorceries he committed. What potion did he give you to bewitch you and make you his ally?"

". . ."

"Whom else have you befriended?"

". . ."

"Whom else have you made pacts or deals with?"

"..."

"What rite, ceremony, or worship were you performing in the cave?"

"..."

"What idol were you worshipping?"

"..."

"What other acts of idolatry have you committed?"

"..."

"Did you make a pact with the Devil?"

"..."

"What did he request in exchange for your soul?"

"..."

"I see you persist in maintaining the attitude of a negative prisoner. No problem. We have abundant time ahead of us and the material evidence we possess of your mortal sins and your capital transgressions is blunt. Nothing offends God more than idolatry. Idolaters and dogmatists should be forced to accept the true religion. If they refuse to accept the Christian religion, they must be compelled. For there is no greater benefit in this life than receiving the faith of Jesus Christ. With Caesar's sword on our right hand and the Gospel on the left, we Spaniards have set out to wage war on the Native inhabitants who had been under the lordship of the Infernal Enemy for centuries."

"..."

"Those of us who were familiar with your record already suspected that you are a dogmatist infected by the Lutheran evil. You think the war we are making to the barbarians is unfair. However, the best thing that could have happened to these idolater barbarians is that we Spaniards came to Christianize, civilize, and humanize them. We are their lords by nature, for natural law states that the superior must prevail and dominate upon the inferior. We Spaniards are superior to Indians in all respects: in prudence, ingenuity, virtue, humanity, and weapons. That is why the pope granted us the legitimate right to conquer, pacify, Christianize, civilize, and humanize them. We are the masters and lords of these territories by both natural and divine law and nothing and no one will prevent these uneducated, barbaric, tainted, ungodly, and clumsy people from being subdued, conquered, and dominated by us."

". . ."

"Don't forget what St. Paul said to the Romans: 'Power is bestowed only by God, and whoever rebels against power opposes the order established by God and condemns himself.' You have condemned yourself in different ways, and your trial in Mexico City will be brief and simple. We won't even need to make use of the deplorable but necessary recourse of torture, because the mutilation your member has suffered since childhood is reason enough to send you to the stake. And this without taking into account the fact that apostasy and treason are punished with even greater severity and inclemency. Your case is already decided. The only recourse you have left to avoid being burned and going to Hell is to admit your grave crimes, abjure Judaism, and accept the true religion."

". . ."

"I know that the judicial procedure of the Holy Inquisition that I have summarized is not new to you. Before you came to New Mexico, your superiors in the convent had already warned you of the great risk you would take if you repeated your mistakes or if you transgressed any of our laws, practices, or principles. I have only come here to fulfill my ecclesiastical and Christian duty. I doubt there is an earthly power or force capable of averting the terrifying destiny that awaits your body. What I do not doubt at all, but I am fully certain of, is that you can still save your soul by abjuring Judaism and accepting the Holy Catholic, Apostolic, and Roman Faith, which is the only true and the truly saving religion. If you wish, I can call Brother Juan del Hierro, who is a reader of theology, to help me persuade you to come to your senses and accept the true religion. This will speed up the long and complicated trial that awaits you."

". . ."

"You don't have to make this decision right now. I'll be back tomorrow during lauds because at seven o'clock they'll come to pick you up to take you and other prisoners to El Paso del Río del Norte. But I warn you, once you board the wagon that will transport you to El Paso and from there to the House of the Inquisition of Mexico City, nothing will stop the slow and overwhelming march of the inquisitorial apparatus."

54

HOW COULD I HAVE ENDED UP HERE LIKE THIS? I DON'T WANT TO die, much less be burned or hanged, horribly humiliated, and without the possibility of defending myself or avoiding death. When am I going to wake up from this nightmare? My intention was just to sleep for a few more minutes. I don't want to be late for work. I need to get up and get ready. I'm thirsty and cold. These handcuffs and this shackle are hurting me. This iron ball weighs too much. How do I take them off? Why did they put them on me if I don't even have the strength to get up? Isn't it enough to keep me locked up here? Why do they want to keep me chained up too? Don't they realize I have nowhere to go and no strength to get away? All I want is to wake up.

What if I'm not dreaming? What am I going to do? Break my silence and admit all charges? What did the custodio tell me in the end? That if I abjure Judaism and accept Catholicism, he will drop the charges and set me free? And what am I going to make up about my so-called Judaism? He's going to want to know details of everything, and I won't know what to tell him. He'll say I'm hiding the truth or I'm lying. He'll want me to implicate others. He'll ask me questions about my past and about a lot of other things and people I know absolutely nothing about.

Why is God punishing me like this? Or is it the Spirit of the North who is punishing me and who set up this trap and this terrible way of dying? Did I offend him so much just by seeing him? Does he hate me so much for being Mexican and American? I know that my countrymen of yesteryear were cruel and ruthless to the Apache, that they enslaved many of them, waged a genocidal war against them until they virtually disappeared them. But it wasn't me. On the contrary, I have tried to prevent the Spaniards from converting them and invading their territory by refusing to fulfill the mission that Brother Antonio and my other superiors imposed on me. I just wanted to get out of here. I didn't want to cause Refugio any harm. If I'd known they were going to torture him and burn him alive, I wouldn't have accepted or asked for his help. I don't know what interest he might have had in helping me or why he was so generous with me. Maybe that's why I'm being punished by the Spirit of the North. But why did he punish him if all he did was try to heal me, make me his spiritual brother, and teach me some things to escape New Mexico and survive in the desert? No, my enemy can't be the Spirit of the North. What if it's the Flayed God? Is he tormenting me? If so, why did he deliver me to his adversaries? No, my tormentor has to be someone else. The Flayed God can use his own warriors and executioners to torture and kill me.

I open my eyes, rub them, and pinch my arm. I visualize my apartment in Ithaca, my futon, my furniture, but I can't wake up. I'm still in this dungeon. I know I'm asleep because I'm listening to Fauré's "Requiem." Why can't I wake up? What's happening to me? Am I in a coma from the accident? Am I witnessing my own funeral? When are they going to give me something to eat? Are they going to starve me to death?

The church bell begins to ring. It's strange. It must be ten or eleven in the morning and, at this hour, there are no Masses. Is it a holiday? I hear distant and unintelligible screams. It looks like a crowd is gathering in the square. What's all the noise I hear? What's going on? I wish I could climb into the window and peek out to see what's happening, but with this shackle and this weakness I can hardly crawl.

Now they're beating the drums of a marching band. A bugle plays the same infantry call I heard the morning when the militiamen of Senecú were summoned to participate in the punitive expedition against the Apache. I guess something similar is going on. Perhaps the Apache have avenged Refugio's death by attacking the village, or perhaps the villagers are preparing for an imminent attack.

The crowd quiets down and someone is speaking. It is the custodio, Father Juan del Hierro. He must be in the atrium because I can understand a few isolated phrases and words. First, he repeats the formulas that are used in comminatory sermons. Gradually I start to realize that he's denouncing some "sorcerers and traitors." He is asking the faithful ones to cooperate with the Holy Office in their investigations; to denounce and not collaborate with the rebels for this will condemn them in this world and in the other. He prays the Creed and some members of the audience join in. Afterward, they show their support through cheers to Jesus Christ, the Virgin Mary, the Church, and the pope.

My godfather, Lieutenant Governor Don Juan de Mendoza, speaks next. He talks about some tragic events that occurred recently in the Magdalena Mountains. The mayor of Socorro, five Spanish soldiers, and six Christian Indians were killed. He claims that the culprits are some Piro rebels from Senecú, who received support from the Gila Apache. He also asserts they had plans to kill Governor Villanueva and instigate a general uprising in the province. Among the rebels, he names Don Roque Gualtoye, Don Pablo Tzitza, his grandson Martín, Tsiké Fayé, and Tambulista. He declares that "these traitors and sorcerers" will be hanged and then burned and that the other captured rebels will be lashed and will pay for their crime and conspiracy by doing six years of forced labor in the mines of San José del Parral.

The public reacts vociferously, and a pandemonium breaks out. Suddenly someone starts hammering the door and I panic. The custodio must have changed his mind and they're coming to take me and burn me at the stake. I crawl into a corner and wait for the agents of the Holy Office hunched with fear. I hear several gunshots. The yelling from the square decreases, but the disorder continues. The hammering is camouflaged by the noises of the mayhem. Two hooded men open the door violently and approach me. One of them is pushing a wheelbarrow. I close my eyes. A series of gunfire and a cannon shot stamp out the disturbance. I get a panic attack and start shaking out of control. Someone taps my shoulder and says:

"Don't be afraid, Diego. It's Pepe, your brother. We're here to rescue you."

They help me get on the wheelbarrow and rush me to the backyard. The Casa Real is deserted. Pepe informs me that all members of the militia, including the dungeon wardens, are in the square witnessing the summary trial and safeguarding the square. We must hurry. A guard could come at any time.

The custodio is speaking again. He's reading the names of the rebels, the crimes they allegedly committed, and the punishment each of them will receive.

On the other side of the wall there are two men waiting for us. They give us assistance and help us climb the wall and get to the other side. I am delighted to discover that two of my rescuers are Pascual Baxcajay and Lucius who, as soon as he sees me, raises his head and neighs with joy.

"Aiiiiiiiiiiiijjjrrrrrrrrr! Jñiiiiiiiiiiiijjjrrrrr!"

"Hush, Lucius. You're going to rat us out!" Pascual rebukes him.

"We take care of the rest, Pascual," Pepe tells him. "You'd better get back to the convent right now. My uncle Bartolomé and all the Romeros thank you infinitely for what you've done for Diego."

"We're at your service. Don Bartolomé has always been generous to my family. Moreover, Lucius and I are fond of Brother Diego. Right, tough guy?"

Lucius whinnies and tosses his head happily again.

Pascual runs away without saying good-bye and without giving me the opportunity to properly thank him for his courageous and generous deed.

"Thank you, Pascual," I mumble with the little strength I can muster. When he gets to the convent's backyard, he climbs the wall, waves good-bye, and disappears.

We're on the edge of the communal lands of the Piro. It is a rugged terrain where only goats can graze. Fortunately, there's no one in sight. Pepe and one of his assistants put me on Lucius's saddle and put the shackle's iron ball in a small basket that is tied to the stirrup. We're almost ready to go. As soon as they hook the wheelbarrow to a cart that Lucius is pulling, we descend the slope and get away from the village.

When we reach a mound, we take a short break. Pepe gives me water and a loaf of bread that tastes like heaven to me. As I devour it, one of my liberators pulls a huge pair of tongs out of a saddlebag and breaks the chains of the handcuffs and shackle. Pepe pulls some clothes out of a bag and says:

"Put this on."

The outfit includes braies, a pair of brown, loose-fitting trousers, a white shirt, a buff coat, black shoes, and a straw hat.

"As soon as you get to the Chupadera Ranch, they'll take the shackles off. Mom and several aunts and cousins will be waiting for you. Uncle Bartolomé and I will get there later. We will have a feast this evening to celebrate your release and homecoming. Uncle Bartolomé is going to sacrifice the fattest calf on his ranch in your honor."

He also gives me a canteen with water and a bag of supplies.

"Inside you will find beef jerky, nuts, and more bread. There are also carob beans for Lucius. Pascual told me he loves them. We have to reward him for helping us rescue you and take you home. Unfortunately, we won't be able to accompany you, so we don't arouse suspicion. We'll disperse here. Each of us will go on a different route. I will return to Senecú, where Uncle Bartolomé will be waiting for me. I will give him the good news and all the details of your rescue, which the two of us organized. He will be thrilled that the operation has been successful."

"And how am I going to get to the Chupadera Ranch?"

"Don't worry. Lucius knows the way by heart. He'll know how to get there without any guidance. It's not far. If you go straight south from here, you'll run into the road to Senecú. Then you'll need to turn to the right and go west. Lucius knows. You'll see. Well, Brother, I have to go. I'll see you again tonight and we'll celebrate your rescue."

"Thank you, *Carnal.*"

"Carnal?" He looks at me strangely.

"Brother, I mean. *Carnal* means brother in border jargon."

"Ah, I understand," he says, perplexed though smiling. We give each other a big hug and he departs. I say good-bye to him and my other liberators, deeply grateful, with tears in my eyes, but unable to utter a word.

55

THE EVENING SUN BLAZES THE LANDSCAPE. CIRRUS CLOUDS DAUB the blue sky and creosote bushes and tumbleweeds cover the pebbly sandstone. Despite the ruggedness of the landscape and the burning sun, Lucius gallops happily as if we were walking on a green, cool meadow bound for the Promised Land. He's singing and dancing to the rhythm of "La morenica."

Morena me llaman
yo, blanca nací,
de pasear, galana,
mi color perdí.

"And why are you so happy, Lucius?

"Because I rescued my body from the flames and saved my soul from eternal damnation."

"Wasn't I the one who got saved?"

"Are you forgetting that you're occupying my body? You're just an astral traveler who's purging a conviction. Don't you this know by now?"

"No, I had no clue."

"You're just ignorant of yourself."

"Believe me, it is not for lack of wanting."

"To know the origin is to find the way."

"And what do I have to do with you?"

"Don't ask me. Ask the one who sent you. All of us in this kingdom are purging a conviction."

"And what crime did you commit?"

"I betrayed my faith and my people. I did not fulfill the mission the Lord entrusted to me."

"What mission?"

"To protect my people from persecution and announce to them the imminent arrival of the Messiah."

"What are you saying?"

"My relatives and many other Spanish and Portuguese Siervos de Dios came to New Mexico and founded the village of Santa Fe to escape the religious persecution we were subjected to in Mexico City. We came to this remote region in search of the Promised Land. My adoptive father, Don Valerio Rosales, sent me to the convent to make me a priest so that I could hold a position in the Church that would protect all Siervos de Dios from persecution, suspicion, and the scrutiny of the Holy Office. I was also entrusted with the delicate mission of announcing the Messiah's imminent arrival in Arzareth and the subsequent founding of the New Jerusalem in these territories."

"Where is Arzareth?"

"North of New Mexico is the Promised Land called Arzareth in the Bible. When the Messiah comes, the Siervos de Dios will found a city on the plains north of the river. There, those who survive the apocalypse will reach Arzareth and will enjoy all the goods promised in the Bible. According to an augury, I will get there only if I purge my sins by rescuing a castaway. Only then will I lose the body of an alboraico imposed upon me by the Lord of punishment."

"What is an alboraico?"

"Someone who keeps no law: neither Moses's, nor Muhammad's, nor Christ's, nor that of any other god or prophet."

"And what were your sins?"

"I became an informant of the Holy Office to save my skin and abjured Judaism. I made false statements against Brother Antonio. I also collaborated with the inquisitors and the slavers. Because of me, many Indians were enslaved and imprisoned. I helped capture children from nomadic tribes and every Indian who was reluctant to convert and rebel against the authority of the Church and the crown."

"I understand."

"I also did not fulfill the task that my Franciscan superiors commissioned me."

"What task?"

"To investigate and report abuse and corruption in New Mexico missions. To my disgrace, I didn't denounce the criminal society that some corrupt Franciscans have with slavers. I should have investigated Lupita's and Chayito's disappearances. I didn't do it out of cowardice and negligence, as you know well, but I should have. It was my moral, civic, and religious duty."

For some reason, listening to this illuminates me and I glimpse a glare on the horizon, a kind of mirage in the desert. I must be having an auroral dream, I tell myself. That flash must be what Dr. Hogan calls "the limpid light of dawn."

I look at that glow and experience the separation of the body and mind that is typical of lucid auroral dreams. I see Diego's entrails, veins, and skeleton. I look up at the sky and clearly distinguish the spindle of Necessity and the eight concentric heavens of the Celestial Sphere. I rise through the air and contemplate the Plain of Oblivion and the River of Forgetfulness. Down there is Diego, waiting to receive the lot that will give him yet another destiny and body. When his turn comes, he chooses the life of a scribbler eager to know himself better and bent on acquiring the perfect and complete awakening.

56

I'VE NO IDEA HOW LONG I'VE BEEN LIKE THIS, OR IF I AM DEAD or asleep. The last thing I remember is the accident I had in Ithaca. The music of my WinPlay3 has died down. All I can sense is the vibration of the cosmos. I hope I wake up soon so I can finally write my novel.

where the

north ends

Editor's Note

On Tuesday, April 9, 1996, in Ithaca, New York, Uriel had a tragic accident. While riding his bike down a steep hill, he lost control, collided with a tree, and was killed instantly. When I was at Uriel's memorial service in Ciudad Juárez, his brother Virgilio approached me and asked if I could curate Uriel's writings into a volume. Out of loyalty to our childhood friendship, I reluctantly agreed to take on this task. Upon reading Uriel's journals, it became evident to me that some of his dreams turned out to be prophetic. From that point forward I dedicated myself to completing this editorial project with the aim of helping Uriel fulfill his most sacred obligation: sharing his dreams with the public. Without Uriel's recorded tapes, however, I wouldn't have been able to make sense of Uriel's labyrinthine notes. *Where the North Ends* is an edited transcription of these tapes and his notes. At the request of an anonymous reviewer, I've modified the ending that, in their view, is "the weakest part" of the manuscript because it "appears a bit vague in trying to close the narrative." They also asked me to add a brief bio, but I declined because this would take away the spotlight from Uriel. He deserves all the credit for the story that unfolds in these pages. I only curated his writings to enhance their readability and to increase his novel's chances of being issued for public distribution and readership.

Acknowledgments

First, I am indebted to Dr. Enrique Lamadrid for his exceptional support throughout the entire process of translating and submitting this novel for publication. I also want to thank Amber Qureshi for her excellent line-editing work on the first draft of this translation, Dr. Juan Luis Longoria Granados for his invaluable assistance in editing the phrases written in the N'dee/N'nee/Ndé language, and Dr. Francisco Lomelí for writing the preface and for his invaluable comments and feedback. Thanks also to Dr. Sonia Dickey for her assistance throughout the review process. Finally, my wholehearted gratitude to my wife, Siobhan Martin, and my two children, Isabel and Sebastián. Their love, support, and grounded approach to life inspire me each day to work hard and persevere.

Notes

1. "Urlicht," *Deutsche Volkslieder*, 372. "O rosebud red! Here man lies in greatest need! Here man lies in greatest pain. So therefore were I in heaven fain. Then came I upon a broad, fair way, there came an angel and would turn aside me. Ah no, I would not turned aside be! I am of God and again would to God! For loving God will give me light for seeing, God will light me onward to eternal blissful being." Mahler, "Urlicht/ Primeval Light," 3–6.
2. "Arise, yes, yes, arise, O thou my dust, / From short repose thou must! / Immortal liveth / The soul the maker giveth." Klopstock, "Die Auferstehung / The Resurrection," 46–47.
3. Opler, *Apache Life-Way*, 304.
4. Klopstock, "The Resurrection," 47.
5. Opler, "Myths and Tales of the Chiricahua Apache Indians," 74–75.
6. Opler, "Myths and Tales of the Chiricahua Apache Indians," 28–29.
7. Müller, *The Dhammapada*, 86.

Works Cited

The Holy Bible: Translated from the Vulgate; Diligently Compared with the Hebrew, Greek, and Other Editions, in Divers Languages. The Old Testament, First Published by the English College, at Douay, A.D. 1609, and the New Testament First Published by the English College, at Rheims, A.D.1582, with Annotations, References, and an Historical and Chronological Index. Belfast, 1836.

Klopstock, Friedrich Gottlieb. "Die Auferstehung / The Resurrection." In *The Poetry of Germany: Consisting of Selections from Upwards of Seventy of the Most Celebrated Poets*. Translated by Alfred Baskerville. Lepizig, 1854.

Mahler, Gustav. "Urlicht / Primeval Light. Alt-Solo aus der Symphonie Nr. 2 in C moll. Alto Solo from the 2nd Symphony in C minor." In *12 Lieder aus "Des Knaben Wunderhorn: für Tiefe Stimme und Klavier."* Vol. 12. Translated by Addie Funk. Vienna: Universal Edition, c1914–1920.

Mittler, Franz Ludwig, ed. and trans. "Urlicht." In *Deutsche Volkslieder*. Marburg, 1855.

Müller, F. Max, ed. and trans. *The Dhammapada: A Collection of Verses; Being One of the Canonical Books of the Buddhists*. Vol. 10, Part 1. In *The Sacred Books of the East*. London: Clarendon Press, 1881.

Opler, Morris. *An Apache Life-Way: The Economic, Social, and Religious Institutions of the Chiricahua Indians*. Chicago: University of Chicago Press, 1941.

Opler, Morris. "Myths and Tales of the Chiricahua Apache Indians." *Memoirs of the American Folk-Lore Society*. Vol. 37. Lincoln: University of Nebraska Press, 1942.